**Sophie Pembroke** has been dreaming, reading and writing romance ever since she read her first Mills & Boon as part of her English Literature degree at Lancaster University, so getting to write romantic fiction for a living really is a dream come true! Born in Abu Dhabi, Sophie grew up in Wales and now lives in a little Hertfordshire market town with her scientist husband, her incredibly imaginative and creative daughter and her adventurous, adorable little boy. In Sophie's world, happy *is* for ever after, everything stops for tea, and there's always time for one more page…

**Cara Colter** shares her home in beautiful British Columbia, Canada, with her husband of more than thirty years, an ancient crabby cat and several horses. She has three grown children and two grandsons.

# CINDERELLA IN THE SPOTLIGHT

SOPHIE PEMBROKE

# WINNING OVER THE BROODING BILLIONAIRE

CARA COLTER

MILLS & BOON

First published in Great Britain 2024
by Mills & Boon, an imprint of HarperCollins*Publishers* Ltd,
1 London Bridge Street, London, SE1 9GF

www.harpercollins.co.uk

HarperCollins*Publishers*, Macken House, 39/40 Mayor Street Upper,
Dublin 1, D01 C9W8, Ireland

Cinderella in the Spotlight © 2024 Sophie Pembroke

Winning Over the Brooding Billionaire © 2024 Cara Colter

ISBN: 978-0-263-32124-1

02/24

MIX
Paper | Supporting
responsible forestry
FSC
www.fsc.org    FSC™ C007454

This book contains FSC™ certified paper
and other controlled sources to ensure responsible forest management.

For more information visit www.harpercollins.co.uk/green.

Printed and Bound in the UK using 100% Renewable Electricity
at CPI Group (UK) Ltd, Croydon, CR0 4YY

# CINDERELLA IN THE SPOTLIGHT

SOPHIE PEMBROKE

MILLS & BOON

To anyone who ever wanted to swap their everyday life for something more exciting…

# CHAPTER ONE

ROWAN HARPER LOVED the little fishing village of Rumbelow on the Cornish coast for many reasons—but most of all she loved it because nobody looked at her.

All her life, people had been staring at her. When she was a child, it was because she was standing next to her identical twin Willow, and people couldn't help but try to find a non-existent difference between them. Later, once they hit their teens, it was because they were familiar from billboards and advertising campaigns that seemed to be everywhere, all the time.

Willow said people stared because they were beautiful. Rowan felt that they stared because they were different. Strange. Wrong, even.

Their mother said they should just be grateful that people looked at all, and they'd miss the attention when it was gone—but Rowan knew that was only because *she* missed it, having given up her modelling career to manage theirs instead, when they were just kids.

But here in Rumbelow nobody stared at Rowan, because there were so many other beautiful things to look at. The arc of the harbour as the sun went down. The tiny boats, bobbing on the shimmering waves. The pretty painted houses along the edge of the sea, and the rambling cottages that continued behind it, fanning off the cobblestone streets with their antique shops and coffee houses.

It was the picture-perfect Cornish village, and Rowan had loved it so much the moment she'd set eyes on it that she'd bought the first cottage she'd found and refused to leave.

That had been six years ago.

In those six years, she'd grown accustomed to the rhythms of the place. The spring festivals and summer regattas. The autumn fires and the special pie they had to eat. The Boxing Day swim in the freezing-cold sea. The local folk club playing and singing the same songs they'd played for decades—longer, maybe hundreds of years. Sea shanties and folk tunes that were older than Rowan's thatched roof stone cottage.

This morning, as she swung a straw bag filled with treats from the local bakery over her shoulder and headed back towards the cottage, the only people who noticed her at all were the locals she saw every day, who waved politely.

Despite the community feel of the village, nobody asked too many questions here. If anyone had realised who she was—or who she had been—they never said. In Rumbelow, your life started the moment you arrived in the village, as if nothing that had come before could have ever been important.

Rowan *loved* that.

She took the last turn past the church, out onto the side street that led down the hill to her cottage, right on the outskirts of the village, humming happily to herself. The sun was high in the sky, if not entirely warm this early in the season, and it sparkled on the ripples of the waves as they crested below against the stony beach. This far along, the harbour had given way to a more natural appearance, and Rowan could see right across to the cliffs and the twinkling sails of the boats out at sea.

She smiled to herself, and waved to her nearest neighbour, Gwyn, as he jogged past her towards the town. Gwyn lived all the way around the curve of the harbour in the old converted lifeboat station that was now a luxury seafront property. He frowned and did a double-take before waving back, which confused her.

Until she turned through the gate onto her own garden path…

And stopped.

Because there, on her doorstep, was someone worth staring at.

Someone she hadn't seen in person in six years.

Someone who looked just like her.

'What are you doing here?' Rowan whispered harshly as she fumbled for her keys. The last thing she needed was someone seeing her and her identical twin standing together on the doorstep and putting two and two together.

Not that they looked exactly identical right now. Oh, they both still had the same long blonde hair, wide blue eyes and slender figure—although Rowan admitted the pastries might have caused a small fluctuation there, but she usually offset that with long walks on the cliffs.

But Willow was chicly dressed in wide-legged beige trousers and leather boots, topped with a simple black sweater and a tan leather jacket. Her hair flowed glossily down her back, her manicure was simple but perfect, and even her make-up was flawless.

Rowan was in a turquoise and pink maxi skirt, a white T-shirt and a hoodie, her hair was scraped back into a messy bun, she couldn't remember the last time she'd had a manicure, and all her make-up had dried up and gone in the bin.

No, maybe not so identical right now.

Finally, she managed to get the door open and turned to Willow to usher her inside. 'Come on, come on. Before someone sees you.'

Oh, she hoped that Gwyn hadn't lingered too long on his run down the street. Or that he hadn't noticed the strangely familiar woman standing on Rowan's doorstep for the last...

'How long have you been here?' Rowan asked as she slammed the door behind them.

Willow's eyebrows arched in surprise at the question. 'In England or on your doorstep?'

There was a slight Transatlantic twang to her sister's voice that she'd only heard on the phone before. A consequence of living in New York for so long, Rowan supposed.

'Both.'

Willow placed her large tote bag on the floor beside the telephone table, and Rowan saw her sister frown at the old-fashioned rotary dial phone that sat there. Phone signal was notoriously patchy in the area, so having a landline just made sense—not that anyone really had the number. Which was why she'd figured she might as well have a phone she liked to look at, since it never rang.

'I arrived in England last night,' Willow said, straightening up again. 'I stayed at a hotel near Heathrow, then got a car to bring me down here this morning. I'd been standing on your doorstep for about ten minutes when you arrived. I did try to call, but...'

She gave the rotary dial phone another dubious look.

'Cell signal can be unreliable here.' Rowan carried her own bag down the darkened hall into the brighter kitchen at the back of the cottage, looking out over her higgledy-piggledy garden, then emptied it out onto the kitchen table. 'Croissant?'

Willow looked nauseous at just the idea of carbs, so Rowan grabbed a plate and bit into one herself. No time for jam and butter this morning. She needed comfort food, stat.

'So. Going to tell me why you're here?' Rowan dropped into the wooden chair she'd found at a second-hand shop and painted lavender, to match the plants growing just outside her window. She nodded at the other chair—another thrifted wooden chair in a different style, painted sage-green, and Willow cautiously sat too.

'I need your help,' Willow said.

Rowan reached for another croissant. 'That doesn't sound good.'

Willow had *never* needed her help. Not once.

As kids, Willow had been the ringleader, the one who decided what they were doing and where. And when Rowan couldn't keep up, Willow had made everyone else wait for her. When their mother was worried that Rowan had put on a few pounds and instigated a starvation diet, Willow was the one who sneaked her enough calories to keep going.

When Mum had yelled and screamed at Rowan for

not wanting success enough, for being a failure, Willow had calmly stood between them and told her to stop.

When Rowan had started having panic attacks before runway shows, Willow had been the one to practice breathing techniques with her, and run interference so that no one else found out. When Rowan had fainted under the lights on a camera shoot once, Willow had literally caught her when she fell.

And when Rowan had wanted to leave, Willow had supported her. More than that, she'd helped her move her own money away from their mother's control, then booked her the damn aeroplane ticket.

They might not have seen each other in person for six years, but they'd stayed in touch via email and videophone. And Willow was the only person in the world who knew where Rowan had gone when she'd dropped off the radar.

Most importantly, Willow had always, always helped her when she needed it.

Which meant that Rowan knew there was no way she could turn her sister away now.

'What do you need?' Rowan asked, and hoped against hope it wasn't something she wasn't able to give.

Eli rapped his knuckles against the wood of his brother's office door, avoiding the frosted glass pane that read *Ben O'Donnell CEO* in a particularly intimidating font.

Refusing to be intimidated, Eli stuck his head around the door. 'Got a minute?'

Ben was on the phone as usual, so he just nodded and waved a pen towards the chair opposite his desk. Eli dropped into it and waited.

Since his brother was still making vague noncommittal noises to whoever was on the other end of the phone call, Eli took a moment to study the office. It had a lot of memories, that room. Not so much since Ben became CEO of O'Donnell Industries two years ago—he'd only visited a handful of times, and never for long.

But when their father had ruled the roost...

After their mother left, Eli had spent a lot of time doing his homework at the second assistant's desk outside the room, because at thirteen he was far too old for a nanny, but his father also didn't trust him at home. Ben, at sixteen, had more often been with his friends—or, as far as their father was concerned, involved in school activities. But sometimes he'd come to the company headquarters building in Manhattan too, and been ushered into the inner sanctum of their father's private office to be initiated in the secrets of how to be a CEO.

At least, that was what Eli had assumed was happening. He was never allowed in to find out.

Growing up, people always told Eli how important his father was, how much his work mattered. People said the same thing about Ben now.

But those same people had also told Eli he was imagining it when he'd worried that his father treated Ben differently to him—loved Ben more than him. His father had said so too, telling him not to be so oversensitive.

He knew now, of course, how right he'd been. As he'd grown up, those same people had stopped trying to keep the whispers from his ears. The ones that said, *'Doesn't he look more like his godfather than his father?'*

They'd still told him he was making it up, though, if

he complained about being shut out of his father's office—of his life.

So had Ben, come to that.

Pushing the memories away, Eli got to his feet and strode across the office to the floor-to-ceiling windows that looked out over the Manhattan skyline. No wonder his father had spent more time here than at home, with a view like that.

Not that the view from the family apartment on the Upper East Side was something to be sniffed at either. Even Eli had to admit it had been a wrench to leave that.

'Right. We'll circle back to that on Monday,' Ben said, and Eli guessed his call was coming to an end.

He turned back to head for his designated chair, but couldn't help but look at his brother's desk as he went.

His father had kept it completely clear, excepting only the framed family photo that sat on one corner— a photo that had been removed after Eli's mother left, and replaced with a staged portrait of Ben and Eli instead. Because whatever his father thought in private, in public he would never do anything at all to suggest that Eli wasn't his son.

And if he wasn't…well, both his parents had now taken that secret to their graves, hadn't they?

Anyway, it seemed that Ben had continued his father's clear desk tradition. There, in the corner, the only decoration was a framed photo of Ben and his on-again, off-again girlfriend Willow, at some awards ceremony or another.

Ben was in a tuxedo, and Willow looked impossibly slender and glamorous in a golden gown, her long blonde hair cascading down her back, her famous smile on show. It looked more like a picture in a magazine than a personal shot. Maybe it was, originally.

In his less charitable moments, Eli worried that Ben was more like their father than he was comfortable with.

He wondered too how serious Ben was about Willow—or if he just liked having one of the world's most beautiful women on his arm when the cameras came out. Ben and Willow had been together—sporadically—for a couple of years now, but Eli had never even met her, only seen them together on TV, or in magazines.

He'd seen other women, though, at Ben's flat, or at parties. He'd always assumed that was during the 'off' periods of their relationship, but he'd never asked. He wasn't completely sure he'd like the answer.

Eli pushed the thoughts away. Ben was his brother, after all. He was rich, handsome, charming, and could probably have any woman at the click of his fingers, if he really wanted. If he'd chosen Willow, it had to be for a reason, and Eli had to respect that.

Ben hung up the phone at last and, following the direction of Eli's gaze, turned the photo face down.

Ah. Off-again, then.

'Things not good with Willow at the moment?' He settled back into his chair and slouched down to rest his elbows on the arms, steepling his fingers in front of him. What Ben called his 'therapist pose', although none of the therapists Eli had ever spoken to had used it.

'I got tired of all the demands, you know? Called time on it for now.' Ben leaned back in his own high-backed, top-of-the-range, ergonomic leather desk chair, silhouetted against the Manhattan skyline behind him. He looked relaxed, confident—and still Eli was pretty sure he was lying. Which meant Willow had probably left him, and he didn't want to admit it. It would diminish his reputation, or whatever.

In some ways, he really was just like their father.

Eli had asked his father once why he didn't turn his desk around so he could enjoy the view while he was working. His father had told him that if he was working, he wasn't looking at the view.

He'd asked Ben the same thing when he'd moved in. Ben had simply said it was more intimidating this way.

Eli hadn't been satisfied with either of the answers. If it had been *his* office, he'd have turned the damn desk around.

But it wasn't. It never would be. Because their father had left executive control of the company, lock, stock and barrel, to Ben. Not that Eli had been left destitute— far from it. Mack O'Donnell would never let it be said he hadn't been generous to his sons—or let anyone suspect he didn't believe Eli to be his biological child. No, Eli might not have got day-to-day control of the company, but he was still technically on the board, even if he never made it to meetings, and he had a share of the family fortune. Eli's father had ensured he'd never have to work a day in his life, if he didn't want to.

But he *did* want to. So he'd made his own way instead.

Which was what had brought him to his brother's office in the first place.

'So if you don't have to escort Willow to any glamorous events this weekend, does that mean you'll have time to look at that file I gave you? The one about the gala sponsorship?'

'Ah, sorry, Eli. I wanted to, really.' Ben flashed him

an apologetic smile that didn't come close to reaching his eyes. 'But I promised a certain glamorous redhead that I'd take her out on the boat this weekend instead. *She* only makes one demand of me…and you can probably guess what that is.' He barked a laugh.

Eli forced a smile. If Ben was taking another woman out publicly so soon, that was more evidence he was lying about what was going on with Willow. Overcompensating.

'Perhaps you can take a look before you go,' he suggested. 'Do you have the file here? We could go through it together. Then I really need to take it back with me…' There was sensitive information in that file—information he wouldn't have normally let leave the locked filing cabinet in his office, or the firewall protected data cloud Launch used. But if showing Ben all the details got him interested enough to sponsor the gala event they were setting up that spring—the biggest event his non-profit ran in a year, and bigger this year than ever before—it was worth the risk.

'Uh, I think I left it at Willow's apartment, actually,' Ben said.

Okay. Maybe *not* worth the risk.

'Ben, I told you that file had sensitive information in it.'

'Yeah, yeah, I know. It's not exactly unfamiliar territory to me,' his brother replied. 'I guess it just slipped my mind. You have no idea how much there is to do as CEO of this company.'

*No, because Dad never let me find out.*

That was an unfair thought. It wasn't Ben's fault that

Eli's parentage was doubtful, and their father had cut him out as a result.

'I know how much running a company can take,' he said instead, working hard to make it sound easy and relaxed. He knew Ben didn't consider Eli's own business ventures in the same league as his own—probably because they weren't. 'And to keep mine going, I really need to get that file back.' *And if you're not going to sponsor my event, find someone else who will. Fast.* 'Can you ask Willow for it?'

Ben yanked open his desk drawer and pulled out a key, handing it across the desk to Eli. 'She's out of town, apparently. But you can go grab it yourself. I'll text you the address and the door code. I left it on the counter, I think.'

Eli hesitated before taking the key. He'd never even met Willow, and the most recent information he had about her was that she'd dumped his brother. Invading her apartment in her absence felt wrong, even if it was to retrieve an important file.

'You're sure she won't mind?'

Ben shrugged. 'I'll shoot her a text and warn her you'll be going, if you like.'

Eli reached for the key. 'That would be great. Have fun on the boat this weekend.'

He turned and left the office, feeling the weight lift from his shoulders the way it always did when he escaped that room.

He had work to do.

Rowan made tea as Willow talked, because it helped to have something to do with her hands. When she'd lived in America, it had been all coffee, all the time—

black and strong and sometimes the only thing she'd consume all day.

Back in Britain, she'd retrained her tastebuds to love the calming, soothing taste of tea.

Even tea wasn't up to this challenge, though.

'You're *pregnant*?' Rowan plonked one of the mugs of tea down in front of her twin. 'How did that happen?'

It was a mark of how serious the situation was that Willow didn't even make a joke about the birds and the bees, or how long it must have been for Rowan if she didn't remember. Rowan almost wished she would. It would make this less…weird.

'It certainly wasn't planned, I can tell you that.' Willow sighed and reached for her mug, blowing slightly over the surface so steam snaked up towards the ceiling.

'Who's the father? Does he know?' That was the next proper question to ask, wasn't it?

'Ben, of course.' Willow frowned at her across the kitchen table. 'What did you think?'

'Sorry. I just…' She'd never met Ben, of course, but she'd seen plenty of photos of the two of them online or in magazines, appearing at glamorous events or holidaying in exotic places. And Willow had mentioned him often when they'd spoken on the phone, or in her emails and texts. 'I guess I figured that if the father was your long-term boyfriend you'd be talking to him instead of me.'

That made Willow wince and look away towards the window.

Hmm. Definitely something her sister hadn't been telling her in those phone calls, then.

'Things with Ben and me…it's not what I'd call a stable relationship environment. Or anything a kid should be involved in.' Willow's words were flat, unemotional. But Rowan read a world of meaning behind them.

'Does he hurt you? Physically or emotionally? Because you do *not* have to go back to him—'

'It's not like that.' Willow sighed. 'He's… I mean, we're…'

'You're really convincing me here, Will.'

Willow huffed a laugh and looked down at her tea again. 'I know. I'm sorry. It's just…the world thinks we're some fairy tale romance, right? The supermodel and the CEO, living our perfect glamorous life together, madly in love.'

'And it's not really like that?' Rowan asked softly. She'd never seen her sister look vulnerable this way before. Usually, *she* was the one who was falling apart, and Willow was the one holding her up.

Maybe it was about time they tried things the other way around for a change. She certainly owed her.

'You know, some days I'm not sure we even *like* each other,' Willow admitted. 'Right from the start…we were together because it was good for our images, our careers. We look great next to each other, and the papers like to talk about us a lot, and that was kind of what we both needed. We could fake the rest.'

'You *faked* being in love with your boyfriend?' Okay, that definitely sounded like the sort of thing that only happened in the bad romcom movies that Rowan usually watched when she couldn't sleep on stormy nights.

'Not…intentionally.' Willow sighed again. Was all this heavy breathing good for the baby? Rowan didn't know.

Maybe she'd have to learn.

'Okay, tell me the whole story.'

The whole story took another pot of tea and several croissants, but basically boiled down to this.

Willow and Ben had met at some society party and realised that they were just the sort of person the other had been looking for. In Willow's case, Ben was successful in his own right so not intimidated by her success, he was rich enough that she knew he wasn't after her money, and they had a lot of the same friends so would inevitably end up at the same events.

In Ben's case, Willow was recognised by the world at large as being beautiful, and that seemed to be enough for him.

They went out on a date and got photographed by the paparazzi. So they went out on another one, and people started talking about them.

'And now it's two years later, and we've never really had a conversation about our future, or our feelings, or if we even like each other beyond spending time in the public eye together and having someone there to have sex with whenever we want to scratch that itch.'

'Do you want to?' Rowan asked. 'I mean, do you want to tell him about the baby? See if the two of you can be a real family together?'

It was something neither of the sisters had ever known. Their father had been out of the picture almost before they were born, and their mother hadn't exactly been mum of the year. She'd always been more interested in how much money they could make her than who they were inside.

Maybe that was how Willow had fallen into such a transactional relationship with Ben.

'I…' Willow looked up and met Rowan's gaze, swallowing hard. 'It sounds awful, but I don't think I do. This is the man I spent the last two years of my life with, sort of. But I know—like, deep down, heart knowledge—that he'd be the wrong partner for me in this. That we wouldn't be happy—and neither would our child.'

Well. That was stark enough.

'You still need to tell him, though,' Rowan pointed out. 'Especially if… Wait. I skipped ahead a step. Do you know what you want to do? Do you want to keep the baby?'

Because if she didn't, why had Willow flown across a whole ocean to tell her about it?

Willow nodded. 'I do. It might be crazy, because what about my career and my figure and my life, and I don't have any support in New York, but I guess I can hire that? I don't know. All I know is that I want to be a mom—a better one than ours was. I want to raise this baby right. And yes, I *know* I have to tell Ben. I just… I need to figure some things out first, about how this is all going to work.'

'I can get that.' Finally, something about Willow's arrival here was making sense. She needed a place to hide, to think, to feel safe.

Rowan knew better than anyone how good Rumbelow was for that.

'I just know if I talk to Ben before I've made some decisions about everything…he'll take over. He'll want things all his own way and I won't be sure enough of anything to fight him on it.'

And in that one sentence, Willow had told her more

about her relationship with Ben than in the rambling story that took two pots of tea.

Rowan reached across the table and grabbed her twin's hand. 'You can stay here as long as you like,' she told her fiercely. 'We'll figure this all out so you can go back with a plan and do this the way you need to.'

Ben would want to have input, of course, but Rowan wasn't going to let him steamroller over Willow's wishes either.

Willow's face relaxed into a small smile. 'Thank you. I hoped… That will really help.'

'Of course. You're my sister. I'll always be here for you.' Especially given how many times Willow had been there for her.

Rowan got to her feet to put the kettle on one last time, and grab her planner so they could start thinking through the essentials—like doctors' check-ups and whether she actually owned any sheets for the spare room.

But Willow stopped her with a gentle hand on her arm. 'Actually, there was one more thing I needed. It's a lot to ask, but…'

'Anything.'

'I need you to go to New York and pretend to be me. So Ben doesn't get suspicious. I need you to be Willow Harper, supermodel, for a few weeks.'

# CHAPTER TWO

WILLOW'S MANHATTAN APARTMENT was pretty much as Eli would have expected it to be—if he'd spent any time at all picturing the home of his brother's sometimes girlfriend, which he hadn't.

Too trendy for a doorman, it had instead some sort of state-of-the-art ID technology that Eli easily bypassed with the code his brother had texted him after he'd left the office the day before. He took the elevator up to the penthouse, barely pausing to take in the stark white and metal industrial chic foyer, or the modern artwork in the elevator itself.

On the top floor there was just one door off the short hallway; Willow clearly had the entire penthouse floor to herself. Eli knocked and waited, just in case. But when there was no response he used the key Ben had given him to let himself in.

Ben had promised to tell Willow he'd be coming by. Besides, Willow was out of the country at the moment.

There was literally no reason for Eli to feel like he was invading a stranger's privacy.

He did, anyway.

But the apartment was empty, as promised. Eli stood by the door, hands on hips, as he scanned the open-plan space. Huge windows meant most of the walls were nothing but glass from the floor to the ceiling; Eli assumed there must be blinds of some sort, or invisible tinting or something, because otherwise living here had to feel like being watched, all the time.

Standing in Willow's own personal space didn't give him any more of a feel for who the woman was. He realised now that his discomfort at invading her private home was unnecessary; there was nothing private or personal here—at least, not in the main living area. It was all white walls, monochrome art, metal bars and neutral furnishings. Not even a magazine on the wood and metal coffee table to give a hint at the owner's personality.

Maybe the private rooms—bedrooms, bathrooms— were different. But the living space that spanned over half the top floor of the building looked more like an event space than a home—with a showcase kitchen and bar, small sitting areas by the windows, as well as the larger living area, and a glass dining table that could seat almost as many kids as they got down at the Castaway Café on a cold Friday night.

Eli shook his head and got down to business.

Ben had said he'd left the file on the counter. Assuming that Willow hadn't moved it since then, that narrowed things down a bit. There was the kitchen counter, the bar over by the window and a few other shelves with some minimalist decor—and it wasn't as if there was a lot of clutter for it to get lost in. If only he'd put the paperwork in a file that was any colour other than white he'd probably have spotted it already.

Of course, if she *had* moved it…

Eli's stomach clenched as it occurred to him that this was *not* a woman who liked clutter, clearly. What were the chances she'd leave her *ex-boyfriend's* clutter lying around the place after he forgot it? Slim, he reckoned.

If he was lucky, she'd have stashed it in a box with any other of Ben's things. If he was unlucky, it had gone in the trash.

With a sigh, Eli moved into the apartment and began systematically checking counter spaces then, when that turned up nothing, looking in cupboards for some sort of container of his brother's belongings.

He had his head in a cupboard full of cleaning supplies—all eco-friendly, expensive and in frosted white bottles—when he heard a key in the front door.

Ducking out of the cupboard, he tried to straighten up and brush himself down—but by the time he emerged above the kitchen counter Willow was already staring at him from the doorway, her eyes wide and terrified.

'Sorry! Sorry, Ben said you were away and—'

He was cut off by Willow's scream, and the crash of her bags dropping to the hardwood floor.

Eli dashed around towards her, narrowly missing the glass coffee table, and slid to a stop just in front of her. They'd never met, but surely she'd recognise him from Ben's photos or something?

'Willow! Don't worry, it's just me. Eli. Ben's brother?' He kept his voice as calm and as reassuring as he could, but it didn't seem to make any difference. The panic had got hold of her, and the fear in her eyes wasn't receding one bit.

Now he was closer, he could see that her hands were trembling—no wonder she'd dropped her bags. Her chest was moving rapidly in and out too, her breaths shallow and desperate.

*A panic attack. She's having a panic attack—because of me.*

Damn Ben and his inability to read a damn file in good time.

Except he couldn't even blame his brother. Because he'd known it was a bad idea to come here and he'd done it anyway, because he needed that file.

He'd caused this. Now he had to try and fix it.

'Okay, Willow?' He moved close enough to meet her gaze, but not so close as to spook her. 'I think you're having a panic attack, or maybe an anxiety attack. Okay? Have you had these before?'

Her pupils darted around the apartment, looking everywhere except at him, but she nodded, just a little.

'I'm going to stay here with you until you're calm again, okay?' Eli went on, still speaking calmly and softly. 'Then I'll leave, once I know you're okay. But for now, how about I take your hand?'

He held out his hand, palm up, and waited to see if she'd accept it. He knew that, for some people, touch could be grounding. But Willow didn't know him, and for all he knew it could be the opposite of what she needed.

After a moment, Willow reached out and grabbed his fingers, her hand clammy and still shaking.

'Okay. Okay, that's good.' He smiled gently at her. Some people needed quiet to process an attack like this, but for others a soothing voice helped too—and Willow seemed to be responding well to his. 'Shall we sit down?' Another nod.

He turned, about to lead her to the sofa, but she was already sliding down the wall behind her to sit on the floor, so he did the same.

From down there, the apartment seemed even more vast and empty. Eli wasn't surprised she'd had a panic attack finding him there. He was more surprised she didn't have one every time she came home to this place.

The sparse apartment seemed to echo with their breathing as they sat in silence, Willow still gripping his hand tightly. The ends of her loose blonde hair tickled the side of his arm, where he'd rolled his sleeves up. The sensation reminded him of another trick he'd learned to help people suffering from anxiety or panic.

He shifted slightly to face her. 'Are you ready to try something else?'

There was a trust now in her gaze that he hadn't anticipated.

He hadn't expected how good it would make him feel to see that look on a virtual stranger's face either.

Willow nodded, and Eli pushed the thought aside. He was here to help. Not bond with his brother's ex.

The world was starting to come back into focus for Rowan as she sat on the floor of her sister's apartment with…some guy?

A big, broad, gorgeous guy in a suit who was holding her hand.

He'd told her his name, hadn't he? But her heart had been pounding so loudly in her chest, her blood roaring in her ears, that she hadn't heard, or at least hadn't taken it in.

Now she was sitting here clutching his fingers tight,

so she should probably make sure to figure out his name at some point.

Also, what he was doing in Willow's apartment when she was out of the country. That seemed like relevant information.

But first, she needed to get her body back on an even keel. God, it had been so long since she'd had an attack as bad as this that she'd almost forgotten what it felt like.

Well, no. That was a lie. She hadn't forgotten. But she'd *wanted* to.

It was just…it had been kind of a day. Or a couple of days.

Ever since Willow had arrived on her doorstep and she'd felt the world shift, it seemed as if she'd been on the edge of something like this. And once she'd realised what her twin wanted her to do…

*'Go to New York and pretend to be you?'* she'd asked incredulously. *'How could I even do that?'*

*'We're identical, Rowan. It'll be easy.'*

Willow had sounded so sure, so convinced that her plan would work, it had been hard to argue with her.

That wasn't why Rowan had agreed to it, of course. She'd done that because her sister needed her help for once, and it was well past Rowan's turn to provide it.

Still. What Willow didn't seem to realise was that the identical thing was only skin-deep. Yes, she could still pass for her twin in a photo. But in person? Rowan wasn't so sure.

Even the journey here had made that much clear. Not to mention the packing session beforehand.

She'd pulled out her old battered suitcase from the top of the wardrobe, only to find Willow shaking her head.

*'That won't do. You'll have to take mine. No one would ever believe I'd travel with that thing.'*

The same proved true about the clothes Rowan had planned to pack, and the skincare products and, well, everything else. In the end, Rowan had been dispatched to Heathrow Airport dressed in her twin's clothes and sunglasses, her suitcase half empty, as Willow told her she could just use her wardrobe and such when she arrived in New York.

New York.

She'd forgotten how busy airports were. How in a hurry everyone was. The way announcements blared out and how a low-level buzz of noise remained constant.

Rowan had been glad of her noise-reducing earplugs at the airport, as well as on the flight. But even they hadn't been enough to protect her against the noise, bustle and chaos of New York in the spring.

Last time she'd been there had been for New York Fashion Week, right before she'd quit modelling, and America, for good. At least Fashion Week was over there for another season, attention moving to other shows around the globe.

Willow had assured her she had no shows booked, no photo shoots even. Mostly what Rowan had to do was leave the apartment often enough to be papped around the city, so people believed she was still there. And by people, Willow mostly meant Ben.

There was a chance she'd get invited out to some events, but Willow seemed confident Rowan could handle those.

Since she was currently battling a panic attack on the floor of Willow's apartment, Rowan was less sure.

Her heart slowed a little at last, her breath rasping less harshly in her chest. The panic was passing, and the fear was setting in to take its place.

Beside her, her companion twisted around to look at her. His eyes were very, very green, she noticed absently. Green eyes under dark hair. 'Are you ready to try something else?'

*Aren't I already trying enough new things here?*

The thought bubbled up and almost made her giggle, which she was sure would convince him she was having some sort of breakdown, so she held it in. Instead, she caught his gaze and, when she saw only concern and comfort there, she nodded.

Maybe she wasn't sure who this guy was yet, but she was almost certain she could trust him. Willow obviously did, if she'd given him a key to her apartment—a thought her anxious brain hadn't been able to process until now. The lock hadn't been broken, after all, and security on the building was pretty good.

She nodded.

'Okay, let's do some breathing together, yeah?' He waited for her second nod before starting.

Using his free hand, the one she wasn't still clutching damply—and oh, yes, she was going to feel embarrassed about that later—he swooped a finger up towards his face as he breathed in, held it there for a few beats, then flew it away again as he breathed out. It should have looked ridiculous, but somehow his sincerity made it anything but.

Rowan tried to mirror his breathing patterns. Breathing techniques always helped her. It was just hard to remember them when she was in the middle of an attack.

Finally, the weight in her chest lifted and an incredible tiredness swamped her instead. She gave his hand one last squeeze then let it go, trying not to miss the connection the moment it was gone.

'Sorry for, well, that. I hope you didn't need the bones in that hand for anything.' Ah, yes, here came the embarrassment. She could feel the heat rising in her cheeks as she realised what this stranger had just witnessed.

But he shook his head firmly. 'Don't apologise, Willow, please. I'm the one who should be sorry, for surprising you here.'

Okay, so she shouldn't have been expecting him. That was a start. Even if hearing him address her by her twin's name was weirder than she'd expected. It used to happen all the time but, after six years away, she'd forgotten how it felt.

Still, at least that meant Willow was right, and they did still look identical enough to pass as each other. As long as Rowan was wearing Willow's clothes and did her hair properly, anyway.

First hurdle jumped.

Now she just needed to try and figure out who he was without giving away that she wasn't who he thought she was. If that made sense anywhere outside her head.

She didn't know what his connection to Willow was yet, for a start. Was there more to the story than her twin had told her, sitting at her kitchen table in Rumbelow?

'Yeah… I know you told me what you were doing here, but…'

'Of course.' He seemed incredibly understanding, anyway. Rowan suspected he must have had experience with anxiety attacks in the past—maybe supporting a friend through them or something, because he hadn't been fazed at all by hers. 'Ben gave me his key because he'd left a sensitive file here…'

'And he sent you to get it?' So did that make this guy Ben's assistant or something? Because, in that case, they were back to it being very weird that he was in Willow's apartment at all.

*But at least he's not potentially the secret father of my niece or nephew.*

Not that that idea should have bothered her, beyond the fact that it would have meant Willow had been lying to her.

'Sort of.' He pulled a face. 'It was my file—it's all the details for this gala event my non-profit organisation is running this spring—you know, Launch? I don't know how much Ben has told you about it, or what you've seen in the press, but we do work among troubled teens in the city—helping with mental health issues, providing refuges and food banks and the like, especially for teen boys who can't go with their moms and sisters to domestic violence refuges.'

'That sounds…great.' She probably didn't sound very convincing, but she genuinely believed it was. She just couldn't figure out what it had to do with Ben or Willow.

'Yeah, but it needs a lot of support every year. And this year we're gunning for something bigger and better than ever, so…' He shrugged, a self-deprecating smile on his face. 'I figured it was time to lean on those old family connections, you know? But Ben left the file here, and now he's away this weekend…' He trailed off, as if afraid he'd said too much.

As if she cared about Ben's plans. Away for the weekend suited her perfectly.

Wait.

Family connections?

This guy was Ben's *family*?

Oh, she needed to get him out of here *fast*.

No matter how gorgeous he was.


Eli wasn't sure exactly what he'd said—maybe she wasn't into charity work? Except who honestly didn't care about other people? Hopefully not someone Ben would have dated for this long—but suddenly Willow was on her feet and eager to get him out of the door.

She wobbled a little when she stood, though.

Eli clocked the suitcases by the door, and the shadows under her eyes—not enough to make her any less beautiful by the world's general standards, but enough to make her look tired.

Tired. She'd just flown in from somewhere, found a man in her apartment and had a massive panic attack.

She had to be exhausted.

'Thank you for sitting with me,' she said with a polite smile. 'But I'm really all right now.' She looked pointedly towards the door.

She sounded more English than he'd expected, considering how long she'd lived in the States now. But maybe the accent was part of her persona.

'Right. I should…get going.' Except he still hadn't found that damn file. 'Um…'

Willow looked blankly at him for a moment, before her eyes widened. 'Your file. Right?'

'Yeah.' He gave her an apologetic smile. 'I'm sorry.

I wouldn't bother—I wouldn't have come here at all—except it's really important. And, well, it has some sensitive data in it.'

'Why on earth would Ben leave it here, then?' she asked, looking baffled.

He shrugged. 'You know Ben.'

'Yes. Right. I absolutely do.' She moved into the apartment a little way, towards the kitchen, then stopped and looked around her, as if lost in her own home. 'I don't suppose he told you where he left it?'

'He said he left it on a counter.' Eli stepped closer, behind her, but making sure to keep enough distance to respect her personal space. 'But I couldn't see it anywhere. I thought maybe you might have tidied it away somewhere.'

Willow gave a weary sigh. 'Probably. Come on then, we'd better get looking.'

For an immaculately tidy apartment, it had a surprising amount of storage shelves and cupboards, all of them stocked with clear acrylic containers and organised in rainbow order. Since Willow seemed surprised by their contents every time she opened a cupboard, Eli suspected the place had been sorted by professional organisers—possibly even while she was away.

Finally, they found the file in a stack of creamy folders stood up in an acrylic holder. It took longer than it might have done, as the scribbled on and reused folder he'd grabbed from the office to put the information in for Ben had been replaced by a sleek, shiny nude-coloured one.

Eli flicked through the papers to make sure they were all there and felt his shoulders relax at knowing he had it back. Of course, the fact that professional organisers were potentially the only people to have handled it since he gave it to Ben didn't bode well for his chances of getting the sponsorship he'd hoped for from the family company, but that just meant he'd have to try some other routes. He had contacts. He'd make it happen.

There were kids relying on him.

'Right, well, that's great, then!' Willow swept towards the door, obviously expecting him to follow. 'You've got your file, I'm no longer in a heap on the floor, everything is great! Lovely to see you.'

She opened the front door and held it expectantly.

Eli hesitated. Of course she wanted him to leave, that was totally reasonable. She'd just travelled back from overseas, found him in her apartment and had a panic attack. She'd wanted him to go *before* they had to hunt for the file, and he hadn't expected that desire to have diminished any. Add into all that the fact that she'd just broken up with his brother—again—and her attitude made perfect sense.

Except…he couldn't shake the feeling that there was something more to it. That she wanted him to leave before something else happened.

And, because he was the curious sort, he couldn't help but wonder what that might be.

Willow vibrated with an energy he recognised—a wary, nervous, almost frightened energy. One he saw all the time in the kids who came through the doors at the Castaway Café when he was serving there on one of his volunteer nights.

Maybe it was just the after-effects of the attack. Or maybe it was something more.

Either way, Eli knew he wouldn't feel right about what had happened here today unless he came back and checked up on her again, soon.

And if the memory of her hand in his, or the way she'd made self-deprecating jokes about the perfect order of her apartment as they'd searched for his file together, made him think that coming back wouldn't be such a bad thing... Well, he was going to ignore those thoughts for now. Because she was his brother's ex-girlfriend, and before long she'd probably be his girlfriend again, and he just wasn't going to go there, even mentally, even for a moment.

'Thanks again for your help.' He flashed her a smile as he held up the file. 'And, you know, for not calling the police on me.'

'You're welcome.' She opened the door a little further.

'I'll get out of your hair now. Goodbye, Willow.'

'Bye...uh...yeah. Goodbye.'

The door slammed so fast behind him that he was almost blown towards the elevator. Eli smiled to himself as he pressed the down button—until something occurred to him, and his smile faded.

He was almost certain Willow couldn't remember his name.

# CHAPTER THREE

ROWAN SLAMMED THE door behind her visitor, turned and slid down it to sit on the floor for the second time that day. This time, though, she wasn't having an anxiety attack. She was thinking. Hard.

Groping for her carry-on bag, she fished out her phone—now housed in Willow's sleek taupe case instead of her own turquoise sticker-covered one—and tapped at the screen until it started to ring.

Willow's face appeared almost immediately.

'Are you there? You should have been there *ages* ago. What happened?' It was moderately gratifying to see the concern in her twin's expression. But it didn't eclipse the pang of homesickness Rowan felt when she spotted her familiar, slightly battered kitchen cabinets behind her.

'I'm here,' she reassured Willow. 'The flight and everything was fine—nobody blinked twice at me using your passport either.' Technically, Rowan was pretty certain that was wildly illegal, but Willow had insisted.

'*Ben might check flight records or something,*' she'd insisted.

Rowan had almost questioned why and how he'd do that, but Willow had been so tense by that point she'd just let it go.

'So why didn't you call before?'

Rowan tipped her head back against the door and closed her eyes. 'Because there was a man waiting in your apartment when I arrived.'

'What?' Willow's screamed word echoed off the almost empty walls of the apartment. 'Was it Ben? What did he say? What *happened*? Rowan, *look at me!*'

With a sigh, she opened her eyes again to look at the screen. 'I'm hoping you can tell me.' She explained everything that had happened, glossing over the anxiety attack as best she could. There was no point worrying Willow when she was all the way across an ocean and couldn't do anything about it.

She also didn't go into too much detail about how gorgeous he was—with his broad shoulders and warm smile and bright green eyes that just begged her to trust him.

She didn't want Willow getting ideas.

'He said he was family? You're sure?' Willow looked thoughtful.

'Very sure,' Rowan confirmed. 'That was when I *really* started to panic. Not— It was fine,' she amended quickly, when Willow's eyes widened with unasked questions. 'I just figured that if anyone was going to know that I wasn't you, a relative of Ben's was probably pretty likely.'

'You'd be surprised,' Willow said drily. 'From the description—and the fact that Ben doesn't actually have a lot of family he's in touch with—I think it must have been his brother, Eli. He runs some sort of charity in the city, I think? I don't really know.'

'Launch,' Rowan confirmed. 'That was why he was here—looking for a file for some event or another. But

Will…he was looking at me a lot. Like, suspiciously. I think he might have guessed I wasn't you.'

Willow laughed. 'I doubt it! I've never even met the man in person over the last two years. If I'd walked in on him I might not have recognised him and just called the cops on him. He was lucky he got you instead.'

Rowan thought about how he'd sat beside her and helped her ride out her anxiety attack. How patient and calm he'd been. How he'd known all the right things to say and do. 'Right. Lucky.' She couldn't tell Willow, but *she'd* been the lucky one.

'Seriously, Ro, don't worry. He won't have suspected a thing.' Willow looked a lot more cheerful on the screen now. 'Ben always says Eli's too wrapped up in that non-profit of his to pay any attention to the real world, anyway.'

'Huh.' Rowan was starting to suspect that Willow wasn't the only one who didn't know Eli very well. She'd only spent a brief time with him, under not the best circumstances, but she could already have told Ben that Eli understood the real world perfectly well—at least, the world she lived in.

'Anyway. I wouldn't worry about it. So, how do you like my flat?' Willow smiled proudly across the phone screen. 'Isn't the view fantastic?'

'I, uh, haven't really had a chance to appreciate it yet. Eli just left.' Also, she had a crippling fear of heights, so looking out of those huge windows was not high on her list of things to do for fun.

Willow frowned. 'Where are you, anyway? Are you… is that the front door behind you? Why aren't you sitting on the sofa?'

'Just tired.' Rowan gave a wan smile. 'Just sat where

I fell after getting rid of Eli.' Probably better not to mention that she was too scared of marking any of the pristine white furniture to use it yet. She still had to replicate the perfect organisation system Willow had implemented throughout the flat.

Eli had assumed she must have got a professional organiser in, and Rowan hadn't corrected him, since it gave her a neat excuse for why she didn't know where anything was. But she knew her sister. Those clear acrylic containers and that rainbow organisational system was definitely all Willow.

'Well, feel free to make yourself at home there, Ro.' Willow's expression turned serious. 'I know how big a favour you're doing me, and I don't take it for granted.'

'It'll be fine,' Rowan said, hoping it wasn't a lie. 'At least there aren't any photo shoots or shows to cope with.'

She wasn't going to think about the last time she did a modelling shoot. About how she'd fainted under the lights, and the booking agent had said she looked unhealthy and unwell, and her mother had screamed at her backstage so loudly that everyone on the shoot must have heard.

That was the day she'd known she needed to leave.

She'd been contracted for three more runway shows before her twenty-first birthday—the day the money she'd been earning since she was young came into her own hands. She'd gritted her teeth and, with Willow's help, made it through them.

And she'd never gone back. Never spoken to their mother again. Moved countries and changed her whole life.

Now she had to try and remember that old life all over again.

'I mean it, Rowan,' Willow insisted. 'My home is your home. My things are your things. You've got my credit card in your bag—use it. Go shopping. Go out for meals. See the sights. Have an adventure for once. Seriously. If you haven't racked up a massive bill on that thing one way or another by the time we swap back, I'll be seriously disappointed. You know I'm good for the money.'

That was true. Rowan had left America with a healthy bank balance for anyone, let alone a twenty-one-year-old single woman. A large chunk had gone on buying her cottage outright, some she'd invested for the future, and the rest she'd needed to make last.

Her childhood had been spent on modelling shoots, not in a classroom. Their mother had pulled them out of school as soon as they were legally old enough, and it wasn't as if she had much in the way of work experience that wasn't basically looking pretty in different poses.

Except, she'd realised, she did. She knew clothes. She knew fashion. She knew how fabrics draped, and how cuts looked on different bodies. And while she might not want to be the one showing them off any more, she *did* love clothes—the way they could express someone's personality in a glance, far better than any multiple-choice test. How they could provide confidence or take it away. How the cheapest fast fashion could look expensive worn in the right way, and the most high-end designer item could look cheap if worn wrong.

Even when she'd been working, she'd been far more interested in what other people were wearing than the clothes she was being dressed in. She liked seeing how the industry insiders chose their outfits. How stylists and stores interpreted the high fashion trends from the catwalk into something celebrities could wear on the red carpet, and then into something anyone could wear day to day.

She'd paid attention to how the outfits were constructed too—the fittings and the alterations made when she needed a couture dress for an event. The design process fascinated her, and she'd started picking up books on it whenever they had downtime.

So, alone in her little seaside cottage, she'd put all that knowledge to good use. She'd started a style blog at first, anonymously, of course. She'd post photos of her outfits, but laid out on her bed, or if she was wearing them, with her head cut off.

And she'd started making her own clothes too. Things she'd never have worn in New York. She didn't worry about fashion or trends, she just made the things she liked. Like retro headscarves in bright floral fabric. Floaty summer dresses and maxi skirts. Things that made her feel like herself, at last.

She'd fallen into making clothes for other people almost by accident. She'd overheard a teenage girl in tears outside the only formalwear shop in the nearest town, her mother helplessly trying to comfort her. She'd needed a dress for the school prom, and none of them fitted her because she wasn't whatever the shop had deemed to be the perfect size for a sixteen-year-old girl.

Rowan had tried to keep a bit of distance with the local community, but this was different.

She'd offered to make her a dress—and the girl and her mum had been thrilled with it. Mum had insisted on paying, and she'd spread the word too. Soon Rowan had business cards and a simple website and an income again.

She was lucky she'd finished her last commission just before Willow came knocking, or she'd never have been able to disappear to New York for weeks on end.

But now she was here, and with her sister's credit card... She knew exactly what she wanted to do with it.

Eli had been told, often in his life, that he had some sort of guilt complex. First by his brother, then by various ex-girlfriends, and even by a therapist or two—although they generally used much more complex terms.

The meaning was the same. Eli felt guilty. About a lot of things. A lot of the time.

Maybe it was because he'd been born into such privilege when so many others had so little. Or perhaps it was because he knew the circumstances of his birth were suspect, but his father could never admit it. Or maybe it was just how he was.

Whatever the reason, it meant he spent a lot of his time, energy and personal fortune trying to assuage that guilt. Running the non-profit was just part of it, as was volunteering at the Castaway Café.

And today he was trying to erase his guilt by checking on his brother's ex-girlfriend.

He picked up flowers on his way, because everyone liked flowers, didn't they? But he went for tulips because it was spring, and because tulips felt more like an overture of friendship than any of the other bouquets on offer. The last thing he needed was Willow getting the wrong idea and giving him something else to feel guilty about.

He'd done a lot of work on his guilt issues, and he liked to think he'd come a long way. He knew it wasn't his fault his father had hated him but still felt socially obliged to support him as a son. He knew he hadn't imagined the bad feelings in his family dynamics, no matter how many people had lied and told him he was making it up, that his father loved both his sons equally.

He'd been almost twenty when he'd learned the term 'gaslighting' but it had been the first step to changing his life.

This time, when he arrived at Willow's apartment building, he didn't use the code Ben had given him to gain entrance, but rang the buzzer instead. No answer.

Eli frowned. He should have called first, perhaps, but he didn't have her number. But if she wasn't here, he was just a guy standing in the street with a bunch of tulips looking hopeful about spring.

Just as he was debating what to do next, Willow appeared around the corner, weighed down with half a dozen shopping bags, and he relaxed into a smile. 'Let me help you with those.'

Willow blinked at him, then smiled cautiously. 'Eli. I didn't expect to see you again so soon.'

At least now the trauma of her panic attack had passed she'd managed to remember his name. She looked better too, like she might have actually slept since he saw her last.

Willow was always, always beautiful—at least, as far as he could tell from the photos he saw online or on billboards. But in her apartment that day she'd also looked…fragile.

Juggling bags with flowers, he nodded towards the

tulips. 'I was bringing you these. An apology for the other day.'

'You really didn't have to.' Her smile tightened as she opened the door.

He followed her with the bags all the same. 'I wanted to.'

They took the elevator up to the apartment in awkward silence.

'Where do you want these?' Eli asked as they stepped inside.

Willow looked surprised, as if she'd forgotten he was carrying her shopping. 'Oh, just dump them by the door somewhere.'

Already there were more signs of habitation in the apartment than when he'd last visited—a sweater slung over the arm of a sofa, a book on the coffee table, coffee mugs on the kitchen counter. All of which reinforced his suspicion that the organisation of her apartment had happened in her absence.

'So, are you replacing things your home organisers decluttered for you?' he joked, gesturing towards the bags.

'What? Oh, no. I just…looked in the closet here and couldn't see anything I wanted to wear. So I went shopping.'

She said it airily, like a privileged woman used to replacing her entire wardrobe on a whim. But there was something in her eyes, something Eli recognised from people he'd worked with before. This wasn't a whim; it was a change.

Willow was making changes in her life. Was it in response to breaking up with Ben?

Eli knew from experience that change could be very positive—or it could be a distraction. Sometimes people changed everything about themselves outwardly, just to avoid dealing with the things that scared them within.

A breakup was a perfectly reasonable time for a makeover—he knew that from romcom movies he'd watched with ex-girlfriends.

So why did he feel like this was something more?

'Can I offer you a drink?' Willow flipped the kettle on, and Eli frowned. Had there even been a kettle in this kitchen the last time he was here? He only remembered the high-end coffee machine. 'Tea?'

'Uh, coffee, if that's okay,' he replied. Maybe Willow was getting back to her British roots after breaking up with her American boyfriend. That would make sense.

She nodded and reached for a jar, rather than the machine. When he frowned, she laughed self-deprecatingly. 'I never did figure out how to use that thing. But if you think you know, feel free!'

It didn't take long for him to make sense of the coffee machine—it wasn't very different to the one he had at home. Willow looked on, nodding politely and sipping her tea as he explained it to her. 'I can write it down, if you like...?'

'No, I'll...' She stopped and blushed prettily. 'Actually, that might be a good idea. Just in case.'

By the time he'd written down the instructions and she'd taped them to the front of the machine, ruining any aesthetic the designer and organiser had put in place for the kitchen, they were feeling more at ease with each other again.

'So, how are things going with your gala?' Willow folded her long legs under her on the corner of the sofa.

Eli, sitting across from her on the other sofa, reflected that this was far more comfortable than the floor. 'They're going.' His contacts had come through—the ones he'd been cultivating even as he'd waited for Ben to read the file he'd given him, knowing that his brother wasn't a sure thing. He didn't have the one big name sponsor he'd hoped Ben would provide, but he'd raised the money he needed through a few smaller ones with just a few phone calls. People wanted to be seen doing good in this city right now, and Eli was perfectly happy to take advantage of that. 'My team are still on the hunt for a few table sponsors, though, if you're interested?'

'How much?' Willow asked without blinking.

'Uh, five thousand dollars for a table of eight.'

'Can you take a credit card?' She was already reaching for her purse.

'You really want to help?' The words were out before he could stop them.

She hesitated. 'Why wouldn't I? I… I read up a bit on your work after you were here and, well, you're doing really important things. Helping the young people of New York City who really need that help.'

'Not all of them,' Eli admitted. 'There are too many that need the help. And a lot of other great organisations are doing just as much, and many are doing more.'

'But you're doing what you can,' Willow said firmly. 'Not many people do even that.'

'Well, if you're sure,' Eli said. Was this a good idea? Letting his brother's ex-girlfriend sponsor a table at his event? Making a connection between them—even an altruistic and charitable one—just as their relationship had ended?

Maybe not. But if he turned away a genuine donation for personal reasons…

'I'm sure.' Willow reached into her purse and pulled out a credit card. 'How do we do this?'

Rowan started to doubt the wisdom of her impulse almost as soon as Eli had picked up the phone to call the office so she could give Willow's credit card number to the fundraiser at the other end of the line. But she'd already had a personal spending spree on Willow's card—buying the sort of wardrobe that was Willow appropriate, but still felt a little bit like Rowan too. Now she wanted to do something more meaningful.

Willow had said she could spend as much as she wanted, on whatever mattered to her—and this mattered. Not just to her, but to lots of people.

She'd researched Eli and his non-profit organisation thoroughly after her call with Willow, and the more she'd read the more she'd been convinced that he was doing good work—and that his brother and her sister had barely even noticed. Ben probably hadn't even bothered to read that file Eli had been searching for the day they'd met.

She hadn't exactly *intended* to sponsor a table at his event or anything but, when the opportunity arose, it seemed like the obvious thing to do. The *right* thing. Given the way his face had lit up, he thought so too.

Eli handed his phone over to her with a smile. 'This is Sandra. She'll take you through the sponsorship form and take your donation, if you're still sure.'

Rowan nodded, and took the phone.

Sandra—a warm-sounding woman with a broad New York accent, the sort Rowan imagined from the movies—was funny, reassuring and made the whole process painless. Right up until the moment she asked, 'And can I take the names of the guests for your table?'

Of course, sponsoring a table meant filling it with people too. Why hadn't she realised that? It wasn't as if she could just call up Willow's friends and invite them to a gala dinner. She didn't even know who Willow's friends were these days, for a start.

'Uh, can I get back to you on that?'

'Sure, honey,' Sandra said. 'Just let me know when you know, yeah?'

A couple more questions and the call was done. Rowan handed the phone back to Eli and he had a few more words with Sandra before hanging up.

Then he turned to Rowan with a small frown line between his eyes. 'So, do you know who you're going to ask to join you at the dinner?'

Because of course *she'd* have to go too. God, she really hadn't thought this through at all, had she?

This was why she didn't usually make spur-of-the-moment decisions. They rarely ended well.

'Actually… I was wondering if *you'd* like to fill the table,' she said after a brief pause. 'I mean, there must be lots of people working behind the scenes at your non-profit who never get to attend the fancy fun stuff. Wouldn't you like to be able to reward them with a table at the dinner?'

There, that solved it! Eli could ask deserving volunteers and staff and she could just pay the money then stay the hell out of it.

'That would be...incredibly kind and thoughtful of you.' Eli was still frowning, despite his words. 'Are you sure?'

Rowan nodded fervently. 'Very.'

'Well, great!' Eli's expression cleared. 'There are definitely some long-time volunteers and staff who would love to be dressed up and enjoying the party rather than behind the scenes on the night—Sandra for one! And I'm sure they'll all enjoy having dinner with a celebrity like yourself.'

'Oh, I—' She broke off. How could she explain that she didn't want to actually attend without sounding like she was too superior to have dinner with the *staff*? 'That will be lovely,' she finished lamely.

So, apparently, she was going to need an evening gown too. Great.

'And since you're going to be there anyway...' Eli looked so hopeful, Rowan knew she wasn't going to like whatever came out of his mouth next. 'Perhaps you'd like to present some of our awards on the night?'

'Sure.' What else could she say, really? Although she was certain her smile must look fake.

'That's fantastic! Thank you, Willow.' Eli reached out and took her hand, his expression so earnest and sincere she couldn't even begin to look away. 'I can't tell you how much this will mean to everyone involved. It's not just the money—although we always appreciate that. It's you lending your name to the cause. It helps us raise the profile, get more people interested in our work, more people donating—everything. I know charity shouldn't require celebrities to get people's attention, but...' He shrugged.

'Sometimes it does,' Rowan finished for him, and he nodded.

She supposed that made sense, in a way. And she knew Willow was always very careful about what brands or causes she lent her name—or, more potently, her face—to for that very reason. People assumed that if she spoke about it, wore their brand or appeared at their events, then she endorsed everything about them. They were linked for ever.

Well, hopefully, her sister couldn't disapprove of supporting vulnerable teens in the city. Otherwise, Rowan was in for an earful the next time they spoke!

'I'm really glad to be able to help,' she said honestly. 'The work you're doing here... I wasn't just saying it when I said I know how much it matters. It's a cause that's...well. Close to my heart.'

She might have not been a teen runaway, or kicked out of her home by junkie parents, or struggling with mental health problems without access to the proper support. She was, in so many ways, hugely privileged and fortunate and she *knew* that.

But she also knew that if she and Willow hadn't looked the way they did, she might not have been.

The luck of the draw. Genetics shouldn't be something to be proud of, since she'd done nothing herself but be born with them.

Eli looked thoughtful. 'I wonder... How would you like to come down to the offices, and maybe one of our centres, and see the work we do up close? You can meet some of our staff before the dinner that way too.'

She should say no. She should be staying out of the way, only appearing as Willow when strictly necessary.

The more people she interacted with, the more chance there was of giving herself away. Of people realising she wasn't Willow at all. And she couldn't risk that, for her sister's sake.

*Especially* with Ben's brother.

But, all the same, she found herself saying, 'That would be lovely,' and a warm feeling spread through her at Eli's smile.

# CHAPTER FOUR

THE FOLLOWING FRIDAY, Eli led Willow into the main offices of Launch through the back door that led to the administrative centre, feeling unexpectedly apprehensive about the whole thing, considering it had been his idea in the first place.

He wasn't even entirely sure why. Willow had been nothing but gracious and generous and—above all—*interested* in the non-profit company he ran, ever since that day in her apartment. But being philanthropic from a distance was one thing, Eli knew. It was easy to throw money at a problem so you didn't have to look at it.

He hadn't expected Ben's ex-girlfriend to show any interest at all in his foundation or the work they did. Most of the people in Ben's circle that he met paid lip service to caring about kids or society's problems, but they didn't get involved. He'd assumed Willow would be the same. But she kept surprising him. She seemed so unlike the media image of her he'd thought he knew, it was hard to remember that she was the same woman who'd hung adoringly on Ben's arm for the last two years.

For starters, she seemed genuinely interested in Launch. He just hoped that interest would outlast a meeting with reality.

From the way she was looking around her curiously as they entered the building, he suspected it would. So what was he really worried about?

Maybe it was because Ben was back in the city. He'd called Eli the night before about an upcoming report due out from the family business. Ben might be the CEO, but Eli was also a stakeholder, so still technically involved. His income from his seat on the board of directors was what had made it possible for him to set up Launch in the first place.

Eli hadn't mentioned Willow when they'd talked. He was still busy pretending to himself that he didn't know why that was.

It wasn't as if they were doing anything wrong. He just…didn't want to have to explain his sudden acquaintance with his brother's ex to Ben.

'So how much work do you actually do here?' Willow asked as they waited for her visitor pass to be printed at reception.

He looked at her in surprise. 'Uh, this is my job. Full-time. So I'm here most days. It's not…it's not like a figurehead position or anything.'

She smiled softly. 'That's not what I meant. I wasn't doubting your commitment to the cause, Eli.'

Behind the reception desk, Addison gave him a cheeky grin as she handed over Willow's pass. Reaching out, he hung the lanyard over Willow's neck as she ducked her head to make it easier for him.

Addison was making hearts with her hands and batting her eyelashes at them. Eli turned Willow towards the elevators before she noticed.

Sending Addison a warning look over his shoulder, he asked Willow, 'So what did you mean?'

'Just that I assume things like the shelters and such are off site? Is this building just for administration, or what?' She stepped into the elevator and he followed, pressing the buttons to take them up to the top floor. They could work downwards, he figured.

'This building houses the helpline staff, the fundraising staff, the admin staff—and through the other entrance on the ground floor we have the Castaway Café, which is actually quite often kids' first port of call with us. I'll show you that later; we can have a coffee.'

'That sounds good.' The elevator surged upwards. 'So, where do we start?'

'My office, of course,' Eli replied.

When he'd been looking for a headquarters, location had been key. Ben had tried to convince him to look at buildings near the company HQ, but Eli had refused. They needed to be somewhere close to the kids he wanted to serve, so that meant moving out of the areas of Manhattan he'd grown up in, and towards the ones that needed his help.

The building he'd chosen, sandwiched between a laundrette and a Malaysian takeaway, had needed a lot of work. But it gave them three floors, kitchen facilities on the first floor for the café he'd envisioned, space for a decent phone bank, and good open-plan offices for the rest of the staff. They'd done up the inside to freshen it up and make it feel new, but left the façade so it matched the surroundings. They didn't want to stand out—not for how they looked, anyway.

Eli wanted their work to stand out for them.

The elevator doors opened, and Eli let Willow step out first, right into the hustle and bustle of the office floor. A few people looked up—one or two even did a double-take, Eli noted with amusement—but they didn't let their latest arrival disturb their work.

The whole floor was buzzing with activity and a feeling of purpose. Eli felt the warmth of pride in his chest as Willow surveyed the scene and smiled.

Then she turned to him. 'Where's your office?'

'This way.'

He introduced her to a few people as they passed their desks, and she asked interested and insightful questions about what they were doing—without getting into the kind of details that were confidential. Eventually, they reached the far corner of the floor, diagonally opposite and as far from the elevator as possible.

'And this is me.' He gestured towards the L-shaped desk with its overflowing in-tray, monitor and laptop stand, and a poster on the wall featuring a quote that read: 'Never doubt that a small group of thoughtful, committed citizens can change the world; indeed, it's the only thing that ever has'.

'Isn't that from the TV show, *The West Wing*?' Willow asked, looking at it.

'It was actually the anthropologist Margaret Mead who said it first,' Eli replied. 'But I had to look that up after watching the episode.'

'Fair enough.' She stared out of the window behind his desk for a long moment, then turned around to look back over the open-plan office. 'You didn't want an office with a door and a view?'

'I have a view,' he pointed out, nodding towards the window.

'You don't face it, though. You face your staff.' He shrugged, and she continued. 'And you're as far away from the lift as it's possible to get, so you have to walk through and see every one of them on your way.'

'I like to be involved.'

'I'm seeing that.' She looked up at him, and this time her smile was considering, thoughtful—and he couldn't look away from it.

At least until the whirlwind that was his assistant, Kelly, came racing across the office from wherever she'd been, doing whatever she'd been doing.

'Eli! I *can't* come to the gala, I just can't!' Kelly's hands were clenched in fists at her sides, and he got the impression that she'd been waiting to tell him this for some time, and working herself up about it.

'That's a shame, Kelly,' he said calmly. 'It would have been lovely to have you there, after all the work you've put in to make it happen.'

'Well, I can't.' Her lower lip was trembling.

'That's fine,' he said. 'It's no problem. But…can I ask why?'

Now tears sprang into her eyes—but it seemed to him they were more angry tears than sad ones. 'Because not all of us look like Miss Supermodel here!' she snapped, waving a hand towards Willow. 'There isn't a dress in New York City that will fit over these hips without making me look like a sackful of potatoes.'

Eli's jaw clenched. He'd never spent any time thinking about his assistant's hips. Mostly, he thought about how she always had the file he needed ready before he needed it, how she cared deeply about the work they were doing and always gave everything she had to getting things done right.

He hated that something as stupid as a dress might stop her celebrating everything she'd worked so hard for.

Tears glistened on Kelly's cheeks as she glanced up at Willow from under her eyelashes. 'No offence meant. I mean, it was very nice of you to offer us the table. Only I'd stick out like a sore thumb at something like that. But that's not your fault. Sorry.'

Eli looked over to see if Willow was offended, but she seemed more thoughtful than angry.

'No, no, I totally understand,' Willow said, smiling graciously. 'Actually, uh, I might be able to help you with that.'

*Help?*

Just when he thought she was done surprising him.

Rowan regretted it almost the instant the words were out of her mouth.

This wasn't something Willow would do. This was a *Rowan* thing, and it was exactly how she was going to get caught out in her deception and let Willow down.

In fact, this was *just* how it had happened with that woman and her daughter outside the dress shop. She hated to see someone upset by something as basic as *clothes*. Hated for anyone to feel ostracised by style or fashion. Not when she could do something about it.

So maybe she didn't regret it all that much. Except for the way Eli was looking at her right now.

'You can help?' he asked, sounding sceptical. 'How? You have…connections, I suppose?'

'I do.' Or, well, Willow did. 'But actually...' She gave Kelly an apologetic look. 'Most of the designers I knew—know—only do sample sizing.'

'Exactly!' Kelly said, vindicated. 'They don't want people like me wearing their clothes!'

'But I *do* have some...experience *making* dresses,' Rowan said quickly. 'My, uh, my sister is a designer, as it happens, and she taught me a lot. If I can get your measurements and some ideas of what sort of a dress you're looking for, I can bring some fabrics in for you to look at, and some draft designs? What do you think?'

Kelly was staring at her in shock. So was Eli, come to that. This *really* wasn't the sort of thing Willow would have done. But actually...neither of them really knew Willow, so how could they be sure?

And she wanted to help. This whole organisation was doing so much good for the young people of the city. If she could help *them*, just a tiny bit...why wouldn't she?

'You *make* dresses?' Kelly asked. 'Seriously? When people must just *give* them to you all the time?'

'Well, it's my sister who's really great at it,' Rowan said. 'But I know enough to make you look good, I promise.'

'It really would be a shame for you to miss the gala,' Eli added persuasively.

Kelly looked between them for a moment, then nodded. 'Okay. We'll try it. How do we start?'

Rowan beamed, then glanced up at Eli. 'Can we use your desk?'

'Go ahead. It's not like I'm going to get any work done this morning, anyway. I'll fetch the coffees, shall

I?' He shot a grin at Kelly, who seemed pleased at this turnabout in their relationship.

'That would be wonderful.' Rowan pulled a notebook from her bag, grabbed a pen and dropped into Eli's desk chair. 'So, what sort of a dress were you thinking of?'

Out of the corner of her eye, she was vaguely aware of Eli watching them and shaking his head, before he went to find the promised coffee. She suspected that there would be a conversation later about this. That he wasn't fully convinced—or at least that he knew something was off.

She'd have to figure out how to deal with that. How to keep lying to him, even as they spent more time together.

This wasn't part of the plan she and Willow had hammered out at her kitchen table in Rumbelow. She wasn't supposed to get close to Eli—she wasn't supposed to get close to *anyone,* least of all Ben's brother.

But it had happened anyway, and she couldn't bring herself to regret it. Not when she was sitting here contributing a very small amount to the work his non-profit was doing—even if only by making his assistant's life a little brighter.

It took some coaxing to get Kelly to tell her the sort of dress she *really* wanted to wear—rather than the sort of dress she *thought* she should wear, at her size.

'It should be black, right?' Kelly said anxiously. 'Black is slimming.'

'Black can be elegant and classic,' Rowan said evenly. 'But if it doesn't really feel like you, that doesn't matter. Other colours can be those things too.'

Kelly sighed. 'I just don't want to look huge and awful.'

Rowan took her hand across the desk. 'I promise you that you won't. You're a beautiful woman, and we're going to create a dress for you that shows that to the world. That makes you feel like your very best you. Okay?'

It was a speech she'd given to girls and women back home a hundred times over the past few years. Girls who thought they were too fat for prom, or that they couldn't wear a classic strapless prom dress because they were 'flat as a board' and had nothing to hold it up. Students who didn't feel at ease in either a traditional prom dress or a tuxedo, and wanted something new, something different—something that felt like them. Women who needed something to wear to an ex's wedding and wanted it to make them feel incredible while also not looking like they were trying too hard.

Finding a dress to match how a person wanted to feel while wearing it? That was Rowan's speciality, and she knew she could do it for Kelly too.

By the time they'd drunk the coffee Eli returned with, Rowan had a page full of notes of Kelly's likes, dislikes, wishes and dreams and fears for her dress—and the start of a picture growing in her mind.

She smiled at Eli's assistant as she closed her notebook. 'Well, I can definitely work with this.'

Kelly's expression grew anxious as her gaze flitted between Rowan and Eli. 'It's kind of you to listen to me chatter about this stuff. But I really can't afford a bespoke dress—or even the fabric for one. He doesn't pay us *that* much, you know!'

Rowan shook her head. 'This one's on me, Kelly. Just call it an extra donation to the cause.'

*Her* cause, of helping women feel confident when people were staring, like themselves even when they were dressed up, and like they deserved beautiful things.

They made their goodbyes, Kelly thanking Rowan profusely as they left, tears sparkling in her eyes.

'That was kind of you,' Eli murmured, one hand against the small of her back as he guided her to the lift.

Rowan shrugged. 'Why not be kind, when we can?'

'An excellent question,' Eli replied. But Rowan couldn't help but notice the way he looked at her as they stepped into the lift. As if she were a puzzle he hadn't quite figured out—but fully intended to.

And soon.

Eli wasn't by nature a suspicious man. He liked to believe the best of people, until they proved otherwise. But Rowan had all his senses on high alert.

The most ridiculous part was that she'd done it by being kind, generous and thoughtful to a fault. Her crimes, such as they were, boiled down to donating to a cause he believed passionately in, helping a woman he was fond of, and now engaging with the kids who found sanctuary at the Castaway Café.

'She seems to really get them.' Standing beside him by the counter, the café manager, Sven, shook his head. 'I wouldn't have expected it from someone like her.'

'Me neither,' Eli agreed softly, watching as Willow drew some of the youths at the table into conversation, asking a question about their hopes for the future, rather than the life they'd run away from.

And that was what it came down to in the end, wasn't it? His own prejudices and preconceptions getting in the way of the reality he observed.

He'd never got to know Willow when she was dating Ben—he'd never had the chance. He'd assumed she had no interest in meeting her boyfriend's less commercially successful brother. He knew he didn't move in the same circles or worlds that Ben and Willow did, because he didn't *want* to. That had been a conscious choice when he'd gained his inheritance at the tender age of twenty-one.

He hadn't wanted to live in that superficial world of celebrity and fame for fame's sake. He'd wanted to do something more than be photographed partying on yachts. It hadn't been a popular decision—with his friends, his brother or his girlfriend at the time.

But he'd done it anyway. And he'd never regretted it.

So he'd assumed, based on the reactions of others, that Willow—who he'd never met and certainly didn't know outside the celebrity gossip pages—felt the same. That was on him.

Why *hadn't* they got to know each other better before now, then? Lack of opportunity? Given how interested Willow was in the work of Launch and the Castaway Café now, he couldn't believe it was because she hadn't wanted to know more. Had she even known what he did for a living? Had Ben spoken about him at all?

Ben. Whichever way he looked at it, it seemed that Ben must have been the one keeping them apart. Why? Because he was ashamed of him?

It was a possibility. Eli wondered what he'd think about their meeting now—and working together, sort of. How he'd feel about Willow getting involved with Launch. Could this be some sort of bizarre revenge scheme she was planning against his brother? He couldn't see how.

But as for what Ben would think... There was no reason for his brother to be concerned. This was a purely professional arrangement, and Ben and Willow weren't even together any more—well, not at the moment, anyway. Eli wouldn't let this evolve into anything that could embarrass his brother or the company in any way. So really, why should Ben care?

And why was Eli so sure he would?

He turned the idea over in his head once or twice, then tucked it away for thinking about later.

Right now, he was focused on Willow.

Willow, who was now being shown around the café, admiring the wall art—created by some of the regulars, in a mix of styles. They had the graffiti wall, the cartoon and manga wall and also some framed sketches and even watercolours on the last wall from an art course they'd run in one of the back rooms a few months ago.

He'd never seen the kids react to someone new like this. She'd got their emotional barriers down in record time, and seemed to genuinely connect with them. How did she do it? And what was it in her past that made her understand them?

Every one of these kids had difficult—often impossible—relationships with their families. Maybe they'd been kicked out, or perhaps they were trying to work through their problems with the help of Launch's trained counsellors. But, as far as Eli knew, Willow didn't have any estranged family in her past. She'd sounded genuinely fond when talking of her sister, for instance.

Her sister. Maybe that was the in.

Whatever it was, he wanted to know more.

Because he just couldn't shake the feeling, unfair as it might be, that this was all an act, somehow. That Willow was hiding something—a secret that would make sense of all the things he didn't yet understand.

He hated not knowing secrets. All those years of sensing people were whispering to each other as they looked at him, but not knowing what they were saying. These days, he just asked them outright.

Which was what he should do with Willow. Maybe over dinner.

No, not dinner.

Except why not? A *working* dinner. A client dinner, like he had hundreds of times a year, persuading people who could make a difference to make a difference at his foundation. That was all.

Nobody, not even Ben, could object to that.

Willow bounced away from the pack of kids, smiling, and made her way over to him.

'This place is brilliant,' she said. 'I can see how at home they all are here. You've given them what they really needed—a place to belong.'

'That was the idea,' Eli admitted. 'I didn't... I didn't always feel at home or like I belonged, growing up. And my experience was definitely at the top, most privileged end of that emotion. So, I guess I wanted to give more to the kids who need it now.'

Give a truth to get a truth, that was how it worked, right? He'd opened up, given her an insight into his own past, so maybe she'd share something of hers—if not now, then soon.

He'd half-expected her to ask about Ben, and how he fitted into that vision of Eli's childhood. But apparently that thought didn't occur to her as she moved breezily on.

'The artwork is fantastic too. There's some real talent there. But, more importantly, they're so *proud* that someone admired their work enough to display it. That really means something to them.' She smiled up at him. 'I love this place.'

He couldn't help but smile back. 'I'm glad. Actually, I was wondering…would you like to get dinner with me tonight? We could talk some more about the work we do here, and maybe how you could be involved longer term?'

Her face started to fall, and he hurried on. 'Only if you wanted to be, of course. I just… You seemed to have a real connection with these kids, and—'

'No, no! I would… I would like that.' Her smile said otherwise, though, wobbling a little as she continued. 'Pick me up at eight?'

Eli nodded. 'Will do.' And then he'd figure out what secrets Willow was keeping from him—one way or another.

# CHAPTER FIVE

ROWAN HADN'T REALLY thought that anyone drove in Manhattan, but Eli did. When Willow went places with Ben she knew he had a driver, but his brother seemed to prefer to do the work himself. He picked her up at eight on the dot and, after a moment of staring silently at her, had driven them to the restaurant he'd chosen.

It was the dress that made him stare, Rowan knew that. Not the fact that she was in it.

Her shopping spree had mostly included clothes for wearing around the apartment, or for running errands in the city. She hadn't really envisioned fancy meals out at that point. So she'd had to raid Willow's wardrobe for something suitable.

And Willow's wardrobe was full of possibilities for a woman wanting to stand out and be looked at. Not so many for a woman wanting to blend in and pass people by.

She'd chosen the least flashy option—a midi-length, fire-engine-red dress that was cut high in the front but very low over her back, and flared out around her thighs—paired it with the only pair of Willow's shoes she thought she could walk in, kept her make-up and jewellery simple, and hoped for the best.

The best being not falling over in someone else's meal because the black heels were still too high.

Oh. And not being outed as not Willow. That would be good too.

She'd had second, third and fourth thoughts about this dinner while she was getting ready. She'd even called the real Willow and asked for advice on how to get out of it.

But her sister had been so excited that Rowan had met someone and was going out for a fancy dinner, she hadn't seemed to care who it was—or let Rowan get a word in to warn her.

'That's exactly *the sort of thing I'd do—go out for din-ner with a handsome man. I mean—he is handsome, right? But yes, you should definitely go. Because I guarantee Ben will have been off being seen with some other woman while we're broken up, so I should too. This is perfect.'*

By that point, it seemed too late to tell her that the man in question was Ben's brother.

Or that it was a working dinner, not an actual date.

Willow had rung off, and Rowan had sighed and put on the dress. And now, here she was.

The restaurant Eli had chosen was thankfully small, not too busy and smelled delicious. Rowan breathed a sigh of relief as she took her seat at the back of the room. From what she knew of Ben, this was the last place he would be seen, which meant that the chances of bumping into him tonight were slim. Willow might have wanted her to be somewhere more high profile, somewhere she might get photographed to prove she was in New York not Cornwall, but this suited Rowan just fine.

'I hope you like Italian,' Eli said as they were handed their menus.

'It's my favourite,' she assured him. 'And the best thing is, in this dress, when I spill spaghetti sauce down me you won't even be able to see it!'

That surprised a laugh from him. 'I wasn't sure if, with your career, carbs were off-limits or something.'

They probably should be, if she wanted to really seem like Willow. But Italian really *was* her favourite. And the restaurant was quiet. Who'd know?

'A well-balanced diet includes all the food groups, as far as possible,' she said instead. Hard-won knowledge she'd had to learn *after* she'd left modelling, but it was still true.

'That's what I always think.' Eli relaxed into his chair. 'Tiramisu is a food group, right?'

'Definitely,' Rowan agreed fervently.

They made easy conversation over menu choices and a glass of wine, and it wasn't until they'd finished their main course that the discussion turned to areas Rowan knew she had to be completely on guard with.

'So, growing up famous must have been weird?' Eli swirled the last of his red wine around his glass before swallowing it. He'd only had the one—and had already ordered a coffee with dessert—because he was driving. She'd also only had one because she didn't want any secrets to slip out if she got even the tiniest bit tipsy.

'I guess…when it's all you know, you don't always realise how weird it is,' she said carefully. 'Like you growing up rich, I suppose.'

'I suppose,' Eli agreed. 'Except… I still went to school and college, did all the usual things a kid was supposed to do. My father just paid more for it.' There was a note in his voice she couldn't place. Not resentment—Eli had been nothing but grateful for his good fortune in life in every conversation they'd had. But maybe…a longing? For something else? She wasn't sure.

'I went to school too, for a while,' Rowan said with a slight shrug. 'We moved around a bit when I was younger, but by my teenage years we were settled in London, and we just flew out for shoots and shows. It was weird going from the classroom to the catwalk and back again, though.'

'I imagine it would be.' Eli pushed his empty glass aside, and leaned his elbows on the table. 'Then after school you moved to New York?'

*After school I was a mess, and barely talking to my family, and on all kinds of anxiety drugs my mother convinced the doctor to give me, just counting the days until I could run away.*

'We split our time between London and New York,' she said, because it sounded better than 'it didn't really matter where we lived, because I was holed up in my room whenever I wasn't needed to be in front of a camera or an audience'.

'Is your mother still in London?'

Rowan shook her head, using the arrival of the tiramisu and coffees they'd ordered as an excuse to look away from his searching eyes. Her mother was *definitely* not a subject she wanted to get into with him.

'LA,' she answered shortly. 'She got remarried, to an actor.'

'Do you see her often?' Eli pressed. No, not pressed. This was perfectly normal first date conversation. He was just being polite.

Not that this was a date at all, she reminded her brain

sharply. As far as Eli was concerned, she was his brother's on-again off-again girlfriend. And she already knew enough about Eli to know he'd never make a move on his brother's girl.

Which was weird in itself. She *didn't* know Eli, not really—and neither did Willow. But she felt as if she did.

He'd been nothing but respectful of her since they'd met, and that slightly stunned look when he'd picked her up was the only hint that he even found her attractive at all. And Rowan knew better than most that external attractiveness meant next to nothing when it came to happiness.

No, Eli had shown no interest in her beyond what she could do for his foundation, and a few polite questions about her life as a model. That was all.

Asking about a person's mother was perfectly normal. It was Rowan's relationship with her mother that wasn't.

She thought back to her last conversation with Willow about their mother. Her twin tended to avoid the subject with her, for obvious reasons, but every now and then it came up anyway. What had she said?

'Uh…sometimes we get together if I'm working out there. But you know how life gets. So busy for everyone these days.' Rowan dug into her tiramisu with gusto, hoping that if her mouth was filled with creamy coffee dessert she couldn't be expected to answer too many more questions.

'What about your sister?' Eli asked. 'The one who taught you how to make dresses. Didn't she used to model with you? Yeah, there's that famous photo of the two of you together. What happened there? Are you still close?'

Oh, this was even dodgier ground, and Rowan really wasn't sure how to handle it.

'She used to, but she decided it wasn't for her.' She gave a light, inconsequential shrug that hopefully covered the full story without having to give any details. 'She lives in Cornwall, in England now. I don't get to visit often, but we talk on the phone a lot.'

'Hmm.' His tiramisu bowl empty, Eli leaned back in his seat and studied her. Rowan tried hard not to flinch under his gaze.

'How about you and *your* brother?' She flung the question back defensively, before realising she should already know the full story about them from Ben. 'I mean, isn't it strange that we never really got to know each other when Ben and I were still dating?'

'Yes,' Eli said, as if the word meant more than it did. 'It is.'

Rowan turned her attention back to her tiramisu and prayed for the evening to be over soon.

Just the thought sent disappointment cascading through her. Because until he'd started asking awkward questions, she'd been enjoying herself far more than she should have been, under the circumstances.

This was supposed to be business. At best, a charade for Willow's benefit. She should want to get home, forget about Eli and get on with acting like Willow. Not hanging out with her sister's ex's brother and getting involved in charity work she had no place getting involved in—especially when she knew she'd be leaving soon and, without Willow's money, wouldn't be able to support them anyway.

She should be grateful to get out of this encounter

without giving anything away. And she should make damn sure not to get herself into such a risky position again.

So that was what she'd do. Definitely.

Except, as they left the restaurant and Eli placed the palm of his hand on the small of her bare back to guide her out, she shivered at his touch. The kind of shiver that betrayed all her protestations that this was just business, that she was just playing a part, that she was only trying to help out a good cause.

The kind of shiver that told her how much more she wanted here.

Oh, hell. She was in trouble now.

Dinner with Willow had been…disconcerting. That was the only word Eli had for it.

Even asking her in the first place had probably been a mistake, but something about her seemed to make him act impulsively—which was not a good thing.

Almost as soon as he'd invited her, the doubts and worries had started flooding in. Yes, he wanted to know her secrets—but what if she got annoyed with his questions and pulled out of the gala? Or told Ben he'd been bothering her? What if Ben saw them in the restaurant? Or heard they'd been seen by someone else? How would that make him feel? Eli knew he'd hate it if Ben was seen with a woman he'd just broken up with—and probably planned to get back together with—however innocent the occasion.

But he'd invited her now. And he *did* want answers. So he'd tried to mitigate the risks by booking his favourite cosy Italian, where no one from Ben's circle would ever be seen dead—only realising too late the romantic vibes it gave off.

And then there was the dress Willow wore. From the front, it looked positively modest, with its high neck and the low hem, but the fire-engine-red colour should have been a warning sign. When she turned around to put her jacket on, the back on the damn thing dipped all the way to the base of her spine, revealing acres of smooth, bare flesh that just begged to be touched.

But he couldn't touch it. Because she was his brother's girlfriend—at least some of the time. And Eli would not be that man. There was a line, and he couldn't cross it.

Besides, they might not be together right now, but Eli knew Ben. He would be expecting Willow to be waiting for him whenever he decided it was time for them to get back together. Ben wasn't used to the world making decisions without him. In Ben's world, everything waited for him to decide.

And if he decided that he wanted Willow back, it was hard to imagine her resisting. After all, she'd gone back to him the last half dozen times, hadn't she?

Eli didn't understand their relationship. He hadn't understood it before either, but now he'd spent some time with Willow it made even less sense.

Willow cared about things, deeply. She connected with other people, she wanted to help, to be involved in people's lives. And Ben...

Eli tried not to think bad things about his older brother. But that didn't mean he couldn't see the influence their upbringing had had on him. All the ways Ben took after their father.

Where Eli had been the black sheep, the red-headed

stepchild, Ben had been the golden boy. The son and heir. Their father's firstborn—and possibly only born, if you listened to the rumours.

And Mack O'Donnell had leaned into that.

He'd paraded Ben around his business associates from the moment he was old enough to wear a suit, making sure they all knew this was the future of the company, right there in a tiny waistcoat. He'd drilled Ben on facts and figures, on strategy and management techniques.

He'd showered him with expectation and information—but not necessarily with love. Mack O'Donnell hadn't been that kind of man.

Of course, Eli hadn't had the love either, but he also hadn't had all the pressure and expectation. Maybe that was what made the difference. Eli never felt as if he had to live up to their father's example, or memory. Ben did.

Eli hadn't seen Ben and Willow together often, but from what he had seen, and from what his brother had said about the relationship, he'd always got the impression that it was more of a convenient arrangement than true love. Oh, he was sure they liked each other well enough, and of course Willow was beautiful, and Ben was handsome, so they looked *right* together...but it had never seemed like the sort of relationship Eli would have wanted for himself. Apart from anything else, if Eli loved a woman, he'd be faithful to her. And there was no way he'd be taking any other women out on yachts, or to parties or dinner, the way Ben always did when they were split up—and sometimes even when they were still together.

He'd felt sorry for his brother, settling for a business-like arrangement that fitted what the media *thought* a relationship should look like for a supermodel and a CEO, rather than holding out for the real thing.

Eli had never found the real thing either, despite his best efforts, but he had faith it was out there somewhere. Ben didn't even seem to be looking.

But now he'd met Willow, spent time with her, got to know her...it all made even less sense.

He could understand, almost, Ben settling for a relationship like that. But why would *Willow?* When she was a woman so clearly open and ready for so much more?

*With someone like me.*

No. Not with him. He was the *last* person who could consider dating Willow.

Something he should have remembered before he'd put his hand on the bare skin at the base of her spine last night to guide her out of the restaurant, before she'd put her jacket back on.

Just *touching* her had sent his mind into a spin—and driven all suspicious thoughts about her from it. Until he'd woken up this morning and remembered how incompletely she'd answered his questions. Nothing she'd told him had explained her affinity for kids estranged from their families, or her sudden interest in supporting Launch.

Something was going on with her.

*And I need to figure out what it is before I let her get any more involved in my non-profit. Or my life.*

And without his brother noticing. Because either Ben would think Eli was making a move on her, or that he didn't trust her, and neither option would end well.

He headed into the next week with that determination in mind, making a conscious effort not to visit Willow's apartment, and leaving communication about the gala to Kelly.

Which was working well until, on Wednesday, he arrived at the office around lunchtime, after a morning of working at home, to discover that his desk had already been taken over by pages of sketches and strips of material.

'Sorry, boss,' Kelly said. 'People were using the conference room, and your desk was the next biggest space. Apart from the café tables downstairs at the Castaway, and we didn't want to risk getting juice or anything on these gorgeous fabrics.' She hugged a gold, shiny one to her chest.

Willow, standing behind his desk, gave him an apologetic smile. 'We won't be long. I think we're nearly there.'

'Then maybe we could grab lunch? Since you're here.' Damn, he hadn't meant to say that. So much for keeping his distance. But seeing her there, her blonde hair bundled up on the back of her head in a clip, her lip between her teeth as she concentrated on what Kelly was saying…how was he supposed to resist that?

He needed to, though. Somehow.

She glanced up again, that same, slightly guilty look on her face. 'Ah, we might be a *little* bit longer than that.'

Eli sighed, even though actually it was with relief. Another intimate, private meal with Willow might be his undoing. 'Well, I guess I'd better go pick up takeout for us then, hadn't I?'

She beamed at that, and the warm feeling it gave him was enough to reignite all the worries he'd had at dinner—at least until Kelly thrust the lunch order clipboard into his hands, and the rest of the office started giving him their orders too.

Rowan laughed as she watched Eli make his way to the lift, a full sheet of lunch orders clutched in his hands. 'You certainly all have a very informal way of working with the boss here.'

Kelly nodded, tilting her head slightly as she studied her. 'I guess it's kind of different at his brother's office, huh?'

Rowan froze, realising the position she'd inadvertently put herself in here. *Of course* Eli's staff were interested in the woman he was spending time with—especially since she was his brother's ex-girlfriend. *Of course* they'd want to know more.

And of course she didn't *know* more. She'd never even *met* Ben.

Oh, she was treading some very treacherous waters here, just spending time with Eli. She knew that—that was why she'd tried to stay away from him since their dinner together. And yet she couldn't seem to stop herself stepping into his world.

'Uh, yeah,' she hedged, since Kelly was still waiting for an answer about Ben's office. 'You know, all very serious business.'

'I'm sure,' Kelly replied, obviously waiting for her to say more.

She didn't.

Instead, she tried to draw Kelly's attention back to the choices they needed to make about fabric and design. But other members of staff were drawing close now too, questions in their gazes.

'We've never actually met Eli's brother,' one of them said.

'Yeah, he wouldn't deign to come here,' another added.

'But we all know what we've heard,' Kelly said, and the staff around her nodded.

This was the father of her sister's child. She shouldn't be gossiping about him with people who'd never met him. But at the same time...she needed an outsider's perspective, and it hardly seemed likely that Eli was going to discuss his brother with her—not when he still believed they'd been dating until a week or two ago.

Yet it was a risk. If they told Eli, or it got back to Ben...or worse, she could blow her cover completely. She was already acting too un-Willow-like. Especially with Eli. But she had to know what Willow had got herself into.

So she took a breath and asked, 'What have you heard?'

A lot, seemed to be the answer.

It was hard to get it all straight, with everyone eager to add to the conversation. *They* at least didn't seem concerned about badmouthing a man to his ex—probably because she *was* his ex, and they figured that had to be for a reason.

But the crux of their issues seemed to be with Ben's lack of interest in Launch, their work and his brother in general.

'Took me three weeks to even get him on the phone for Eli to talk about the gala,' Kelly said. 'That snooty secretary of his kept telling me he was "far too busy to be bothered". Bothered! By his own brother!'

'You weren't here when he *did* get him on the phone, though,' another woman said—Rowan thought it was the same Sandra who'd taken her sponsorship money on the phone.

'What happened?' Rowan asked curiously.

'Well, Eli was just trying to tell him about the gala, and the sponsorship, and how this year he's trying to make it a real spectacle—bigger than ever before—and how he wanted the family name blazoned across everything as the main sponsor.' Sandra glanced around to make sure Eli wasn't returning before she continued. 'But his brother wasn't listening. Kept talking about how the company already did plenty of high-profile charity work, that it didn't need to start associating with the dregs of society too.'

A gasp went around at that. Rowan wasn't surprised. She felt her own jaw tighten at the description of the kids Eli and his team were trying to help.

'And then Eli asked if he could at least drop off some information about the event, and the work we were raising money for, and Ben finally agreed,' Sandra finished. 'But I don't know what happened to it, because he sure as hell hasn't forked out any money for the cause.'

'No. He didn't,' Rowan said thoughtfully.

Instead, Ben had abandoned the file, probably unread, in Willow's apartment, and gone off on a yacht with his latest flame, according to the gossip websites. Rowan hoped Willow wasn't reading them, back home in Rumbelow.

'I'm sure there must be something good about the

man,' Kelly went on, shaking her head. 'I mean, you dated him, honey, and *you* seem perfectly lovely! But the way he treats his brother…he sure makes it hard to see it. You know?'

'I know,' Rowan said with feeling.

She needed to call Willow tonight. Find out if there was more to why she was hiding out in her cottage, while Rowan paraded around New York pretending to be her, than she'd originally thought.

Because if Ben treated Willow the way he apparently treated Eli… Rowan wasn't surprised she didn't want to bring up a child with him as the father. Because why would he treat a child any differently than grown people?

Ben seemed the sort to ride roughshod over everyone, without listening or considering what they wanted or needed. Rowan had grown up with a person like that as her mother.

She wouldn't wish it on anyone. Let alone her own nephew or niece.

# CHAPTER SIX

'LUNCH IS SERVED!' Eli strolled into the office, laden with food, to find almost his entire staff gathered around his desk—and around Willow.

Oh, good. Because that wasn't suspicious—or alarming—at all.

Eli knew he'd built a good team here—a family, almost. And he wasn't surprised they were all interested in the new woman in his life, even if she was only there because she was his brother's ex-girlfriend. Even if there could never be more between them.

Kelly wouldn't see that. Or Sandra. They were romantics, at heart.

Maybe they all were, really. Thinking they could change the world. What was more romantic than that?

People scattered with their sandwiches as he handed them out, and he was actually allowed to sit at his desk finally and check his emails—although his focus was shot because Willow was sitting opposite him, making notes in her notebook, a stack of sketches and fabric teetering beside her, as she nibbled at her lunch.

More than once, Eli thought he was composing a response to an email, only to discover that he was actually just watching Willow, thinking how different she was to the woman he'd expected. Willow, who was sitting there oblivious to him. Just being...beautiful and adorable and absorbed in doing something nice for someone else...and still his brother's ex-girlfriend.

He'd actually spoken to Ben the night before—an unusual occurrence in itself, more so when his brother was off on his boat, enjoying himself. Apparently, there was a board meeting being scheduled in the next few weeks—there'd be an email coming out—but Eli shouldn't worry about being there. Ben knew he had a lot on with the upcoming gala, and all the follow-up that would entail, and didn't want him to overload himself trying to do both when the meeting would just be a boring routine one.

Hearing his brother's concern about his workload, and the fact that he'd remembered the gala at all, had only made Eli feel more guilty about his dreams the night before. Because of course they'd been about Willow. Willow in that fire-engine-red dress with no back, looking over her shoulder at him as she slipped the straps down her arms and let it fall to the ground...

God, he was a terrible person. He'd even let the memory of the dream run in his mind for a moment or two, until Ben said, 'Hey, did you get that file from her apartment, by the way? Do you know if she's back in the country? I think she's ignoring my calls, unless our time zones are completely out of whack.'

Eli had started so violently he'd almost knocked over his drink. 'Uh, she's back in New York, I think.' *I know.* 'I bumped into her when I was picking up the file. She, uh, actually came on board to sponsor a table at the gala.'

Ben just laughed at that. 'That's a new one in her

repertoire for making me feel guilty when we're apart! Well, good. At least one of us is getting something out of this current separation. Just keep an eye on her for me, will you? I don't want her doing anything stupid that means we can't get back together again next time one of us needs the PR boost.'

Keep an eye on her. Well, yeah, he could definitely do that.

But now, watching Willow eat a chicken salad wrap, and frown when she dropped lettuce on a sketch for Kelly's dress, it was impossible to believe he and Ben had been talking about the same person. The Willow Ben described sounded as mercenary about love as he was, as absorbed in appearance and what others thought, caring more about being seen in the right places and with the right people than helping others.

The Willow Eli was growing to know—care for, even—was a million miles away from that.

So which one of them was wrong?

Ben had known her intimately for years, so Eli had to assume it was him—he only had a couple of weeks of friendly encounters with her, after all. She could be putting on an act for him to get back at Ben.

Except…except Eli would bet his whole life savings that he knew her better than his brother did.

And that just made no sense at all.

'Do you need help getting all that home?' he asked, long after lunch, when she packed up to leave. It was an idiotic thing to say, a stupid offer, just asking for trouble. But he made it anyway because he couldn't resist spending just a little while longer in her company. To prove that he was right about her.

That she was honest and good and not the woman his brother talked about.

Willow hesitated, her arms full of fabric samples and who knew what else. How had she even got them all there? He hoped she'd taken a cab.

'Don't you have work you need to do here?' she asked. 'I know I've been taking up a lot of your time lately.' The way she chewed on her lower lip as she awaited his answer told him she knew they were playing with fire here too. But she hadn't asked him not to come.

Eli looked at the screen, full of unanswered emails he hadn't been able to focus on anyway. They'd keep until he was at home tonight, unable or unwilling to sleep. 'Nah.'

And so he found himself back in her cavernous apartment, drinking a beer she'd insisted he stay for, while she got on with the job at hand. He couldn't even bring himself to regret it, even if the whole situation was bound to blow up in his face sooner or later.

The sewing machine that dominated the oversized coffee table hadn't been there the last time he'd visited, he was sure. Neither had the stack of glossy magazines with designer dresses and gowns in them. Or the basket full of fabric samples and what he assumed were the things his maternal grandmother had always referred to as 'sewing notions'.

'Are you making Kelly's actual dress right now?' he asked, as she measured out a fabric on the floor that looked a lot plainer than the ones Kelly had been sighing over earlier.

Willow shook her head, not looking away from the task at hand. 'This is the mock-up for her to try on, to make sure it works right, before I start cutting the actual fabric she chose—that's a lot more expensive, so I want to make any mistakes on this stuff first.'

'That makes sense.' Sitting down on the sofa to watch her work, he realised that this small living area was the only part of the apartment that looked lived in at all. The rest was still bare and empty, while the area around the coffee table looked like a sewing shop had exploded in it. 'Wouldn't this be easier at the dining table?'

'Better light over here,' Willow answered. 'Besides, I'm scared of all that glass.'

'I can understand that.' But not why she chose to live here. An apartment less suited to the woman he was coming to know was hard to imagine.

Maybe Ben had helped her choose it.

Eli swallowed down the guilt that rose in his gullet at the thought, and focused on the woman in front of him. It was easy, watching her work, to forget that she was anything to do with his brother's supermodel girlfriend. She seemed a whole different person around him.

For a while, he just watched her as she drew around pattern pieces and measured cut fabric, her bottom lip trapped between her teeth as she concentrated. It was fascinating to him. He wondered if Ben had ever seen her like this.

And that was the thought that stunned him out of his silent reverie again.

'How did you learn to do all this?' he asked, just to stop himself staring obsessively. 'You said your sister taught you?'

'Uh...yeah.' Willow placed two pieces of fabric together and started to pin them. 'One summer when we were about, um, seventeen, I think, she got it into her head to learn to make her own clothes—rather than relying on the ones designers gave us. I'd…um, she'd been spending a lot of time with the stylists back stage at our shows, and she was always fascinated by the way they made clothes look perfect, even as we were halfway onto the runway—tacking up a hem, fixing a shoulder seam, anything that had been missed at the fitting or what have you. Anyway, she spent a whole summer in our London townhouse teaching herself from videos on the internet. And she got kind of good at it.'

'So you asked her to teach you too?'

'Exactly.' Willow looked away, her focus completely on the dress in front of her.

Eli was missing something here. He wasn't sure what it was, but there was definitely something. Something to do with her sister? Something she was afraid of telling him?

Afraid? That couldn't be right. Could it?

But he knew this feeling. The rising bubbles of frustration in his chest. The heavy weight of being left out in the cold, the only one who didn't know the truth.

He'd felt it his whole childhood, with the rumours about his parentage.

But he'd felt it as an adult too—when he'd realised the girl he thought he'd loved, or at least *could* love, was sleeping with his brother. Ben had denied it, of course, until the girl confessed all. Ben had apologised profusely—but in a way that had somehow left Eli feeling it was *his* fault for not realising the girl wasn't serious about him sooner.

He felt as if he was waiting for another one of those apologies.

Except this time *he* was the one in the wrong, wasn't he? He was the one lusting after his brother's girl—although at least they were actually broken up, this time. For now.

Maybe that was it. Maybe Willow just didn't want to tell him that she still loved his brother, that whatever he thought was happening between them, the connection he felt, it was all in his mind.

Yeah. That had to be it. What else *could* it be?

Eli drained the rest of his beer, put the bottle down on the table and got to his feet.

'I'll leave you to it, then,' he said.

Willow looked up sharply. 'Okay. Thanks for…well. I'll see you soon.'

He nodded. 'Soon.'

But only if he couldn't avoid it.

He needed to stay away from Willow Harper—at least until the charity gala.

Otherwise, he was afraid he might lose his mind.


The mock-up dress was finished.

Rowan studied it through narrowed eyes as it hung on the adjustable dress form she'd ordered on Willow's credit card. Obviously, it was nowhere near as grand as the finished dress would be, but already the lines hung well, and she could imagine it on Kelly's curvaceous body, looking fantastic.

She'd hoped to have it done sooner, but, well. It had been a couple of nights since Eli had left the apartment so abruptly. She hadn't been able to concentrate with him watching her, but she'd found she couldn't concentrate with him gone either. Not when she didn't know what thought process had made him leave.

Had he begun to suspect something? She'd almost slipped up when he'd asked about 'her sister' learning to make dresses—almost let slip that it was her, not Willow. And after that he'd been watching her so closely, asking questions about her 'sister'…and she'd wanted to tell him everything. To tell him about herself, her past, her life, with him knowing she was talking about *herself.*

She wanted to tell him she was Rowan, not Willow.

But how could she?

She'd made a promise to her sister. To her unborn niece or nephew. After everything Willow had done for her, this was all she needed in return. Rowan couldn't screw it up.

No. The only thing to do was to try to carry on as if everything was normal. Not normal for Willow, as she'd never be in this position, and not normal for Rowan, because that was home in Rumbelow. Normal for Rowan *pretending* to be Willow.

It was giving her a headache, this feeling that she was two different people at the same time. She wasn't even sure which one was most real any more.

But normal, in this bizarre version of reality, was heading down to the Launch offices with this mock-up dress for Kelly to try on, so she could make any adjustments she needed to before she started cutting the fabric for the real thing.

She grabbed a coffee on her way, hoping it would give her a little more energy after three nights of little sleep, and also because it meant Eli couldn't offer her one at the office and she'd be able to make a quick getaway.

In fact, she lucked out—Eli wasn't even there when she arrived. The receptionist gave her a friendly smile before handing over the visitor lanyard Rowan had started to think of as her own, and waving her towards the lifts.

In the office, she found Kelly organising files on Eli's desk.

'Boss isn't in,' she said. 'I assumed he was slacking off with you.'

'Afraid not. But it doesn't matter.' Rowan held up the dress bag with the mock-up in it. 'I'm here to see you anyway.'

Kelly squealed and grabbed the bag, disappearing into the ladies' bathroom to put it on.

'Don't forget, it's just the mock-up!' Rowan called after her.

She perched on the edge of Eli's desk while she waited, casting a glance over the papers Kelly had been sorting. She wasn't snooping, she told herself. Just... surveying her surroundings.

Which happened to include a bright yellow sticky note, right on the top of the pile, with the words *Your brother—call back!* in stark black letters.

Ben had called Eli. *Call back.* Did that mean he wanted Eli to call him back, or that he was returning Eli's call? Rowan couldn't be sure.

And if Eli had been calling Ben...what if it was about her? What if he *knew?*

At that moment, Kelly emerged from the bathroom— beaming and strutting as if she were on a catwalk, not weaving between the desks of her office. Rowan clapped her hands in delight at how well the mock-up dress fell around her. Then she turned a more critical eye on her work, and busied herself making the tiny alterations that made all the difference in a bespoke dress.

She accompanied Kelly into the bathroom to help her out of the dress again, since it was now filled with pins and probably a dangerous solo task. By the time she came back out, Eli was sitting behind his desk, frowning at the sticky note on top of his files.

Rowan's heart did a quick double beat, and she silently told it to act normal. If Eli was starting to suspect something, the last thing she should do was panic. In fact, she needed to behave as if her life was perfectly ordinary.

Even when that was the furthest possible thing from the truth.

He looked up as she approached and smiled—but it wasn't the smile she was used to. It wasn't the open, friendly, welcoming smile she loved to see. It was tight and reserved and she didn't like it one bit.

*He knows.*

*He can't know.*

*And he can't find out.*

Already, she could feel the alarm rising, her chest tightening, and she forced herself to focus on her breathing. On the present moment, right now. Usually, she did that by noticing things around her.

*Five things I can see. Four things I can hear.*

Except this time all she could see, hear or think about was Eli.

'I thought you might be here,' he said, and her heart

stuttered again. Then he nodded towards her bags, abandoned by the side of his desk. 'Those were a giveaway.'

'Right. Sorry.' She gathered them up over his protestations that it was fine. 'I had the mock-up ready for Kelly to try on. And now I'm going to go home and start sewing the real thing, so—'

Juggling her bags, the mock-up dress and her empty reusable coffee cup, she lost her balance, and everything tumbled to the ground—including her. Or she would have done, if it hadn't been for Eli's strong grip on her arm.

'Willow,' he said firmly. 'I wasn't asking you to leave.'

He was so close now she could see the fine lines around his concerned eyes. And apparently he could see the shadows under hers because he said, 'You look tired.'

She pulled away from his grip and began gathering her things again. 'Just what every girl wants to hear.'

She regretted the words as soon as she'd said them. Why should she care what Eli thought about her looks? She was supposed to be pining after his brother or something, wasn't she?

He flinched anyway. 'I just meant…is everything okay?'

Oh, he meant had she had any more anxiety attacks without him there to talk her down. 'Everything's fine.' Even if the only thing making her anxious right now was him.

Or the secrets she was keeping from him, more accurately.

'Okay. Good.' He looked at her for a long moment, his eyes moving as if he was searching for something in her own gaze. Then he sighed. 'Listen, there's a cocktails and canapés thing for gala sponsors tonight. I meant... I should have invited you earlier. I know it's short notice, but it would be great if you could come.'

Off to the side, Kelly was giving her boss a puzzled look Rowan couldn't quite understand, but it gave her pause all the same. 'I...' She glanced down at the desk, at the sticky note about Ben, almost involuntarily.

'Ben won't be there,' Eli said quickly. 'If you're worried about bumping into him. That...that message is about something else.'

Something he wasn't telling her. Not that there was any real reason he should.

Rowan considered her options. Say no, offend Eli, let down the charity perhaps, and spend the evening alone, fretting over what he suspected.

Or go to the event, enjoy Eli's company—and maybe even figure out why Kelly was looking at him that way, and what was going on with his brother.

Put like that...

'I'd love to come,' she said.

Eli picked Willow up from her apartment that evening, braced for a night of trying not to touch her. Or even look at her, probably, if he didn't want to give his feelings away.

Kelly at the office already suspected, he knew. Hell, half the staff probably did, if they'd seen them together. But Kelly was particularly suspicious because he'd told her, when she was finalising the list for that night's event, that Willow couldn't make it.

And then he'd gone and asked her in front of Kelly,

making it obvious that he'd never mentioned it to her in the first place.

Way to give himself away.

He hadn't intended to invite her at all. His plan of trying to keep his distance had been working well, at least until he saw her there in the office, looking tired but proud. He was proud of her too. Kelly's dress might not be finished yet, but he could already tell it would be stunning. More than that, just the time she'd given his assistant counted for so much. He was fond of Kelly, in a big brother sort of way, and it was so nice to see someone else realise how special she was.

So yes. He'd tried keeping his distance from Willow. But really, what was the point? She was in his life now. A sponsor at his gala event, and yes, maybe as his brother's girlfriend again once more. He couldn't change that. He wasn't even going to try.

Whatever else had passed between them over the years, Ben was his brother. He wouldn't betray him.

But Willow... He'd grown to care for her since the day she'd found him in her apartment. They had a connection. And perhaps it was foolish to try and ignore that too.

So he'd invited her tonight. And if part of his reason was that, knowing Ben was back in the country, it was only a matter of time before their easy friendship would have to come to an end, he intended to ignore that. At least for tonight.

Thankfully, she wasn't wearing that fire-engine-red dress again. Tonight's outfit was, instead, a shimmering golden dress that fell halfway down her calf. The thin spaghetti straps admittedly looked like they could give way at any moment, and Eli knew he'd be dreaming that night about peeling them from her shoulders. She had paired the dress with matching high heels, her hair piled up in some sort of complicated fashion on top of her head. She looked every inch the supermodel—and completely out of his reach.

He had to remember that.

*No touching.*

If he touched her, he might lose his mind.

'So what is tonight about?' Willow asked as she settled into the front passenger seat of his car.

'It was Kelly's idea, actually,' Eli replied. 'She had the thought that, if all of these rich people were supporting the same charity, they might have more in common than they thought. So if we brought them together before the main event, it would give them a chance to mingle and network.'

'Potentially giving them new business contacts as well,' Willow said. 'Clever. You've given them more than they expected—more than just a chance to do good. You've given them a business opportunity too.'

'That's the hope,' Eli said as he pulled away from the kerb. 'We need these people to do more than donate just once a year for this gala night, even if it is our biggest fundraising opportunity on the calendar. We need regular ongoing support to keep our work going. If our sponsors feel they can get more value from us by being part of what we're trying to do all year round, that can only help us out.'

The venue for the night's event was a hotel uptown that Eli had never made it to before, but was supposed to be the next big thing. Willow, he was sure, must have been there a hundred times before, but she still managed to look impressed as they walked into the flashy lobby, and through to the bar area Kelly had hired for the evening.

Already, the room was bustling, and as they walked through to the bar Eli heard numerous conversations between unlikely companions about everything from golf to family to business. One or two of them were even talking about the work Launch was doing there in the city, which was gratifying.

It didn't take long for Eli to get drawn into conversation with a backer or two. To start with, Willow stayed by his side—but then Sandra appeared and the next time he checked, the two women were off together by the bar.

It *was* a work event, so Eli tried not to be frustrated that so many supporters wanted his time and attention. Normally, he'd be in his element—he loved talking about Launch, the work they did, the kids they'd helped and where they were now—at college, or undertaking apprenticeships, or setting up their own businesses, or starting families that had the right tools to be better adjusted than the ones they came from.

But tonight he just wanted to be with Willow. To enjoy what was left of his time with her.

Ben was out of town again this weekend and, from the way he'd gone back to dodging his calls—the message on the sticky note on his desk had proved to be a call from Ben's assistant saying that Ben didn't have time to speak to him this week—he might even have a suspicion of what was up. He and Willow hadn't been discreet in their adventures around town, and people always did love to talk. Plus, he knew there was always a chance of a photographer being about when Willow left her apartment. Just because they hadn't seen the camera flash, or spotted any resulting photo on the internet, didn't mean it wasn't there—or that Ben hadn't seen it. Hell, if he suspected something, he might even have hired a PI to tail her.

So this could be his last night with Willow. And he was spending it talking to other people.

No wonder he was frustrated.

He had to make do with glimpses of that shimmering dress across the room, as Sandra introduced her to anyone and everyone she might like to meet. Or, knowing Sandra, donors who would be excited and grateful to meet Willow—and maybe give a little more next time. She wasn't his best fundraiser by chance.

But as the event started to wind down, and he was just allowing himself to think about asking Willow to join him at the jazz bar around the corner that he liked, he realised that Sandra was by the door saying goodbye to people—and Willow was nowhere to be seen.

'If you'll excuse me.' He extricated himself from his current conversation with an apologetic smile, and set out to find her.

It took only a moment to establish that she wasn't in the main bar—the crowd had thinned out enough that he could see it all in a glance. Perhaps she'd gone to the ladies' bathrooms? He should have thought of that sooner. Willow was hardly likely to thank him for storming in there in a panic looking for her.

But he was *responsible* for her. He'd brought her here. And the funny, unsettled feeling behind his ribs told him that something wasn't right here.

When Sandra confessed she hadn't seen her for a while that feeling solidified, and Eli decided he didn't care how mad she was with him for overreacting, he was going to find her. Now.

After just a few words with the concierge, he had a team helping search inside. Which left him the outside. It was possible she'd wanted to get some air; the room had been stifling at its most crowded. And overwhelming, perhaps.

The thought of Willow suffering another panic attack without him set him into even faster action. Eschewing the elevator, he took the stairs three at a time to the fourth floor, and then up one more to the roof terrace. He burst out into the high-level garden, and spotted a tell-tale shimmer of golden light almost instantly. Not wanting to alarm her, he put a hand out to stop the doors slamming shut. And then he watched, and listened.

'No, really, I need to get back inside now,' Willow was saying, firmly but politely. 'Thank you for showing me the sights—you're right, the view is spectacular. But my date will be waiting.'

Date. She had to mean him, even if it wasn't strictly an accurate term. But the fact she felt she needed to use it…

Willow made to move towards the doors, where he stood hidden in the shadows, still unseen. But the man at her side reached out to grab her around the waist, pulling her close. She pushed him away, but he only held her tighter.

Eli blinked away the red mist that threatened to fill his vision. Willow didn't need him to come in fists flying. She needed an accomplice to get her out of there without a scene.

He pulled the roof terrace door open again and, this time, let it slam closed. 'Willow? Are you up here? I just asked the guy to bring the car around. Shall we get going?'

The man beside her let go at the sound of his voice, just as he'd hoped. Eli didn't recognise him as anyone *he'd* spoken to that night, but he made a point of memorising his face so he could quiz Sandra later about who he might be.

Willow hurried to his side. 'Of course,' she said brightly. 'I was just taking a look at the view. But I'm done now.'

Eli held the door open for her and, this time, headed for the elevator. They waited in nervous silence for the car to arrive, but the man didn't follow.

'Who was he?' Eli asked, once the elevator doors had closed behind them, and he'd punched the button for the ground floor.

Willow shook her head. 'I don't know. Someone from the party. I was trying to politely excuse myself by saying I wanted to get some air, and then he insisted on taking me up to the roof garden and, well. You saw the rest, I imagine.'

Eli shook his head. 'If I hadn't come up when I did…'

'Then I would have kneed him in the groin and come down alone,' Willow said firmly. 'And if that didn't work, I had pepper spray *and* a rape alarm in my bag. I didn't need you to save me, Eli.'

'No. I know.' That didn't change the fact that he was glad he *had* been there. Just in case.

They travelled down in silence for another second or two before Willow slipped her hand through his arm, and he realised she was shaking a little. 'I'm really glad you did, though.'

He covered her hand with his own. 'Me too.'

# CHAPTER SEVEN

'WELL? HOW DO I look?' Kelly stepped out of the women's bathrooms at the Launch offices to a full-on round of applause, and more than a few whistles—mostly from the women.

The dress Rowan had spent the last week sewing looked *exactly* like she'd imagined it in her head, more so even than it had on paper, and she beamed at Kelly as the relief flooded through her.

She'd done it. Even while pretending to be her sister, she'd created a dress that made someone smile. Made them feel like Cinderella going to the ball.

Maybe it wasn't as noble a calling as Eli's, but it was hers, and she was proud of it.

'You've done an amazing job,' Eli murmured next to her ear as he leaned against his desk beside her. 'I've never seen Kelly smile so much. Thank you.'

'It was a pleasure,' Rowan said honestly, ignoring the slight shiver that found its way down her spine at the feel of his voice by her skin.

She couldn't help but imagine those lips *on* her skin. Even though she knew she mustn't.

Ever since the night on the roof terrace, the week

before, the pull between them had seemed stronger than ever.

Rowan hadn't been lying; she could have handled herself with that man. She'd been in worse situations before and managed alone. And she knew his type; he was all talk, but he wouldn't have taken it any further. Especially not in such a public place.

She wasn't blasé about the risks a woman faced alone in the city, though. She hadn't been lying about the pepper spray or the rape alarm either. In fact, she'd had the first of them tight in her grip inside her bag when she'd heard Eli's voice.

It was funny, she supposed, that an event like that hadn't sparked an anxiety attack, whereas the thought of Eli finding out her secret made her breathing catch instantly. Perhaps because she'd known she was in control, had known her next steps and what she would do to save herself.

If Eli found out the truth… Rowan had no idea what she would do next, then.

But if he went on believing she was Willow, that she was in love with his brother, until she left New York… if he never knew the truth at all…she wasn't sure what she'd do then either.

This hadn't been the plan. She was never supposed to meet Eli, let alone grow so close to him.

She wasn't supposed to be lying to anyone she cared about. Just a few photographers or designers who cared more about what she looked like than who she was, anyway.

Eli cared who she was.

But she wasn't who she said she was.

*That* was a problem neither she nor Willow had seen coming.

She'd lain awake for nights, wondering what would happen when the real Willow returned. Would she just avoid Eli for ever? Feign amnesia of the whole affair?

In the end there had only been one answer.

Once the gala was over, Rowan needed to walk away. To prove to everyone that all of this had only been about helping the children who needed Launch to make their lives better. After that…what reason would she have to see Eli again, anyway?

So she'd walk away. And then, when Willow came back to New York, she'd have no reason to see him. Especially if she really didn't plan to get back together with Ben.

If she handled this right, she and Willow could keep all their secrets. And Eli might wonder, might even feel let down, but that was all.

And it was something Rowan would have to live with.

'Willow? Can you help me out of this thing?' Kelly asked as she turned back towards the bathrooms. 'I don't want to risk getting *anything* on my perfect princess dress before my big night!'

'Of course.' Rowan pushed away from the desk and forced herself not to glance back at Eli as she followed Kelly. She felt his gaze on her all the same.

Kelly was bubbling with excitement about the gala and her dress as Rowan helped her change back into her office-wear, storing the dress carefully in the protective bag she'd delivered it in.

'What are *you* wearing, though?' Kelly asked, as she fluffed her hair in the mirror.

'I haven't really thought about it yet,' Rowan admitted. She'd have to, though, and soon. Willow would have something suitable in her wardrobe, she was sure.

Kelly gave her a sideways look. 'You do realise that that gala is *tomorrow,* right?'

'I know, I know. I just…well, I've been more worried about your dress than mine!'

'Girl, I know you look incredible in anything, and you must have a closet *full* of gowns. But don't you want to wear something that really knocks the boss's socks off tomorrow night?'

Rowan froze, aware that in the mirror her reflection looked paler than ever. 'Um… Eli and I…it's really not like that. I mean, I'm his brother's ex-girlfriend.'

'*Ex* being the important word in that sentence.' Kelly turned to rest a hip against the sink and gave her a serious look. 'Willow. If any man looked at me the way Eli looks at you? I'd have him down the aisle faster than he could blink.'

'I don't—'

Kelly held up a hand. 'And the way you look at him? That's no better either. You want him, and he wants you, that much is obvious to anyone with eyes. But more than that… You two are good for each other. I've never seen Eli as happy—in himself as much as in work—as he has been these last few weeks. And as for you…' She shook her head. 'I don't know much about that brother of his—and I want to know even less—but from what I've seen and heard and read…he's not the right guy for you. Is he. Honestly?'

Rowan shook her head. That much, at least, was easy to agree on.

'So why let the past—or him—ruin what could be a really great relationship for you and Eli?' Kelly asked.

'It's not that simple.' Because it wasn't the past, or Ben, keeping them apart. It was the lies she'd been telling since the day they'd met. And if she walked away he'd believe those lies for the rest of his life.

But it was the only answer. Unless...

*I tell him the truth,* she realised suddenly, and a weight landed on her chest at the same time as another one lifted from her shoulders.

Because the truth might only make things worse.

'Just think about it,' Kelly advised as she took her dress from Rowan and opened the bathroom door.

'I will,' Rowan promised.

An easy promise, since she already knew that question wasn't going to let her sleep tonight.

Eli had intended to pick Willow up for the gala dinner, like he had on every other night they'd gone out together. But by mid-afternoon on the day of the event it was already clear that wasn't going to be a possibility.

'I'll meet you there,' he told Willow, his phone jammed between his ear and his shoulder as he scanned the pile of forms Kelly had just thrust into his hands. 'Will you be all right getting there on your own?'

'I think I can just about manage,' Willow said dryly.

And now the night they'd been working towards all year was finally here. But rather than enjoying the moment, Eli found all he could do was scan the crowds looking for one particular woman.

The venue they'd chosen was stunning. Somehow, Kelly had managed to find a botanical garden he'd never heard of that was looking to get into the wedding venue business, and given them an incredible deal to come in and try it all out.

It had been a risk, Eli knew, but the more money they could save on running the event, the more the final total raised. And so far it seemed to be paying off.

'I can't believe you found this place,' he told a beaming Kelly as, together, they surveyed their surroundings. Lights had been strung everywhere, hidden amongst the foliage and wound around wooden pagodas and structures that lined the paths. A band played in one corner of the gardens and people were even dancing to the big band music that filled the air. One of the smaller vintage-looking glasshouses had been transformed into a bar, with a silent auction ongoing inside, hoping to draw a few more big donations.

Later, they'd wind their way down one of the starlit paths to the larger glasshouse, where dinner would be served. Eli had already seen it, with its crisp white linen on the tables, the lights hanging from retro wires from the roof, and the greenery wound all through it until it was impossible to tell where the garden ended and the dining room began.

While most of the guests were donors—and people they wanted to impress—there were also staff, thanks to Willow, sitting at the Launch table. Also present were some of their success stories, as Sandra put it. Kids they'd helped out of terrible situations and, with the kids own hard work, supported them onto better paths. Eli knew Sandra had briefed them all, asking them to talk up the work they did, to show how well it worked.

*'Social proof,'* she'd told him seriously. *'Anecdotes*

*from those kids will work better than any statistics we throw at them.'*

But Kelly had also made a suggestion that Eli had embraced, and they'd invited a number of the kids they were helping right now too. Ones who *weren't* success stories yet—but could be.

And right now, Eli could see those kids mingling with some of the biggest names in NYC business, eyes wide, helping themselves to canapés. If nothing else, they'd have shown them the sort of life that was possible—something they might never have known, otherwise.

'Seriously, Kelly,' he said. 'This place is incredible.'

She smiled smugly. 'New York Botanical Garden? Brooklyn Botanical Garden? Those are for suckers.'

'And out of our price range for the events budget,' Eli added, which was rather more the reason they hadn't picked either of the more famous gardens.

'And that,' Kelly allowed. 'But the point remains; this is the place to be. And I am dressed to party!'

'You are that.' The dress Willow had made fit Kelly like a dream, and enhanced and celebrated her personality, her body, and her confidence. He'd never seen his assistant look quite so alive. 'You should go enjoy it.'

'You sure?' Kelly gave him a worried look. 'I can wait with you until Willow gets here? Or just drag you over to talk to all the people you're *supposed* to be schmoozing, if you weren't too busy mooning over a certain model we both know.'

'I'm not mooning.'

'Boss.' Kelly laid a hand on his arm and looked up at him, her eyes serious. 'You really, really are.' Then her gaze flicked away to something happening to his right. 'So why don't you go do something about that?'

Kelly melted away into the crowd as he turned around, and there was Willow, the people parting to let her through as if the whole botanical garden was her catwalk.

He tried not to let his mouth fall open at the sight of her, but he honestly wasn't sure if he'd succeeded or not. If he'd been blown away by the dresses she'd worn on previous nights, nothing had prepared him for tonight's gown.

It was black and white, fell all the way to the floor and—crucially—was strapless. In fact, Eli assumed the thing was only staying up from sheer force of will. Or perhaps because it fitted so closely to her torso, before flaring out into a wide skirt with a slit that ran…oh, God. It ran all the way up to her mid-thigh.

She looked stunning—a point that was lost on none of the people she walked past.

She looked…she looked like she always did in the photos in magazines. The ones where she was on Ben's arm, going to some flashy event or another.

That thought brought him back down to earth, fast. And when she reached him, he struggled to return her smile.

'Everything okay?' she asked, looking concerned.

'Everything's fine.'

*Except I've fallen for my brother's ex, who he probably expects to get back together with any moment. And she's so far out of my reach I shouldn't even be able to see her.*

But he could. And that fact was doing things to him.

'Is it the dress?' Willow looked down at herself, dismayed. 'I was worried it was too much. But when I sent Kelly a photo, she said it was perfect.'

'It is perfect.' His voice sounded gravelly, even to his own ears. 'You look perfect.'

Perfect for Ben. Not for him.

'Okay. Good.' Willow was still eyeing him sideways, like she was trying to figure out what was wrong with him.

But it wasn't like he could tell her, was it?

Kelly came to his rescue, thankfully, although she shot him an accusatory look as she did it. 'Willow, you're here!'

The two women appreciated each other's dresses, and then Kelly whisked her off to chat to some of the kids she'd met at the Castaway Café the other week. But not before she paused to whisper at him, 'That was lame, boss. Very, very lame.'

And the worst part was, Eli knew she was right.

Rowan had decided, even before leaving the apartment, that she was going to channel Willow for the evening.

Everyone at this event would be expecting Willow Harper, supermodel and socialite—not her anxious, awkward and uncomfortable minutes-younger sister who hadn't sashayed down a catwalk in years.

So she'd picked the most Willow-like gown she could find in the wardrobe, and even helped herself to her sister's lipstick and perfume. And she'd given herself a stern talking-to in the mirror while waiting for her cab too.

'You are Willow tonight. And Willow would walk

in there with her head high and her back straight. She wouldn't notice all the people staring at her. She'd smile and be gracious and charming, and make friends with all the important people who matter. So that's what you'll do too.' Then she'd nodded at her reflection, grabbed her clutch bag and headed down to the lobby to wait for her cab, hoping she'd get used to the high heels before she arrived.

To start with, things had gone exactly to plan. People had stared as she'd stepped out of the cab, but while she'd felt their gazes on her, she'd focused on her own body—on her senses, and her breathing—to help her ignore them.

She'd mastered the heels—grateful for the solid path through the gardens that meant she didn't sink into the grass. She'd even managed a small sashay as she walked.

But then she'd reached Eli. And while she'd hoped that his stunned expression might just be her breathtaking beauty, she hadn't really been all that optimistic. Because all along, what she looked like was the thing Eli had cared about least.

There was something wrong there, and she couldn't ask what it was—not here, not tonight. Maybe he'd already figured out the truth, or maybe there was something else going on with Ben he didn't want to tell her about. But she couldn't ask him tonight.

She needed to tell him the truth about who she was, if he *hadn't* figured it out. She'd already decided that. Walking away just wasn't an option any more, which meant confessing was the only way through.

And while part of her wanted to do that right now and get it over with…

Not tonight.

Eli and his team had been working for *months* on tonight's gala event, and she was damned if she was going to make it all about her, when he should be enjoying the spotlight and doing the good work that mattered so much to him.

So she didn't press, after her initial polite query. She let Kelly lead her away gratefully—and pretended she didn't hear her whispered comment to her boss.

With a glass of champagne in her hand she was happy to do the rounds with Kelly—but even happier when she got to talk to some of the kids she'd met at the Castaway Café, rather than the titans of industry she'd been preparing for. Their overawed excitement about the event echoed her own; they'd certainly never had anything like this in Rumbelow, although she wasn't sure she wouldn't rather be at folk night at the local pub.

Before she'd left home, and modelling, behind for good, she'd always tried to avoid the big events. At least this one was outdoors, which meant she got plenty of fresh air. The worst were the ones where she could feel the walls closing in, as the voices around her grew louder and louder, matched only by the thumping of blood in her ears.

She didn't see Eli again until they were led through for dinner. She looked for him as the staff—dressed in white dinner jackets—started to usher them down a path through a tree tunnel towards the dining area, but she couldn't spot him. She assumed he must have gone on ahead to get things sorted, and took the arm of a kindly-looking older gentleman in a tailcoat to lead her through.

The glasshouse where the dinner was being served

was spectacular; Rowan gasped when she saw it, and from the noise around her, she wasn't the only one.

'It's like a magical garden,' she whispered. 'I half expect a talking bird to flutter past at any moment.'

The man beside her chuckled. 'I wouldn't put it past that brother-in-law of yours. He'll do anything to help his cause—an admirable trait, I suppose, but it does strain the wallet rather!'

He wandered off to find his table, leaving Rowan to wrap her arms around herself at his words. *Brother-in-law.*

He wasn't, of course, not even Willow's. But the guy clearly wasn't up on the celebrity gossip and thought Ben and Willow were still together. Maybe most people in the room did.

She'd have to remember that. She didn't want to trash her sister's reputation by being seen mooning over her supposed boyfriend's brother—especially if, in the end, Willow went back to Ben to raise their child together.

There was a beautiful seating plan, edged in vines and flowers, that guided her to the table she'd sponsored—on Willow's credit card. She was pleased to see that she recognised most of the people sitting there—either from the office, or from the Castaway Café. With Kelly on her right, keeping the conversation flowing, she was able to relax a bit and enjoy the meal.

But not completely. At the edge of her awareness, she couldn't ignore the pull to look at Eli, sitting up with the big donors at the front table. He seemed perfectly relaxed, enjoying his evening, and oblivious to her sitting across the room.

Good. That was good.

'I'm sure he wishes you were sitting up there with him too,' Kelly murmured in her ear, thankfully quiet enough that no one else at the table seemed to hear.

'I don't know what you're talking about,' Rowan lied, and made a point of not looking over at Eli's table for the rest of the meal.

It wasn't until after dessert had been served and eaten, and Kelly and several of her other tablemates had disappeared to the bathrooms, when she felt that awareness again. Someone was watching her—she could feel all the hairs on the back of her neck standing up. *Eli*.

She turned towards his table, but he was deep in conversation with the woman next to him, and not looking her way at all. So who—?

'Willow!' A tall, handsome man about her own age tumbled into Kelly's chair, and reached out to pull her into a hug. 'It's so good to see you again! Where's Ben?' He looked around him rather obviously at the lack of Eli's brother. 'You two aren't on the outs again, are you?'

Rowan smiled tightly, desperately scanning her memory for any picture of this guy from Willow's press photos, but coming up with nothing. She had no idea who he was, but he clearly knew her—or, rather, Willow—very well.

'He couldn't make it tonight,' she said shortly. That was simple enough, right? It was reasonable to assume that if he *could* have made the most important date in his brother's year he would have done.

But the man gave a short, nasty laugh. 'I bet he couldn't. So, he sent you to represent, did he? Good of you to still do it, given those photos that came out earlier.'

'Photos?' Rowan blurted, before she could stop herself. Of what? They couldn't be of Willow in Rumbelow, could they?

'Oh, don't say you haven't seen them? I've really put my foot in it now, haven't I?' He pulled a face that was probably supposed to be remorseful, but somehow just looked smug.

Rowan pushed her chair away from her table. 'I'm sorry. I just need to—' She didn't elaborate, stumbling blindly through the tables towards the exit, just hoping she didn't break an ankle in Willow's heels.

She'd been an idiot to think she could do this. Of course she was going to bump into Willow's so-called friends, and she had no idea who any of them were, or what their agendas were—because they clearly had them. And what the hell had Ben been photographed doing, anyway?

Outside the glasshouse, she leaned against the cool bark of the nearest tree and pulled her phone from her clutch bag to do an internet search. It only took seconds to find the photos of Ben cavorting on the deck of some yacht somewhere with a curvaceous brunette in a tiny bikini.

Rowan rolled her eyes. Fine. As long as Willow was still safe and enjoying some privacy back home in England, she didn't much care what her sister's ex was up to.

'Willow?' Eli appeared from the glasshouse, his bow tie skewwhiff and his eyes concerned. 'Are you okay? I saw Jack corner you, dripping his usual poison, I assume. What was it this time?'

Rowan turned her phone towards Eli with a wry smile. 'He just wanted to make sure I'd seen these.'

Eli studied the photos for a second and went very still, his mouth little more than a line above his tightened jaw. Then he said, 'My brother is an utter, utter idiot, Willow, and he never deserved you.'

'We're broken up,' Rowan said evenly. The last thing she wanted to do was start some sort of feud between the brothers at this point.

'Again,' Eli replied. 'And he'll expect you to come back to him again when he wants you, and ignore anything he did when you were apart, right?'

'Probably,' Rowan admitted, even though it wasn't exactly *her* Ben would be expecting. And she wasn't sure that Willow would go this time either, given the baby.

Eli met her gaze with his own burning one, and she realised there was more to this conversation than she'd expected. 'And that doesn't bother you? Because, Willow…if you were mine, the idea of anyone else touching you, even if we weren't together at that moment, I have to tell you, it would drive me insane.'

The heat in his words, the sincerity in his eyes, filled her with an emotion she'd forgotten, it had been so long since she'd felt it.

And when he leaned in closer, so near she could feel the heat of his breath against her mouth, she wanted nothing more than to kiss him. To feel his arms around her and his mouth on hers and his body—

Rowan pushed him away. 'Eli, no.'

# CHAPTER EIGHT

ELI STUMBLED BACK so fast he almost fell over the vine growing up the tree behind him, or maybe his own feet, he wasn't really sure.

All he could hear was her 'no' echoing around the caverns of his mind.

He'd been wrong. Everything he'd thought was between them—the connection, the attraction…everything—had only been inside his head. He'd imagined it all.

It was almost enough to make him doubt his own sanity. Or, at the least, everything he thought he knew.

He'd been so *sure* she felt the way he did.

'Willow, I'm sorry.' The words tumbled out of him. 'I misread the situation. It's entirely on me, and I can't apologise enough for putting you in that position. I—'

But Willow was shaking her head. 'You didn't misread anything.'

Eli froze, staring back her. Her eyes were wide, her pupils blown, and standing there in the glow of the tiny fairy lights wound around the branch above her head, she was the most beautiful thing he'd ever seen in his life.

'Then…is this about Ben? You're still in love with

him?' Even after everything he'd done and said, if Willow really loved him and thought they could make things work, Eli couldn't get in the way of their possible happiness. He couldn't do that to his brother.

But Willow blew that idea out of the water too. 'It's not about Ben. I don't... I don't love him. *I* never did.'

The strange stress she put on the word *I* only confused him more. He shook his head to try to clear it, but it didn't help.

He made sure to keep back, not to crowd her, to give her the space to speak and think without him looming over her. Even if all he really wanted to do was pull her into his arms.

Whatever she said next...he hadn't imagined things between them. And she hadn't lied to him and told him that he had. That had to count for something.

Eli had been lied to enough in his life. Told that something he believed was wrong, when it was right. He didn't think he could take it if Willow did that to him too.

But she hadn't. She'd admitted the chemistry between them was mutual. And if the problem wasn't Ben...

'I don't understand, Willow. Can you explain it to me?'

She met his gaze, her expression open and vulnerable. 'I want to. But I... I'm scared how you're going to react.'

That hit him like a blow. 'You know I'd never hurt you, Willow, surely?'

'Of course.' That got him a small, tight smile. 'You just might not like me very much any more.'

'I honestly don't think that's possible,' he admitted. 'And I don't see how we can move forward from this moment if you *don't* tell me.'

'I know. And I... I'd already resolved to tell you the truth, anyway. I just didn't want to do it *tonight*. Tonight should be about you and your team, and all the hard work you've put in. Not about me and my sister and all our issues.'

'Your sister?' Eli frowned. 'The one who taught you to make dresses? What does she have to do with us?'

And then he knew. Before she even said the words, before her eyes dropped to the ground before she spoke so she wouldn't have to look him in the face. Before *everything* changed. He felt it, the truth of it, in his bones.

She wasn't Willow.

She took a breath. 'My sister didn't teach me how to make dresses. I taught her. Because I'm not Willow. I'm—'

'Rowan. You're Rowan.'

She nodded in confirmation, and Eli's whole world fractured.

He'd fallen for a woman who didn't exist. Who had lied to him about everything—even something as basic as her name.

He'd tortured himself with guilt over wanting his brother's ex. He'd told himself nothing could happen, that he was crazy for even thinking it.

But worst of all...he'd known there was something. Known she was keeping something from him, and he hadn't called her on it because he'd wanted so badly to believe her. To trust her.

And she'd blown that trust to smithereens.

'I'm sorry. I didn't want to lie. Hell, I didn't want to do this at all! Willow just showed up on my doorstep and—'

He held up a hand to stop her. He couldn't take any

of this right now. Inside the glasshouse, servers were clearing away the desserts and bringing out coffees. Any moment, someone was going to introduce him on that stage and he needed to be there to make a speech. To thank everyone for their donations, their support, their time—and encourage them to give more of all three.

He'd been writing and revising it for weeks. Now he couldn't remember the first line.

'Eli…' Willow started again.

*No, not Willow, Rowan.*

He shook his head anyway. 'I… I have to go give a speech.'

She stepped back, apology heavy in her eyes. 'I know. We can…can we talk about this later?'

He knew what she wanted to hear—that they could talk this out. That he'd listen to her explanation and try to understand what she'd done. That they'd work through their feelings together and build something stronger now they finally had a foundation of truth.

But he couldn't give her assurances on any of that right now. Not when he didn't think he could even *look* at her again.

So he just turned around and walked away, back into the glasshouse, towards his real life, and all the people who were counting on him.

They were the ones that mattered right now.

And *they* hadn't lied to him.

Rowan watched Eli give his speech, her stomach churning and her head aching with all the could-have-beens and regrets spinning in it. Watching him, she was sure none of the other guests in the room could tell that she'd just ripped his heart out and stamped on it. That he'd just been betrayed in a horrible, horrible way.

She saw it now, more clearly than she had from inside her own deception.

She'd been thinking of Willow, of protecting her sister, protecting herself too if it came to it, and protecting her niece or nephew most of all. She'd thought that nobody needed to know. That no one would care.

But she'd been so very wrong.

From the other side of the lie, everything looked different.

She'd allowed herself to grow close to Eli—and for him to grow close to her—without being honest about something as basic as her name, her identity. She'd allowed him to believe that she was his brother's girl, so to speak. To feel guilty about everything that was brewing between them.

At the most basic level, she'd lied. When he'd felt there was something wrong, she'd brushed him off. She'd told him everything was fine, that she was Willow, that the world was flat and the sky was green—and he'd believed her. Because he'd trusted her.

But she wasn't worthy of that trust.

The audience laughed at one of the jokes in Eli's speech, and Rowan glanced up again to find his gaze on her. He put down the papers he was speaking from and stepped forward, right to the edge of the small platform they'd erected for the speeches.

'The kids we help…they get told a lot of lies in their lives,' he said, the tone of the room suddenly far more serious than it had been so far. 'From their parents, from their teachers, from their friends, from the world around them. On the one hand, you have a society that tells them they're nothing, worthless, and will probably end up dead or in prison. And on the other you have an American dream that tells them if they work hard they can be rich and happy and respected. Which one is lying? Well, that, we've found, tends to be up to them.'

Eli wasn't looking directly at her any more, but she still knew, somehow, that his words were for her.

'When we lie to these kids and tell them they're worthless, that they can't make anything of themselves, we betray them, because sometimes all they need is a little faith to do incredible things. And at the same time, if we tell them that success and happiness is just a matter of hard work, that's a lie too—that path to the American dream looks a lot different depending on the circumstances you're born into, after all, and why should these kids judge themselves against someone with a trust fund and a family company to be given shares in—someone like me.'

That got a laugh, as Eli gave a self-deprecating shrug.

'The one thing we always promise the kids who come through our doors at the Castaway Café, or who make contact with Launch for help, is that we will never lie to them. Not about the ways we can help them, or—and this is the most important one—about *who they are. They* are the only ones who get to define that. We just want to help them—and we hope all of you will too. Thank you.'

He stepped down to overwhelming applause. Rowan joined in, but her mind was still whirling.

Was that what *she'd* done? Told Eli who he was by not telling him the truth about who she was? She supposed she had, in a way. He'd been defining himself in relation to her and their growing closeness, based on the idea that she was Willow.

And she really, really wasn't.

'Go talk to him,' Kelly said from beside her. When Rowan looked up, she rolled her eyes and continued. 'Whatever happened outside between you two, it's got you sighing and him ad-libbing the most important speech of his year—not that he didn't do a great job, of course. But go make it up before he does something else stupid that doesn't work out as well.'

'I'm not sure he wants to speak to me,' Rowan admitted.

'And that means you're not going to even try?' Kelly asked, brows raised.

No. No, it didn't.

But Rowan couldn't get close to him for the rest of the night. He was surrounded by donors, by friends, by the people this night was *supposed* to be about. So, in the end, she crept off to the taxi rank and headed home to Willow's apartment to make a call.

She needed to talk to her sister.

She needed to sort all this out.

Willow wasn't particularly pleased to be woken in what had to be the very early morning over in Rumbelow, but through her yawns she listened to what Rowan had to say all the same.

'Wait a minute,' she said, once Rowan was done. 'Are you sleeping with Ben's brother?'

'No! We're just friends,' Rowan insisted. 'I couldn't

do anything more when I was still lying to him about something as basic as my actual name.'

'But you wanted to, right?' Willow guessed. 'That's why you felt you had to tell him the truth. I can get that.' She sighed heavily, and Rowan was pretty sure this was something more than tiredness.

'Is everything okay? With the baby? The cottage?' she asked. 'Ben hasn't been in touch, has he? Because, honestly, the more I hear about that guy, the more I think you had the right idea, hiding out in Rumbelow.'

'Even if it meant you had to make "friends" under false pretences?'

'Even then,' Rowan promised. 'Seriously, Will. Is everything okay?'

'Everything's fine,' Willow replied unconvincingly. 'There's just…stuff. But I had my next scan and we got to hear the baby's heartbeat and see it wriggling about and everything! Not enough for us to tell if it's a boy or a girl though. It had its legs crossed.'

'I want photos!' Rowan paused, and frowned. 'Wait. We?'

'Me and the ultrasound technician.'

Rowan was almost certain she was lying. But who else could possibly have been there with her? Nobody even knew she was in England.

'Right,' she said anyway. She had enough to worry about in New York without fretting about what was happening in Rumbelow too. Willow would tell her if she needed to worry. 'Well, send me photos.'

'I will,' Willow promised. 'If *you* talk to Eli. Tell him whatever you need to, just make sure he doesn't tell Ben where I am or what's going on.'

*Tell him whatever you need to.*

No. She couldn't do that.

There was only one thing she *could* tell Eli.

'I'm going to tell him the truth, Will.'

Eli hadn't wanted to come. Even now, standing outside Willow's apartment—or Rowan's, he wasn't really sure on any of that any more—he half wanted to turn around and walk away. More than half, if he was honest.

But Rowan had sounded so open and honest on the phone. She'd called and called until Kelly got sick of him refusing to take the calls, and told him it was a sponsor on the phone with an urgent problem who would only speak to him.

Which was, as she pointed out afterwards when he complained, strictly speaking, completely accurate.

So he'd spoken to Rowan—under false pretences—and she'd asked him to come. More than that, she'd promised to tell him *everything.* No lies, no confusion. Everything.

He wouldn't have come for anything less.

The door to the building opened without him buzzing or putting in a code, and suddenly Rowan was standing there in the open doorway.

'Are you coming up?' she asked, her head tipped slightly to the side as she watched him. 'Only this isn't really a conversation I can have in the street. That's why I asked you to come here.'

Oh, Eli had a very bad feeling about this. He had no idea what could make Rowan pretend to be her sister for weeks on end, but it wasn't going to be anything good, he was sure of that much.

His head had been whirling with possibilities ever since he'd realised the truth. He barely remembered anything of the gala after that moment with Rowan—not even the speech he gave which, apparently, went down thunderously well. Maybe someone had recorded it.

He'd barely slept afterwards, thinking of all the reasons Rowan might have had to lie to him.

He needed to know what the truth was.

'I'm coming up,' he said.

She didn't even look like Willow any more—which Eli knew was a ridiculous thing to say, since they were identical twins. And they *were* identical—in their physical looks, at least. But now he knew what he was looking for, Eli saw differences.

Whenever she'd been at the office or events as Willow, she'd carried herself a certain way—with a bearing that said she knew she belonged. She'd held her head high, and always seemed on a slightly different level— and not just because of her height in heels.

He'd seen glimpses behind that façade, though. The first time they'd met, at the apartment, when he'd helped her through an anxiety attack. And again at the Castaway Café, or when she was working on Kelly's dress.

Maybe those moments were the real Rowan.

And, if so, he knew he'd never forgive himself if he didn't at least give her the chance to explain.

So he watched her as she moved around the apartment kitchen, fixing drinks for them both. Her long blonde hair was caught up in a simple ponytail, and she wore plain slim-fitting jeans and a white T-shirt with a picture of a pineapple on it. Her feet were bare, the nails

unpainted, and she had no make-up on her face, no jewellery at her throat or ears or on her fingers.

There was a tiny frown line between her eyebrows
as she battled with the coffee machine and, God help
him, he wanted to kiss it—the line, not the coffee machine. Although, after the lack of sleep he'd had in the
three nights since the gala at the Botanical Garden, it
was a close-run thing.

But, most of all, he just wanted to know who this
woman he'd spent weeks falling for really was.

And why she'd lied to him.

'So,' he said, when they were finally seated on separate squashy white sofas, either side of the coffee table—
which had been stripped of its sewing room accessories.
'What the hell has been going on, Rowan?'

She winced at the harshness of his tone, but he refused to feel guilty about it. He had every right to be
angry about being lied to.

Rowan placed her coffee cup on the table—then hur-
riedly reached into a drawer and pulled out a coaster
and put it on that. Now that he knew the truth, he could
see how ill at ease she was in this apartment. He'd put
it down to an interior designer and home organiser setting everything up without her input. But the truth was,
she just didn't belong here—and he couldn't believe it
had taken him so long to see it.

Looking up, she caught and held his gaze, her expression open and her eyes clear. Whatever came next, he
had faith that it would be the truth.

This time.

'I'm going to tell you everything,' she said evenly.
'The whole story, from start to finish. And when I'm

done, well. It's up to you what you do with the information. But I really hope you'll stay and listen to the reasons why I would appreciate it if you could keep my presence here—and my sister's whereabouts—a secret for now. Especially from your brother.'

Oh, he didn't like the sound of that at all.

His brain had been right. This was bad.

'Start talking,' he said. 'And I'll listen.'

# CHAPTER NINE

ROWAN WATCHED ELI'S face carefully as she explained the strange sequence of events that had brought them to this moment.

The three days when he'd refused to answer her phone calls had given her plenty of time to figure out what she was going to say. She'd contemplated going down to the Launch offices and confronting him directly, but, given the open-plan nature of the place, she'd thought better of it.

She needed privacy for this conversation, just in case he blew up completely.

She started with an explanation of her own history, and Willow's, and how she'd walked away from her modelling career and the fame that came with it several years ago. She talked about how Willow had always supported and defended her—even though she didn't understand what Rowan was feeling. She talked about the anxiety attacks, the pressure, her mother, and the summer locked away in that London townhouse learning to sew.

Eli nodded thoughtfully. 'That explains a lot. But not why you're here and Willow is... Where *is* Willow?'

'Rumbelow,' Rowan replied. 'It's a tiny fishing village in England where I live. You'd love it. Well, for a visit.' Because, now she thought about it, she couldn't imagine Eli in Rumbelow. Eli belonged to the city. To the kids he helped, and the society he was born into— even if his role now was more making that society see the problems they'd rather ignore. He was designer suits and swanky hotel bars and events at botanical gardens that felt like magic.

And yes, he was also quiet dinners and a beer while he watched her sew, and holding her hand sitting on the floor through a panic attack.

But that didn't mean he'd fit in back home in the place she loved. If she was out of place here in New York, he'd be just as much so in Rumbelow.

'Rumbelow?' Eli asked, frowning. 'What the hell kind of name is that?'

Rowan sighed. 'I know. Anyway. Back to the story.'

This was the difficult bit, of course. Explaining why Willow had come to her. And, more than that, why Rowan had agreed not just to keep her secret, but also to take part in this masquerade.

She'd decided, lying awake at night, that the only way to tell it was exactly as it had happened.

So she did.

Eli listened in silence, but she could see him going stiller, feel him drawing away with every word she said. By the time she'd reached the end, she was shaking.

'And then I arrived here and found you in her apartment and, well, I guess that was the last straw after a very stressful couple of days.'

He squeezed her hand. When had he started holding

her hand? She couldn't even remember, it just felt so right. 'I bet it was.'

Eli took a deep breath, then let it out again, as if he'd thought he had something to say and had forgotten it. Rowan watched him carefully as he processed everything she'd told him.

Finally, he said, 'She's really pregnant?'

'I can show you the ultrasound photo.'

'And it's Ben's baby? For sure?' Rowan gave him a filthy look, and he shook his head. 'Sorry. Of course it is. I just... I have to ask because...'

'Because?' she prompted him when he trailed off.

'A secret for a secret?' Eli said suddenly, sitting up a little straighter and pulling his hand away from hers. 'Not that mine is much of one, really. Most of New York probably knows.'

'Knows what?' Rowan shifted a little in her seat, leaning in towards him.

'That my father—Ben's father—probably wasn't mine.'

Rowan's shock must have shown on her face because he shook his head lightly, a rueful smile playing around his lips. This was old news to him, she supposed, something he'd come to terms with, but still shocking all the same.

'When did you find out?' she asked.

'That's the thing. I always knew there was something different in the way our father treated me compared to Ben. Ben was the golden child, the heir apparent, the one who got all the schooling in the way of the company, the one who went to functions and events with Dad, who met everyone that mattered. And I was the one who was shut outside with his secretary, doing my homework.'

He spoke plainly, evenly, but all the same Rowan couldn't help but imagine a lonely little boy, not understanding why he didn't matter the same way his brother did.

She knew that feeling. The feeling of not measuring up. She'd felt it too, every time she'd started shaking before a fashion show and her mother had snapped at her, wanting to know why she couldn't be more like her sister.

'When I was old enough to notice and mind, I started asking questions. Asking people why my father didn't love me the way he loved Ben,' Eli went on. 'They all told me I was imagining things, that I was making it up.'

'They gaslit you,' Rowan said, softly. 'They lied.'

'Basically, yes,' Eli agreed, his jaw tight. 'That's why I have such…issues with lies, even now.'

And she'd lied to him for weeks about something as fundamental as who she was. No wonder he'd refused to take her calls. The only miracle was that he was here now at all.

'How did you find out the truth?' she asked.

Eli shrugged. 'I'll probably never know for sure—unless Ben agrees to a DNA test, which I doubt. With both my legal parents dead, there's no one to ask. But eventually, as I grew older, after my mother was gone, people got less careful about what they said when I was around. The gossip mill loves a scandal here in the city, and if the parents were talking about it the kids knew as well, and they weren't afraid to let me know.'

'Did you ever ask your father?'

'What was the point? He'd only have lied too.' Eli looked away from her, reaching out for his coffee. It had to be stone cold by now, but he drank the remaining dregs anyway.

'Would you like another?' She reached for his cup, but he shook his head.

'No. I need to get going.' He was already standing before he'd finished the sentence.

Rowan stood too. 'Going? Where? We still need to talk about—'

'We've talked,' Eli interrupted. 'You've told me the truth, and I appreciate it. But now I have to go.'

Oh, Rowan had a really bad feeling about this. 'And do what?'

'And tell Ben the truth.'

'Eli, you can't!' Rowan's plaintive cry caught at his heart, but he turned towards the door anyway.

He couldn't let a pretty face distract him from doing what he knew was right. Even if Rowan was so much more than that.

'My brother has a right to know he's going to be a father.' For all he knew, his own, real, father had never been given that chance. He wouldn't be the one to deprive Ben of it.

'I absolutely agree.' Rowan put a hand on his arm to stop him and met his gaze with wide, honest eyes. 'I told Willow the same thing. It was part of our agreement for me coming here.'

'Then why are you trying to stop me?'

'Because Willow also has a right to figure out what

she wants to do before talking to Ben,' she said, and Eli's heart contracted.

'She's thinking about not keeping the baby? Rowan, she *has* to talk to Ben before she makes that decision.'

Rowan shook her head. 'That decision, at least, is already made. She's keeping it.'

Relief flooded through him. While he fully supported a woman's right to choose, if it came to him keeping that knowledge from his brother for the rest of his life, he knew he'd never have been able to live with the guilt.

'But if she's keeping it, what else is there to think about?'

'She and Ben aren't together right now, remember?' Rowan pointed out. 'In fact, he's been off swanning on his yacht with another woman.'

'True.' Eli let her tug him down to the sofa again, and this time she sat beside him, close enough to touch.

He *could* touch now, he realised. If he wanted. Because she wasn't his brother's girl any more.

Just the woman who'd been lying to him.

'Willow just wants some time to figure out how it will all work. I don't think…they're not going to get back together this time, Eli. She wants to go this alone. But obviously Ben will need to be involved, if he wants to be, and I think Willow wants to decide for herself what she wants that to look like, before he comes in and steamrollers all over her and dictates the way it will work.'

'Ben wouldn't—' Eli stopped. Because he suspected Willow was right. Ben absolutely would.

He was a lot like their father, that way. He saw the way he thought things should be done, and demanded that was what happened.

'How long?' he asked instead.

Rowan shook her head. 'I'm not sure. But it can't be much longer, I don't think. I told her I need to be back in Rumbelow before too long, anyway. I've got dress commissions to get started on. I'm doing what I can from here, dealing with emails and sketching designs, but it's kind of a hands-on process, you know?'

'So I saw.' He thought of Rowan spending all that time with Kelly, perfecting her dream dress—then standing back and watching her glow on the night of the gala.

Maybe that was the clearest sign that the woman he'd fallen for over the past few weeks was Rowan, not Willow. Willow was used to standing in the limelight, the centre of attention, while Rowan hid away in her ridiculously named fishing village.

The fact that *Willow* was now the one in hiding… maybe that was something to think about too. That she felt she couldn't be in the same city as Ben while figuring this out.

What did that say about his brother, and their relationship?

Eli pushed the thought aside. Ben was his brother and, despite their differences, he still loved and trusted him—the same way Willow clearly trusted Rowan. Ben deserved the truth—and Rowan deserved to go back to living her own life again.

*Except then she'll leave New York.*

The thought stopped him in his mental tracks.

Somehow, he hadn't made that connection yet—that Rowan wouldn't be staying. Perhaps because it felt so much like she belonged here, with him.

But she didn't, did she? The first day she'd arrived she'd had an anxiety attack—although, to be fair, that was mostly his fault. But still. He could recount numerous occasions over the past few weeks where she'd stepped outside to get air, or where her smile had seemed too tight to be real. She found this city hard to navigate, and he'd known that and ignored it.

She didn't want to be here.

And he really didn't want her to leave.

But how could he ask her to stay?

'So another couple of weeks, at most?' His voice came out a little hoarse, and she looked at him strangely. He cleared his throat. 'Until you swap back and Willow tells Ben the truth?'

'I guess.' She looked down at her hands. 'I really should be getting back soon. And she'll be…pretty pregnant by then. At least halfway, I think. She'll need to have a plan.'

'Right.' For a moment, his head swam with an image of Rowan pregnant, and he swallowed, hard.

'Do you think…could you just wait until then, to tell Ben, I mean?' Rowan fixed him with her pleading gaze. 'Just give her the chance to do it herself.'

'If he ever finds out I knew before he did…' He loved his brother, but he didn't love his temper. Ben hated being the last to know anything. And this…yeah, he'd be furious. Rightly so too.

'Why would he?' Rowan asked reasonably. 'He doesn't even know we've been spending time together, right?'

'Right.' And they needed to keep it that way.

Before, he'd kept his connection with the woman he'd

thought was Willow a secret from his brother because of
the guilt he felt about his feelings for her. Now, when he
was free to feel however he liked about Rowan, he had a
new reason to feel guilty. A worse one, in lots of ways.

He should walk out of there right now, find his
brother, and tell him the truth.

But he already knew he wasn't going to. Not because
Willow needed more time.

Because Rowan had asked him to.

'Two weeks,' he said. 'That's all I can promise. And
in return...'

'Anything,' Rowan said quickly, already beaming.

'You have to...' What? What could he ask of her,
really? 'Help me out at the Castaway Café this week.'

'Deal.' Her smile faded and she gripped his hand
tightly. 'Thank you, Eli.'

'It's just two weeks,' he said.

But he didn't know if he was reassuring her or himself.


The relief that Rowan felt at Eli's agreeing to keep Willow's secret was short-lived. Because when she called to
tell her twin about their new deadline for getting things
sorted, Willow dropped another unexpected bomb into
her life.

'You need me to *what?*' Rowan squealed. 'You said
I wouldn't have to do any of that!'

The deal was that she'd come to New York and be
seen around the place so Ben wouldn't get suspicious.
No photoshoots, no fashion shows. That was the *deal*.

'I know, I know,' Willow said apologetically. 'But
this is for a friend, and I owe her. It's only a little—like,

absolutely tiny—preview of her new collection. That's *all*. There'll hardly be anyone in the room even watching, Rowan, I promise.'

That wasn't the point, though, and Willow knew it as well as Rowan.

The point was that the last time she'd tried to set foot on a catwalk, she couldn't.

Their mother had been furious, but Willow had talked her down. Convinced her to just let Rowan do the photoshoots while Willow handled the shows. Nobody was happy about the arrangement—everyone wanted the identical twins walking down that runway together, for maximum impact—but Willow had stood firm, which meant Rowan had been able to too.

Otherwise, she was pretty sure she'd have had a major meltdown on camera at a New York Fashion Week show, and that wouldn't have been good for anybody.

But now Willow was the one asking her to step onto that catwalk again.

'I don't know if I can, Will,' she said softly.

'*I* know,' Willow replied. 'You've grown so much since then, Ro. I think you can do anything. I saw the photos online of you at that gala at the Botanical Gardens—you were glowing. There were cameras and hundreds of people and it didn't faze you one bit, did it?'

'Well…' Rowan wasn't sure that was completely true. But she *had* managed the evening, hadn't she? She'd just pretended she was Willow when anyone she didn't know spoke to her or looked at her and—

Oh. Maybe that was all she had to do at the fashion show too.

Could she do that?

If Willow had asked her at the start of this switch, she'd have said no. But now…

'Maybe,' she said slowly. 'Maybe I can do it.'

'I know you can,' Willow reassured her. 'Piece of cake.'

But Rowan's hands were still trembling as she handed over plates to the kids at the Castaway Café the next day—and Eli noticed.

After she almost dropped a tray full of hotdogs, he steered her away from the counter and into the back room, his hand warm at her back, and just the scent of him was somehow reassuring.

'What's wrong?' he asked, once the door was shut behind them and they were alone. 'Has something happened?'

'Willow called yesterday. She needs me to do a small fashion show. As her.' There, just the simple truth. It definitely sounded less terrifying when she said it out loud.

Okay, it didn't. But she was pretending it did, anyway.

Eli didn't fall for it, though. 'And you're freaking out. Understandably.'

'I'm not freaking out,' she snapped. Eli gave her a look, and she slumped down to sit in the ancient armchair by the window. 'Okay, maybe a bit.'

'I can't believe she asked you to do it.' Eli paced in front of the door, his hands thrust deep in his pockets. 'I mean, she knows what happened last time you had to do that. You told me—it's what set off your biggest panic attack ever, and made you leave modelling in the first place! I thought your deal was that you wouldn't have to do any of this stuff?'

'It was. But…things come up. And this is a favour to a friend. And…'

'And?' Eli pressed, when she trailed off.

Rowan sat forward, her forearms resting against her thighs, and focused hard on the door handle on the other side of the room, thinking.

'Rowan?' Eli said, when she stayed silent.

'I think… I think this might have been part of Willow's plan all along,' she said finally.

'You mean she got pregnant just so you'd have to come to New York and do a fashion show again for the first time in years?' The incredulity in Eli's voice was plain. 'I think that might be pushing it a bit.'

'No, of course I don't mean that.' Except…in a small way, she did. Sitting back, she tried to explain. 'You realise that Ben hasn't been near her apartment, the whole time I've been there?'

'Well, no. Because he was…'

'Off on a yacht with that other woman, yes,' Rowan finished. 'And Willow must have known he'd do that. From what I understand, it's his modus operandi.'

Eli winced, obviously not enjoying thinking of his brother as that kind of man. 'I wouldn't know. But… yeah, perhaps.'

'Maybe it was useful for her to have me here, being seen, so no one—especially the media—would start speculating about where she'd gone,' Rowan continued, still thinking aloud. 'But it wasn't exactly essential. She could have hidden out in Rumbelow with me, and if anyone got suspicious we could have said *I* was the one who was pregnant, and that was why she was there.'

'That would have been a lot to ask of you,' Eli said.

'And coming to New York wasn't?' Rowan shook her head. 'No, I get that this worked out well for what Willow needed—time and space away from Ben, without him or anyone else wondering where she was. But it was kind of extreme, don't you think? This whole sister swap scheme?'

'You think she had another reason too?'

Oh, Rowan was almost certain she had. After all, she knew Willow. And Willow always had at least a dozen reasons for every decision she made.

'I think she wanted to get me out of my comfort zone, and back into the real world again.'

As soon as she said it aloud, she knew it was true.

And from Eli's face, he did too. 'And you're… How are you feeling about that?'

Rowan couldn't think about feelings just yet. She was still on logistics, and trying to read her sister's mind from across an ocean. 'I think she thought that if I came here I'd find my confidence again. I don't think she imagined I'd suddenly want to get back into modelling—that was never really me, anyway. But maybe she thought I'd retreated and hidden myself away a bit *too* much, so this was her way of forcing me to face up to that. While also conveniently giving her everything she needed too.' That would be very Willow.

'Suddenly I'm understanding why your sister and my brother were together for so long,' he said dryly.

'Given what I know of your brother, that's not exactly complimentary to my sister.'

Eli shook his head. 'He's not a bad man. He just…he has that same sort of mind. The sort that sees a situation and finds a path of action that addresses half a dozen problems all at the same time. It's what has made him so successful in his business. And his personal life, to a point.'

'I can see that, I suppose.' The only problem with that plan of action, in Rowan's experience, was that it didn't always solve all the problems equally well. And sometimes it forgot about the people at the heart of it.

'Of course, sometimes he just manages to screw up all the things at the same time,' Eli went on. 'Like losing Willow, not knowing she's pregnant and being stuck on a yacht with the most vacant woman of all time.'

That surprised a laugh from her, and Rowan relaxed back into her seat, thinking hard.

'So, what are you going to do?' Eli asked. 'Now you've figured this out?'

'I'm going to see if she's right,' Rowan said slowly. 'If I really am ready to do this.'

It was a risk, of course. But she'd already come so far. Why not take it the whole way?

# CHAPTER TEN

ELI HAD NEVER attended a fashion show before—he'd never had any desire or need to either. But wild horses wouldn't have kept him away from today's.

As Willow had promised, it really was only a small affair, with just a few rows of chairs filled with people who all seemed to know each other. The catwalk jutted out into the room between the seats and long black curtains hid whatever was going on behind the scenes from sight.

Eli took a seat to one side, as close as he could get to those curtains, his phone gripped tightly in his hand. He hadn't been allowed backstage—and Rowan had told him he'd only make her more nervous anyway—but he wanted, no, needed, to be close at hand. Just in case.

His phone was on silent, of course, so he stared at the screen, waiting to see if it would light up with a desperate plea from Rowan to come and help her. What if she had another panic attack? Or just couldn't do it and needed him to drive the getaway car?

'I have techniques and methods to deal with this, Eli,' she'd told him in the car on the way over. 'I've learned a lot about how to manage my anxiety since the last time I was on a catwalk. I'm not the same person I was back then—and, even more importantly, my mother isn't there to be unbearable about everything either.'

It was still a risk, though, as far as Eli was concerned. Not just because of how Rowan might react to being backstage at a fashion show again, but because the designer was a friend of Willow's. A real friend would surely realise that the woman wearing her designs *wasn't* Willow at all. Wouldn't she?

Rowan hadn't thought so, when he'd suggested it in the car. 'She'll be too busy flapping about the show going smoothly to notice. As long as we don't hang around afterwards we'll be fine. And Willow has already told her she'll have to make a sharp exit because of another commitment.'

So now here he was, just sitting there, willing his heart to slow down, more nervous than if he was the one preparing to parade about in the latest fashions for an audience.

The phone in his hand buzzed, and he looked down to see a message.

Stop gripping your phone so tight; you'll break it.

He smiled, even as it buzzed again.

And stop glaring at the catwalk. If the wind changes your face will stay like that.

That made him laugh out loud, much to the concern of the people sitting around him.

Eli looked up to try and find where Rowan was

watching him from, but saw only the flutter of a curtain. At least he knew she was doing okay so far.

The lights dimmed, and the small crowd settled, as music started over the speakers. Eli sucked in a deep breath, and had to remind himself to let it go again as he waited for Rowan to appear on the catwalk.

She wasn't the first model to appear, or even the second or third. Eli suspected she was the surprise extra appearance on the runway to win over the audience— and, sure enough, she was the last one out. Afterwards, Eli couldn't have said what any of the others had been wearing, but the outfit Rowan had been dressed in would be burned in his memory for all time.

Apparently, chain mail was a thing this season, or maybe Joan of Arc chic, Eli wasn't sure. Fashion wasn't his specialist subject. But the diaphanous white fabric that clung to Rowan's body, anchored only by strips of fine silver chains, was something he was willing to study at great length.

Preferably while removing it. With his teeth.

Hell, she couldn't be wearing *anything* under that, or it would show through. All he could see was the rosy glow of her skin peeking through the fabric...

There was a murmur of excitement as Rowan made her way down the catwalk, hips swaying gently, her gaze focused straight ahead, a Mona Lisa non-smile playing around her lips. Her hair had been slicked back into a low knot at the base of her neck, her face mostly bare of make-up except for a shimmery finish on her cheeks and collarbones.

She looked beautiful. Ethereal. Untouchable.

But God, he wanted to touch her.

'How the hell did she get Willow Harper to appear here?' someone behind him asked in an astonished whisper. Eli glanced back just in time to see their companion shrug their confusion too.

Designer friend or not, Eli suspected Willow would normally have turned this down, if the woman up there in the breathtaking dress really *had* been Willow. This must be another of Rowan's sister's ploys—a way to get her sister to dip her toe back into the world she'd left behind, without being too terrified.

When Rowan had first mentioned her suspicions about Willow's motives, he'd had to swallow down the anger they raised. Who was she to trick Rowan into doing *anything* she was uncomfortable with? Willow had used her twin's love for her to force her into a situation she didn't want to be in, and that was not okay.

Except if she hadn't, he might never have met her. Never have fallen for her as hard as he had—something he'd basically given up denying even to himself at this point.

It still didn't make it okay.

But watching Rowan up there, owning that catwalk, reclaiming a life she'd walked away from in fear and anxiety…it was hard to stay angry with Willow right in that moment.

The show reached its conclusion before Eli had managed to reconcile his thoughts on the matter, and he joined in the rapturous applause as all the models—and the designer—took a final bow on the catwalk.

'I heard Willow is designing gowns herself now,' he heard someone say as the audience got to their feet and headed towards the drinks and nibbles set up in the next room. 'Maybe that's why she agreed to do this show—contacts are everything.'

Another person scoffed. 'It's not like she doesn't have enough of those by herself. If I were her, I'd be more worried about having the *talent*. It's a long jump from wearing clothes to designing them.'

'I don't know,' their companion said. Eli turned towards the voices in time to see one of them showing the other their phone screen. 'Says here she designed this dress for some woman at a charity gala event...not too shabby.' Were they talking about *Kelly's* dress? How had *that* got out on the internet?

The same way everything did, he supposed. They'd had an official photographer, but plenty of other people had been taking photos on their phones and posting them to social media. Kelly could even have put it up there herself, and it wasn't as if they'd told her not to mention Willow was the designer. Even if they had, everyone in the Launch offices knew 'Willow' had been working on it.

Maybe the real surprise was that it hadn't got out sooner.

The other person took the phone and studied it. 'That's not bad, actually. Although if she's planning on making a niche out of designing dresses for the imperfectly proportioned the internet will pile on for sure.'

They wandered away before Eli could hear any more of their conversation, and he headed over to find Rowan to make their swift getaway, still thinking.

When she emerged, at the back door as planned, Rowan was back in her jeans, T-shirt and jacket, her hair up in a ponytail, and only the slight shimmer on her cheeks a sign that she'd ever worn anything else at all.

She'd done it. She'd walked down that catwalk like a pro—and, more importantly, she'd faced her demons and she'd won. And he was so damn proud of her he could hardly see straight.

'Did I look okay?' she asked as he wrapped her up into a tight hug.

'Magnificent,' he murmured against her shoulder. 'You were…you were incredible.'

She pulled away, blushing slightly. 'Thanks. So… uh… I suppose we should get out of here before someone stops us and drags us back for the party. What do you want to do now?'

'I am taking you out,' he told her. 'For a celebratory New York tour.'

It wasn't what he *wanted* to do, exactly. But their relationship, such as it was, hadn't reached that stage yet for everything he wanted to do. So, for now, they'd stay in public, where he wouldn't be tempted to rush them to that next level. There was still a lot of trust to build up between them first.

Not *too* public, though. Places where Ben wouldn't even think to go, and it wouldn't get back to him that they'd been out together.

Maybe Rowan should wear a hat or something, just in case.

'Sounds great,' Rowan said, beaming. She was bouncing on the toes of her tennis shoes, and he knew the adrenaline had to still be racing through her body. Getting out and active would help her burn that off too. And in her street clothes she looked so much more like *her* than her more famous sister. Odds were she might not even be recognised at all, if they were careful.

Somewhere, a door banged. Rowan's eyes widened, and he grabbed her arm to lead her to where he'd parked.

'I don't suppose you get to keep the see-through dress with the chains, do you?' he asked casually, as they headed to the car.

She laughed. 'You liked that one, huh? Well, sorry to disappoint, but I had to give it back. Maybe I could make something similar, though. Just for wearing at home...'

'I would not object to that,' Eli replied, grinning.

'Good to know.'

Rowan had a feeling that Eli's idea of a tour of New York City wouldn't be in any of the tourist guidebooks, and she suspected the reason for that had more to do with avoiding his brother and anyone who might recognise her and report back than anything else.

'You already saw all the obvious stuff when you were living here as a teen, right?' He tucked her hand through his arm as he led her along the pavement away from where they'd left the car. 'So I figure we'll do some things I bet you *didn't* see.'

They stopped outside a large red brick building with classic black metal fire escapes down the side. Rowan squinted up at the sign. 'The Tenement Museum?'

Eli nodded. 'It's my favourite New York museum. Come on. I've booked us on a tour of the apartments of nineteenth-century immigrants, and it's about to start!'

Rowan couldn't help but grin at his enthusiasm. Of course this was his favourite museum.

An hour later, she had to admit he'd been right; the tour was fascinating.

The only slightly distracting thing was the way her phone kept beeping with new emails, voicemails and messages—all of them forwarded from Willow, and all of them asking for details of her bespoke gowns. Which didn't exist.

Rowan switched her phone off and concentrated on learning about the lives of immigrant Americans in the nineteenth century instead.

After their tour, Eli dropped her home and, when she invited him in, shook his head. 'Not yet.'

'Yet?' Yet implied that one day he'd come in again—and with purpose.

Eli nodded, then ducked his head to touch his lips to hers. Surprised, Rowan gasped, and Eli deepened the kiss with a groan.

The sound reverberated through her body, making every nerve-ending tingle, and her blood heat. Her hands reached around to hold him closer, until he was pressing her against the door, and she could feel how much he *wanted* to come in...so why wouldn't he?

Suddenly, Eli pulled away, panting. Resting his forehead against hers, he said, 'If I come in now, I don't think I'll be able to leave. Definitely not for a few days. And there's more of my New York I want to show you first.'

'That's the only reason?' Because it didn't feel like it. They only had a couple of weeks left together, and she didn't want to waste a moment.

Eli just gave her a small sad smile, and she knew

he wasn't quite ready to trust her that far, not yet. But hopefully soon.

'I just want to know you as *you,* first,' he explained.

And then, with a last burst of self-resolve that, from the expression on his face, might have been physically painful, he was gone. Leaving her breathless against her sister's apartment door, her mind filled with images of what the next few days might have looked like if he wasn't so damned principled.

True to his word, he was back the next morning, ready to take her on an app walking tour from his phone that took them to all the best delis, showcasing international foods from around the world. Once they were stuffed, they visited his favourite second-hand bookshop, where Rowan found a fantastic selection of vintage dress patterns stuffed into a wicker basket at the back.

Then he left her at her apartment door again, with another mind-bending kiss, and the basket full of sewing patterns he'd insisted on buying for her.

With a sigh, Rowan went inside to check the dozen or more messages on her phone.

On the third day, he took her somewhere she hadn't even imagined could exist in New York.

'No, really. How does this city have actual medieval cloisters?'

Eli laughed. 'They're part of the Met Museum,' he explained. 'And they were actually built in 1933, but using medieval European-style architecture. Come on, let's go see if we can find a unicorn.'

'A unicorn?' Rowan echoed as she followed him through a Gothic chapel. But really, nothing would surprise her at this point.

They *did* find the unicorn—actually a series of unicorn tapestries, but magical enough for Rowan—then took a walk through the cloister gardens.

As her phone buzzed again in her pocket, Eli looked down at it. 'Not going to answer that?'

Rowan shook her head. 'I don't think mobile phones were encouraged in medieval Europe. Just pretend it doesn't exist.'

Eli smiled, but it didn't quite reach his eyes. 'Okay.'

Then she realised—the real reason he kept saying goodbye at her apartment door, even now.

He thought she was keeping something else from him, but she wasn't, not really. She just didn't want to deal with it at all.

Maybe later. Later, she'd tell him about all the requests and commissions, and the interviews Willow kept turning down, and how everyone out there thought that Kelly's dress was *Willow's* work, and she had no idea how she was going to untangle that mess, or if she even wanted to.

Right now, she just wanted to soak in the peace of the cloister gardens, and imagine a unicorn running through them. Was that so bad?

She leant her head against Eli's shoulder as they walked, arm in arm. 'Thank you for bringing me here,' she murmured.

'Thank you for coming,' Eli replied, and the emotion in his voice told her he wasn't just talking about the Cloisters.

They lingered in the Cloisters a long time. Eli had always loved the place for the quiet, and the space for reflection, and he'd guessed Rowan would too. It hadn't occurred to him until they were there that, living in England, she probably got to see the real thing all the time, if she wanted.

But Rowan had shook her head when he'd suggested it. 'I don't leave Rumbelow much,' she'd explained. 'And there are no medieval cloisters there—just rotting fishing boats!'

He hadn't mentioned it again, but he couldn't help but wonder what was so wonderful about Rumbelow that she never left the place. Or was it more that everything outside it was so terrible—or terrifying?

She'd come to New York, though. Perhaps she was ready for other new adventures too.

Maybe even with him.

After the Cloisters, they headed to Giovanni's— which Eli firmly believed was the best ice cream parlour in the world—and took their cones for a walk through the park.

'It's good,' Rowan admitted after a few mouthfuls. 'But you should come to Rumbelow and try Marco's ice cream.'

'Maybe one day,' Eli replied, even though he couldn't really imagine it. He was a city boy through and through—and the idea that anywhere had better anything than New York was clearly absurd.

As he stole a lick of Rowan's strawberry shortcake cone, her phone buzzed again in her pocket. She reached in and flicked it off, but that didn't stem Eli's curiosity.

She didn't want to talk about whatever was blowing up her phone, that much was clear. But that didn't mean she shouldn't. Eli had a feeling that Rowan was enjoying avoiding reality right now—but that didn't mean it wasn't going to come back and bite them both anyway.

He'd been so determined to spend time getting to know her as *Rowan,* not Willow, before they took things any further, but now he wondered. How much time did they really have?

At some point, they were going to have to have the difficult conversations. Life wasn't all unicorns and ice cream. Unfortunately.

Her phone buzzed yet again, and Rowan gave a heavy sigh.

Eli tugged her arm gently to get her to sit down beside him on the nearest bench, where they could stare out over the other parkgoers.

'You don't have to tell me what's going on that you don't want to answer your phone about,' he said cautiously. He wasn't sure what the right or wrong thing to say was, and the last thing he wanted to do was put his foot in it now. 'But if it would help to talk about it...'

With another sigh, Rowan pulled her phone from her pocket, opened her email app and passed it to him.

Frowning, Eli scrolled through what looked like a screenful of messages from Willow. Until he looked a little closer.

'These are all dress commissions,' he said, still scrolling. 'Or requests for them, at least. People are going to Willow thinking she designed Kelly's dress for the gala?'

'Apparently.' Rowan took the phone back. 'There are voicemails and texts too. Willow's getting pretty fed up of having to forward them all, since I won't answer any of them.'

'Do you think maybe you should?' Eli didn't want to presume. Everything between them was so tenuous and new—a few longing kisses and a distance he kept in place without even fully knowing why. It wasn't his place to decide what she should do or not—it never would be, no matter how close they grew. But if she wanted his advice... 'This sounds like the sort of thing that isn't going to go away in a hurry.'

Rowan sighed. 'It's only because they think it was Willow—that *I* am Willow. Which... I know that was the plan, but this is different. Designing and making bespoke gowns...that's *my* thing, I taught myself how to do it and built up a small business back home making clothes I cared about for people who deserved to feel beautiful. I did that. Not Willow. And now...'

'Now you think people are cashing in on the name and the moment and wanting to get close to a celebrity?' Eli guessed. When she nodded, he eased the phone from her hand again and scrolled through the messages. 'You know, some of these don't even mention Willow's celebrity. They just really, really liked the dress. Look at this one... "As a plus size woman of colour, I can't tell you how much it meant to me to see a bespoke gown like that. To know that I could have clothes that make me feel beautiful just the way I am. I can't afford it yet, but maybe one day! Please keep making the dresses for people like me. I'm saving up!"'

Rowan looked up. 'I didn't... I didn't read them all,' she admitted.

Or any of them, Eli was willing to bet.

'I don't think they're only interested because they think you're Willow,' Eli murmured. 'Just like I wasn't.'

She gave a watery chuckle at that. 'You really wished I *wasn't* Willow for most of the time we've known each other, didn't you?'

'Damn right, I did.' Those days of crippling guilt about lusting after his brother's girl had now been replaced with the guilt of lying to him, but knowing that Rowan was *Rowan* was still a relief. 'Looks like wishes can come true, after all.'

She met his gaze, and what he saw there felt like everything that had been building inside him over the past weeks.

*Finally,* they were on the same page.

'You should respond to some of those messages,' he said, his voice sounding hoarse even to his own ears.

'What's the point? I'll be going home soon, anyway. I won't be here to make the dresses.'

The words hung between them, and Eli wondered if all the other things she wouldn't be there to do were racing through her head too.

He looked away. 'I should take you home.'

'Right.' She paused, and he couldn't help but sneak a glance up at her. 'Will you come inside this time?'

The wanting in her voice, the heat in her eyes, left him in no doubt of his answer.

'Yes.'

# CHAPTER ELEVEN

ROWAN STRETCHED AGAINST the sheets of her sister's bed the next morning, her body pleasantly aching and every muscle relaxed.

Well.

That had been worth waiting for.

She smiled at the curve of Eli's body beside her, the sunlight pouring in and warming his bare skin. He had one hand flung out towards her, the other tucked against his chest, as if he was both giving away his heart and holding hers close and safe at the same time.

She knew how he felt.

Last night had been incredible. Turned out, all that pent-up longing and unconsummated desire was good for one thing—when they'd finally given in, they hadn't held back. From the moment they'd stumbled through the door, already kissing, it had been a race to see who could get the other naked first. Then she'd fallen onto the bed and he'd lowered himself over her and...

Maybe she should wake him up for another round.

Eli gave a light snore and burrowed deeper into the mattress, and she abandoned the idea with a fond smile. Apparently the three rounds last night would have to suffice for now.

She could live with that.

As long as they were exploring each other's bodies, they weren't exploring the far trickier subject of what happened next. When Willow came back to New York, and she headed home to Rumbelow.

The thought ruined the warm and hazy morning-after feeling, so Rowan slipped out from between the sheets without waking Eli, to go find some coffee. Spotting his white shirt on the floor—and remembering stripping it from him and humming her approval as she examined the broad, lightly muscled shoulders underneath with her mouth—she smiled. Maybe, just for this morning, she could be that girl in the movie. Living in New York, having incredible sex with a new, gorgeous and considerate lover—who also made it his life's mission to care for the less fortunate. And, most critically in this moment, gliding around a sunlit penthouse apartment in Manhattan on a lazy morning wearing nothing but her lover's expensively tailored white shirt.

She was a tall woman, but Eli was even taller, and the tails of his shirt covered the very top of her thighs at least when she slipped it on. It wasn't something she'd wear out in public, but for the very limited plans she had for the rest of the morning it would do just fine. She fastened the most crucial buttons and headed out into the kitchen to wrestle with the coffee-maker, already imagining Eli's expression when he finally woke and came to find her.

She'd *almost* managed to make a latte, and was about to tackle a plain americano for Eli, when she heard the front door to the apartment open.

*Willow.* Rowan spun around, expecting to see her sister, fresh off the plane and here to tell her it was time to go home.

Instead, she found herself face to face with a man she only knew from photos. Magazine shots with Willow. And that family photo on Eli's desk.

*Ben.*

Oh, this was not good. At least Eli was still in bed. If she could just get rid of him without Eli waking up, maybe this would still be a good morning after all.

But her chest was already tightening, and she had to focus hard on her breathing to even get any words out at all.

'What are you doing here?'

'What, I can't come visit my girlfriend when I get back to town?' Ben asked, an amused smile on his face.

'We broke up. Remember?'

He rolled his eyes. 'Like that's never happened before. Listen, I've got this awards dinner next week. Want to patch things up in time to appear on my arm in all the glossy magazines?'

Rowan swallowed. What would Willow say?

Well, based on past evidence, she'd probably say yes—she always had before. But that was before there was the baby to consider. And since Rowan *wasn't* Willow, she could make the right choice here, on her sister's behalf.

And the fact that his brother was naked in her bedroom had practically nothing to do with it.

'No, Ben. I don't want to patch things up. I told you, things are over this time. For real. I'm not playing these games any more.'

Wow. That sounded good, even to her own ears.

Strong and determined. Exactly the way she wished she'd been able to talk to her mother, when she'd decided to leave modelling behind for good.

Back then, she'd been too scared, too damaged. She'd stolen away in the middle of the night without so much as a note, and left Willow to explain things for her.

Maybe it was appropriate that she was here now, to do the same for her twin.

It felt…right. It felt like closure.

Ben, however, didn't appear to feel the same. His pleasant façade fell away, and his expression twisted into something ugly and entitled.

'What the hell are you doing lately, Willow?' He stalked across the room towards her, and Rowan backed up against the counter instinctively. Her sister had said that Ben had never hurt her physically, but that didn't mean he wasn't still damn intimidating when he wanted to be. 'Designing dresses instead of modelling them? Leaving me high and dry? What's it all about? Is our arrangement not working for you any more?'

Rowan swallowed, trying to get her throat to open enough to answer, but Ben's focus suddenly shifted away from her and over to his left.

To where the bedroom door had just opened.

*Oh, help.*

Eli stood, mussed and still half asleep, wearing nothing but his boxer shorts, in her bedroom doorway. Even Rowan had to admit that really didn't look good.

'Ben?' Eli blinked a few times, and then his eyes widened as he awoke to the reality of the situation. 'Wait, we can explain this.'

No, they really couldn't. Not without giving away Willow's secret anyway.

Fortunately, Ben didn't seem in a mood to listen to his brother.

Turning on Rowan again, he pressed her up against the counter, his snarling face too close to hers. She gripped the edge of the counter and focused on her breathing. Willow wouldn't have a panic attack at his behaviour, and neither would she. He was all hot air and no substance.

His brother, however, was the opposite. And he was right there if she needed him.

She could sense how much he wanted to come and save her, but he held back, waiting for a sign from her. She didn't give it.

'If you wanted my attention, Willow, you know how to get it—on your knees,' Ben purred. 'You didn't have to sleep with the runt of the family to win me back.'

*How can he talk to her that way?*

In that moment, Eli wasn't sure he even recognised his brother. The big brother he'd looked up to, admired, all these years…he would never have spoken to a woman, or to anyone, like that.

Except… Eli had been on the wrong end of Ben's sharp tongue before. He knew his brother's temper of old. He'd never imagined he'd speak to a woman that way—but why not? He cheated on them, said things about them behind their backs—so why not to their faces too?

He'd just wanted to believe the best of his brother, the only family he had left. He'd hoped that Ben was a good man, under all the conditioning their father had put him through. He'd wanted to believe that Ben could choose to be a better man, now their father was gone.

But that hope had fled now, and he finally saw the man his brother truly was before him.

Bile rising in his throat, Eli started towards Ben, determined to rip him away from Rowan, but the calm expression on her face stopped him. She had this under control, and she wouldn't appreciate him bursting in like a knight in shining armour.

Sure enough, Rowan let go of the counter, placed her hands on Ben's chest and pushed. Surprised, he stumbled backwards a few paces, staring at her.

'I don't want you back, Ben,' she said firmly. 'We're done. And nothing between me and Eli has anything to do with you at all.'

One day, probably soon, Willow would have to explain all this to Ben. Eli suspected that would be one hell of a conversation.

Ben looked between the two of them slowly, before settling his gaze on Eli. 'Oh, I see what this is. Tired of trying to live up to my legend in the business world, you thought you'd take on my sloppy seconds instead, huh? Well, brother, I can tell you now, she's too much woman for you to handle.'

Eli gritted his teeth. 'That's not what this is.' If they could just tell him the truth... He looked towards Rowan for guidance, but she shook her head subtly.

Unfortunately, Ben caught it. 'Oh, what's that? Keeping secrets are we—more than the fact you're screwing around behind my back in the first place? I wonder what they could be...'

He turned back to Rowan, obviously assuming she was the easier target. 'What's my little brother been telling you, then? Business secrets? What do you think you know?'

Eli frowned. 'I don't know what you're talking about. I haven't been telling her anything.'

'I want to hear it from her.' Reaching out, Ben grabbed her arm, and Rowan flinched.

And that was all he could take. 'Get off her.' He wrenched his brother away from her, then covered her with his own body against the counter as he checked she was okay.

'I'm fine, Eli,' she said, but her voice was shaking.

'We have to tell him, Rowan,' he whispered.

But not quietly enough.

'Rowan?' Ben echoed, confusion in his voice. Then he repeated it with more certainty. 'Rowan! You're not Willow at all, are you? Well, that makes more sense.' He pushed a hand against Eli's shoulder, but Eli stood his ground. 'Couldn't bag the real thing, so you nailed the sister instead. *Now* I get it.'

It was almost more than Eli could bear. Spinning around so that Rowan was behind him, he faced down his brother. 'You get *nothing*. You don't understand anything here. And neither do I. How could you speak to her that way? The woman you're supposed to love? The—' He broke off sharply as Rowan dug her nails into his arm.

Oh, God, he'd been about to say *the mother of your child*. They might have given away Rowan's identity, but it was definitely up to Willow to tell Ben about the baby.

'What the hell do you care how I speak to my woman?'

'She's not *your* woman,' Rowan snapped, stepping out from behind Eli before he could stop her. 'She's her own person, and she's chosen to be a long way away from you.'

'Where is she?' Ben demanded, zeroing in on Rowan again.

'There is nothing in this world that could make me tell you that,' she replied calmly.

'And you, *brother*?' Ben spat the word. 'I suppose you're keeping her secret too?'

'I am.'

A slow, sly smile spread across Ben's face. 'Then there must be a very good reason for that. I mean, why else would she go to all this trouble? Sending you here to pretend to be her. No, there's something going on she doesn't want me to know about. And that means I'm *definitely* going to find out. I don't need either of you to tell me.' He turned and covered the floor to the door in long strides. 'But first, I've got a board meeting to attend. Something that you're clearly too busy to make a priority.'

And with a last, satisfied smile at Eli, Ben walked out of the door.

But he left behind a feeling in Eli's gut that something was very wrong.

Rowan slumped back against the counter as the door swung shut behind Ben.

'Well, that could have gone worse. Somehow.' Right now, it was hard to imagine a way in which it *could* have been more of a disaster, but she was sure there was one. Probably.

'There's something else going on,' Eli said, sounding distracted. 'I don't know what, but that wasn't the brother I know. And why was he so desperate to find Willow if he doesn't even know about the baby? No, there's something else at play here.'

'Like what?' Rowan asked. As far as she could see, the only real mystery was why on earth Willow would have dated that jackass in the first place.

'I don't know.' Eli turned to her, running a hand through his hair. He was still only wearing his boxers, she realised with a smile. Although the mood from that morning—or last night—was well and truly shattered. 'But I need to find out what.'

Rowan frowned. There was something more to this. 'What aren't you telling me?' They'd had enough secrets between them already—okay, mostly hers. But it was time to try something new. Honesty.

Eli paused and for a moment she thought he wasn't going to tell her. That he'd lie, or spin a line.

But this was Eli and so, when he spoke, she knew it was the truth.

'The way he was acting then—towards you and even towards me—I've never seen Ben quite like that. He has a temper, but that…he sounded totally desperate. On the edge. I've never seen that before. And I hope you know that if I'd *ever* seen him behave like that towards your sister—or any woman—I'd have called him out, done *something*.'

'I know that,' Rowan murmured. 'I know you.'

It was true, she realised, even as she said the words. She did know him. They'd only been in each other's lives for a handful of weeks, but she *knew* him. The heart and soul and bones of him.

And she was pretty sure he knew her too. Better than anyone except Willow ever had. In some ways, even better than her.

Under other circumstances, the revelation would have been a good thing—something to fill her with light and happiness and possibility for the future.

As it was, all she could think about was what she was going to have to say goodbye to, soon.

Maybe he'd come back to Rumbelow with her. Not to stay, but for a while. Maybe they could have some more time to figure all this out, at least. And she'd like to show him Marco's ice cream shack on the edge of the beach. Give his big city parlour some competition.

It was a flicker of hope, at least.

But Eli wasn't finished.

'He was… It was like being in the room with my father all over again.' He shook his head. 'Something must have happened.'

'Like finding his girlfriend and brother in bed together?' Rowan suggested. Eli himself had said that the idea of someone else touching her would drive him insane, hadn't he?

Eli wasn't convinced. 'He knew you weren't Willow soon enough. And he'd been off with someone else since they split up, anyway. No, the way he spoke to you, when he thought you *were* her…that wasn't love. That wasn't anything beyond a frustration that a convenient business relationship no longer worked the way he wanted it to.'

Rowan couldn't argue with that; she'd got exactly the same impression. Ben didn't want Willow back because he loved her, but because she was convenient. She looked good on his arm, gave the right message. That he was a successful, attractive businessman who could have any woman he wanted—but also one in a stable, long-term relationship with one of the world's most beautiful women.

He'd been happy to give that impression up though, not so long ago. Happy to be filmed with another woman on a yacht. Was that part of it?

Investors didn't want a playboy; they wanted someone reliable at the helm. Was that why he was so eager to get Willow back?

She glanced at the troubled expression on Eli's face. 'You think it's something to do with the business?'

'The board meeting he was rushing off to... He told me a while ago I didn't need to attend.'

'Do you usually?'

'No,' Eli admitted. 'Ben doesn't like me meddling with the family business, and I'm only a shareholder really, not an employee. Well, technically, I'm supposed to be on the board of directors, but it never seemed to mean much. My focus was on Launch, so I always left the family business to Ben.'

'So if you don't normally go to the meetings anyway, why did he feel the need to tell you again not to bother going to this one?' Rowan asked.

'That's what I'm wondering.' Eli met her gaze and gave her an apologetic smile. 'I think I have to go. I need to find out what's happening.'

Rowan nodded. 'I understand. Besides... I need to pack.' Ben knew the truth now. She had to get to Willow and Rumbelow before he did.

And, just like that, any small part of the bubble they'd built around themselves the night before that had survived Ben's arrival, disappeared.

Reality was firmly back in charge.

Rowan didn't think she liked it.

# CHAPTER TWELVE

ELI REGRETTED LEAVING Rowan the moment the apartment door swung shut behind him. But the relief on the other board members' faces when he arrived at the company offices told him he'd made the right choice.

'Nice to see you decided to show your face for this one, at least.' Eli's godfather, Jeremiah, collared him the moment he entered the meeting room, dragging him off to one side before the other board members could talk to him.

'Where's Ben?' Eli asked, scanning the room. He'd left Willow's apartment before Eli—long before him, by the time Eli had showered and dressed and kissed Rowan goodbye. And left her dragging her suitcase out from under the bed, although he couldn't think about that part now.

'Oh, he'll be watching and waiting until we're all here, making sure we know he's the one in charge by showing up late.' Jeremiah waved a hand. 'I don't want to talk about him. I want to talk about you. Finally taking an interest in the family business, are we?'

'I barely have a *financial* interest in the company,' Eli reminded him. 'Everything important was left to Ben, remember?'

His godfather sighed heavily at that. 'You got short shrift, that's for sure. Whatever your father suspected… you were his son, and he didn't always make you feel that way. That was wrong of him, and you have to believe I told him so, often. But you were your mother's son too—there's so damn much of your mother in you, and I think that hurt him more than anything. Seeing that.'

Eli opened his mouth to respond, but Jeremiah put up a hand to stop him.

'I'm not making excuses for him,' he went on. 'The man was my friend for a lot of years, and I watched him change, as he grew older. I've been watching your brother change too, and you haven't been here to see it.'

Guilt pinged in Eli's chest. He wasn't his brother's keeper, he knew that. But Ben was still his brother, whatever the differences between them. If there was something going on with him, he *should* have been there.

'What's happening here today, Jeremiah?' he asked.

The older man shook his head. 'We'll see, when Ben arrives. A lot of it depends on him, and his attitude, I suspect. But if he carries on the way he has been…'

'I don't know what you expect me to do, though,' Eli said. 'I don't have a controlling share of the company. I don't have any influence here—most of the shareholders barely know me.'

'And that's something you're going to need to do something about.' Jeremiah put an arm around Eli's shoulders. 'Every leader needs someone to keep them in check. To remind them that they're not lord of all they survey—they're there to do what's right. For your father, it was your mom—and once she was gone, well, that's when the wheels started to come off the whole thing. For

Ben... I don't think he's ever found that person. There was that supermodel he was seeing, but I never got the impression she had the kind of influence over him she needed.' He gave Eli a sly look. 'Plus, I think I saw her on *your* arm more recently, didn't I?'

'That was her twin sister,' Eli muttered, but Jeremiah was already moving on.

'The point is, Ben needs that someone. And if he can't find them himself, you're going to have to step up and do it for him. Be his reality check. His conscience. I have a feeling you'd be good at it.'

'What if Ben doesn't want that, though?' Eli asked. 'He tried to keep me from even coming to this meeting, you know.'

Jeremiah sighed. 'What it comes down to is, it's still your name over the building. I'd think you'd want to make sure that means something. Or doesn't mean the wrong thing, anyway.'

Well. That sounded ominous.

'Is it going to? I saw Ben earlier. He seemed...agitated.'

Jeremiah barked a laugh. 'That's one way to put it. He sees the writing on the wall, then. That's good. That will make things easier. Or at least more interesting.'

Eli wanted to ask *what* it would make interesting, when Ben burst through the doors, still fizzing with the same anger he'd displayed earlier. He scowled when he spotted Eli, but didn't acknowledge him any further.

'Right then,' Ben said. 'Let's get this show started.'

Rowan got as far as laying her suitcase out on her bed and then realising that almost all of the clothes she'd been wearing were either Willow's or bought with Willow's credit card, and stopped. Instead of packing, she stretched out on the side of the bed not currently covered by a suitcase, and reached for her phone.

'Rowan? What's going on?' Willow asked. 'I've got, like, eight voicemails on my phone from Ben, suddenly telling me he knows everything, and then you weren't answering yours and—'

'He doesn't know about the baby,' Rowan said quickly. 'He does know I'm not you.'

'How?'

Rowan explained the events of the morning. Willow did not seem to be focusing on the most important parts.

'Wait, so Eli was naked in bed with you when Ben walked in? Oh, my God! When did this happen? What's the deal with the two of you? Is this a drunken hook-up or something more…?'

'It's…not a drunken hook-up.' Rowan felt her cheeks heat up and hoped that the video on her phone didn't show the blush. From the wide smile that split Willow's face, she suspected it did.

'So it's something more.' On the video, Willow sat up straighter at Rowan's kitchen table, in Rowan's little cottage, in Rowan's village of Rumbelow, and said, 'Tell me everything.'

Rowan opened her mouth to do just that. But what came out was, 'What's the point? I'm packing to come home right now. So, whatever it was, I just have to leave it here in New York.'

Willow's eyes widened on the screen. 'Okay. This is clearly a conversation that needs tea. Go put the kettle on, and I'll do the same, and while it's brewing you can tell me exactly what's been going on over there between the two of you.'

She reached for the teapot from the top shelf in such an easy, familiar movement that Rowan almost cried. That was her teapot. Her cottage. She should be there doing this for Willow, the way it had always been. Willow had the adventures, and Rowan heard about them later over pots of tea.

Now, everything was different.

'I don't know where to begin,' she admitted.

'Start from the beginning,' Willow advised. 'Right from the moment you arrived in New York and found him in my apartment. Because I'm pretty sure you've been leaving things out in your accounts of your Big Apple adventures, haven't you?'

Rowan couldn't deny it. So, instead, she told her sister everything—from the first panic attack to the realisation that their time was almost over, and their race home to bed, and onto their rude awakening that morning.

Willow mostly listened—although, being Willow, she obviously had to interject with a few important observations. Like, 'I knew this wasn't just all about some dress you made!' And, 'Wait, there's a unicorn in New York?'

'Well, it all sounds pretty much fairy-tale-perfect to me,' Willow said when she'd finished. 'Up until the part where my ex-boyfriend walked in. But he's *my* problem, not yours. So why aren't you happy? Why aren't you loved-up and making dresses for celebrities and living your best life with Eli right now?'

'Because...' When she put it like that, what she needed to do sounded obvious. But Rowan knew it wasn't. Maybe it could have been for Willow, but she *wasn't* Willow.

And that was the point.

She took a deep breath and tried to explain.

'When I came here, I was pretending to be you. So I lived life as if I *was* you, as best as I could. I took chances and put myself out there…all that stuff I haven't done since I walked out on you and Mum years ago. And I know… I know that was probably the idea—and don't think we're not going to have a conversation about why you decided sending me to New York was the best solution to your situation because we are, once I'm over this particular crisis.'

'I have no idea what you're talking about,' Willow said, far too innocently. 'But go on.'

'These last weeks here in New York…they haven't felt like real life. My real life is *there,* in Rumbelow. And the person I've been here… I can't be sure if she's real either. I miss my cottage, my home. And I miss the person I am there too, a little.'

'So come home,' Willow said. 'Leave Eli behind as a fond memory. A holiday fling.'

'I would. Except…'

'Except you're in love with him,' Willow crowed triumphantly, almost upsetting her cup of tea as she thumped the table with one hand.

Love?

Oh, God, Rowan hadn't even really *thought* about love. Love definitely felt like one of those things that was for other people. She hadn't been looking for it, even here, on her escape from reality.

She'd fallen for Eli in increments. One touch, one

word, one insight at a time. Until she was in so deep it was hard to see a way out.

'Oh, God, I'm in love with Eli.'

But did it change anything?

No. Not really.

'I still can't stay here.'

'Why not?' Willow demanded. 'You love him, you're glowing, he makes you happy, it's the greatest city in the world, you've conquered your fear of being out there again… You *can* do this, Ro.'

And she was right, Rowan realised. She could. But *should* she?

'I… I feel like two people right now, Will. The old Rumbelow Rowan, and the new New York one,' she said, trying to explain. 'I need to find a way to make those two people one, before I can really move forward with my life.'

'And you need to come back to Rumbelow to do that?'

'I think so. Yes.'

Maybe not for ever. But she needed to get her head straight before she made any huge, life-changing decisions for herself—or for Eli.

She wasn't a city person. She didn't *want* to be either. But she couldn't imagine Eli anywhere except New York.

And if there was something going on with the family business…this was where he was going to need to be. She'd already caused enough friction between him and his brother—not to mention Ben and Willow. The person she'd been here in New York might have wanted to be altruistic and compassionate—giving to Launch, helping out at the Castaway Café, making Kelly's dress— but in the end she'd been selfish.

She'd given in to what she wanted—Eli—rather than holding out and doing what was right, even knowing how much it could cost Willow, and even Eli himself.

And she wasn't sure *that* was the version of Rowan she wanted to be.

'Then come home.' Willow's smile on the phone screen was gentle. 'You have to be sure, and you have to feel right about the decisions you're making. That's why *I* came here, after all. So come home and see if Rumbelow can work its magic on you.'

'Did it do that for you?' Rowan asked.

Willow nodded. 'Yeah, I think it did. I'm ready to face the music now, anyway. This place has taught me what I want, and now all that's left is to make it happen.'

'That's good.' Rowan wanted to ask exactly *what* Rumbelow had taught her twin, but the closed look on her face stopped her. Willow would tell her, when she was ready.

'Perhaps Eli will come to Rumbelow with you,' Willow said hopefully.

'Perhaps,' Rowan echoed.

But she knew as she said it, it wasn't true.

This was something she needed to do on her own.


Eli returned to the apartment to find Rowan's bags already packed by the door.

'You're leaving?' he asked, as she appeared from the bedroom with the last of her things.

She answered with another question. 'What happened at the board meeting?'

Heavy with the memory of one of the least enjoyable afternoons of his life, Eli sank down to sit on the sofa.

Rowan settled beside him, and just her hand on his arm made him feel a little better.

'The board had evidence that Ben had been making some…not illegal, but not entirely sensible or ethical decisions, behind their backs. Keeping things from them as far as the terms would allow. They were…unhappy.' To put things very, very mildly.

He'd never seen his godfather so angry. And he'd been one of the more reasonable board members in attendance.

'What did they do?' Rowan asked. 'I mean, I don't really understand how boards of companies operate, but I guess they had the power to do something about it?'

Eli nodded. He wasn't sure *he* really understood how big corporations—or at least O'Donnell Industries—operated either. It wasn't as if his father had ever taught him, the way he'd taught Ben, and his experience and education was mostly in the non-profit sector. According to Jeremiah, the way their father had left the business— the uneven split between the brothers, the power that remained with the board—wasn't exactly typical anyway. So no, he didn't really understand how it worked.

But it looked as if he was going to have to learn.

He'd taken his eye off the ball. He'd avoided his brother for weeks because of his guilt over his feelings for Rowan—especially when he'd thought she was still Willow. And maybe this had been going on for longer, but the point was, he hadn't been paying attention. Hadn't noticed the hole his brother was digging for himself and the company, because he'd been too caught up in his attraction to Rowan.

He'd gone after a woman he knew he shouldn't want.

And even when he'd learnt her true identity, he'd kept lying to everyone all the same, even though he knew it was the wrong thing to do. All because he hadn't been ready to say goodbye to her.

This mess was at least partly his fault. And it was his responsibility to put it right.

'They wanted him to step down—resign in disgrace—I think. But we managed to reach a compromise.' He took a deep breath. 'They want me to run the company with him. Keep him on the straight and narrow, and get the company's reputation back where it belongs.'

It had turned out that Ben's cut corners and underhand dealings were getting them quite a name for themselves on the internet, and before long it would be in the papers too. That was what the board wanted to avoid most of all.

Rowan winced, and patted his thigh sympathetically. 'Working with your brother. That's going to be... What about Launch?'

He sighed. 'I've got a great team in place there. I'll still be involved, but I'm going to have to scale back the time I can spend there, until I can get O'Donnell Industries back on track.'

It was going to be a steep learning curve too. Eli relished a challenge, normally. But right now... Right now, he just wanted to pack his own case and go wherever Rowan was heading, and say to hell with the company.

Was that so bad of him?

He knew he wouldn't do it, though.

Whatever his father might have thought of him, he was still the only father he'd ever known. This company was the legacy he'd left him, even if only a sliver of it.

And the company wasn't just his father's either. As Jeremiah had reminded him, it was his mother's passion too, for a long time, when they were young and just married and building it up together. Eli had a right to it.

None of that was why he was doing it, though.

He was doing it for Ben, even if his brother didn't appreciate that right now.

To be the brother he *should* have been all along. And maybe to model to Ben that there were other ways to be the head of a company, other than the way their father had. Other ways to live. Other ways to be a person, even.

'How did Ben take it?' Rowan asked, as if reading his mind.

That called for another sigh. Because this was the really difficult part.

'Badly. He…he doesn't have much of a say in the matter, because the board have the power to appoint me to the role regardless.'

Rowan frowned. 'He could make things difficult, though?'

'He could,' Eli said. 'But I'm hoping he'll see reason. Eventually. But there's another problem to deal with first.'

Rowan stared at him for a moment, then her eyes widened. 'He's gone to find Willow?'

'I'm afraid so.' Eli wasn't entirely sure how the two situations had got conflated in Ben's head, but they had. 'He seems to think that this is all our fault—the three of us, I mean. That if Willow had just been there to hang off his arm and smooth situations over and convince people that he was a settled, responsible man—or at least that his celebrity mattered more than what he was doing with the company—it would all have worked out for him.'

'I'm guessing that people seeing us together and thinking I was Willow didn't help the situation either?'

'Not exactly. Basically, he thinks we all set out to trash his reputation, and now he's off to yell at Willow about it to make himself feel better.' He *hoped* yelling was the worst of it. He didn't believe his brother would hurt another person, let alone a pregnant woman, but he didn't like the idea of Willow waiting there for him alone either.

'Does he know where she is?' Rowan asked.

'Not yet. But I can't imagine it'll take him long to find out.' Ben still had all the connections of the company, and his own personal ones. Now he knew to look, he could probably have Willow's location in a matter of hours.

Rowan got to her feet. 'Then it's just as well I've got a flight home late tonight. I just need to call a taxi to the airport.'

'I'll take you,' Eli said, even though the last thing he wanted was to send her away.

If he could keep her here, with him, for ever, he would, he realised. He'd get down on one knee right now if it would make her stay.

And maybe it would. But it wouldn't be the right thing to do.

She needed to go.

They'd made this mess. Maybe not alone. And perhaps it wasn't their fault they'd been drawn into it all the same.

But they'd made the whole situation worse by falling

for each other. Choosing each other now would be selfish, and it could have even more catastrophic results for
Ben and Willow and their futures.

Right now, they had to keep their focus where it belonged—on helping their siblings, who needed them
more than ever. They had to take the responsibility for
muddying the waters and causing more pain and hurt.

And they had to fix it.

Their fingers met on the handle of her suitcase, and
when Rowan looked up at him he saw tears in her eyes.

'I don't want to go,' she admitted.

'I want you to stay. But I know you need to go.' They'd
talked a lot the night before, in between everything else.
He knew how torn she felt, between the woman she'd
been in Rumbelow and the woman she was here. How
she didn't want to be Willow, but she wasn't sure how
to be Rowan any more either.

That was something she needed to figure out for herself. And he had to give her the space to do it.

'I want you to come with me,' Rowan said with a very
small smile. 'But I know you need to stay.'

'I do.' And he cursed his brother for that. But also…
New York was his home. Could he really give that up—
turn his back on everything he'd built there, all the work
there was still to do—and move to England, just to be
with her? What would he even do in a fishing village?

No, there was too much work here in New York for
him to walk away.

'So…' Rowan trailed off. He didn't blame her.

'We'll go and do the things we need to do,' he said.

'Apart.'

'Yeah.'

'Well, that sucks.' She sighed again. 'I can't help but feel that me coming here, pretending to be Willow…it's actually made things worse, not better. For her, but for everyone else too.'

He knew what she meant. Willow had wanted time to decide on her future so she could discuss it rationally with Ben with a clear head, and instead she'd get him flying in furious and spoiling for any fight he could win. Not to mention that Rowan being her had given them both a taste of something they couldn't have—and that would leave them both wanting.

And yet…

They were saying goodbye. He might never see her again. So he wasn't going to let her leave on a lie.

He gripped her hand tight. 'I wouldn't change it, though. Not for the world. Not if it meant never getting to know you.'

She met his gaze, and this time her eyes weren't the only ones that were wet with tears. 'Neither would I.'

# CHAPTER THIRTEEN

RUMBELOW WAS GLORIOUS in the sunshine. The waves in the harbour glittered in the sunlight, the brightly coloured boats bobbing gently on the sea. The cobblestone streets were lined with bistro tables and tourists eating breakfast, bunting and flags strung well above head height, zigzagging across the paths. The air was filled with the scents of freshly baked bread, coffee and the ever-present tang of salt.

Rowan waved to one of the shopkeepers as she passed, and smiled as they called out a good morning. It *was* a good morning. It was an almost perfect morning in the village she loved. Her home.

It just didn't seem to have quite the same magic as she remembered from before she went away.

Willow had returned to New York not long after Rowan came back here—although not before Ben had tracked her down. Still, her twin seemed to have that whole situation under control—she was more steady and settled than Rowan had thought her capable of being. It had gone a long way to assuaging her guilt about making Willow's situation worse—as had a lengthy heart-to-heart with her after Ben had left again, where her twin had reminded her that it wasn't all or nothing. She could be a loving sister *and* have whatever life she wanted. Willow had never wanted her to mortgage her own happiness for her.

Besides, looking out at the old lifeboat station now as she turned the corner towards her cottage, Rowan suspected Willow would be back in Rumbelow sooner rather than later.

Probably not to stay, though. Hardly anybody did.

Rumbelow was a place for locals and for tourists. The tourists came in their droves in the summer months, then disappeared with the sunshine. While they were there, the streets buzzed with activity, with noise—and with money. There were never enough hands to do everything, and always more people than space. But when they were gone... Rumbelow was a different place altogether.

The locals stayed year-round, despite the weather or the storms, or the empty holiday homes standing forlornly on the edge of the sea. They stayed when the fish weren't biting, or when the sea raged and breached the walls. In many cases, they'd stayed for generations already, and would stay for generations more.

Or they wouldn't.

People left, of course they did. For love or work or opportunities—or just to see the wider world. Nobody blamed them for that, and they were always welcome to come home and visit.

And then there were people like her. Transplants. People who came as tourists and stayed. They never quite became local, but they were the nearest thing.

When she'd settled down in Rumbelow, she'd never imagined leaving. It was her safe place, her haven. Her cottage was her sanctuary. She loved the winter months best of all, because the village emptied out and she could batten down her hatches against the weather and stay hidden away.

She'd thought that would be enough for her for ever. But now...

Willow and her schemes had given her a taste of the outside world again. And while she knew she never wanted to go back to the kind of high profile, visible career she'd had before, knowing that she *could* do it without breaking was a surprisingly potent thing.

The world was bigger than Rumbelow. And she wasn't too small and scared to enjoy it any more.

*You're just making excuses because you miss Eli.*

The voice in her head could be her own or it could be Willow's but, either way, she couldn't deny the pull in her heart that led her back to New York. But could she really live in a city again? Give up all of this? This life she'd worked so hard to build for herself?

She sighed as she turned into her garden gate, ready to trudge up the path to her cottage door...

And stopped.

Because there, on her doorstep, sat a tired-looking Eli, licking an ice cream cone from Marco's.

'You might be right,' he said, as he got to his feet. 'I didn't think it was possible, but this *is* better than Giovanni's.'

She took a cautious step forward, half afraid that he was some sort of mirage that would disappear if she got close enough to touch.

'What are you doing here?' she asked.

'I shouldn't be,' he admitted. 'I should be back in

New York. There's a million things still to straighten out with the company, and Ben is being…well, Ben, and the board as a whole are generally making things difficult, which my godfather seems to find endlessly amusing, so I really should be in New York. But…'

Rowan's heart seemed to swell in her chest. 'But?'

'I missed you,' he said simply. 'And I know you belong here, so I came to you.'

Rowan stared at him so long that Eli started to worry he'd said something wrong.

'The thing is… I'm not sure that I do any more. Belong here, I mean.'

He blinked. 'You're not?'

He hadn't come here with any expectations. Hadn't even allowed himself much in the way of hope. He'd just needed to see her, that was all.

Running the company with Ben was…it felt like jumping from a skyscraper and hoping someone would be there to catch him. It was hard and intense and even though he *knew* it was the right thing to do, he also knew it could take over his life if he let it.

Could turn him into the sort of man his father had been and his brother had been becoming, before he'd stepped in.

Eli couldn't risk that. He needed to hold onto the important things. The things that mattered.

The *people* that mattered.

When he was with Rowan he felt grounded. He felt at ease. At home.

He'd thought home was New York. Now, he was starting to believe it was wherever she was. And Rumbelow looked like a nice enough place. With a good Wi-Fi connection and regular red-eye flights back to the States, he could probably make it work. The ice cream alone was pretty good compensation.

Except now she was saying she didn't belong here. What was he supposed to make of that?

'I thought that Rumbelow was where I needed to be, because it was where I was safe. Where I felt protected and secure. But I realised, coming back here, that what it really gave me was a place to hide,' Rowan explained. 'And I don't want to hide any more. Not from who I am, or what I can do—or from who I love.'

Her voice grew stronger with every word and Eli found himself drawn nearer, without meaning to, until his arms were around her waist and her gaze was locked on his.

He saw everything he'd ever hoped for in her eyes. But he still needed to hear the words.

'What does that mean for us? Am I going to be eating Giovanni's or Marco's ice cream this summer?'

She smiled, a dimple appearing in her cheek. 'How about both?'

He raised his eyebrows. 'Both?'

'Yes. Both.' She took a quick breath, before the words came tumbling out. 'I've already wound up my dress commissions here. And I even answered some of those emails and voicemails. I've got meetings set up in New York next week.'

His heart stuttered in his chest. 'You were coming back anyway?'

She gave him a shy nod. 'Yeah. Is that okay?'

'It's better than okay,' he said fervently. 'It's everything.'

'I want to be close to Willow and the baby, wherever they end up. And I want to be out in the world again, not just in this tiny bubble of safety I've built myself. I'll always want to come back here too—it's a place that means so much to me. But most of all… I want to be with you. Wherever that is.'

'That's the conclusion that got me on that plane last night, straight out of my last meeting, without even an overnight bag,' Eli admitted. 'I had to buy a toothbrush at the airport. I just had to see you.'

'I don't ever want to go two weeks without seeing you again,' Rowan said—and then she was in his arms and kissing him and Eli knew that it didn't matter *where* they were, as long as they were together.

'Then we won't,' he promised, when they finally pulled apart. 'We can split our time between here and New York—and anywhere else in the world you want to be. Of course…' He grinned as the thought occurred to him, the weight of the box in his pocket a happy reminder. 'All that international travel…the passport controls would be easier if we had the same surname.'

She raised her eyebrows at him. 'Is that seriously the most romantic proposal you could manage?'

'How about this?' He dropped to one knee and, fishing the ring box from his pocket, opened it to reveal the ring he'd travelled thousands of miles to give her.

Rowan's hands flew to her mouth as her eyes widened. 'Yes!'

Okay, he could have phrased that better.

'Yes, it's more romantic, or yes—?'

'Yes to all of it.' Rowan bent down to kiss him again. 'I'm only saying yes to things from now on. And a life with you is something I could never say no to.'

* * * * *

# WINNING OVER THE BROODING BILLIONAIRE

## CARA COLTER

MILLS & BOON

Margo Louise Jakobsen

1948–2023

Beloved

# CHAPTER ONE

SHELBY KANE SLAMMED on the brakes, and the tiny car skidded to a halt. For a moment frozen in time, the leaping deer was so close to her front windshield that she felt as if she could see each individual hair on its shoulder and stomach.

She closed her eyes, held her breath and braced herself.

Nothing happened.

She dared to open her eyes. The deer bounded away through tall grass the color of wheat, though it was spring. As she watched, the animal—with the same graceful effortlessness with which it had cleared her car—sailed over a barbed wire fence. It paused and looked back at her, eyes liquid, soft, deeply brown. One ear twitched and then it trotted off, winding its way through a herd of fat, oblivious cattle.

She had never been so close to a wild animal. The truth was, despite the extraordinary beauty of the deer, she hoped she never would be again. The experience had been an unwanted challenge to her decidedly new driving skills.

Her heart still racing, Shelby got out of the car, leaned on the fender and drew in deep breaths of sun-on-grass-scented air.

She took in her surroundings with a mix of awe and trepidation. She had never been this close to a real live cow before, either. The humongous creatures, separated from her by only the thin wires of that fence, seemed, thankfully, disinterested in her.

She was in the Foothills Country of Southern Alberta. Nothing could have prepared her for the immensity of the land, the endless sweep of the grass and the undulating hills that looked as if they were covered in suede. The Rocky Mountains, brilliant against an endless blue sky, loomed in the near distance, peaks craggy and snowcapped.

Though it seemed impossible, the mountains appeared to be the same distance away as when Shelby had started down the numbered range road. When her GPS, at the turn-off from the main highway, had instructed her to go sixteen kilometers—a measure that, as an American, she was not totally familiar with—she had thought it would put her right in those mountains.

She had pictured herself, white-knuckled, on a narrow, winding road that had unforgiving rock on one side and steep, water-gushing ravines on the other. The Mountain Waters Ranch was her destination, after all.

But no, many flat, straight kilometers later along the dusty gravel road, she seemed no closer to the mountains, and certainly there was no ranch in sight.

She was a city girl, through and through, most recently calling New York home. Though her past lifestyle had allowed her to experience more wonders in the world than most people could even dream of, she had never experienced anything like this.

Rugged beauty.

Endless space.

And an almost terrifying sense of acute aloneness.

Where was the nearest person?

Taking one last look around, Shelby got back in the car. Her GPS told her she had only traveled ten of the sixteen kilometers.

She was somewhat grateful she'd opted for the GPS feature in the rental, instead of a bigger vehicle, though at the same time, she was so aware that her *new* life required her to weigh such choices: bigger car or GPS. The tiny economy car may have fit her admittedly limited budget, but it certainly did not align with the first impression she wanted to make.

She glanced down at her clothes. She'd chosen a classic tailored pair of dark teal slacks and a matching jacket, with a colorful silk blouse underneath. All were designer, as were the shoes, a three-inch spike heel that might not be exactly appropriate for a ranch—or for driving, come to that—but that boosted her five-foot-four height to five-foot-seven in a way that had proved irresistible. A practiced eye would know her clothing choices were not on trend anymore, but how practiced an eye would anyone have who lived on a ranch?

Speaking of first impressions, she adjusted the rearview mirror and took stock of the things she could control.

Her hair, while no longer colored and cut to perfection by Frederique's on Fifth, remained one of her best features. It was naturally honey-colored, and fell in a thick and shiny wave to her shoulders. Looking at it critically, Shelby was pleased with the result she had achieved herself with a blow-dryer and a curling iron. She even wondered if the extraordinarily expensive Frederique had ever actually improved it.

Her eyes, brown flecked with gold and green, still looked wide and startled from her encounter with the deer. Her lashes looked luxuriously thick, and she allowed herself to be newly amazed at how mascara that fit her budget seemed to do just as good a job as the fifty-dollar Epais brand she had preferred in the past. Ditto for her budget lip gloss.

*Budget*, she thought, not without a familiar surge of astonishment, as she put the mirror back the way it had been and started the car.

As the only child of billionaire business mogul Boswell Kane, Shelby had been raised breathing the rarefied air of the extraordinarily wealthy. She had grown up in family homes all over the world—Paris, Lisbon, London, George Town, Los Angeles, New York—though *family* and *home* would not be accurate descriptions of any of those houses. Each was a mansion, with multiple pools and media rooms, staff quarters and manicured grounds. Each missed the "hominess" mark by about a million miles.

Her mother, Jasmine, had died when Shelby was ten, and even at that young age, She had recognized her father was in some way trying to make it up to her. Her every whim was indulged. There was not a single thing she had ever wanted for.

Shelby had lived the lifestyle of the rich and famous that everyone dreamed of: private jets, fashion events, exclusive designers, spas, parties. She had skied the Alps and scuba dived the Great Barrier Reef. She had been on photo safari in Africa. She had dined with royalty and been backstage with the most well-known bands in the world. She had been to the Oscars and the final game of the World Series.

Had she even appreciated what she'd had when she'd had it, though? Because despite "having it all," there had always been a restless sense of something missing.

Until she had fallen into an opportunity. Her friend Kylie had become engaged and was endlessly debating the perfect venue for the wedding.

Shelby happened to know someone with a villa in France. She'd put the two parties in touch and then, because she'd attended so many exclusive events, she had acted as an adviser on details like menu and decor and accommodations for the guests. It had been fun in a very different way than other things in her life had been fun. That restless sense of something missing had been held at bay for the entire time she'd been involved in Kylie's wedding.

The wedding had turned out so well that soon another friend had asked for Shelby's help with an event.

And so her company Eventually had been born. Despite the fact getting the first check for money she had actually earned had been more heady than the very expensive champagne served at Kylie's wedding, Shelby was aware her company was really nothing more than a fun little hobby. Still, that didn't stop her from thinking about it. A lot. When she wasn't dabbling in actual event planning, she was collecting a growing portfolio of perfect locations.

Each time she collected a picture and information on a new potential location, she would have a wonderful, dreamy sense of exactly the kind of event that belonged there.

And then, into her life had come a wicked stepmother. Though Shelby still hated to admit this, it might have been one of those blessings in disguise.

Lydia Barkley was not like the kind of women Shelby's father, Boswell, usually dated. His taste usually ran to women, admittedly like Shelby's own mother, who were coiffed, sophisticated, fit society women—or cleverly disguised wannabes.

No, Lydia was stout. Her brutally short hair sometimes looked as if she had cut it herself. She wore makeup badly. Shelby doubted she knew Prada from Gucci, though she owned both. She was blunt rather than subtle. Still, her father found her refreshing.

Lydia had a successful law practice. She *liked* working. From the outset, it had been apparent she viewed cosseted, pampered women with very thinly veiled contempt.

Which Shelby deduced meant Lydia held her died-too-young mother in contempt. You didn't really need an excuse to dislike your stepmother, but Shelby was glad to have one.

Not that it mattered, anyway. Shelby had been twenty-six when her father had married Lydia, well past the age where she needed a mommy. In fact, for the most part, she was able to avoid the newlyweds. If her father and Lydia let her know they were arriving at the location Shelby was at, she quickly vacated it.

Still, there was no avoiding the obligatory "family" gatherings. Which was how she'd had her deduction about Lydia's contempt for her mother confirmed.

Her father—or maybe Lydia—had selected the Chelsea house for Christmas. Shelby thought it was a poor choice. She found London drab in the winter. Her current boyfriend, Keith—the latest in a long string—had refused to come, so she had bought him a ticket for the Cayman Islands, where she planned to meet him at the Kane property as soon as it was humanly possible.

Coming down the stairs to join Lydia and Boswell, Shelby—dreading making excuses for Keith, whom she knew her father did not approve of—stopped dead in her tracks outside of the double doors of the parlor at the sound of her own name coming off Lydia's lips.

What she had heard changed Shelby's entire existence and cemented her dislike for her stepmother.

"Boswell, I'm concerned about Shelby."

*Sure you are*, Shelby thought. She waited for her father to protest discussing his daughter with an interloper, and a dowdy one at that, but no, all she heard was her father's mild "Oh?"

It was all the encouragement Lydia needed.

"She's obviously being used by Keith."

Her father, again, was given an opportunity not to indulge in this kind of backstabbing gossip, but he did not.

Instead, he said with a sigh, "Obviously."

*Obviously?* That hurt! The truth felt more complex. Shelby sometimes wondered if she wasn't using Keith.

He suited her. He filled the need for companionship without ever bringing up any sense she would have to commit to him.

Commitment could lead to other things.

Like children.

Shelby liked children. She liked them a lot. In fact, she got on famously with most of the children she knew.

Probably because, until Eventually at least, her maturity had matched theirs. She was pretty sure she'd make a terrible mother.

Still, aside from the qualification of being commitment-phobic, when was the last time Keith had paid for anything? Or even offered to pay for anything?

"In fact, Bosley—"

Ugh. How Shelby hated Lydia calling Boswell that horrible little endearment.

"I don't like the people she surrounds herself with. They're superficial, frivolous or users."

This was patently untrue! Wasn't it? Besides, Shelby thought huffily, the people she hung around with wouldn't like Lydia, either.

Because of the way her step-mother wore her hair? Didn't that kind of prove Lydia's point?

"I've feared the same thing," her father said.

*What?*

"But Bosley, dear, it's really on you. You've overindulged poor Shelby to the point of ruination."

*Poor Shelby? Ruination?*

"I tried to make up for the fact she had no mother," Boswell said.

"Of course you did, dear. But, in fact, I fear she did have a mother, and I fear she will end up just like her if you don't sort it out."

Shelby felt a familiar shiver of dread at the mention of her mother, which she shrugged off in favor of indignation.

Here was her father's opportunity! To leap to her defense,

and the defense of her mother! It wasn't as if it was her mother's fault she had died.

*Or was it?* a voice in Shelby's head insisted on whispering. There were still so many unanswered questions around her mother's death, a topic she had been shielded from since it had happened.

Willingly shielded from. Her father had protected her from the inevitable gossip that surrounded such a beautiful, young, well-known woman's demise, and Shelby was grateful for that.

*Wasn't she?*

Of course she was! She could have searched the details online at any time if she needed more information. The thought of looking up her mother made her feel sick to her stomach, as if she was spying or prying or being disloyal to her memories.

"I've had some thoughts," Lydia said. And then she had outlined, in quite great detail, what those thoughts were.

So, Shelby had been 100 percent prepared when, after an awkward Christmas dinner, her father had suggested a meeting and they had all moved to the stuffy library of the Chelsea house.

Lydia, Shelby noticed, was wearing her lawyer face.

But before Lydia could announce the plan Shelby had already overheard—that she would not receive an allowance, or have access to the family jet, or any of the residences around the world, or their lovely staff who cooked and cleaned and looked after her, or even a driver—Shelby made an announcement of her own.

"I've started a little business," she said casually. "It's doing quite well."

Okay, that was a bit of a stretch, but the look of skepticism on Lydia's face egged her on.

"I've decided that I'm perfectly capable of making it on my own."

Her father had looked flummoxed, and Lydia had looked put out at having her wicked-stepmother scheme snatched out from under her. Both their expressions had made Shelby's announcement well worth it!

And given her just the incentive she needed to show them by taking her business to the next level.

Now Shelby was eighteen months into Eventually.

Annoyingly, her father and Lydia—and her own niggling doubts—had been absolutely on point about Keith.

Starting her own business had brought out a surprisingly pragmatic side in her. Shopping for your own toilet paper could do that.

And, increasingly, she had seen that she had imbued Keith with poetic qualities of romance and charm, when in fact, he was lazy and lacked goals, focus and ambition. He did not pull his own weight or pay his own way, even when her funds dried up. Instead of offering to step up to the plate, he sulked.

She was not sure why she had set such a low bar for herself. She had fallen into a relationship apparently on a shared value of not wanting to get married and not wanting to have children. Recognizing this aversion to commitment, she swore off love with a sense of relief, rather than loss, and gave herself over to her business with her whole heart and soul.

Shelby had not so much left Keith as let him fade from the picture, not as angry with him as she was with herself.

What had she been thinking?

She threw herself—gratefully—into surviving her new and shocking reality.

She was a young woman who had never fried an egg, driven a car, paid a bill. She had always been surrounded by luxury and now she lived in a cubbyhole about the same size as any of her closets around the world. It felt as if she had been thrown into a new country where she had no map and did not speak the language.

Still, she was shocked—and delighted—to discover a hidden truth about herself. Shelby Kane was a fighter!

She *liked* making it on her own. She *liked* conquering the challenges that she faced every day.

And, as extra incentive for success, she was determined to show her father and Lydia she was not going to be the ruined object of their pity!

# CHAPTER TWO

THOUGH HER TALENTS might have been born of complete desperation, Shelby found she had a knack for business as she pushed Eventually to the next level.

Shelby's connections had helped her to survive and thrive. While walking a fine line—"I'm doing this for fun not because I have to"—her business was becoming the go-to among the rich and famous for the best birthday party or anniversary or family reunion or charity fundraiser.

She'd quickly established that her specialty—what set her apart from all the others—was venue. She knew people who owned some of the most spectacular real estate on earth, and she was able to use her name to talk them into sharing it for the right cause and the right price. Her father allowed her to use Kane properties if it was for her fledgling business, though, annoyingly, he seemed to find her business pursuits *cute* and she had the feeling he was just waiting for her to either fail spectacularly or lose interest.

But she wasn't losing interest. If anything, she felt more interested in life every single day. That portfolio of collected photos and locations that she saved for extra-special events kept getting thicker and thicker. When she approached people, even strangers, they were usually surprisingly amenable to her enthusiastic vision, and to having their property enjoyed by others. For the right price or even the right publicity.

And so Angela Fillmore's eighth birthday had been held

at a 150-room castle in the Blue Ridge Mountains outside of Asheville, North Carolina.

Kate and Landon Whitley had hosted four hundred guests to help them celebrate fifty years of marriage on a private island in the Caribbean.

The Wellingtons had welcomed four generations of family for a reunion on board a superyacht off the coast of Greece.

The Ladies Aid League of New York had held their charity ball—their most successful event ever—at a luxurious Martha's Vineyard estate.

The learning curve was steep. Sometimes, when the smoke had cleared, Shelby had not made as much money as she had hoped, and on one disastrous occasion she had even lost money, and the stress of planning events was often unrelenting.

She lay awake at night thinking of bills. And of juggling Peter to pay Paul. And going over all the hundreds of details involved in creating a successful event.

And yet, she was succeeding. She had been able to hire an assistant, Marcus. And underlying the hum of worry and stress was a sense of satisfaction. Accomplishment. The truth was, she was finding herself—her strength, her creativity, her confidence and even her leadership abilities—in the task of being responsible for people's hopes and happiness.

And then Lydia had thrown her a curveball. She wanted Shelby to plan her father's sixty-fifth birthday party.

Shelby was not sure if it was, on Lydia's part, a test or a fledgling act of trust.

What she did know was that she *needed* not just to take this on, but also to make it her most spectacular event ever. She needed them to see how far she had come, she needed to prove this wasn't just some cute little game she was playing that she would soon lose interest in and come back begging for their assistance.

Shelby had refused Lydia's money. And said she would be happy to give the party as a gift to her father.

And she had known exactly where to have it.

In that folder she kept, there was one place that stood above them all. She had come across it in a magazine in the waiting room of a corporate office whose CEO's anniversary she was planning. The magazine had been about ranching, of all things.

It had drifted open to a photo that had taken Shelby's breath away and made her heart sigh with longing, or maybe even knowing.

The magazine article had been about the history of ranching in that part of Southern Alberta. The photo that captured her soul had been of a huge timber-frame barn, with a traditional gambrel roof. It sat, solid, on the edge of a wooded ravine, the mountains beyond that.

The description said the 150-year-old structure was on the Mountain Waters Ranch and had been decommissioned as a barn for over fifty years. It was now used exclusively to service the surrounding ranch community, hosting graduations, weddings, family reunions, birthday parties and anniversaries.

She had looked at that photo as if it was a long, cool drink and she was dying of thirst. The photo was taken outside the huge, wide-open double doors that led into the barn. One might expect a barn to be dark, but surprisingly, light poured in from double doors, also open, at the other end of the structure. Those doors framed a painting-like vista of valleys and mountains.

The cavernous barn interior was both majestic and cozy with open beams and rafters. Again—surprisingly—gorgeous, gigantic chandeliers hung at the center of each of the four crossbeams. The slatted wooden ceiling and the walls had aged to the color of maple syrup.

Though there were no people in the photo, it was obvious the space had been set up for a wedding. At least two hundred matching chairs, white, with pale blue bows on the back, faced those incredible open back doors and the views beyond them.

Shelby, of course, had recognized her own weakness because of the horrible Keith choice, and was totally sworn off romance.

It felt like way too close a call, a brush with disaster. What if, caught in the thrall of romantic illusion, she had actually married him? It made her shudder to think!

And yet, when she had seen that photo, it was as if every lesson she'd learned evaporated. It was as if some much-suppressed part of herself surged to the forefront. Shelby—who didn't even have a boyfriend, and hoped to never have one again—had had the completely ridiculous thought *This is where I will get married.*

Why would she need to get married? Running her business took all her time and energy and was fulfilling in ways she had not expected in the least. She was free of the *neediness* of women who pursued a relationship—and marriage—as if that was some kind of holy grail that would give them every single satisfaction they had ever sought in life.

Still, even knowing it was not rational—lying to herself that her interest was strictly professional—she had surreptitiously torn that picture from the magazine and folded it carefully into her handbag to put in her portfolio.

Since she knew—rationally—that she was not getting married, why not impress her father with this location for the most spectacular sixty-fifth birthday party ever?

That, however, was proving to be a major problem, because Samuel Waters, the reclusive widowed billionaire who owned the ranch, turned out not to be one of those amenable owners who could be persuaded to share a special place.

Even with all her sources, Shelby could not lay her hands on a phone number for him. She did find an email.

But Mr. Waters had only answered one of her three dozen emails. With a single word.

*No.*

Without having met him, Shelby was pretty sure she disliked Samuel Waters nearly as much as her wicked stepmother.

Which was not mature.

Really, she had hoped her perseverance over the many challenges of the past eighteen months would be worth something. She had hoped she would be much more grown-up by now than to dislike someone sight unseen.

Though, she hoped to be seeing Mr. Waters very soon. She was not taking his *no* as a final answer. She was sure she could convince him. She was going to beard the lion in his own den.

Or on his own ranch as the case might be.

The range road, finally, began a gradual uphill climb. It wound through lovely copses of trees, the green of their leaves new and vibrant. Every now and then Shelby caught sight of a creek meandering beside the road.

She opened her window and sure enough, she could hear the babbling of the waters. And birdsong. The air had a purity and a crispness to it she was not sure she had ever experienced before. She suddenly did not feel the aloneness as a burden.

She came to the top of the hill and stopped. For the second time, Shelby got out of the car, taking in the incredible view of the valley below her.

The road wound down to a ranch and entered under a wooden archway with a wrought iron sign hanging from the thick log crossbeam. The sign had a single cowboy in relief, gazing off into the distance, and the words *Mountain Waters Ranch*.

From her viewpoint on the hill, the buildings looked as if they belonged to a child's toy set. It was obvious this was a very prosperous operation. There was a white barn, and some outbuildings, corrals, and a sandy riding arena. There was also a runway and an airplane hangar, which was good because she was not sure about asking people to drive this far for a party.

She was pretty certain the wicked stepmother could arrange for the Kane private jet to ferry people from the Calgary International Airport. And maybe Lydia could even pony up for some helicopter transport.

The view gently swept the preoccupation with logistics from Shelby's mind. In the distance, where fields gave way to a valley, was *the* barn, perched on the edge of a ravine carved out by thousands of years of water flowing through it.

The photos had not done it justice. The weathered building, hewn, weather-grayed logs with thick chinking between them, was huge and spectacular.

But at least as spectacular as that barn, situated at the center of the ranch, like a hub, was a sprawling log house that had not been in the photo Shelby had seen.

Several gigantic trees shaded the wraparound porch, but smoke chugged out of a river-rock chimney a defense against the mountain crispness in the air.

Shelby felt the oddest longing looking at the place.

Somehow, the house and the buildings fit here, as if they had been here forever and would stay here forever.

There was a solidness about the Mountain Waters Ranch that made her sigh with a deep and surprising sense of yearning. That cluster of buildings in that wide valley whispered of tradition and history and family. A place, isolated from the world, where people had found safety and sanctuary, and made *home* for a hundred years, or maybe longer.

Her feeling that it would be perfect for her father's sixty-fifth deepened to a conviction that it was the *only* place that would do.

And she discovered how invested she was in wanting to be the one to give him that extra-special day, to show him she loved him, despite his falling under the sway of her wicked stepmother. And that she was worthy, somehow…

She got back in the little car and drove the shaded road down the hill. The road curved left to the house and right to the barn and outbuildings. She took the left turn and found herself at a parking pad, in front of a neat yard. Again, she felt that sigh, almost like recognition.

A swing dangled from a branch of one of those trees. There was an expanse of well-tended lawn, vibrantly green. A bed of red tulips formed a half circle around the veranda, and the thick green leaves stirred in the breeze.

Wide stone steps made their way up to a deep veranda scattered with furniture, though Shelby's eyes rested on the two rocking chairs, side by side, which looked out across the sweeping yard and beyond to the buildings, and beyond that to the endless mountains.

A child's shout, high-pitched with excitement, drew her attention away from the house. She turned, shaded her eyes and saw *him*.

The man, probably fifty yards away, was the quintessential picture of a cowboy. Booted and hatted, he was leaning on his elbows on the top rail of a wooden pole fence that enclosed a riding arena. One long leg was hitched on the bottom rail. He had on a dark denim shirt, jeans faded to nearly white and, of course, the cowboy boots and the hat. There was something in his stature, the broadness of his shoulders, the leanness at his waist and hips, that suggested both power and grace.

He turned and gave her a cursory look, the brim of his white cowboy hat keeping his face shaded.

Even though she couldn't see his features, she could feel something stir in her.

*Be still, my heart*, she commanded herself. She thought he would come to her—how many strangers would show up here, after all?—but no, he turned his attention away from her, as if her appearance held no interest to him whatsoever.

Shelby felt *dismissed*, in the same way she had when she'd received that single-word response to her emails. It was a somewhat new feeling in her Kane world. She was also aware that, despite the rudeness of the email, she had expected a certain rural friendliness, a tipped hat, a *howdy, ma'am*.

She debated. Go knock on the door of the house? The tulips held some promise of hospitality, didn't they?

But then she spotted the source of that shout that had drawn her attention in the first place.

Oh, for heaven's sake. Of course the cowboy hadn't come over! He was supervising a child. A small, adorable child. She looked to be about five, and she was sitting on a chubby palomino pony on the other side of the fence from the man.

Shelby started to make her way toward the riding arena, but the heel of one shoe sank deep into the spring soft ground. She contemplated that for a moment. Shoes of this quality were not in the *budget* if she broke the heel.

She took both shoes off and went forward barefoot. Despite her control of the first impression going somewhat awry, Shelby reminded herself of her mission. She also reminded herself maturity was required.

The little girl suddenly saw Shelby. Her expression was anything but curious. The child looked furious!

As Shelby approached the rail at the far end of the arena, the little girl pulled the pony around, pointed him in Shelby's direction and laid her heels to him. He reluctantly broke into a trot, and then a clunky canter as she pummeled him with her legs.

She arrived at Shelby in a cloud of dust. As it settled, Shelby took her in. Dark, wild curls tumbled out from under a pink cowboy hat. She had a leather-fringed vest on over a Pawsy-Poo T-shirt. The only reason Shelby knew who Pawsy-Poo was was because she had done a themed party for a little girl obsessed with the cartoon character.

The child had on a leather skirt that matched her vest, with black tights. The ensemble ended at her feet, which were encased in pink cowboy boots.

She had beautifully delicate features, eyes that reminded Shelby of the deer that she had encountered earlier. She had a tiny bow of a mouth, though her loveliness was distorted by her scowl and the downturn of said bow.

Peripherally, she was aware of the cowhand now striding along the arena toward them.

"Hel—"

She was given no opportunity to finish her greeting.

The child pulled a toy from a holder at her waist and pointed it directly at Shelby.

"Bang."

If Shelby was not mistaken, she had just been shot with a fashion doll.

She had no choice. She dropped her shoes, staggered backward and clasped her chest. She closed her eyes, let her knees fold under her and fell to the ground with as much drama as possible.

"I've been shot," she whispered, hoping the grass was not staining her outfit, because like the shoes, she did not have the means to replace it.

When she heard a reluctant giggle, Shelby quit worrying about the outfit, or about being mature. Maturity was not all it was cracked up to be, anyway.

# CHAPTER THREE

SHELBY LAY THERE, STILL, until she felt a shadow fall over her. She opened her eyes. Then she felt as if she really had been shot.

The man gazing down at her, from underneath the wide brim of that cowboy hat, was 100 percent gorgeous. And he emitted a kind of power and confidence that whispered a warning to Shelby: *Not just a cowboy.*

His eyes, identical to the child's, were one shade darker than the most decadent of dark chocolates, and fringed with an abundance of lashes that Epais would have killed to be able to use for an advertisement.

His hair was off his face, held back by the cowboy hat, but it escaped out over his ears and brushed his neck, with a promise of dark curls just like the child's. His hair was too long, and yet the look was undeniably sexy.

He had high cheekbones, a straight, strong nose, full lips and a hint of a cleft in his chin.

He gazed at her for a moment, and his eyes narrowed, as if he was debating what to do. He was obviously not amused by her reaction to being downed by the doll.

There was definite reluctance when, after a moment, he held out his hand to her. Which was still a long way from *howdy, ma'am.*

A feeling engulfed her, like a premonition. Not that Shelby had ever been given to such things.

If she took his hand, her life would be changed forever. In ways she could not control. Shelby Kane liked control, a lot.

What she did not like was powerlessness.

And yet that was what she felt as she reached out to his proffered hand. Powerless. As if she had given in to a spell, one loaded with a kind of savage sizzle rather than sweet enchantment.

The sizzle was confirmed as his hand closed around hers with pure and breathtaking masculine strength.

Shelby had never experienced a touch that was quite that real or that raw before. As she was yanked unceremoniously to her feet, his easy strength made some awareness—primal—tingle up and down her spine.

For a moment, she was sure he felt it, too, as she saw a flash of startled awareness in his eyes. But then he let go of her hand abruptly and scowled.

Unfortunately, his stern look was extraordinarily sexy, especially because of its contrast to those untamed curls.

"Hannah," he snapped, looking away from her and to the little girl, who still sat on her pony, "it's not polite to shoot at the guests."

"You can't shoot someone with a doll," Hannah pointed out. She wagged the doll at him—it was wearing an outfit not unlike her own, minus the hat—and tucked it back in her waistband.

Shelby caught a look on the man's face. Vulnerable. Unable to counter the inarguable logic of a small child. For a man who looked as if the whole world belonged to him, as if there was no situation he would not bring indomitable confidence to, he seemed to be in over his head.

"Besides, I don't like her," Hannah announced.

"You're shattering my myths about farm friendliness," Shelby said, smiling at her.

"It's not a farm," the child said, not charmed. "It's a ranch."

"You're being very rude," the man said.

A puffy lip stuck out in an unrepentant pout.

The man presented Shelby with his hand. For the second time.

"Sam Waters," he said.

This was Sam Waters? It confirmed her initial intuition that he was more than a cowboy. It occurred to Shelby her allergy to internet sleuthing had not stood her well this time.

Had she known he was not old and stodgy, she could have been better prepared.

Though gazing at him, she was not quite sure how you prepared for *this*.

"Shelby Kane," she said, taking his hand. She should have been ready this time. But she wasn't. His grasp was mind-blowingly strong, warm, sexy. And brief.

"This is my daughter, Hannah."

Hannah glowered at her.

"Say hello to Miss Kane," Sam said sternly, "and then apologize for assaulting her with your doll and telling her you don't like her. You don't even know her."

"Hello, Miss Kane. I'm sorry I don't like you."

Shelby giggled at how Hannah had circumvented the apology, which earned her a dark look from the very sexy daddy.

"I wasn't expecting you. The agency told me they weren't going to send anyone else," he said, taking off his hat and running a hand through glossy hair. Loose curls sprang up under his touch.

That hair! Unfairly gorgeous.

*What agency?*

"I don't need a nanny!"

Sam regarded his daughter for a moment, then slammed his hat back onto his head.

They thought Shelby was a nanny!

"Of course you don't," Shelby said, earning her a look of

reluctant interest from the child and a glance of grave annoyance from the man.

That wasn't exactly *I am not a nanny.*

"You're a city girl, aren't you?" Sam asked. His voice had a gravelly tone to it that felt as if it was scraping across her skin. And not in an unpleasant way.

Best not to let him know that!

"I prefer to think of myself as a woman," Shelby said.

*Especially around him.* She thought about how she had earlier contemplated the phrase *boyfriend.*

He would never be anyone's boyfriend.

And she didn't want to be seen as a girl around him.

Something extraordinarily adult was swirling in the air between them. It was a good thing Shelby was now 100 percent a career woman!

Sam Waters cocked his head at her.

"Woman," he said, his tone flat. "Noted."

That was not *exactly* how she wanted him to notice her. Still, they were getting off on the wrong track.

"I'm from New York," she said.

He nodded, as if this was not entirely unexpected, and not a good thing, either. He rocked back on his heels and looked into the distance.

"I guess that's why they're called International Nanny Services. Though I'm surprised *nanny* is still a politically acceptable term."

There was lots of sarcastic emphasis on *politically acceptable*—clearly a dig at her correcting him about being a girl. Shelby realized that she had to tread very carefully at the moment.

For some reason the lines were blurring. It actually felt as if she *had* arrived here as a nanny, not looking to him to provide his ranch for a sixty-fifth birthday party. She allowed herself to glance off toward that timber-frame barn.

Though the barn would be absolutely perfect.

"You know, if you're going to bring your city sensibilities here with you, you can just get back in—" he leveled a look at her vehicle "—that toy car and go back where you came from."

"It looks like a car a clown drives at the circus," Hannah chimed in.

"Hence the agency being reluctant to send people," Shelby said to the pair of them, diplomacy be damned.

He looked at her narrowly. It occurred to her he was not a man accustomed to being challenged.

Given what she wanted from him, couldn't she, just this once, have held her tongue?

She had to tell him the truth and she had to tell him right now. On the other hand, Sam Waters did not look as if he was going to be amenable to giving over his ranch for a party.

What if he knew her better? What if she knew him better?

She was kidding herself. Somehow this wasn't even about the party anymore. Shelby didn't just want to see inside that house, it felt as if she *needed* that. To set foot in a place where stockings had hung on the same mantel for a hundred years or more, where people had sat on those porch rockers, maybe holding hands...

Sam sighed. "Can I assume you don't ride?"

"You can. I don't actually like horses."

She was treated to identical aghast expressions from the father and daughter duo. She looked at the pony.

"Toy horses excepted, of course."

She watched a reluctant smile twitch at Sam's lips.

"I don't need a nanny," Hannah said again. "Buckie is fine! I love him. He takes care of me."

"The pony?" Shelby asked. A pony was looking after the child?

"No, that's Rascal," Sam said. "Buckie is the ranch cook."

"Buckie?"

"Nicknames tend to go hand in hand with ranch work. He does childcare in a pinch, but it's not ideal. We're pretty much a society of men out here. She needs a woman."

"I don't!" Hannah cried. "You can't be my mommy. My mommy died."

For a moment, the angry mask slipped, and all Shelby saw in the little girl was immense and bottomless pain.

"My mommy died, too," she said quietly.

The connection between them was brief and intense. Suddenly she knew this little girl *needed* her.

It was shocking to realize that in her twenty-eight years on the planet, she had never, ever felt that before.

*Needed.*

She wondered, briefly, why she had such an aversion to having children when, really, who needed you more than them?

She felt a sudden, totally unwanted tickle down her spine. She could suddenly remember herself, at about the age of this child, *needing* with a terrible desperation.

It wasn't quite a memory. The realization was followed by that familiar feeling of blankness that she always had about her early childhood.

She shook it off, and watched as Hannah whirled the fat pony around and took off down the arena, stirring up clouds of dust behind her.

Shelby glanced at Sam's face as his daughter rode away.

Maybe because some secret of her own had threatened to surface, she saw his with stunning clarity. He was a man who obviously had complete control of an empire. When she had searched for his contact info, she had found out his business portfolio and holdings were immense. They easily rivaled her father's.

But all his billions and all his power had not been able to save his daughter from sorrow.

As a daddy on his own, it seemed possible he was in way over his head.

Maybe, for once in her life, Shelby could put the needs of others ahead of her own. Such a noble sentiment made going along with a little white lie—committing the sin of omission—okay, didn't it?

No, it did not.

She drew in a breath. The woman she had been eighteen months ago would have gone along with the mistaken-identity thing, played it out for a bit.

But she couldn't. It wouldn't further her cause in the end, anyway.

Or maybe it was something about him, about Sam Waters, that made anything short of 100 percent integrity seem as if it was not acceptable.

"Look, I'm not—"

A sound stopped her midsentence. A man was thundering directly toward them on a horse. She could not be certain he was in complete control. Was the horse running away? Stampeding? Were they about to be crushed?

Shelby thought about jumping over the nearby fence to avoid a collision, but she felt oddly protected by Sam, who made no evasive move as the horse came closer, standing his ground, calm and strong.

Just when it seemed as if the horse was going to crash right into them—she slid behind Sam, though he did not even flinch—the horse slammed to a halt, practically sitting down on his back legs the stop was so abrupt.

"Boss," the lean cowboy on the horse said. "There's been an accident at the round pen. I think we might need to chopper Jim out of here."

Sam's stillness was gone. He was already running.

He turned back. "Have you got this?"

Shelby nodded. Of course she had it. What other option was there?


Sam called Hannah from the hospital to make sure she was okay and to tell her good night.

He thought his daughter would be beside herself at his sudden departure and being handed over to the brand-new nanny, but her first question was for Jimmy. It was a small thing, but her ability to be concerned about others gave him hope that, in the sea of single-parenting confusion, maybe he was managing to get the odd thing right.

"Is he okay?" Hannah asked with touching and genuine concern.

"Yes, he's fine. He broke his arm."

"Does he have a cast?" she asked, not *when will you be home*, not *I hate the new nanny*.

"Yes, he does."

"Can I draw on it?"

The mystery of his daughter: How did she know people drew on casts? She had probably seen it on television.

*Did he let her watch too much TV? So convenient, sometimes...*

Would the woman who'd appeared in their lives so unexpectedly know things like that?

"How's, uh, Miss Kane?"

"She said I can call her Shelby. I like her."

"You do?" He tried to strip his genuine astonishment from his voice.

"Yes. She's nice."

"She is?"

"She's not really a nanny. She's just going to be my friend."

# CHAPTER FOUR

*CLEVER*, SAM THOUGHT, for Shelby Kane to recognize his daughter's aversion to nannies and skirt around it.

He allowed himself to feel marginally hopeful that this time it was going to work out, even while he experienced a shiver of discomfort.

Miss Kane, in their very brief acquaintance, had made him feel something.

He didn't like it when he realized what that feeling was. Some awareness of her as a woman had shivered along his spine, even before he had taken her hand. Since the death of his wife, he knew all about the painfulness of firsts: birthdays celebrated without her, Christmas. You could sort of brace yourself for the swamp of feelings if the event was on a calendar.

But this first had taken him entirely by surprise, like a hit up the side of the head: finding a woman attractive.

For a man who had lost way too much to love, Sam recognized that shiver he had felt for what it was: a warning.

It was flashing brightly in his brain like a neon sign: *Danger. Stay back.*

He'd traveled the treacherous path of love and loss a few too many times now. Only a fool would embark on that journey again.

It was dark by the time he landed the helicopter back at the ranch and helped a drowsy Jimmy to the bunkhouse.

"Take it easy for a few days," he told the hand.

"I hate leaving you shorthanded at this time of year."

"You know ranches," Sam said, even though he hated being shorthanded, too. The ranch was the least of his many business obligations, but it always seemed to be jostling for more time than he had to give it.

Still, he had every hope the new nanny might make his schedule a little more manageable.

"Sorry, boss."

There was injured pride in that statement. No cowboy wanted a hospital visit after getting tossed from a green colt.

"Hey, stuff happens." Only Sam didn't say *stuff*. He said a word he couldn't say when he was wearing his daddy hat and that he was pretty sure the nanny would not approve of.

He walked back through the darkness to the house. He stopped before he arrived. Someone was sitting on the front porch in one of the rocking chairs, wrapped in a blanket against the chill of the mountain spring evening.

It was the new nanny.

He felt a shiver of doubt. Should he call her Shelby? Or Miss Kane? He was annoyed at the uncertainty. He made decisions where millions of dollars were on the line with less thought than this.

He knew, from that jolting awareness of her, that the uncertainty ran deeper than what to call her, so he hesitated in the darkness awhile longer, studying her.

Sam remembered how her hand had felt in his when he had lifted her off the ground. Some dangerous current had passed between them, and he had seen awareness of it pass through her eyes, too.

But that was probably a natural reaction. He had not touched a woman since Beth had died. Such impulses could be controlled.

It was the other thing that seemed more dangerous. Sam

remembered how she had looked at him a little too intently, as if she saw something he did not want her to see.

As if his every uncomfortable uncertainty was on full display. Especially when it came to raising his little girl on his own.

Every day, he tried to find balance between his business and his parenting obligations.

Business was easier, cut-and-dried.

Parenting, not so much. He walked in the unfamiliar land of not having answers. How much television was too much? Was it okay to let Hannah play the occasional game on his phone? What was he supposed to do with all that hair? Should she be picking her own outfits?

And bigger questions. The ranch was as close to happy as either of them had gotten since Beth had died. But was it okay to raise her here? Didn't she need *more*? More friends her own age, more things to prepare her for school?

School. Next year. He had to make decisions. He was good at decisions. Usually.

Now they nagged him. Did Hannah need more women? Even though Hannah had reacted violently to the suggestion, didn't she need some of that softness around her, that feminine energy that was in pretty short supply at the ranch?

Feminine energy. Shelby Kane had that in spades, even with her slender figure hidden in the folds of a blanket.

She was way too pretty for this job. Sam didn't like that he had noticed, especially her eyes. He might have initially said her eyes were brown, but that wasn't true. Up close, he had seen they were so shot through with flecks of gold and green that he wasn't quite sure what color they were.

Her hair was loose and thick. Earlier in the day, the spring sun shining on it reminded him of honey in a jar. And her mouth...

He wished the agency would have sent a nanny like that

one on television. The one who looked like a refrigerator in a pantsuit.

Shelby represented a complication of the variety he didn't need. When he'd helped her up off the ground, he'd felt that *complication* jolt through him.

Still, Hannah had actually said she liked her.

Had they connected because Shelby—he had decided to call her that, instead of Miss Kane—knew what it was to be a little girl drowning in sorrow?

That gave him a hope that maybe they could make this work.

Because when he'd first seen her, out of the corner of his eye, when she had walked up to the arena, he'd seen her get that heel stuck in the ground. The footwear choice alone signaled she didn't have the slightest idea what she was getting into.

When he'd observed her up close, he had recognized the name inside those shoes. Once, he'd been a part of that world.

Like generations before him, Sam had been born and raised on this ranch. But unlike those who came before him, and to his family's distress, he'd wanted a bigger world.

In university he'd been pulled toward technology, a field as far removed from the gritty realities of cows and land and weather and hard, physically demanding work as a man could get.

And yet, he was well aware, it was the combination of the worlds that had allowed Sam his rocket ride to success. His upbringing had given him drive and toughness, a relentless work ethic, an ability to think on his feet and handle challenges. He'd chased success and found it beyond his wildest dreams.

For a blink in time, he'd been the man with success and money and power beyond imagining.

And then he'd found love. In a way, Beth had been like

him. She came from hardworking roots, but she had found fame in the culinary world, and by the time he'd met her, she was a celebrity with her own restaurants, cookbooks, internet channels and television specials.

For a blink in time, they had been the "it" couple. They had graced the covers of magazines and conquered the world. From the outside and from the inside, they had been the couple with everything.

Though Sam had redefined *everything* when he had held his baby daughter in his arms for the first time. The ranch—family—suddenly called him. He liked spending time there. He and Beth loved bringing Hannah to Mountain Waters for weekends, longer stays in the summer, at Christmas. Hannah had ridden with her grandfather, tucked into the front of his saddle, since she was a baby.

And then, Sam Waters's time in the sun had been over.

His father had gotten sick and died. His mother, her heart broken, followed with stunning swiftness.

Still reeling from those losses, Sam listened as Beth told him she wasn't feeling well. He knew, right away, that she had been trying to protect him because of his other heartbreaks. Had that delay mattered? If she had told him sooner—if he had *noticed*—could the outcome have been changed?

The diagnosis was devastating, as was the illness.

And then Sam, who only a moment ago had every single thing a man could ever dream of, was alone in the world, save for a small child who was trusting him not to break under the weight of all his shattered dreams.

Sam was left with the crushing knowledge that a man's sense that he was powerful was a complete illusion. When it counted, he was not.

And he was also left a single dad, in a world that wanted to feed on his grief and vulnerability.

Suddenly, the ranch he'd left behind—the life he'd left

behind—offered sanctuary. He figured out how to run his other businesses from there. Technology—and access to an airstrip—made it possible.

This was the place where his daughter was happy and protected from the public eye. This was the place where he could occasionally lose himself in the kind of hard, physical work that was a balm for the unrelenting pain, his awareness of his own powerlessness.

He was shocked how just seeing a woman on the porch had triggered all these thoughts. He hesitated, then went up the steps through the darkness.

Was that warning sign *Danger* flashing a little less brightly?

"Miss Kane," he said out loud.

"Shelby," she said.

He was aware he had been hoping for that, and that it felt like a weakness to harbor such a hope.

"Sam," he responded, even though the familiarity took a board out of the high fence he needed to keep up between them.

*Employer, employee*, he told himself sternly. "How did things go with Hannah tonight?"

"She wouldn't take a bath, or let me touch her hair, but other than that, good."

"Her hair," he said. "It's a good thing I know how to wrestle calves, because once a week I have to pin her down and get the tangles out of it."

He didn't admit how many times he had thought of cutting Hannah's wild hair short. He hadn't because it would feel like a failure of sorts.

"You wrestle calves?" she asked. "Is that as exciting as it sounds?"

He did not want her to find anything about him *exciting*.

"It's hard and it's dirty. There's nothing romantic about it."

He wished he had not used that particular word. "Anyway, I said I know how. I'm not very hands-on with the ranch these days. I have a foreman who looks after the day-to-day operations. I'm pretty much an office guy now. And dad with hair challenges."

"Her room is a delight, by the way," Shelby said. He wondered if she wasn't trying to let him know that, despite the hair failure, he was doing something right. "I like the little tent in the corner. We sat in it to read a storybook."

He slid Shelby a glance. He was relieved things had gone well. It probably said way too much about his parenting that he wondered what contortions she'd had to do to squeeze into that tent.

"How's the injured man? Jim?"

It warmed him in a way that he didn't want to be warmed that there was such genuine concern in her voice for a stranger, a man she had never met. And that she'd remembered his name.

"I brought him back with me. He'll be okay. Broken arm. He'll be laid up for a bit."

"What happened to him?"

"He was riding a green colt. Things went sideways. It's a ranch. Stuff happens." This time he did say *stuff.* "What are you doing out here?" he asked.

She gazed up at him with those luminous eyes, which, in the moonlight, looked more green than gold or brown.

He'd rather she wasn't pretty, because that was just a complication on a ranch full of men. It was the same as putting a mare in with the herd. Pretty soon all those old reliable guys were acting silly and vying for attention.

The hands would probably all be picking the tulips and bringing her bouquets within a week.

Who was he kidding? It wasn't the hands he was worried about.

It was himself.

And it was the first time he'd had such a thought since Beth died. Shelby was bringing firsts he hadn't expected, and he didn't like it. It made him feel faintly resentful, as if she was intruding in a sacred place.

He needed to turn the wattage back up on that *Danger* sign.

"Didn't Buckie show you where to put your things?"

"Yes, that lovely room above the garage. It's very nice," she said.

"It's set up for you to cook for yourself if you want to. But the nearest grocery store is a long way away. Buckie does all the cooking until you're set up, or if you'd rather not."

"Alvin's adorable, by the way."

"Alvin?"

"Oh, that's his real name."

Sam contemplated that. The ranch cook had been on the Mountain Waters Ranch long before he had. He'd been part of raising him. Of course, he knew his name was Alvin, because he signed the checks. But he'd never heard him called that before, ever.

The cook was a man whose idea of knowing the alphabet was having a swear word to match every letter.

Every single letter.

He wondered what the new nanny would think of *that*.

Adorable, he was not. Of course, Buckie, like every other guy in the place, would probably be on his best behaviour.

"It's so beautiful out here," she breathed, answering his question about what she was doing outside. "I wanted to just enjoy it for a bit."

*Don't sit down with her.*

But suddenly he felt exhausted, the day catching up with him. He took the rocker next to her. Why wouldn't he sit down with his daughter's new nanny? Wasn't it part of his parental responsibility? To get to know Shelby Kane?

But he knew that wasn't exactly why he'd taken the seat. And it couldn't totally be blamed on exhaustion, either. It was the look on her face.

Wonder. It pulled at some place in him that had not felt that for a long, long time. He should have heeded it as the danger level increasing, but he was too tired.

"I don't think I've ever seen stars like this," Shelby said.

He looked out at the star-encrusted night. He was astounded by the beauty of it, as if he'd been blind and suddenly could see. How long had it been since he'd had a moment like this? When he just felt so aware?

"And the sounds," she pointed out. "I thought it would be quiet in the country, but it's not."

Sure enough, he heard the cry of an owl, the deep lowing of faraway cattle, crickets chirping, a chorus of frogs down by the creek.

"I smell something, too," she said. "It's so pure. Like opening a bottle of champagne and the bubbles tickling your nose."

He noticed a scent as well, but it had nothing to do with the fresh fragrances of mountain air, pine, the clean breeze coming down off the snowcapped mountains, cattle.

It was her. The fact it was so subtle—not perfume or soap—made it shockingly sensual. He could not pinpoint it, but it was like a combination of flowers and spice and feminine mystery.

Sam felt—despite the fact he was trying to heed all the danger signs—for the first time in a long, long time, fully alive. He did not like it!

It occurred to him he had a professional duty here that he was neglecting. He should be finding out about her.

There was a little more to entrusting a person with your daughter's care than your daughter's endorsement.

*She's nice.*

Tempting to think that was enough, but it wasn't.

"I'm sorry I wasn't expecting you," he told her. "I haven't checked my personal email for a couple of days."

"That must be wonderful," she said wistfully.

*Yeah, she'll see about that when a late spring storm comes through and knocks out all the power for a week or so.*

She was, of course, completely unsuitable for this position, even if she did read storybooks in a tent.

# CHAPTER FIVE

SHELBY KANE. By her own admission she was a city girl.

But, so far, every one of the nannies Sam had tried out had been completely incompatible with the job. Sometimes they had been run off by his daughter before he even had a chance to see how unsuitable they were.

Certainly Hannah had never once said, of any of them, *I like her.*

Besides, unsuitable or not, he had several business trips coming up, and now he was down a hand. If Shelby could get him through the remaining days of spring calving, that was all he could ask.

"You must like children a lot to become a nanny," he said, trying to feel his way into what he supposed was an interview of sorts. "I'm surprised you don't have your own. A family of your own who will miss you when you take these assignments."

A husband had not occurred to him, until right this second. He slid a look at her ring finger.

Bare.

What about a boyfriend, waiting in the wings? He told himself the only reason he would care about her personal life, at all, was because of any effect it might have on her duties.

"I've never wanted children," she said softly.

He frowned. That was an odd comment from someone who made her living tending children.

She hesitated for a moment. "I wasn't just enjoying the evening. I was waiting for you, actually."

It was a small statement, and yet it made him *feel* something. Again. Having developed quite a skill for avoiding pesky emotions, he didn't like this. And especially when he pinpointed the pang as longing. To come home and have a woman waiting for him.

*Danger.*

Again, she was the nanny. Professionalism. Employer, employee. He barely knew her. He was just tired. His defenses—which were considerable—were down a bit. Because defenses, like the endless miles of fences on a ranch, needed constant vigilance, repair, maintenance.

"I didn't put anything in the room Alvin showed me."

She hadn't settled in. What did that mean? A new record for leaving? She'd already figured out it was way too isolated up here?

"I have to tell you something," she said, her voice low, as if she was about to make a confession.

Her gallows tone made Sam brace himself for a multitude of possibilities.

*I'm pregnant. I've already decided I'm not staying. Can my boyfriend come? Can I have the weekend off? Where's the mall?*

"I'm not a nanny."

After telling him that simple truth, Shelby watched Sam Waters's face carefully.

He had removed his hat and was twirling it between long fingers. He really was unfairly gorgeous, with those loops of too-long curls framing his face. Here, sitting on the front porch, with his features illuminated by moonlight, his rugged good looks were even more obvious than they had been at their initial encounter.

She noticed his lashes again. The luscious darkness of his eyes. The masculine, symmetrical cut of strong, perfect features. The firmness of his lips, the faint puffiness of the lower one.

The stubble beginning to darken his cheeks and his chin accentuated his masculinity and made him look faintly roguish and entirely sexy.

She had talked about the scent on the air, but in truth she had noticed that before he sat down.

After, her senses had been engulfed by *him*, and the unexpected intimacy of the moment. She had been super aware of his nearness, his distinctive aroma, the hard line of muscle on his forearm as he rested it on the arm of the rocker. Despite the chill in the air, Sam was still in the same dark blue denim shirt—no jacket—and yet he seemed in no way cold, which made her even more aware of the robust appeal of the man.

He laughed at her announcement.

She liked the upward quirk of those firm lips, and the light that danced in the darkness of his eyes. She *really* liked his laughter. It was warm and engaging. It made her aware Sam Waters carried a weight, and that the laughter, however briefly, lifted it.

He actually looked relieved by her announcement, as if he'd been expecting something else.

"That's what Hannah said when I called from the hospital to tell her good night."

Something in Shelby's heart just melted. She must have already left the little girl when he'd called. There was a sweetness to his calling his child to say good night that a person wouldn't expect from the stern lines in his face.

That shadow of something like memory passed over her again. *A little girl waiting for a call that did not come.*

"Hannah told me that you're not a nanny. Given her aversion to them, I congratulate you on being so clever."

There. She could leave it at that. She had done her due diligence. She could take false credit for him thinking she was clever.

Maybe she could spend a few days here, before she revealed the truth. Mountain Waters Ranch was doing something to her heart that made her not want to let go of it right away.

When Alvin had shown her around the house, she was not sure she had ever been in a place that felt so like *home*, despite the fact it was large and utterly magnificent. The kitchen was state-of-the-art. She had glimpsed a theater room.

It had been exquisitely renovated, with no expense spared, and yet, while having every modern amenity, it had remained true to its traditional roots.

Shelby had recognized the quality and timelessness of many of the furnishings and decorations. Like the Kane properties, this house held gorgeous, tasteful antiques, priceless rugs, rare paintings, authentic collectibles from many cultures.

But the polished golden log walls, the paned windows and the heartwood pine floors gave it a feeling of hominess that none of the interior designers of her father's many houses had ever achieved.

There was a sense here—worn into the floors and radiating from the magnificent log walls of that ranch house—of stability, of generations of gatherings around that harvest table in the dining room for special occasions, but ordinary ones, too.

The house had the layers of charm that came only when people actually called a place home. There were toys on the floor and a jigsaw puzzle, partially built, on the kitchen island. There was a calendar hanging with the boxes crowded with markings in a strong hand. Vet coming, dentist appointment, a birthday party—all the daily details of lives where people actually stayed and lived in one place.

In the living room there was a book, opened and face down, abandoned on the coffee table, and a sock peeked out from under an old, comfy-looking easy chair. A teddy bear with only one ear and the thread for his mouth half removed was flopped over on a sofa.

The focus of the room was a floor-to-ceiling river rock fireplace, the inner firebox burned black and with remnants of charcoal and ash in it. On the chunky wooden mantel, Shelby could clearly see the nails where socks were hung at Christmastime.

Alvin appeared to be the only staff member. It was more than obvious there were no servants discreetly in the background, slipping around returning everything to perfection as quickly as possible.

Her glimpse into the real lives of the Waterses had filled Shelby with a longing. To know more.

Or maybe deeper, and certainly more frightening, to fit. To belong.

Something tickled up her spine. Fear. Of wanting things she had decided, many years ago, that she could not have.

It would be almost a relief to get sent packing before those hidden desires got out of control. But her experience told her that to long for a sense of family was to set herself up for disappointment.

"I'm *really* not a nanny. I wasn't sent here by International Nanny Services."

Sam's frown deepened. He looked hard at her through narrowed gaze. His eyes, which had seemed the color of chocolate in the light of day, looked nearly black in the stripped-down light of the moon.

The laughter was completely gone from his expression.

"Who are you, then?" There was no friendliness in the question. That moment of connection between them was erased.

Completely.

She took a deep breath. "I *am* Shelby Kane. I'm just *not* a nanny."

"Then what are you doing here? Mountain Waters is not exactly on the beaten path. People don't arrive here by accident."

She took another deep breath. "I can see why you would assume I might be a nanny, then."

"I don't recall you correcting that assumption."

"I was in the middle of telling you who I really was when we were interrupted."

He was silent, and expressionless, but a muscle jumped intimidatingly in his jaw.

Shelby took a deep breath. "In my defense, I thought we were about to be trampled."

If she thought his look might soften a bit with sympathy, she had been mistaken.

"I actually run a company called Eventually," she said in a rush. "I contacted you, by email, about hosting an event at the timber-frame barn?"

His frown deepened. "I left my daughter with you," he growled. "Thinking you had qualifications."

It was as if he hadn't even heard the part about the event.

"Yes," she said, keeping her tone agreeable, "There was a misunderstanding."

"You could be *anybody*," he said, his tone low and dangerous.

"Well, yes, that's true, but—"

"Who are you?" he interrupted, and then he said a swear word. "I trusted you. Because the agency does thorough background checks. Their nannies are trained to look after small children."

For a moment, she felt her own ire rising. "Are you suggesting that I might be some sort of unsavory character, derelict in my duties to your daughter through lack of formal training? If you're that uncertain about me, maybe you better go check and make sure Hannah is safely asleep in her bed. With no signs of neglect."

Sam didn't move, but his expression didn't soften, either.

"I *helped* you," she pointed out, miffed.

"You lied to me."

"I did not," she sputtered.

Suddenly, below his anger, she saw his underlying insecurity about being a good parent. A wisp of wistfulness flitted through her mind. Had anyone ever held themselves to this fire for her?

"You didn't fail in the parenting department because there was a misunderstanding about my credentials," she said quietly.

"I didn't?" he snapped back, not soothed. "You could be a reporter from one of those despicable rags that feed on human misery, while *pretending* compassion."

At least he didn't see her as a potential kidnapper.

"I hope that hasn't happened to you."

His glare spoke volumes.

"You could," he continued, "have been one of those women who has decided my daughter needs a mother and I need a companion, and coincidentally, they'll be set for life if they snag me."

She didn't have to ask this time if that had happened. It was written in every cynical line of his face.

"I'm sorry. I'm familiar with the hazards of wealth and fame."

He cocked his head at her.

"I'm Boswell Kane's daughter."

There. That should reassure him that a gold digger hadn't tracked him down and inserted herself into his life. "I told you. I'm just here because I want to rent the timber-frame barn."

For a moment, he looked only puzzled. And then understanding dawned on his face.

"Now I recognize your name. You've sent me about thirty thousand emails."

"Three thousand, at the most," she came back with.

He did not look amused.

"And if you would have answered them," Shelby continued, "I wouldn't be here."

"I did answer. And you're still here."

It was pretty hard to argue with that.

"It just wasn't the answer you wanted, was it?" he asked, his tone cold.

Somehow, the way he said that made her feel like the spoiled girl she had once been, unable to take no for an answer, unable to believe she could not get her own way.

"And if I had answered the way you wanted, if I'd said yes, you can rent the barn for your event, you would still be here, wouldn't you? Taking measurements, and making plans, and disrupting the quiet and the routines of this place with constant air traffic, and shipments of stuff and staff coming, and finally people arriving for the *event*."

He managed to load that word with contempt, as if she had suggested a three-ring circus, or a carnival complete with a sideshow.

"How would they arrive?" Sam went on softly, and held up his hand when she went to reply. "No, no, let me guess. Private jets and helicopters and maybe a Mercedes-Benz bus or two. And then people traipsing all over the place, breaking off their heels in soft dirt—"

That landed! Shelby felt herself wince.

"And getting lost," he continued, "and spooking the livestock, and distracting the hands, threatening to sue me."

"I've done many large events on private properties as nice as this one," she said stiffly.

"Good! Get one of them."

"I'm a professional," she went on, with pride. "I know how to troubleshoot, and I also know it's a privilege to use a property like this. I would never abuse that privilege. I can provide references."

"That won't be necessary. Because I don't rent out the barn."

"Yes, you do," she said.

"How about if you don't call me a liar?"

"You called me one! I saw a photo of an event there."

"Look, I don't want to spar with you. I don't *rent* out the barn. I make it available to friends and neighbors for the *right* occasion."

"The right occasion," she repeated. "Such as?"

"Sometimes a private function like an anniversary, or a wedding, but usually community events. The high school graduation ceremony and dance will be here in a little over a week."

"You don't even know what my occasion is."

"I don't know you. I don't care what your event is."

"What's the difference?" she demanded. "The disruption to your precious routines would be just the same."

"The difference is that these are the people who have stood with our ranch in good times and in bad. The difference is these are the people we've grown up with and grown old with. The difference is that I would know the first names of almost every single person who set foot on the place. The difference is we share the history of this valley."

There was that longing again, dangerous, and so appealing, as many dangerous things were.

A yearning for what she had never had.

Community. But she would not let him see how he had stung her. She would not beg!

# CHAPTER SIX

SAM REALLY COULD not remember the last time he'd felt so angry with a person.

How dare Shelby Kane just waltz up here to his ranch thinking she could charm him into changing his mind? Impersonating a nanny?

"The difference is," he finished softly, "that I don't let people use this barn to make money. It's to give joy."

"You know," Shelby said with her chin titled and her tone haughty, as was befitting of the daughter of one of the world's richest men, "in our short acquaintance, I would say that is a topic you seem to know nothing about."

That stung! Not that he would ever let her see that she had landed an arrow.

There was more than a grain of truth in it. He had known joy, once. It had gone hand in hand with love. He was terrified of both now. Because once you had known them, the loss was shattering in every way it was possible to be shattered.

"And just for your information," Shelby said, "I didn't want to hold an event here to make money. I wanted to have my dad's sixty-fifth birthday party here."

*Don't bite*, he ordered himself, but then just like a fish circling, he couldn't resist, even though he knew there might be a hook buried in the bait. "Why here? Your father has probably experienced every wonder the world has to offer."

"Exactly! My dad *has* seen everything in the entire world. But I just knew he'd never seen anything like this."

She looked out at the immensity of the sky. Her face was unguarded for a moment. Wistful.

The problem with a woman like her was that she could make a man weak when he most wanted to be strong. She could make him lean toward a temptation, even when he was aware there might be a hook buried in it.

"You can stay the night," he said coolly. "I don't want you attempting the roads in the dark."

"How thoughtful," she said snippily.

"Not really. I don't have the manpower to be staging a rescue if you go off the road."

"I'm quite capable of tackling the roads."

He heard something in her tone that made him suspect she was not quite as confident as she wanted to appear. "The deer and elk are out at night."

He saw something flicker in her face. What was he doing? What did he care if she got in her little toy car and drove away and he never saw her again?

He *cared.* Already. Even though he was irritated. Which just meant it was wiser—imperative, even—to send her on her way. In the morning.

"Bears come out at night."

She glanced around the yard warily, as if a bear might be hiding behind the tree swing. "I'll leave first thing in the morning."

"Animals are worse in the morning. At dawn."

"So, since you need to be in control of the whole world, when do you want me to leave?"

*Control. The one thing a man doesn't really have, no matter what illusions he harbors.* Still, he would do his best to protect her while she was in his domain.

"After breakfast would work."

"Are you inviting me for breakfast?"

"I'm feeding you. There's a difference."

"Fine."

"Good."

And yet, as he got up from the rocking chair and went into the house, snapping the screen door shut behind him with a little more force than was strictly necessary, Sam was aware he didn't feel *good* at all.

He had found solace from his grief in hard work. His business ventures benefitted from his single-minded drive to escape the pain of a loss he had not been able to control. He was more successful than he had ever been, and if it exhausted him, he saw that as a good thing. He always fell asleep the minute his head hit the pillow. But tonight, he tossed and turned, and the weariness did not work in his favor. Fences tumbled down and Sam thought of what he least wanted to think about.

He thought of Beth. He recognized he was still angry with his wife even though it was closing in on two years since she was gone. How could she do this to him? He knew getting sick was not her fault, and that made his resentment even more shameful. But he felt abandoned, left alone with a pile of broken dreams and a little girl to raise.

It pierced the ire how much he missed her. Wasn't the anger—like so much of his life—really about keeping the sorrow at bay? He missed her when he was raising Hannah, and on those special days, like Christmas and birthdays, but he especially missed her in moments like this one.

Moments that called for something more than he had to give. Qualities he thought of as feminine. Empathy. Intuition.

And suddenly, Sam knew Beth would be disappointed in him, and in the way he had handled all of this.

Shelby had driven all this way to try and make him see something. That she—a woman with access to anything—

wanted to do something special for her dad, to give him something he had never had.

She *had* helped Sam out of a tough spot, and he was pretty sure it was the circumstances that had prevented her from telling him earlier that she wasn't from International Nanny Services.

He suddenly remembered Shelby telling them she had lost her mom, too.

Was it possible he wanted to get rid of her because of how she was making him *feel*, rather than anything she'd done?

Beth had always required him to be a better man. He knew he needed to be the best man he could be to raise his daughter. In these circumstances, what did that mean?

It meant he didn't repay Shelby's kindness in taking Hannah under her wing when he was in a pinch by being rude and selfish. By protecting himself at a cost to someone else.

It meant maybe he needed to apologize. He hoped it didn't mean he had to rethink his decision about the old timber-frame barn. Because that meant his life would be tangled with hers for longer. And look at how he *felt* after just a few hours of her acquaintance.

Tumultuous. Self-doubting. Insensitive. In danger.

When the first fingers of dawn began to paint his bedroom a faint blush, he gave up on sleeping. Sam felt as if he hadn't slept a wink. Hannah was not up yet.

He got up, showered and dressed, went down to the kitchen. Beth had designed it to her exacting standards. It reminded him those standards applied to him today.

*Be a better man.*

Buckie slammed a coffee cup down in front of him as soon as he entered the room. He glared at him.

"She's leaving," he told Sam.

Sam wondered if Shelby had been as restless as he, and if that was why she was up so early.

"Yeah, I know."

"Hannah likes her. I like her."

"She's not who she said she was."

"Anybody who can't tell who that girl is from lookin' in her eyes is just plain dumb."

"She likes to be called a woman. And she's not a nanny," Sam said tightly. "She came to rent the old barn for an event. After I'd already told her no."

"For her *dad*," Buckie said.

Jeez, had Shelby confided her whole life story in Buckie? What time *had* she gotten up? The sun was barely out of bed.

"Where is she right now?" He said this carelessly, as if he didn't care, except that she might be getting into trouble somewhere with her city ways. Getting her shoes stuck in the mud. Trying to pet the bull.

"She said she was going to go look at it."

"The barn? I don't know why she would. I told her no."

"Yeah, well, she said she wouldn't rent it from you now if her life depended on it."

"Quite the little tête–à–tête you two managed to have this morning," he said sourly.

"Just 'cause you speak French doesn't make you a class act," Buckie told him. "I know some French, too."

He said several words he must have learned from French sailors. Even though he massacred the accent, and Sam did not speak French, his meaning was abundantly clear.

This was the problem with having staff who had been around since before you were born, and who had wiped your nose and fussed over your bruises. No respect.

"You can't say stuff like that with a child in the house," Sam admonished him.

"You grew up on stuff like that. It didn't seem to hurt you."

"A *girl*," Sam reminded him.

"She ain't even up yet."

"Don't let that fool you. If you whispered *ice cream* right now, she'd be down here in three seconds."

Buckie just glared at him, as if he thought the possibility of Sam being a better man was pretty much hopeless. Then he turned and stirred a briskly bubbling pot. Porridge. Sam hated porridge. It smelled like it was scorching.

"She'll be staying for breakfast before she's on her way," Sam said, shamelessly vying for a change in menu. Buckie could—and often did—produce cuisine as good or better than five-star restaurants Sam had dined in.

"She grabbed a yogurt and an apple and said that was all she wanted."

It looked as if Buckie had made enough porridge to last a long, long time.

Sam told himself it was to appease Buckie and to get out of eating that porridge—nine days old just like the rhyme said, if the size of the pot was any indication—that he went in search of Shelby. But he knew that wasn't the whole truth.

Not even close.

It wasn't all about being a better man, either.

He found her sitting cross-legged in the very center of the old barn. She had opened both the front-and back-facing doors. She was facing the back view, the valley dazzling as the first rays of sun pierced the heavy morning mist that had settled over it.

He froze for a moment, watching the light spill around her, play with the curve of her neck, the roundness of her shoulders, the slender, straight line of her back. Her hair was wet and that turned it a shade darker, more golden.

He cleared his throat and she froze, then turned, a half-eaten apple in her hand.

Buckie had been right. Sam could see who she was in those amazing gold-green eyes.

"Don't get up," he said, when she scrambled to find her feet. She hesitated, then sank back down.

"Don't worry," she said, her voice tight, "I'm leaving. I'd be gone except I thought I should wait for the bears to get off the road. And say goodbye to Hannah."

Did she have to make him feel like more of a jerk by being thoughtful? Hannah would be upset if their visitor left without saying goodbye.

"Do you mind if I join you?"

She lifted a shoulder and he walked over to her. The stuffy suit from yesterday was gone. She was wearing black, form-fitting yoga pants and a sleeveless white tank top. Sneakers had replaced the impractical heels.

It was obvious from her ease at sitting on the hard concrete floor that she did yoga. That probably explained her getting into the tent in Hannah's room, too.

A bra strap, impossibly white, was visible on one shoulder. For some reason, it made his mouth go dry. She shot him a look as he lowered himself to the floor beside her, making a manly effort not to groan.

He noticed that the indescribably beautiful smell of a woman in the morning wafted off her.

She glanced at him. His efforts to hide his discomfort did not succeed, because she smiled, though it seemed reluctant.

He was not sure he was strong enough to handle the smile *and* the enchantment of the morning light caressing her.

"You're more used to sitting on a horse," she concluded.

"You're right. Plus, there are lots of old injuries."

"From what?"

"Like every young guy who grows up around here, I had to try my hand at rodeo."

"Oh my," she said, sounding way too impressed.

"It's like wrestling calves. Not romantic."

Why did he have to keep using that word around her?

"Anyway, I sucked," he said. "I'm lucky I'm not in a wheelchair. For a sport that's so dangerous, it's really underpaid."

*Get it over with*, he instructed himself firmly, *then go*.

"You were right about the animals," she said. At his look of puzzlement, she passed him her phone. "The deer come out in the morning."

He smiled when he saw she had captured a shot of four cow elk, their bellies round with unborn calves, looking up from the new, dew-encrusted grass that sprouted in front of the barn. Their gazes on her were alert and curious. They didn't look at all nervous, as if they, too, could see who she really was.

He passed her back the phone. Their hands touched. He could feel the jolt up to his shoulder.

"They're elk," he said. "Not deer."

"Oh! City slicker mistake." She studied her phone for a moment.

"I wanted to tell you I'm sorry," he said gruffly. "I overreacted last night."

"I understand how it must feel like the biggest job in the world to protect Hannah."

He was silent, not wanting her to know how her *seeing* that, how her easy forgiveness, touched him.

"I'm to blame, too," she said. "I shouldn't have come here after you said no."

# CHAPTER SEVEN

SAM RESISTED THE desire to agree with Shelby. She shouldn't have come here.

"I've held a lot of events," she went on, her voice low. "And in some pretty spectacular places. But from the moment I first saw this, I *felt* something. It's magnificent, but solid, too. It's like the past and the future are combined here. I felt as if this building was telling me what it wanted. It's even better up close. So many places disappoint when you see them for real, but not this one. It's better than anything I could have imagined."

She stopped. She blushed. She looked away from him. "I'm sorry. I'm gushing. You probably think I'm silly."

He was silent for a bit. He realized the silence was oddly comfortable between them, as if they had known each other longer than they actually had.

"My wife felt the same way about it," he said, reluctantly. "From the minute Beth first saw it, she started planning, *seeing* how it could be. She, too, had a vision of holding gatherings here. She thought of invitation-only events, with the best food, world-renowned musicians, celebrations of friends and family. She was eventually going to build a permanent kitchen in a separate building. She was a chef. Bethany Britannia."

"Oh my goodness. I watched her on television. I ate in her

restaurant in Paris once. It was sublime. I'm so sorry for your loss. And Hannah's."

Just words, but it felt, again, as if his fences were coming down. He, of all people, knew the danger of downed fences, but still, he engaged when he should have been disengaging.

"Yours, too," he said. "You told Hannah your mom died."

A shadow crossed the loveliness of her features.

"It was a long time ago, though I still feel I know exactly how Hannah feels. There's something about losing the person who loves you best of all that it's hard to heal from. Especially when you're young. I wasn't as young as Hannah though. I was ten."

Sam wanted to say he also loved Hannah best of all, but he knew, no matter what he did, it would never be the same as a mother's love.

"It was like my dad tried to shield me from life, after that. To make up for it, somehow."

He could hear affection in her voice for her father's efforts. And he could also hear that it had been a failure. Which he filed in the *notes to self* compartment of his brain.

"What happened to your mom?"

She hesitated. "It was a car accident. Even as shielded as I was, there were whispers around it. I think there's lots I don't know. And here I am, eighteen years later, still not wanting to find out."

"I'm sorry," he said, and found he meant it from the bottom of his heart.

"What happened to Bethany?" she asked softly.

He never talked about it. Part of the reason he had retreated to the ranch was because he didn't have to. This was a society of men, and they did not talk about their broken hearts.

And yet it suddenly felt compelling to do just that.

"After Hannah was born, Beth realized something wasn't quite right. She didn't want to tell me, because I'd lost both my parents that year. She—we—waited too long. By the time she got a diagnosis, it was too late."

"Oh, Sam." Somehow, her hand was on his arm.

Just as he could see who she was in her eyes, he could feel who she was in that touch. Stronger than she looked. Compassionate. Empathetic.

"So much loss," she said. The words were simple. And yet so heartfelt.

"What are the dates for the birthday party?" he said, sliding his arm out from under her hand before he was tempted to lay his head on her shoulder and drink in the comfort she offered.

Shelby tried not to flinch when Sam pulled his arm away from her touch.

Suddenly, what she had wanted most—this barn as a venue—faded. She could feel the danger in the air.

Not just in how she had felt when he sat beside her, his long legs stretched out in front of him, not just how she had felt when she touched his arm, but how she felt now.

As if she wanted to be with him.

To tell him things. *I don't really remember my mom. How do I know if she loved me best of all?* It had actually felt strange saying that, that her mother loved her best of all, as if it was a lie.

Something snaked along her spine, a realization that the secrets around her mother—the things she could not remember, which was pretty much everything before age ten—was what kept her from wanting the things other people wanted: families, children, commitment. She shivered.

Why was being here, just for this short time, making her feel as if the past she had managed to outrun was catching up with her?

All kinds of danger lurked here.

And maybe the worst one was the desire to be needed. Whatever she had felt in her childhood, it had not been that. She had not felt, even after the death of her mother, needed. Isn't that what most families did? Leaned on each other, needed each other, to get through bad times?

Really, the first time she'd ever felt needed was when she had put together the wedding for Kylie. And her business had made her feel that way ever since.

But compared to the needs of Sam and Hannah, it felt superficial.

She wanted to help him heal. To be the one who made him laugh again, and live again. To help Hannah. It felt as if that desire to tangle her life with theirs was intensifying. As if, in some deep way, the part of herself she had lost when she was ten lay in this direction.

And this direction only.

On the other hand, wouldn't she be the worst possible person to think she had anything to offer anyone else? Her whole life had been an avoidance strategy.

Better to get away from the temptation to leave her map for life behind and take an unmarked road. Better to get away from Sam Waters and his adorable daughter, and the enchantment of this ranch and especially this building they now sat in.

She had a plan for life—since aversion to commitment had been solidly cemented into place even before her last fiasco with Keith—Eventually was going to be her whole life. It was going to fill every need in her, satisfy her, give her a sense of belonging and accomplishment and fulfillment.

A commitment to a business, and all her plans for it and her life, felt so safe.

Sam Waters was the kind of man who left plans like that in a burnt pile of smoldering ash.

"I was planning his party for the first weekend in September. But it's okay," she said, inserting a breezy note into her voice, "I decided last night I'd find a different place for it."

Juggling her half-eaten apple, she scrolled through her phone. "I understand the concern you voiced about disruptions to the ranch routine. I imagine you would have felt those were more manageable if it was your wife doing the event. I can also understand your reluctance to let someone outside of the community use it when it meant so much to Bethany."

Not to mention she would now feel an added pressure to do Bethany Britannia's vision justice.

She found the photo she was looking for and held it up for him to see. "It's a vineyard. Tuscany."

He regarded it, his brow furrowed.

"Buckie told me you wouldn't rent from me now if your life depended on it."

Her life—or at least her life as she knew it—did feel as if it depended on *not* going any further down this road. She scrambled to her feet—before he got up first and offered her his hand, again—and dusted herself off.

He got to his feet, too. He winced. "I might need to take a few yoga lessons from you."

*Wouldn't that be fun?* she thought.

Without the high heels, Sam was taller than her by a head. So broad across the shoulders and narrow at the waist. He looked incredible this morning in a pressed white shirt, his legs long and lean in dark denim jeans. There was something about his polished cowboy boots that was undeniably sexy.

She had the entirely inappropriate thought that she wanted to step not away from him, but into him. That she wanted to wrap her arms around his waist and lay her head on his chest, and tell him all those thoughts she had just had.

That she would help him through it.

That he would help her.

That together they would help each other.

*That she did not really remember her mother, let alone whether she had loved her best of all.*

*Stop*, Shelby ordered herself, with desperate firmness. *Just stop indulging these fantasies. That one man and one woman could take on the world.*

Instead of stepping into him, she stuck out her hand, all business. She couldn't let him see how frazzled she felt. She realized she still had a half-eaten apple in her hand. She looked around and then stuffed it in her back pocket.

"Nice to meet you," she said formally, offering her apple-sticky hand. "I'll go say goodbye to Hannah and be on my way. Hopefully the elk are off the road. And the bears. Imagine the damage one of them could do to my little toy car."

She was aware she was babbling. Trying to outrun something. He wasn't taking her hand. No doubt because of the apple, not because of the electricity. Maybe she was the only one who felt it. Maybe she was like this woman who hadn't been touched in so long that a bump of hands practically made her swoon with longing… She was babbling inwardly now.

"What if I didn't rent it to you?"

"Sorry?" She let her hand awkwardly drop away.

"Shelby, what if you stayed?"

It was unfair how her name sounded coming off Sam's lips, she thought. It was unfair how his words stirred some deep longing in her.

To just see.

Where it could go. Where the unexpected could take her.

"You know," she said, noting her voice sounded high and squeaky, "I really can't. I have a business to run. We're putting finishing details on a debutante ball right now. Who knew that such a thing still existed? I've secured a refurbished mansion in Mississippi for it."

She let her voice drift away. Babble. Babble. Babble. She had *never* been a babbler.

For a moment he didn't say anything, and she jumped into the silence. "Besides, I didn't pack for a stay. I have no clothes to wear. Look what I'm wearing today. My gym clothes."

His eyes flicked to her, moved away, but not before she saw she was not the only one feeling the electricity.

All the more reason for him to jump on her excuses.

Though she wished he would jump on—where had that thought come from? She didn't just need to get out of here, she needed to get out of here at top speed. She needed to act as if she was the fox and the hounds were at her heels.

Sam lifted his shoulder, as if *no clothes* was nothing. She noticed, again, how broad it was. She wondered how no clothes would look on him.

She hoped she wasn't blushing.

"It's quite pressing that I leave," she squeaked. Pressing. As in them, pressing together, the hard lines of his body up against hers, with no space between them.

"I was hoping we could negotiate a trade," he said, oblivious, thankfully, to the wayward ways of her mind.

"A trade?" Again, her voice had that odd squeaky note to it, and her mind was negotiating all kinds of trades. Mostly involving lips. She tried to think if she had ever had this visceral a reaction to a man. Her mind was blank.

"If you could help me with Hannah for the next ten days, until calving is over, and I have some business trips out of the way—that would be the Sunday following the grad event— I'll give you the barn to use for your father's birthday."

He'd give her the barn! It was a gift! Why did she feel compelled to talk him out of it?

"It's probably just not a good idea. I mean, I have friends with kids, but other than that my experience is zero. You need a qualified nanny."

"I've tried the experts. All their so-called experience didn't seem worth a whit. I think you could muddle through."

"You want to trust your child to a complete amateur?"

"Everybody's a complete amateur at kids," he said softly. "You should see how it feels the first time you hold your baby."

The stab of longing Shelby—the one who had never wanted children—felt was nothing short of shocking.

It was another clue of what needed to be done.

*Say no.*

Of course she had to say no! A week? With this man? And his precious daughter? It could change the well-planned course of her whole life! It could change her belief system! She had just felt a stab of longing to hold a baby! If that wasn't a warning, what was?

But the barn itself seemed to be whispering to her. As was the mist-shrouded valley beyond it. As she watched, before her very eyes, the sun came out with force and the mist burned off.

And she could see so clearly.

"Hannah likes you," he said softly.

Everything in her weakened.

Why not say yes?

She had Marcus now, her assistant. The details for the debutante ball were nearly completed. She had a phone. She could still be there, virtually.

She also had to admit that the ball seemed suddenly frivolous in light of Sam's proposal.

Proposal. The whole English language now seemed rife with double meanings. But Shelby was so aware it wasn't really Sam's proposal—suggestion—that she was saying yes or no to.

It was the absolute adventure of life, with all its twists and turns and its propensity for the unexpected, its seeming delight in leading an unsuspecting traveler down dark paths and through unknown woods, where everything you thought you knew would be challenged and where your destination could equally hold danger or enchantment.

It was the type of decision someone should take time to think about. Time in absolute solitude, if possible, like a monk deciding whether or not to take a final vow. It was not a decision that should be made in such close proximity of an unfairly attractive man, in a barn that was putting a spell on her. Or maybe that was the unfairly attractive man.

But *I need time to consider my options* is not what came out of Shelby's mouth. Not even close.

"Yes," she whispered.

# CHAPTER EIGHT

SAM'S SMILE WAS the very same as the mist burning off the valley—as if something that had always been there was suddenly revealed—and it was so beautiful it was nearly soul shattering.

They walked back to the house together, Shelby aware of the easy grace and strength in his stride, how much taller than her he was, how one misstep could cause their shoulders to touch. She was aware of how the morning suddenly had a shine to it that could not be fully explained by the burning off of the mist or the surprising strength of the spring sunshine.

"You can toss what's left of that apple," he said.

"I was going to wait for a garbage can." She made a note to herself: he noticed everything.

"Those *deer* you saw this morning would like it. I should probably show you a picture of a bear so you don't think it's the cutest big dog you ever saw."

She smiled. He was *teasing* her. And she didn't need any more coaxing than that. She fished the chewed core out of her pocket and dropped it on the ground.

As they entered the kitchen, she saw Hannah was at the table, her hair adorably sleep tangled. She was in pink, fuzzy pajamas with feet in them that could almost make someone who had sworn off children of her own reconsider.

*Why, exactly, was she so adverse?*

"Daddy," Hanna cried, as if Sam was returning from the wars. She got up and flew to him. He hoisted her up with ease, planted a kiss on her nose and set her down, trying to hide the obvious consternation her tangled hair was causing him.

It was clear that Sam loved Hannah best of all, and that the little girl was completely secure in that knowledge.

Boswell had never been demonstrative. There had been an awkward hug every now and then, a kiss on the cheek, a pat on the shoulder.

Never this, that she could remember, an unspoken action that said *you are my world, my reason.*

She could not remember her mother being demonstrative, either. Wasn't that the sort of thing you should remember?

There was that voice again, from the shadows, a little girl, her past self, watching her carefully. Had Shelby been her mother's world? Her reason?

The question—the fact she was asking herself questions like this, and even reconsidering her beliefs about having children—was disturbing. What had she let herself in for?

"Shelby's going to stay for a bit," Sam said. "Just to help out around here until calving is done and the grad event is over."

There was, wisely, no mention of that help being Hannah related.

Shelby had the odd feeling the announcement about her staying might have actually been for Buckie's benefit, as much as Hannah's, because a look she couldn't quite decipher passed between the two men.

"What's for breakfast?" Sam asked, casually.

"Buckie is making us mouse pancakes," Hannah said.

"Mouse pancakes?" Shelby teased, shaking off her own shadows. "I cannot eat a mouse! And I don't care if it does make me a city girl!"

Hannah chortled. "No, the pancakes aren't made out of mice! Ugh! They're shaped like Mickey!"

As Shelby watched, the cook took a big pot off the stove and scraped its mushy contents into a pail.

"What's that?" she asked.

"Just mash for an orphaned calf," Buckie said, but he shot Sam a look.

"Oh! An orphan!" Hannah said happily. Apparently this was ranch life, because the child did not seem the least saddened by the circumstances that brought about an orphan. "Can we go see it? Shelby, do you want to?"

"Sure, if that's what you'd like to do."

It occurred to her that Hannah had accepted that Shelby's role would be childcare.

Shelby shot Sam a look. The relief on his face was palpable. He did a gesture with his hands, which she took to mean *can you manage the hair?* She nodded, and his look of pleasure made her feel as if she would do anything for him.

She was getting in deeper and deeper.

It was because he was a daddy, not because he was just about the most attractive man she had ever laid eyes on.

"I'll have regular pancakes," Sam said, sitting down at the head of the table. Shelby took the seat beside Hannah.

But when Buckie put a big platter of pancakes on the table, they were all mouse pancakes. Even though she had already eaten, Shelby couldn't resist taking one of them.

It took up her whole plate, with its two smaller round circles for ears and one large one for the face.

Hannah showed her how to make the features come alive with chocolate wafer cookies for eyes and a string of liquorice for the mouth.

"Isn't this a special occasion kind of breakfast?" Sam asked.

"It is a special occasion," Buckie said. "We got company."

Sam considered that for a moment, then cast her a glance. Then to Hannah's—and Shelby's—delight, he surrendered. He took the cookies and carefully added eyes to his pancake. Not satisfied with that, he made liquorice eyelashes.

"Ha," Buckie said, wandering over to regard Sam's handiwork. "This work of art from the person who wanted regular pancakes."

*And this enjoyment*, Shelby added silently, putting a mouth on her mouse, *from the person who didn't want children*.

When they finished decorating mouse faces on their pancakes, they all admired each other's masterpieces. And then Hannah picked up a spray can of whipped cream from the middle of the table and obliterated the face her father had made on his pancake.

"Take that," she said, gleeful.

"Oh, yeah?" Sam replied. He grabbed the whipped cream from her, but then turned to Shelby and the face on her mouse pancake disappeared under a blob of cream. "Take that."

Hannah chortled with absolute and fiendish delight.

Spitting with equal parts of indignation and laughter, Shelby tried to grab the whipped cream from him, but he was too fast. He leaned away from her. She leaned harder, but he got up from his chair and moved away, holding it high. She had no choice but to follow him.

"You wrecked my mouse!"

"It's not personal," he said. "It's a tradition!"

Shelby backed him into a corner, and then made a leap to grab the whipped cream. Just for a moment, the movement pressed her full against him. It was just as she'd imagined it when that word *pressed* had crossed her lips earlier. Sam Waters was all heat and hard lines and male strength. At the moment, the fact that he was a daddy was the least important thing about him.

It had felt so easy to fall toward the comfortable domestic routines of the household. But now, she could feel an underlying tension, a sizzle that had nothing to do with mouse pancakes! Which was more dangerous to her commitment to noncommitment?

He stared at her, and his grip loosened on the whipped cream spray can. She grabbed it, wanting to make the moment light, to disperse the intensity of it.

She aimed the spray can straight at him, the way Hannah had aimed the doll at her yesterday.

He put his arms up in surrender. She giggled. As soon as she did, he dropped his arms and caught the wrist of her hand that was holding the whipped cream.

She pressed down the nozzle. Her shot went wild and whipped cream squirted onto his cheek. For a moment, the whole kitchen went very still at her obviously crossed boundary. He let go of her arm.

"Take that," Shelby said, and Buckie and Hannah roared with laughter.

Sam wiped the blob from his cheek and licked it off his fingers. Way too slowly. He gave her a look that somehow seemed loaded and very personal, indeed. It felt, suddenly, as if the two of them were all alone in the kitchen.

But the sizzling look was only a distraction because, just as his fake surrender had been, quick as lightning, he took the spray can from her. For a moment, he seemed to consider his options.

His gaze let her know what he could do with the whipped cream. And maybe wanted to. But he turned on his heel, went back to the table and squirted cream on Hannah's mouse pancake.

"Take that," he said. Then, he grabbed his own pancake off his plate, folded it in half like a sandwich, and took a bite. With his other hand he took his cowboy hat off the back door, grabbed a briefcase, and was gone, the screen door snapping quietly shut behind him.

"A briefcase?" Shelby said.

Buckie snorted. "You didn't think those was going-to-work-cows clothes, did you?"

Actually, she had, but now that she thought about it, that crisp white shirt and the polished boots probably were not cowhand clothes.

Buckie sat down with them, and regarded the mess of whipped cream nearly obliterating the pancakes.

"It's our tradition," Buckie explained to Shelby. "We decorate the pancakes then we whip cream-bomb each other's. We've done that since he was a little boy."

The big cook's features softened, remembering Sam as a child. Shelby could see that though this house had been hit by way too much tragedy, the love was so strong here. It was holding them up, whether they knew it or not.

Shelby had had so many spectacular moments in her life that she probably could not count them all. She'd had many moments that other people could not even imagine. She'd swooped down slopes on skis, snorkeled the most famous reef in the world, ridden in some of the world's rarest and most fancy sports cars.

She had dined at five-star restaurants, been to charity balls in palaces, been to movie openings with the actors who had starred in them.

How could this moment of pancakes and laughter and flying whipped cream—being part of a silly family tradition—feel as if it was the best one she had ever had?

In Shelby's world, had there been love to hold her up when she needed it? Of course, her father had loved her, in his awkward way. Of that, she had no doubt.

But she was aware a door that she kept tightly closed had opened a crack. Where had her mother been when she needed love? Why was that whole part of her life shrouded in darkness?

She wrestled that door firmly shut.

And thought instead about the layer of tension between her and Sam. That definitely fell outside of the perimeters of family tradition, and yet it was part of the light that infused the day and the moment.

What had Sam felt when they had made full-on body contact like that?

Something.

Otherwise, why would he have left so suddenly?

"Well, well, well," Buckie said enigmatically. "It's good to see the boss laugh."

That made her feel guilty for telling Sam joy was a topic he knew nothing about.

Buckie looked at Shelby for a moment, then turned away, whistling tunelessly, and trying to hide his smile.

"Do you know how to make braids?" Hannah asked, as they finished up their absolutely delicious pancakes.

She felt a little smug. Sam had indicated hair was an issue, but Hannah was already trusting her with it!

Even though she was not a kid person, she had been a kid once!

"I used to have a doll, a little bigger than the one you shot me with yesterday, and that was my favorite thing to do with her. Should we try it on you? Do you think you'd like a single plait down your back, or two braids?"

"On me?" Hannah said, wide-eyed. "I was thinking of Rascal!"

Buckie snorted with enjoyment over Hannah's misunderstanding.

"On you," Shelby confirmed.

Hannah considered this. "I guess we could try," she said, but without much enthusiasm.

"Girl things," Buckie muttered with approval, waving off Shelby's offer to help clean up the kitchen.

Hannah's bedroom was fit for a princess. Aside from the delightful tent for reading, it had a twin bed with a pink canopy, a window seat filled with plump pillows and stuffed toys, and shelves and shelves of books.

Shelby was willing to bet Sam hadn't had much to do with the design and planning of the room.

The room had an adjoining bathroom and Shelby convinced Hannah—with lots of bubbles—to get into the tub. She gave the mop of hair a thorough washing, and added lots of conditioner to detangle it.

She wondered why she had avoided children so scrupulously all her adult life. There was something very lovely about their trust and innocence.

Hannah's thick, curly hair was gorgeous. And an utter mess. It had been surface controlled for a long time.

"Let's put on some music," Shelby said, after Hannah was out of the tub and wrapped in a big white towel. She got out her phone. "Who do you like?"

Hannah named the pre-teen popstar of the day, and Shelby found it on her phone, and they sang along as she worked her way through that glorious head of hair. When she was done, a single thick plait fell over Hannah's shoulder, tied with a ribbon Shelby had stolen from one of the teddy bears on the window seat.

Together, they picked out an outfit for the day: bright yellow shorts with a top covered in drawings of lemon drops. Rather than fighting her, Hannah seemed to be lapping up the feminine input. Then they went to visit the orphaned calf and both were allowed to feed it milk from a bottle.

Again, she was aware the experience was enriched by sharing it with a child.

"He's very greedy," Shelby said, when it took all her

strength to keep the calf from pulling the bottle right out of her hands with his desperate sucking.

Rascal was in a stall in the same barn as the calf, nickering softly at them.

"He wants a cookie," Hannah said.

They fed the tiny horse—who was at least as greedy as the calf—cookies and then brushed him.

"Can you show me how to braid?"

Shelby showed Hannah and soon the pony was sporting a clumsy new hairstyle that he seemed—if the shaking of his head was any indication—less thrilled with than his owner was.

Shelby was shocked by how the morning had evaporated. After the whipped cream incident, she had felt a tension—she didn't want to call it hopefulness—about seeing Sam, but she had not seen him, and eventually the tension of that expectation dissipated.

She reminded herself this experience had a ten-day time limit, and so she gave herself over to exploring this new world of the ranch through the wondrous eyes of a child.

Hannah delighted in everything. Not just big things like the orphaned calf and her pony, but ladybugs and new leaves and the color of dandelions, which she demonstrated made a really nice stain.

"Look! I can use dandelion juice to make my hands match my shorts!"

"Dandelion juice and mouse pancakes. I'm not sure about life on the ranch."

"I won't make you drink any if you let me dye your hands, too."

What choice did a person have, really, when it was put like that? And so, she let Hannah dye her hands, the little girl's tongue caught between her teeth with her intensity of focus.

Shelby felt a stirring of incredible wonder as Hannah

stepped back from her work, and Shelby looked at her yellow-dyed hands. It felt as if she was having childhood experiences that she had missed.

*Had she missed them, or were they part of what she could not remember?*

# CHAPTER NINE

SHELBY DECIDED NOT to spoil these delight-infused moments being given to her with too much contemplations.

After they had finally managed to scrub the dandelion stains off their hands, she and Hannah sat down with Alvin on the wraparound porch to a delicious lunch of thick roast beef sandwiches on homemade bread.

"Oh, look, dandelion juice!" Hannah declared of the hand-squeezed lemonade. She laughed fiendishly when Shelby looked at her glass with pretend trepidation. "And we're having lizard juice with supper, aren't we, Buckie?"

"Fresh out of lizards," Buckie said. "Maybe tomorrow. By the way, Hannah, your hair looks really pur-ty." The little girl preened.

Again, Shelby felt the love that surrounded Hannah.

In Shelby's various households, there was a preference, unspoken as it might have been, that the staff remain as invisible as possible. She liked that Alvin seemed to be more a member of the family than an employee. Shelby noticed neither the cook nor Hannah seemed to be expecting Sam.

After lunch, Hannah fetched a storybook—they seemed to be all over the house, which Shelby loved—and they curled up together on one of the deeply cushioned rattan sofas on the deck.

The little girl snuggled deeper into her as she read.

Shelby had had a nanny who liked to read to her, but didn't recall Boswell ever reading to her. Had her mother? Surely you would remember sweet moments like the one she was experiencing right now, forever. So, why didn't she?

Despite a ceiling fan lazily moving air around the porch, it was unseasonably warm. A fat bee buzzed by. Hannah's head drooped, and then she slumped against Shelby's midriff. A gentle snore came from her, and then saliva pooled on Shelby's top.

She felt her own eyes grow heavy as contentment enveloped her like the hug of a weighted blanket.

She woke up when Hannah stirred against her. Her tank top and her yoga pants were sticking to her. Hannah looked flushed. Her hair was stuck to the sides of her face.

"I'm hot," Hannah said, plucking at her yellow shorts. And then she brightened. "We should play water blaster."

*We.*

How quickly that had happened. The child's quick trust and their comfort with each other, seeing the world through Hannah's eyes.

"What's water blaster?"

"I have these blasters that you fill with water and you squirt each other. And you run through the sprinkler at the same time. You get *really* soaked."

"That sounds much more amazing than only getting partly soaked, but I don't have a bathing suit."

"You don't need a real bathing suit. Just a pair of shorts and a top."

"I don't have shorts, either."

"If I find you a pair, will you play water blaster with me?"

Really, given the heat of the day, the clinging yoga pants, and Hannah's sweet pleading, it was too tempting to resist. "All right."

Hannah disappeared into the house and Shelby looked over the landscape and contemplated the surprise life had given her. It had not only brought her to the ranch, but had also given her the gift of a perfect day.

Well, except for shadowy memories and questions.

Still, how long had it been since she had experienced a day that was not planned? How long since she had a go-with-the-flow kind of day?

Hannah came back after a while, in a one-piece bathing suit. She held two large purple contraptions that looked as if they would hold a gallon of water each, and a pair of shorts.

"Here," she said happily, handing the shorts to Shelby.

It wasn't until she was holding them that she realized Hannah had handed her a pair of men's boxers. Obviously way too small to be the cook's.

Which meant they could only belong to one person, which also answered the age-old question: boxers or briefs?

She realized—not that she had thought about it, but that if she had—this was not quite what she would have expected for Sam's choice of undies.

She would not have expected playful. And yet, there it was. Bright pink shorts with green fish all over them.

"Where did you get these?"

"Daddy's drawer. I knew my shorts wouldn't fit you. Buckie helped me pick them for him for Christmas."

So, they weren't Sam's style. A novelty item. He had probably never worn them. Which somehow made the fact she was touching them less intense.

"I'm not sure I should wear your daddy's shorts." Actually, she was pretty sure she should not.

"Pleeaassee," Hannah said, leaning into her and blinking adorably.

How could she resist that? Or the pull of playing in a sprinkler on a hot afternoon? It was such an ordinary thing to do, and yet Shelby was so aware it was among the many ordinary childhood things she had never done—or at least, couldn't remember doing.

She went into a bathroom off the porch, pulled off the yoga pants and put on the shorts. She left on the tank top.

She was pretty sure she looked like a tourist in Hawaii, baggy-bottomed and white-legged.

But it didn't matter one little bit.

When she emerged from the bathroom, Hannah handed her a "weapon" and led her onto the rolling expanse of lush green grass in the backyard. Already squealing with anticipation, she went and turned on the tap that was connected to the hose.

A fan of water shot out of the sprinkler, which began oscillating back and forth.

"Look, rainbows," Hannah shouted excitedly, abandoning the water blasters. "Pretend we're at a horse show, Shelby, and we're jumping rainbows."

Hannah led, galloping through the lines of water. Shelby should have known from Hannah's shout just how cold the water was going to be, but it took her by surprise. She howled at the shock of the cold.

But then couldn't wait to turn around and do it again.

Soon, they had the water blasters filled up and were romping around the yard, in and out of the sprinkler, and squirting each other.

Shelby was not sure she had laughed so hard in her entire life.

Infused with their laughter and squeals of delight, an ordinary hot afternoon became a magical place of imaginary horses leaping over rainbows.

It became the childhood Shelby had never had.

Sam could hear them before he saw them. It was incredibly hot given that they were still days away from summer. His shirt was sticking to him after just a short walk up from the helicopter pad.

He'd had a good day in Calgary, signing off on a deal that had been in the works for months. He had been aware, though, of feeling preoccupied. Both eager and reluctant to head back to the ranch.

And this was the reason right here.

He could have avoided the commotion in the backyard and gone through the front door, but somehow he was drawn to the screams of laughter like a magnet drawn to steel.

He paused when he came around the corner of the house and saw them in the backyard.

Hannah and Shelby were totally unaware of him as they chased each other, water blasters in hand and shrieking with laughter, through the sprinkler.

His daughter had on her bathing suit. He noticed her hair was in a thick braid. But even the new, tidy hairstyle was totally eclipsed by her radiance, by the happiness pouring off of her. It had been a long time since he had seen Hannah give herself over to just having fun.

How had Shelby so effortlessly accomplished what he had not been able to?

His attention shifted.

If he was expecting to impersonally analyze Shelby's reason for success, he was in for a shock.

Sam felt his mouth go dry. Since the whipped cream incident this morning, he should have been prepared for the fact that cool-headed analysis had already gone out the window. Hadn't he already been having an awful time not feeling preoccupied with the new nanny, who was not a nanny at all?

Now, he could see there were some things that overrode a man's ability to be rational.

Shelby had given herself over to water play. As he watched, she gave her soaked head a shake and droplets flew off that honey-colored hair and cascaded around her. Water sluiced down her face. Her shout of pure enjoyment shivered along his spine.

Unlike his daughter, she was not wearing a swimsuit. She was barefooted and long legged, like that filly that had been born this morning.

As he squinted at her, Sam was pretty sure she was wearing a pair of his underwear. Which seemed way too personal!

His underwear was plastered to her. So was that little white tank top she'd been wearing this morning.

It left very little to the imagination. The litheness of her body was completely outlined. The fabric of the tank top had become transparent. Underneath it was the lacy bra that he had glimpsed the white strap of earlier.

He felt, suddenly and embarrassingly, like a peeper. He turned to slide away and go in through the front door, after all.

"Daddy!"

Too late.

And here Hannah came, running on chubby legs, her braid flying behind her, her water blaster poised for attack.

Again, he was totally entranced by the look on Hannah's features. A man lived to see a look like that on his child's face.

"Take that," she said with glee, unloading most of the contents of the water blaster on him. She cackled happily. Shockingly, Shelby-in-his-shorts joined his daughter in the attack, racing up to him and blasting his face. Deliberately. Not a slip, like with that whipped cream this morning.

He held up his arms, but Shelby took aim at his hat, and knocked it right off his head.

"Hey! Didn't anyone tell you a man's cowboy hat is sacred?"

"I must have missed that part of the introductory tour."

Did that mean he should have given her a tour, instead of running out of the kitchen this morning as if his hair was on fire? It seemed it might have been the reasonable thing to do. He'd been a reasonable man his whole life.

Why did it suddenly feel as if reason was going out the window?

Hannah shot from below, and Shelby unloaded a stream of water down his shirt.

The cold water felt shockingly good. Reason be damned, retreat was out of the question. He pushed through his attackers, bent down and picked up the sprinkler. Armed, holding the sprinkler in front of him like a sword, he whirled back on them. They both ran.

He caught Hannah first, and held her under the spray while she wriggled and shrieked. His other attacker didn't let up the whole time, shooting him with her water blaster, going for the back of his neck, drenching his shoulders. He let go of Hannah, who collapsed on the ground laughing and turned on her.

Shelby darted out of his way. He ran after her, sprinkler in hand. Running was awkward in cowboy boots and it was slippery. She could have easily outrun him, except she was the one who lost her footing on the water-slick grass.

She went down, sliding through the grass, water blaster held out in front of her. She hit his hat at crushing speed. She was laughing so hard—especially after she hit the hat—that Sam was not sure how she could breathe.

"Don't," she begged, rolling over on her stomach, even as she continued to fire away at him with her water blaster. He was not sure why she would resist the sprinkler. It was not as if she could get any wetter, or any more see-through. He caught her ankle and held it. She tried to pull it away, but he directed the full force of the sprinkler at her.

The ribbons of water hit her and sluiced off of her. When

she realized escape was futile, she gave herself over to it, arching her back, and opening her mouth to taste the droplets.

He was pretty sure he'd seen a movie with a scene like this.

It was much more erotic in person.

Some shocking wanting shot through him. He was not sure if she had planned this, but he dropped the sprinkler as if it had burned him. Hannah, thankfully totally unaware of his very adult reaction to Shelby, had been waiting for the opportunity. She swooped in and grabbed the abandoned sprinkler, giving chase around the yard.

Shelby didn't rejoin the game. Instead, she lay in the patch of sunlight, panting, her knees up, her arms thrown open.

Unaware she was a goddess. Or maybe she *was* aware, and deliberately tormenting him.

He fervently wished he could take back his own awareness.

"Ice pops," Buckie shouted from the porch. "Raspberry."

Hannah dropped the sprinkler and ran to the cook, who handed her a towel and the flavored ice-on-a-stick, before he went back in the house. Hannah wrapped herself in the towel and went around the side porch to sit down.

It made Sam feel oddly alone with Shelby who, with sensual grace born of what he assumed were long hours of yoga, unfolded herself and got up.

How was she making those shorts look like that? Shouldn't he address the fact he didn't want her wearing his shorts, and he certainly didn't want her rummaging around in his drawers. Had she gone in his drawers?

Gone in them. She *was* in his drawers.

"Hannah lent me your shorts," she said, adding mind reading to her list of superpowers. "I hope you don't mind."

He *did* mind. Sam was unfortunately aware it would be churlish to say so. She'd already told him she didn't have any clothes here with her.

What was most important? She had made his daughter happy!

He was aware that his jeans were heavy and soaked and uncomfortable. His shirt, too. He was aware he certainly did not want to see Shelby's mouth closing around an ice pop, her luscious pink tongue darting out to catch drips.

He beat her to the porch, went in and let the door snap behind him. The house felt cool and dark, a sanctuary for rational people. He brushed by Buckie.

"You going to go through the house drippin' like that?" the cook asked, disapprovingly.

"No," Sam snapped, then added in an undertone, "I'm going to strip off right here in front of the whole world so I don't get puddles on your damned floor."

"Ain't nobody here but you and me," Buckie said mildly.

The man was being deliberately obtuse. "Somebody could be coming in for her damned ice pop."

Buckie backed up, eyes wide, hands up. "Hey, no need to get mad."

"I'm not mad."

No, he wasn't mad, but there was no denying the fire that was burning.

"Huh," Buckie said skeptically.

"Ice pops?" Sam said. Since Buckie thought he was mad anyway, he might as well air all his grievances.

"What's wrong with ice pops?" Buckie asked, all innocence.

They both turned as Shelby approached. They could see her through the screen door, coming up the steps. She was wringing out her wet hair.

*Watching her eat an ice pop would be X-rated*, Sam thought.

Buckie gave him a smirk. Another damned mind reader

on the property! With one final glare, Sam moved by him, dripping water the whole way.

Some more cold water was in order. *Tout de suite.* Not that knowing the odd French phrase made him a class act, as Buckie had so helpfully pointed out.

# CHAPTER TEN

SAM TOOK A LONG, cold shower and a miss on dinner. He was pretty sure Buckie would be having a good smirk over that, too.

As far as Shelby was concerned, Sam considered avoidance to be as good a strategy as any. In fact, four days later, like a prisoner marking his time, he found a pen and got ready to put one more highly satisfied X through a day on his calendar. He'd managed to find business away from the ranch for most of those days.

He had one last meeting in Calgary tomorrow, so that would be five down, five to go.

If his daughter had noticed he was leaving early and coming home late, she hadn't complained about it. Which, okay, hurt a bit, but Hannah knew the realities of ranch life. There had been lots of times before now she'd had to hang out in the kitchen with Buckie because the ranch—or one of his other businesses—needed attention.

The trade-off for not being missed was well worth it. From a distance, Sam made note of Hannah and Shelby, playing dress-up, building a house out of sticks in the wooded area behind the house, and having extravagant tea parties there. They read stories and drew pictures and did things with each other's hair. They were being girls.

Their laughter, their voices formed a backdrop to his days.

He couldn't help but notice that Shelby was playful, like a big kid, which was the only safe way to think about her. Her makeshift wardrobe accentuated that. Buckie had found a few pairs of small jeans somewhere, which she had to wear rolled up. The men's shirts she had to knot at the waist to keep them from going down to her knees.

The look, thankfully, was more Huck Finn than sexy farm-girl.

The heat was holding so there was, of course, the daily sprinkler escapade. He had made it a point not to join in, but word of the water fun had gone through the barn like wild-fire. Sam had to forbid the hands from finding excuses to go up to the house in the heat of the day.

He had just finished the *X* when his phone pinged. Sam looked down at the message. It was an invitation for Han-nah to have a playdate at the neighbor's. He glanced at his watch. Was she still up?

He opened his door a crack and listened to the sounds coming from the bedroom down the hall. Shelby was still with her. He could hear them laughing.

He looked at the message again. Really, he should ask Han-nah what she wanted to do. A playdate was a big deal when the nearest child Hannah's age lived twenty-five kilometers away. On the other hand, Shelby was with her. Maybe he should just make the decision.

He contemplated that. Avoidance was a fine strategy, but he was acting like a teenage boy who was scared of getting a hard-on in the presence of his crush.

*Crush?*

Okay, he had been watching her from afar, but *crush* was a little strong. This was simply what too much isolation did to a man. Too much avoidance.

Was he really at a point where he would put his Shelby-avoidance strategy ahead of Hannah's well-being? He literally needed to take the bull by the horns. Especially if he was that bull!

He took a deep breath. Tucked in his shirt. Ran a hand through his hair. Had a quick look in the mirror. Just like that teenage boy about to meet his crush.

"You're pathetic," he muttered to himself. Still, he felt like a warrior heading to battle as he marched down the hall.

He paused at the closed door of Hannah's room. He could hear them in there. Shelby was singing "Old MacDonald." She was at the pig part.

"With a—*snort snort*—here…" No wonder Hannah was laughing!

Did he knock? It was *his* house! He took a deep breath, and opened the door. They were on Hannah's bed, Shelby sitting cross-legged on the edge of it, and Hannah kneeling behind her.

Hannah was braiding Shelby's hair.

They were both in their pajamas. There was nothing remotely sexy about Shelby's attire, pink cotton drawstring pants, and a tank top not unlike the one she had worn the other day in the sprinkler. Except maybe this one was a little thinner.

If she got wet in that top, he was pretty sure he wouldn't see a bra underneath it. It was obvious she didn't have on any underwear.

The teenage boy in him clamored.

"Here an *oink*, there an *oink*, everywhere an *oink-oink*—" She suddenly realized they were no longer alone. She stopped, turned her head to look at him, and blushed.

Her hair was falling out of the clumsy braid, curling around the sun-kissed delicacy of her face. He'd forgotten—or had been trying to forget—those eyes. Brown, but so generously flecked with green and gold that just to say brown seemed like a crime of inadequate use of the language.

He saw, despite the laughter, the depth in her, layers. And shadows, too.

"Don't stop for me," he said, and hoped his voice wasn't a tiny bit hoarse, though he was sure it was. "That's a mighty fine *oink* you got there."

He swore to himself. Of all the things he could have said, had he just told Shelby Kane that she did a mighty fine *oink*?

He told the clamoring inner boy that it was just as he had been telling himself all week.

Shelby Kane was like a big kid.

The inner teen wasn't buying it.

"Isn't it?" Hannah said. "Daddy, you should hear her do a duck. Shelby, do your duck for Daddy."

"Um, not right now," she said, embarrassed.

"Daddy. Come look at what I'm doing."

*I can see from here, thank you.* No sense letting Shelby know what she was doing to him. He walked over.

"Very nice," he said, with what he hoped was zero inflection.

"Do you want to try?" Hannah asked.

"No!" There was some inflection in that!

"But you could learn how to do mine," Hannah said.

He didn't have any desire to learn how to do hers. Did that make him a bad dad? If he changed his mind, that's what the internet was for.

"I had a text from the McKinnons," he said, changing the topic, even as he could imagine his hands in Shelby's hair. "Do you want to go over there tomorrow and play with Crystal?"

"Yes!" Hannah squealed. And then her face crumpled and she slid a look at Shelby's back. "Oh. Maybe not."

Even not seeing Hannah's face, Sam understood instantly his daughter was trying not to hurt Shelby's feelings by choosing a different playmate. Sometimes, he felt as if—

hair braiding aside—maybe he was doing something right in the daddy department.

"Hannah, I want you to go!" Shelby said. "It would be perfect if you did. I need to go shopping for a few things. I'm getting tired of rinsing my—"

She stopped. Her blush deepened.

There was something so appealing about this young woman, daughter of one of the richest people in the world, having no masks.

"You need a bathing suit!" Hannah said.

Apparently her need of a bathing suit was right up there with the unmentionables hanging over her bathroom shower rod.

"I think I need some pants that fit better."

"No, you *need* a bathing suit," Hannah said officiously. "Because we play in the sprinkler every day."

"All right," Shelby said. "I'll see if I can find a bathing suit."

"Do you like one-piece or two-pieces?" Hannah asked.

*Lord have mercy,* Sam thought.

Shelby seemed to consider, tilting her head thoughtfully. Did she cast him a quick glance? "I think for the sprinkler, one-piece."

*See? The occasional prayer was answered.* If word got around that Shelby was cavorting through the sprinkler in a bikini, he probably wouldn't be able to stop a full-fledged stampede up from the barn in the heat of the day.

"And what about on the beach?" Hannah asked.

"You're not going to the beach anytime soon," he snapped.

Hannah gave him a *what's up with you?* look.

"But if we did," Hannah insisted.

This time it was Shelby, not the good Lord, who showed him mercy. "Let's not worry about that right now. I'll go to the nearest town tomorrow and see what I can find."

He could not help but appreciate how she had so quickly and skillfully allowed Hannah to do what she wanted, without feeling guilty about her choice.

"You'll come back?" Hannah asked, and he made note of that. Was his daughter already attached? Worried about loss? Had a temporary arrangement with Shelby been a mistake? Was he reading too much into it? Way too much?

"Of course I'm coming back!"

Hannah visibly relaxed. So did he. Only he hoped not visibly.

"Where is the nearest town for shopping?" Shelby asked him. "I know I came through a couple on my way here."

He suspected the little towns she had passed on her way here would have a good selection of work boots, plaid shirts, and farm and ranch supplies. No bathing suits.

Another thought occurred to him.

*Don't do it*, he ordered himself.

*Be a better man*, another part of him insisted.

She had made his daughter happy. It was one thing to avoid her, it was another not to let her know how much he appreciated her.

"Um, I'll be taking the ranch helicopter to drop off Hannah and then to continue to Calgary. Why don't you come with us?" Well, *us* for part of the way. He and she alone, for the rest of it.

For Pete's sake! He'd be piloting a helicopter, an activity he thoroughly enjoyed because it required such intensity of focus. And not on her hair, either!

When Shelby didn't answer right away, he felt compelled to convince her.

Because he owed her for his daughter's happiness.

The teenage boy inside him snickered.

"It'll save you a couple of hours of driving on lonely roads."

He wondered if she might be feeling as awkward about spending time with him as he was with her. Had the avoidance been working two ways? For some reason that hurt in the same way that Hannah not appearing to miss him had hurt.

"I'll be in meetings, so you'll be free to shop to your heart's content. You should get a dress for the grad."

"The grad?" she said, surprised. "I'm invited to that?"

"Of course, silly," Hannah said, "*Everybody* goes."

"It's a really small high school," Sam said. "We only have seven grads this year. But Hannah's right. *Everyone* comes. Grandparents, aunts and uncles, cousins, babies. This year they've called it *Taking on the World!* It's kind of *the* event around here."

Why was he suddenly invested in her attending? He didn't want her to know that.

"I thought it might interest you," he said. "You know. Professionally. To see how a small, rural community holds an event. They always do a pretty amazing job."

"I *do* enjoy seeing how other events are put together. What kind of dress would I need?"

Which meant she was going to say yes, didn't it? He didn't quite know how to respond to that. How many kinds of dresses were there?

"A nice one," Hannah supplied.

"That's helpful. Calgary it is," Shelby said with a tentative smile.

What the hell was he doing?

"We'll leave around nine tomorrow morning."

"Sounds great."

Did it?

"Good night, Hannah-Banana," he said hastily to his daughter, and forewent his nightly hug in favor of getting out of that room as quickly as he could.

* * *

Shelby had done her best to freshen up the slack suit she had arrived in, but the truth was she was deliriously happy to be going shopping. She was sick to death of the nightly washing of undies, rolled jeans and ill-fitting tops.

*She was sick to death of not being noticed by Sam Waters.*

She felt ridiculously obsessed with him, straining her eyes to catch glimpses of him in the distance, straining her ears to hear him come in the house, feeling her heart start to pound hoping he would join them.

Playing in the sprinkler.

Or for a good night story.

But, since that afternoon in the sprinkler Sam Waters had become as elusive as a ghost.

But when she came down to breakfast she had to acknowledge her delirious happiness had so much less to do with fresh undies than it had to do with him.

# CHAPTER ELEVEN

SAM WAS, for the first time since they had shared mouse pancakes, in the kitchen when she arrived.

His preference for dress seemed to be business casual, and often with a Western flair, like a suit accompanied with boots and a cowboy hat, but this morning Sam was in full businessman mode. And he looked every inch the billionaire that he was.

"You've had a haircut," she said. Maybe she should have pretended she hadn't noticed. But how could she not notice that? And how was it, even without those curls, she still wanted to run her fingers through his hair? Just to see if it felt as silky as it looked.

"Yeah, Buckie took the shears to me. Does it look okay?"

"Fine," she bit out, instead of saying, *of course it looks okay. Better than okay! Sam Waters, you look ready for your GQ cover shoot.*

She really was not sure which look she liked best on him. This morning, the cowboy had been banished. As well as the business-ready haircut, Sam was freshly clean-shaven. In the same way his hair begged for her touch, that shaved skin made her want to put her fingertips on the tenderness of it.

Sam was sharply dressed in a pale gray suit. Shelby could tell from the way it fit him to absolute perfection—the jacket hugging the broadness of his shoulders, the pants skimming the large muscles of his thighs—that it was custom-made by a really exquisite tailor. With it he had on a crisp white linen shirt and a black silk tie. The knife-pressed pants finished with a polished black dress shoe.

"Dresses up pretty good, huh?" Alvin said, coming into the kitchen. Shelby blushed that she had been caught staring, and wished she was not in a suit that was still crumpled despite her efforts to steam it in the bathroom beside the shower.

She was happy for the distraction of getting Hannah ready to go, but then they were all in the helicopter, and Sam was piloting.

"You fly?" she asked, as he settled Hannah in the back and directed her to the seat beside him.

"The pilot called in sick. I thought I'd give it a whirl."

Shelby realized he was teasing her, like he had about her mistaking a bear for a dog, way back on day one. Why did that already feel as if it belonged in a different lifetime?

The tiny intimacy of his teasing sent a tickle up her spine. She adjusted her headset and gave in to the temptation to tease him back.

"You know, you could do a whole beefcake calendar by yourself. Cowboy. Businessman. Pilot."

Pilot was *very* attractive, the headset, the mirrored aviator glasses, his calm and confidence as he began to flick switches.

"What's a beefcake calendar?" Hannah asked innocently through her own headset.

He looked up from his control panel and raised an eyebrow at Shelby, mocking her knowledge of such things without saying a word.

"Oh, it's a calendar with a picture of a cute guy for every month of the year. They represent different jobs, like a fireman and a policeman," Shelby choked out. She wished she could take that back and omit the cute part.

"I might be a police when I grow up," Hannah said. Then

she leaned forward in her seat, and regarded her father solemnly. "He's not cute," she decided. "He's my dad."

"Hey!' he said, mock-offended. "Dads can be cute."

*Can they ever*, Hannah thought.

Then, thankfully, the blades began to spin, slowly and then faster and faster, until the helicopter lifted off the ground. The takeoff took the focus off of cute dads, though Sam's competence at the controls of the helicopter was at least as appealing as his cuteness and the way he was rocking that suit!

Shelby, totally aware that the broadness of that shoulder nearly touching hers was adding to the exquisiteness of the experience, took in the absolute beauty of the country they were flying over.

Sam pointed out the boundaries of the huge ranch and— she was fairly certain—deliberately detoured to allow her to see more of it. There were forests and meadows, herds of fat cattle, a pasture of horses, the meandering creek, a spectacular waterfall.

They landed briefly at a neighboring ranch and off-loaded Hannah, who was excited to see her friend Crystal. She waved goodbye and then never glanced back.

And now they were alone.

"You're really good with Hannah," Sam said. He was piloting the aircraft with the casual confidence with which most men would handle a car. She liked the way his voice sounded coming through the headset. Raspy. Close.

"I just love hanging out with her." In fact, she was already wondering about the hole that was going to be left in her life when her ten days here were up.

There were only five days left. She was counting. How had five whole days gone by in such a flash?

"Your mom must have been terrific."

The question caught her totally off guard. "I don't know if she was or not."

He gave her a quizzical look.

And she said something she had never said to anyone before. "I don't remember my mom."

"What? You don't?"

"Do you think that's strange?" she asked. Why was she asking him this? Was it too personal?

Maybe there was something about having your life, literally, in the hands of someone that inspired trust. "I mean, I was ten. You'd think I'd remember something. But I don't."

He glanced at her. "You were probably traumatized by her death. I think people handle trauma in different ways. I try to make sure Hannah knows who her mom was. As painful as it is, I go through the baby albums with her, and tell her stories about things Beth and I did together, the things we did for that short time that we were allowed to be a family."

Something shivered along Shelby's spine. Why hadn't her father ever done anything like that? She recalled, with sudden intensity, feeling very alone with her pain after her mother's accident.

She frowned.

"What's wrong?" he asked softly, glancing at her, and then returning his attention to piloting.

"I just... I don't remember my dad ever doing anything like that. I have photos of my mom, but I don't recall us ever looking at them together. In fact..." She went silent. She did remember something, after all.

"In fact?" he prodded her.

"In fact, I think my dad may have been relieved."

He was silent for a moment, and then he looked at her with a look so authentically caring that it felt as if it could melt a place in her she had not been aware was frozen, until just this moment.

"I'm sorry," he said.

Shelby's memories of that time in her life felt as if they

were shrouded in fog, and that one thing—her father's relief—had poked through for a startling moment. Though she
had a few photos of her mom, hadn't other traces of her disappeared from their lives with rather astounding rapidness?

Or was that memory playing tricks on her? No wonder
she didn't recall that time of her life! It was painful and con-
fusing.

But somehow, being part of a household had made her
realize her aversion to commitment, her reluctance to have
children, were related to the things she could not remember.

She couldn't remember? Or she didn't want to?

"Are you okay?" Sam asked.

Again, there was something in his voice that made her
want to lean into whatever he was offering.

Strength. Trustworthiness. The comfort of a shared burden.

But she didn't lean into it. She leaned away from it.

"Yes, of course," Shelby told Sam, her tone deliberately
breezy. "I'm fine. How could I not be? What a spectacular
day."

Even though his eyes were hidden by the sexy sunglasses,
his expression was dubious, as if he saw right through her, to
something she had never even allowed herself to see.

*The pain was still there. Right below the surface. It had
probably controlled almost every single decision about her
whole life.*

But she was not going to let it spoil today!

"You're a good dad," she told him, anxious to take the
focus off herself and avoid this feeling of weakness, as if she
wanted to share deep confidences with him.

He smiled, something a little weary in the expression.
"Some days are better than others," he said. "Parenting a little girl, particularly alone, feels as if I'm navigating a mine-

field. When I get through another day without a catastrophe, I feel euphoric."

"What kind of catastrophe?" Shelby asked.

"Let's see, the no ice cream for supper one, the bath one, the bedtime one, the hair one—especially the hair one…"

"But I haven't seen any of that."

"That's why I thought you must have had a really good mom. Because you're so natural at it."

*A natural mommy?* Her? The one who had never wanted to have children? The one who, when women her age started talking about having children, felt terrified?

"She's done really well since you came," Sam continued. "No tantrums. No pointing her dolls at anyone in a threatening manner. Tamed hair."

"Hannah is confident and creative, empathetic and fun. That's all the proof you need that you are doing so much right."

"Well, maybe it's Buckie," he said.

And they both laughed. But he wasn't as distracted as she hoped he would be.

"Was your dad a good dad?" he asked softly.

She thought about that. "I think he tried a little too hard to make it up to me that I didn't have a mom. I was overindulged."

"All the more impressive that you've started your own business."

"Thank you. Given that I was basically raised to believe I was a princess, I think I've managed to shock quite a few people by being hardworking and practical and quite good at what I do. My dad didn't understand that people need a purpose. My business gave me one."

And so, she thought, did being with Hannah. And Sam.

"And, you know, my dad did his best. I see that more now than I ever did. Even though he was clumsy about loving a child, I always felt as if he had my back. Even when I was bratty."

"You, bratty?" He had that teasing tone again, and she liked it. Again, she could feel herself, emotionally, leaning into him.

"I acted like I was thirteen until I was about twenty-three."

"In terms of Hannah, I'm scared of what thirteen is going to look like."

"And well you should be."

"Particularly if it lasts ten years!" he said with mock panic.

They both chuckled over that.

"Anyway, that's why Boswell's birthday party is so important to me. To let him know how much I appreciate him doing a job alone that usually takes two... Just like you," she finished softly.

He gave her a look of gratitude. The moment passed, and yet it felt as if they had shared something important, a trust springing up between them.

They landed and Sam had a car and a driver waiting at the small airport on the outskirts of Calgary. They sat side by side in the luxurious back seat, leaning close as he used his phone and showed her some of the downtown shopping areas. They exchanged phone numbers so they could arrange to meet when his meeting was over.

The car pulled over to drop her off. Sam got out before the driver could, and held open the door for her.

The noise and bustle of downtown Calgary was a bit of a shock after the quiet of the ranch, and he read her expression.

"You'll be okay exploring on your own?" he asked. Again, she was taken with his ease in reading her, his very genuine concern, and his old-fashioned chivalry.

"Of course," she said. "I'm from New York!"

He reached into his pocket and handed her a credit card. "This is preloaded. Get whatever you need."

She tried to hand it back. "No—"

But he wouldn't take it. "Let me do it for you. I owe you one. For making Hannah happy."

"You don't owe me anything for that. We've done a trade and I'm more than happy with it."

"It would give me pleasure, really. And if you see something Hannah might like…"

"Alright," she said, and couldn't help but be pleased again at his chivalry and thoughtfulness, warmed by how his daughter was never far from his mind.

"My meeting won't be long. I'll let you know when it's over and we'll go for lunch. I have a special place I'd like to show you."

He had a special place he wanted to show her? What was taking shape between them? It felt frightening and wonderful at the same time. Or maybe she was reading too much into it. He was being hospitable. Maybe that was all.

Then Sam got back into the vehicle, and it slipped quietly back into traffic and was gone.

# CHAPTER TWELVE

IT WAS A beautiful day and Shelby adored downtown Calgary with its wonderful combination of old historic buildings and innovative modern ones. There was a vitality about the city famous for its Western culture and its Stampede.

Though the Stampede was weeks away, she could feel the city gearing up for it. It seemed as if it would be an exciting time to be here, but she would be gone and it would be too early to come back to start on her father's party.

*Gone.*

Gone from Hannah. And Sam. And Buckie. And Rascal.

How could she feel faintly bereft over that? Probably just because she had been so intensely immersed in a world different from her own. It was only human that she would miss it. Though she knew, a week ago, if someone had told her she would miss playing nanny she would have scoffed.

It made her feel as if she didn't know herself, at all!

She gave herself over to discovering Calgary instead of indulging self-contemplation. Much of the downtown was connected by walkways, which functioned as protection against the many months of winter weather, though they were unnecessary today.

The shops and boutiques were world-class, and she gave herself over to the pure enjoyment of shopping. It had been a long time—since starting Eventually—that she'd had the time or inclination—or budget—to pamper herself. Despite Sam giving her the credit card, she used her own on everything, including the cutest little dress she found for Hannah.

When Sam called her, time had evaporated. Shelby had gotten all the essentials to get her through a few more days: underwear; socks; suitable shoes; shorts and tops; a pair of casual slacks, but she was no closer to picking out a dress for *Taking on the World*.

"Ready for lunch?" he asked. His voice over the phone was warm and sexy and felt like a touch on the back of her neck.

She looked at the sea of dresses she was surrounded by. "Hang on," she said. "I'm sending you a picture."

She took a photo of one of the dresses, on its hanger, and sent it. "Hannah said nice. What does that mean? Formal? Summer? Cocktail?"

"Hang on, it just came in."

Silence.

"Well?"

"It's a little, uh, I-hate-this-dress-but-I'm-still-hopeful bridesmaid," Sam said.

"That's a lot to tell about a dress. It sounds as if you've been to way too many weddings."

"Weddings are important in our part of the country. Community events. Right up there with grad nights."

She felt a tickle of longing for that kind of community. It made her feel the same way the first glimpse of his house had. As if there was a promise there. Of family. History. Stability. Tradition.

She ordered herself to focus and took a picture of the second dress. She pressed send and heard the ping of it arriving on his phone.

"Wasn't that in *Beauty and the Beast*?" he asked. "I think it's a bit too ball gown."

"Your areas of expertise are taking me by surprise."

"Spent the winter on a ranch with a five-year-old. There were at least a hundred viewings." He hummed the theme song.

She laughed. She snapped a picture and sent it. "Okay, this one."

"Definitely not."

Only this time, that sexy voice wasn't coming through her phone, it was practically in her ear. Sam was standing right beside her, looking at the dress.

"What the heck? How…"

"Magic," he said.

She stared at him. Her mouth had fallen open. She'd only left him a few hours ago, how could his pure presence be so newly shocking?

Maybe it was the contrast of all that masculinity in the distinctly feminine atmosphere of the dress boutique.

"M-Magic?" she stammered. Oh, yeah, she was definitely feeling that! "No, seriously, where did you come from?"

"I caught a glimpse of the shop tag inside the first dress you sent me a photo of. I was practically standing outside."

Something—pure delight—shivered along her spine that Sam was standing beside her, apparently game to help her pick a dress.

"I'm glad you clarified," she said, not wanting him to see how pleased she was by his presence, "otherwise it might have seemed as if you were a stalker."

He tilted his head at her. She was pretty sure she wasn't hiding anything from him. He was used to females plying him with unwanted attention. He'd said as much the first day they'd met.

Out of the corner of her eye, Shelby saw the three sales-clerks exchange glances. One fanned herself and another pretended to swoon. Sam cast them an irritated glance, evidently well aware of his ability to cause a flutter in female hearts.

"Believe me," he said. "I'm not a stalker."

"Okay," she said, "I believe you." More like the stalkee!

"Thanks," he said dryly.

"This is the final of the three I've narrowed it down to," Shelby said, trying for an all-business tone. She held up the pale blue backless dress to him.

He looked at the dress for a long time. She saw his Adam's apple bob as he swallowed. "You'd steal the show in that one."

She felt like it was her turn to swoon, but she kept her tone light. "Taking on the world!" she reminded him.

"Maybe we should let the grad girls be the ones who steal the show."

"Oh! You're right." Again, his sensitivity impressed. Of course it was the grad girls' night to be the stars. But the fact that he understood that boded so well for Hannah's future.

"Something a little more subdued," she said.

"Mature," he agreed.

He turned to a rack beside him, skimmed through it, looked her up and down, and handed her two dresses.

"Try on these ones for me."

*For him?*

It was just an expression. Still, she gulped. She looked at the labels inside the dresses. Her size *exactly*.

"Excuse me, ma'am?" Sam called.

The salesladies, all three of them, rushed toward him. "Could you see what you have for shoes that would match those two dresses?"

They scurried off, eager to please. What kind of man thought of stuff like that? She realized Sam was not just a good daddy, he had been a fabulous husband. She felt a funny little ache in the region of her heart. Because her life had not had men like this in it? Because she had convinced herself that she was not the marriage type?

She put on the first dress, way too aware that Sam was

only a few feet away from her on the other side of the door as she undressed. The dress was a beautiful butter-yellow cotton summer dress, button-down and short-sleeved, with a belt dividing the bodice from the wide skirt. She slipped on a pair of matching flats that had been put under the door for her.

She felt really shy when she stepped out to model it for him.

Sam cocked his head.

She did an experimental turn, and loved the way the dress swished around her legs, and how as she completed the turn, she saw his eyes resting there, heated, before he quickly masked it.

"It's nice," he said. "Really nice."

"But?"

"Maybe too, um, fifties housewife."

"Sexy fifties housewife," one of the salesladies chimed in.

*Sexy?* She thought maybe she should take it!

Or maybe not. It would not take much to push things into the danger zone between them. As if they weren't halfway there already.

Actually, hadn't they been flirting with the danger zone since that day they had chased each other through the sprinklers?

He knew it. That's why he'd been avoiding her ever since.

She tried on the other dress. Shelby had cut her teeth on beautiful clothing. She had closets stuffed with the designer duds she had collected, casually and carelessly, before she had chosen the path of poverty.

Okay, not exactly poverty, but not two-thousand-dollar dresses, either.

This dress was not two thousand dollars, not even close. And yet it held more pure enchantment than some of those very expensive dresses had.

The dress was a dark mossy green, fitted, with a dark under sheath and a layer of laser-cut lace, one shade lighter, on top. It was a nice length, ending just above her knee. Coupled with the matching high heels, it made her look extraordinarily, but subtly sensual, oozing feminine power and mystery.

She realized she looked very grown-up. And she realized she wanted to live up to what that dress said she was. She realized she wanted to be the woman who looked back at her from the mirror, a woman who had come fully into herself, who knew exactly what she wanted, and knew how to get it.

What exactly did she want? Shelby was shocked by the immediate answer that blasted through her brain.

She wanted to taste Sam Water's lips. She'd wanted to taste them since the day they had negotiated the trade. And every day since.

Time was ticking. Loudly. She was pretty sure she could hear it. Sam would probably take up avoiding her again the second they got back to the ranch.

Something inside her felt as if she *had* to know the taste of him. Before it was over, in five short days, one of those days half-finished already.

Sam tried not to let his mouth drop open when Shelby emerged from the changeroom in the second dress he had picked for her.

On the hanger, it had looked lovely—exactly the kind of *nice* dress Hannah had suggested and not the kind—at all— that could make a man lose his mind, like that sexy blue number Shelby had shown him.

*Maybe we should let the grad girls be the ones who steal the show*, he'd said, and she'd fallen for it, never guessing how terrified he'd been to see her in that dress.

*This* dress had lied to him. On the hanger it had looked like something a woman might wear to tea at Buckingham Palace.

Off the hanger, subtly clinging to her soft curves, it was way worse than the overtly sexy one would have been.

Shelby looked simply, impossibly, stunning. Her eyes looked suddenly completely green, the hints of brown and gold gone. Why was he noticing her lips? They didn't have anything to do with the dress! She wasn't even wearing lipstick. Maybe, now that he looked, a hint of gloss...

Gone completely were any remnants of the playful child who played in the sprinkler and who could do great pig snorts. He felt as if the tomboyish girl in her borrowed clothes had transformed to a full-blooded woman before his very eyes.

"What do you think?" she asked him.

He was pretty sure she knew what he thought!

He hardly trusted himself to speak. He ordered himself to say, *sure, it will do.*

But he didn't say that. He breathed, "Beautiful."

*The dress. The woman. The possibilities...*

Some awareness of each other passed between them, shocking and intense. He broke his gaze first, deliberately looked away from her.

"Ready for lunch?" he asked. "I'm starving."

"Me, too," she said.

But for food?

Was her voice husky? Were those eyes, made smoky green by the color of the dress, fastened on his lips? Was she noticing his lips the same way he had noticed hers?

This was just wrong. He had to pull himself together while she went and changed. Hopefully, without that dress weaving some kind of spell around him, he could go back to the boss/nanny relationship.

But when she came out of the changeroom, she was wearing different clothes than what she'd been wearing this morning.

The rumpled business suit was gone.

And she certainly did not look like she was impersonating Huck Finn.

She was wearing slender-fitting navy blue slacks, and a white sleeveless top. While not as flattering as the green dress, now that he had seen her like that, *that* Shelby lingered like a shadow.

He could see what a beautiful, sensual, all-grown-up woman she was. This hunger he was feeling, he told himself sternly, had nothing to do with his goal of being a better man.

Shelby Kane was his daughter's nanny.

Not technically, a voice inside him insisted on crowing. She was kind of an un-nanny. The terms of their agreement were based on a trade. He wasn't really her boss. She wasn't even an employee.

His guest, then.

His daughter's protector and caretaker. He thought of all of them running through the sprinkler. That moment had been almost as sizzling as the dress. Maybe more so.

But it cemented the fact that over the past few days, Shelby had quickly become his daughter's friend. He could not do anything to jeopardize that. These feelings Shelby was stirring up in him were explainable.

He'd been on his own for a long time. He had not even looked at another woman since Beth died. It felt disloyal to be doing it now.

Five days left.

Since he was relying on technicalities, all of a sudden, four and a half. She would leave right after *Taking on the World.*

Anybody could do anything for four and a half days. A person watching their weight could give up cookies. A person who shouldn't drink could give up booze.

He could fight off his base instincts for four and a half days. He could be a gentleman and a better man. He could be grateful for all she had done for his daughter. And he could show her that. And only that.

# CHAPTER THIRTEEN

"LET'S GO FOR LUNCH," he said.

"Yes, let's. Are you going to show me Calgary's finest?"

"I am. But it's probably not what you're expecting."

She sighed and her eyes met his. "Nothing has been what I'm expecting."

She didn't say that as if it was a bad thing.

He made a call, and had his driver come and pick up her many packages and deliver them the lunch he had made arrangements for earlier. Then, insulated bag in hand, he walked with her to the Devonian Gardens. Calgary's indoor botanical garden was an absolute marvel, a one-hectare oasis in the heart of downtown. It was spectacular with its ponds and fountains, hundreds of plants and trees, butterflies flitting about.

"I'm in awe," she said, taking out her phone and snapping pictures. "I'm adding these to my dream file. This would be the best place for an event."

She tapped her lip thoughtfully. He wished she wouldn't do that.

"I'd like to do a Christmas party here. Can you imagine? The juxtaposition of snow falling on the glass roof and the tropical atmosphere inside?"

He found himself enjoying seeing her in the zone, her enthusiasm and professionalism residing side by side. Again, he was so aware she was not his daughter's playmate. Shelby

Kane was all grown-up. Finally, she had enough pictures, and they found a quiet place to sit.

"This is utterly amazing," she said with a sigh of contentment.

He was pleased by her enjoyment. See? He could be the perfect host. To prove it, he opened the lunch container and handed her a box.

She flipped the lid and her eyes widened.

"I figured you've experienced just as many five-star meals as I have. I wanted you to taste the real Calgary."

"Oh, this looks so yummy! But did you have to pick such a messy lunch? This top is brand-new."

"I didn't want you to leave Calgary without sampling Ray's Ribs. Don't worry. They sent bibs."

*Bibs! That should take the awareness factor down a notch or two.*

But it didn't. He shook out the large plastic bibs, and then found himself leaning close to her to tie the strings at the back of her neck. His fingers grazed the delicate skin there. Her hair had a scent to it that reminded him of the world after rain. Clean. Pure. And something else…

And then she took the other bib from his fingers, leaned into him, and he felt her fingers on the back of his neck, trailing heat. He could, shockingly, imagine her lips tracing that same line.

He reared back from her. Beware of a woman who could make a bib sexy!

She took a rib out of the container, nibbled it, drew it into her mouth, and pulled the meat off the bone, then licked sauce from her fingertips.

And he had thought it would be hard to watch her eat an ice pop! What had he been thinking! Sandwiches would have been a safe choice.

He looked at her lips, and thought *maybe, maybe not.* Maybe nothing was going to be safe in his world ever again.

No, that wasn't right.

Four. And. A. Half. Days.

"Earth-shattering," she said with a contented sigh. "I wonder if Ray caters?"

Earth-shattering is what it had been when they had run through the sprinkler together. Earth-shattering is what she had been in that dress. Earth-shattering is what he felt leaning into her, tying the strings behind her neck. All of life, even the simplest of things, had become earth-shattering.

"Tell me about growing up on a ranch," she said.

Sam did not consider himself much of a talker, and so no one was more surprised than him about all he had to say.

About his mom and dad, and his first pony, and hard work and bad weather, and the utter magic of the Mountain Waters Ranch.

"Of course, just like those grads who can only think of taking on the world, and not the world they already have, I had no idea what I had while I had it. I wanted something else. I wanted bigger. And more exciting. And more choices."

She smiled. "That's the song of youth, isn't it? More, more, more?"

"It is. Anyway, I came to university here in Calgary, and given my outdoorsy, kind of rough-and-tumble upbringing, I had a surprising knack for tech. I loved it. I started writing code, which if you're good enough at, you can name your own price. Instead, I started my first company before I graduated, and it got me all the *more* that I craved, and then some.

"Within a few years, *I* was going places I would have never predicted. My business was exploding. I had employees, I had offices around the world, I was making the kind of money a ranch—even a really prosperous one—could never dream of making.

"And I loved it all. The new people, the worlds that opened to me, the adventures, the successes, the accomplishments.

"But after Beth and I got married, we started coming back to the ranch more. She loved it there. She helped me see it through fresh eyes."

It occurred to him that he was talking about his wife without pain. For the first time, he remembered their partnership with deep appreciation, not tinged with regret or anger or guilt or what-ifs.

"She loved all things family," he remembered softly, and there was a stab not of pain, but of longing.

Family.

He realized it was what he wanted for Hannah: huge family dinners, games around the dining table, weddings and anniversaries.

And at the same time, he wanted to protect her from the loss that inevitably came from all that. The very thing that should have been most solid in all the world—that should be every person's safe place—could be snatched from you in the blink of an eye.

Love, that by-product of family, had left him shattered and unsure of everything. Most of all his own ability to be in control when it really mattered.

"With Beth, I came home to the realization of what a special place Mountain Waters was. We both started juggling our commitments to spend more time at the ranch.

"I'm so glad of that now. My dad was diagnosed with cancer just before Hannah was born. We got time with him, with both my parents. They got to hold our baby. My dad died before Hannah's first birthday, my mom before her second. It think my mom literally died of a broken heart. And then, still reeling from those losses, we found out Beth was sick."

Shelby's hand had found its way to his arm. She'd done

that once before, that morning in the barn when he had also talked about Beth.

It was this—as much as the laughter, as much as her subtle sexiness, as much as how good she was with his daughter— that was the most dangerous to his battered and bruised heart.

His strength and been tested, almost beyond what he could endure.

Sam was not ready for any other battles.

And he was not sure he ever would be.

Sam contemplated all the things he felt Shelby's touch held. It was as if her strength flowed into him, filling up a reservoir that had emptied.

There was a kinship in her touch. They had both known sorrow and somehow, he was sure neither of them knew exactly how, they had survived.

And, in those fingers resting on his arms, he felt maybe the worst thing of all.

Hope.

That the light would come on in the world again. Isn't that what had been happening for the last five days?

The sun had risen in his and Hannah's dark world. His daughter was like a little plant that had survived the harshest of winters, poking strongly out of the ground, moving unerringly toward the sun, lifting her face to it.

"I see the ranch now," Sam said, "as the best place in the world to raise a child."

"To heal," Shelby said simply. And he felt entirely seen.

"Yes," he said, softly.

A quiet unfolded between them. It should have been comfortable, but an awareness of her zinged in him.

She took her hand off his arm. He missed it.

"I feel as if I have sauce from my hairline to my fingertips."

It was exactly the right moment to insert some levity, and

he was grateful to her for it. Shelby lifted the bib and dabbed at her face.

"You missed some right—" He took his own bib, and touched the edge of her lip.

Something went very still between them. And it was not comfortable, at all.

He could feel his heart beating hard, as if it planned to leap out of his chest.

She leaned toward him. He had time to move, but he didn't. He felt frozen. She reached up and mirrored what he had just done. She dabbed the corner of his lip with her napkin.

Her eyes were intent on his.

"Don't," he whispered.

"I have to," she said.

And then she kissed him.

Her kiss was light, the briefest touch of her lips to his. And yet it was a long, cool drink of water to a man dying of thirst. It was an oasis in a life that had become a desert.

"Why did you do that?" he asked. He hoped his tone was harsh. He missed the mark. It came out huskily.

"Just to say thank-you. For a perfect day. For telling your story to me. And inviting me into your space. And saying yes to letting me use the barn for my dad's birthday. And for helping me pick a dress. For these gardens. And the ribs.

"And most of all, for sharing your beautiful daughter."

A butterfly went by her, and she followed it with her eyes.

"Maybe," she said softly, "I'm not even thanking you, so much as life, and its unexpected gifts."

*Well, they were his lips she had chosen to bestow her gratitude on.*

But he understood perfectly what she was saying. They were alive. That kiss was part of acknowledging they were alive and that life—all of it, including the chemistry between a man and a woman—could be unexpectedly and breathtakingly beautiful.

And seductive, beckoning a person back toward the land of the living.

"We can't," he said, his voice a croak.

"Oh," she said, "I know that. Don't worry. I'm the woman least likely to want anything from you. I'm not the forever kind."

For some reason, instead of feeling relieved that she was not getting ready to post banns at the church because they had kissed, her words made him feel sad for her. His vow to keep her at a distance wavered. He could just accept the gifts of this moment. No, more than that. He felt *compelled* to accept them.

When her hand crept back into his, he let it stay. No, he closed his hand around hers, felt the perfect fit of their two hands together, felt all that softness against his own work-roughened palms.

He knew he was saying yes to the gift even though, underneath that bright wrapping, that gift might hide shards of glass waiting to embed themselves in his already tattered heart.

It was just for this moment. She had made that crystal clear.

The kiss had been a mistake. So why did it feel so good?

The truth was that mistakes often felt good, didn't they?

Tasting Sam had been everything she could have dreamed of. It had confirmed things about him, as if she had tasted his soul. It had told her that Sam was strong, but sensitive, practical, and extraordinarily deep.

The problem with a kiss like that was it triggered a longing for more. Shelby was determined to fight that longing, because *more* with Sam would not be the same as *more* had been with any other man she had ever been with.

She was aware she had chosen men who did not require much from her. He would not be that guy.

If Sam had been avoiding her before the trip to Calgary, it was her turn now to avoid him and all the complications he represented, and that the kiss had made all too apparent.

Thankfully, on Thursday, people began to arrive to get the barn ready for *Taking on the World*. It was a wonderful distraction from Shelby's awareness of Sam as she threw herself into what was truly a community event.

The whole high school seemed to show up, not just the graduating class. And with them came teachers and mothers, aunts and grandmothers. Fathers and grandfathers and uncles showed up for heavy lifting and ladder work, to wire electrics and to build props.

Shelby and Hannah were welcomed into the fold of activity. It felt like a beehive with so many people purposefully buzzing about. There were jobs for everyone. Hannah was soon engrossed in making tissue flowers while Shelby painted panel backdrops representing some of the countries of the world.

Over the next few days, the old barn was transformed into a global community. The grad committee had already done so much work doing props for their international theme.

Shelby suggested they set up the barn into zones: an outdoor area, comfortable places to sit and converse, a food and drink space, a game space, a place for the DJ, a place to dance, and lots of selfie zones. Shelby loved loaning her expertise to the group.

The grads set up a zone for each of their selected countries and themed it for that. So, you could have a quiet conversation in Paris, grab something to eat in Rome, have a game of beanbag toss in Los Angeles. You could dance the night away in Dubai, or go sit under the stars in Reykjavík.

Shelby's favourite was the selfie zones at the entrance

to the barn. The first thing a guest saw was a huge papier–mâché globe that looked as if the students had spent most of the year constructing it and painting it. It was now suspended from the ceiling, and with the right setup, it looked as if the person in the picture was holding the whole world in their hands, literally *taking on the world.*

She loved all the prep for the big night, but most of all, Shelby loved how Sam and Hannah's community—their family—accepted her with open arms. She was totally embraced.

On Friday, Shelby and one of the grad girls, Sandra, were putting up the grad date on the wall in tissue flowers, threaded through with fairy lights. Tomorrow, the event they had all been working toward would welcome the entire community.

In a low undertone, Sandra confided, "I don't really want to take on the world."

"Oh?"

"I mean, most of the grad class wants to. They want to see a bigger world and explore new things."

Shelby remembered how Sam had told her he felt that way.

"I don't want to," Sandra said. "I don't want to leave here at all."

At that moment, Sam and the Mountain Waters Ranch hands came in. Under Alvin's supervision, two of them were carrying a huge vat of soup. Jimmy, his arm still in a cast, was juggling a tray of buns still steaming from the oven.

"I'll break your other one if you drop those," Alvin said.

If Shelby was not mistaken, Sandra's eyes followed Jimmy with an intense longing. Would Shelby have even recognized that kind of longing a week ago? She was pretty sure she was looking at Sam the same way. She hoped it wasn't as obvious, she hoped that maybe she only recognized that secret look because her heart recognized it.

"You know what I think?" Shelby said. "Most of the kids

who leave will only know what they had once they don't have it anymore. Sam told me that's how he felt when he left and then came back."

"Really?"

"I think you have a special gift, Sandra. You already know what you have."

"But I don't know what to do! Not all ranches are helicopters and thousands of cattle and acres. Ours is a family operation, but my two older brothers already work with my dad. It can't support me, too. I live a long way from the nearest job opportunity."

Shelby contemplated that for a moment, and then a light bulb went off in her head.

"Maybe you don't," Shelby said with sudden inspiration. "Sam needs someone to help with Hannah. He hasn't been able to get a nanny who will stay."

"That would be my absolute dream job," Sandra breathed. "And I just love Hannah. Do you think he'd consider me? Really?"

"You won't know until you ask," Shelby said gently, but she already knew that she was standing with her replacement.

Soon Sam and Hannah would not need her anymore.

And she knew she was as uncertain about the future as Sandra was.

There had been so much activity and so much anticipation that it had almost made Shelby forget that after the Saturday night event, she would be leaving.

She had twin terrors warring within her. One, that her feelings for Sam had reached a dead end, and two, that they hadn't. Was it over, or was there a future?

A future? She was the woman who could be counted on not to burden people with claims on their futures!

One possibility made her feel despondent, and one frightened. She had a terrible history with relationships. Why would a relationship with Sam break the pattern? No, it would be best if she got off the Mountain Waters Ranch without encouraging any more complications.

# CHAPTER FOURTEEN

BUT NOW SHELBY had allowed the forbidden thought: *a relationship with Sam.* As might be expected of a forbidden thought, it caused Shelby to tremble, and not entirely with fear, either.

Still, Shelby refused to spoil her final moments on the ranch by contemplating a world without Sam and Hannah.

She had to break the spell she was under. That she *belonged.* Because wasn't hope the most dangerous thing of all?

She frowned at that thought. When had that core belief formed? That hope was dangerous.

Shelby felt her younger self trying to whisper to her.

She shrugged it off. She knew she and Sam were both suppressing an electric attraction. That kiss had told her that.

But since then, she felt how his eyes lingered on her. She wondered if he could see the pulse in her neck pick up tempo every time he was around.

And yet, didn't they both know that following that sizzle could lead to disaster. Because then what?

It felt as if *Taking on the World* had become a pivotal point in her life, as if her whole world was never going to be the same, no matter what happened next.

So, when the event actually started, Shelby felt as giddy with fear and anticipation as any of those grads.

Hannah was also giddy with excitement, which was a lovely distraction. In her new dress she looked like a princess.

As they walked from the house to the barn, Sam and Shelby indulged in a rare moment of togetherness. Hannah insisted on taking her daddy's hand on one side and Shelby's on the other, and she kept leaping up, and they would swing her between them.

It was such a lovely, simple moment. Infused with that dangerous thing.

Hope.

That a future could look like this. Mommy and daddy and their little girl.

Shelby realized, stunned, why this evening felt so pivotal.

She had guarded herself against this exact thing her entire life, and yet here it was.

She longed for what she had experienced here on the ranch. She loved Hannah, and the little girl loved her.

But that made everything more complicated with Sam. A little girl could be badly hurt by a misstep between them.

She cast him a look out of the corner of her eye. He was gorgeous tonight, in a suit with an ever-so-subtle Western cut. He wore a black cowboy hat pulled low over his eyes and black boots.

What was going to happen between them? A fling? Leading where?

She ordered herself not to try and see the future, to put away the crystal ball, to just enjoy the moment and the evening they had all worked so hard toward.

They walked by the field that had been set aside for parking, which was packed with pickup trucks. Several parties had arrived by helicopter. Two planes had landed. Everyone from a hundred miles and beyond had come.

The grads—particularly the young women—shone like stars in the night. Their dresses were spectacular. Their hair and makeup perfect.

People mingled, enjoying the games and each other, laughing over selfies. Children, including Hannah and Crystal, darted in and out of the crowds, safe, watched over by their entire community.

The room hummed with an air of celebration.

"I'll go find us a drink," Sam said over the noise. "What would you like? A glass of wine?"

He said that as if they were together. She shivered at the thought of what being together with Sam would mean. It felt as if they were suddenly barreling toward an inevitable conclusion.

One thing she knew was that whatever happened tonight, she was not going to blame it on wine. And the fact that something was going to happen was popping in the air between them, like a downed power line snapping on the ground.

"Just water is fine."

He nodded and she watched him move away, appreciating his long lines and casual power, the way he stood out from the crowd.

He was waylaid long before he made it to the bar. It was Sandra, looking stunning in a mauve silk backless dress. She was looking up earnestly at Sam, and over the heads of the crowd, he sent Shelby an apologetic look, but she smiled and waved him off. She appreciated how he cocked his head, listening intently to Sandra, giving her his full attention.

Suddenly, they were both smiling, and Shelby guessed Sam had just found his perfect nanny.

He moved away from Sandra, but he was soon stopped by someone else. This time it was an elderly woman, and again he found Shelby's eyes, ever so subtly lifted one of those broad shoulders, before honoring that grandmother with his full and undivided attention.

She liked seeing him among his community. He was a man who could fit in anywhere in the entire world. He could walk with equal ease with kings and princes and probably had.

But it was obvious that he was fully in his element here.

She liked seeing how much this community loved him and respected him. She liked that almost everyone here had known him forever, since he was a little boy.

He was liked and loved for who he was, and that affection had not been caused—or corrupted—by his enormous success in the world.

It made Shelby's heart happy for Sam—and for Hannah—that they so obviously were in the place they belonged.

And where did she fit into all of this? She had never really felt as if she belonged anywhere in her life. There had never been a real sense of family or community. Could that change?

Even as she had longed for it, she wondered, did she really want it to?

Belonging involved commitment, the one thing she had consistently failed at her entire life.

Except for her business, and she was not sure that counted.

Shelby wondered if she had just been a temporary interloper in Sam and Hannah's world. If she was like a rock dropped into a pond and sank from sight, creating a temporary ripple that quickly disappeared.

But she forced herself to shake off all the troubling thoughts. This might be her last night ever on the Mountain Waters Ranch. There was no room for those kind of thoughts when the very air seemed to be infused with joy.

As she watched, Jimmy came in, his eyes searching the crowd.

And finding exactly who he was looking for.

He moved toward Sandra with a certainty that could make a person feel hopeful about the future and commitment and the whole world.

The music started and there was absolutely no moment of hesitation.

Suddenly the barn was hopping! Shelby lost sight of where Sam was.

"Could I have the first dance of the night?"

It was Alvin, looking very spiffy in a Western-style suit. He swept off a bonanza-sized hat and bowed to her.

"Of course!"

After that it was a complete whirlwind. She had always been popular, but at the back of her mind, Shelby might have wondered how much her popularity had to do with her last name.

Since it definitely wasn't that, she wasn't sure what it was tonight. Being the new gal in town? The amazing dress? Or was she, like Sandra, glowing with the soft light of someone open to possibilities?

Whatever it was, she just said *yes*. To every invitation and every new experience. One lovely older gentleman patiently taught her how to do the polka. She took part in the hysterically funny chicken dance. They danced the Hokey Pokey. The Bunny Hop was a fun-infused variation on a conga line.

Through it all, she waited for Sam to come and claim her.

But he did not.

And Shelby was not sure if she was relieved or irritated that her instinct that tonight would somehow be pivotal in her life was so off.

When had she begun to think she could trust her instincts?

Sam had long since given the bottle of chilled water he had finally managed to get for Shelby to someone else.

He couldn't get anywhere near her.

Which was maybe just as well.

At nine thirty or so, Hannah came and informed him, excitedly, that she had been invited to a sleepover at Crystal's. An hour later both sleepy, protesting girls had been packed into the neighboring ranch's truck.

So, he was not on daddy duty, and Shelby Kane was not his nanny anymore. Sandra Jefferson was going to take over on Monday.

Sandra's stepping up to the task was nothing less than heaven-sent, really.

And even though Shelby had never officially been employed by Sam or the ranch, her position had kept a nice little barrier in place between them. As had Hannah's constant presence.

Now those barriers were teetering on the edge of total destruction, as he kept an eye on Shelby. They were lined up three deep to claim a dance with her.

It was nearing midnight, and Sam had not danced a single dance. But, boy, she had. Shelby was the belle of the ball. Well, in that dress, and with that radiance pouring out of her, it was little wonder.

Buckie was suddenly at his elbow. "Quit scowling," he said.

"I'm not scowling."

"Tell your forehead."

Even though he didn't want to admit Buckie was right, Sam deliberately tried to loosen up his facial muscles.

"Just go ask her to dance," Buckie said.

"Who?" he said, innocently.

Buckie snorted. "The night's nearly over. What are you waiting for?"

Maybe for the night to be over, for the moment to be gone, for the temptation to be successfully fought off. Tomorrow, she'd be gone.

"What are you afraid of?"

Sam wanted to tell Buckie he didn't want to wait in a lineup to dance with Shelby. He wanted to tell him he wasn't afraid of anything. But no words came out. Instead, he looked at the man, wordlessly.

"Oh," Buckie said, giving him a long look, as if he was a book, too easily read. He gave him a clap on the shoulder. "*That*. You're afraid of that."

Embarrassing to be so obvious.

"I remember the first time you fell off a pony," Buckie said quietly. "Come to your daddy bawling your eyes out. You remember?"

"Oh, yeah."

"He told you to get out there and get back on that horse, or he'd give you something to cry about."

"And there went his parent-of-the-year award," Sam said.

"I know folks do it differently now, but there were things to be said about the way it was done back then. Your daddy was teaching you to be a man. He was teaching you pain is temporary, but giving in to fear is forever."

"And yet if I ever talked to Hannah like that, you'd whup me up the side of my head," Sam pointed out.

"Huh. Well, the girl-children are an entirely different species," Buckie admitted. "She could help you with that."

He nodded toward where Shelby was bent over double with laughter, one of the final participants in a round of musical chairs.

As they watched, she shoved a man nearly twice her size out of the way and plopped herself down in the last chair.

Everything was in that: her fire, her sense of herself, her strength. She was the girl-child who had been raised without a mother and still, despite it all, she had become this. A woman who could wear a dress like that, a woman who every man here recognized for what she was.

"You need to get back on the horse, Sam," Buckie said softly.

Sam didn't go ask her to dance right away. There was no sense letting Buckie think he was going to take relationship advice from a man who had never actually had one.

Except, he realized, he had. Buckie had had a relationship with this family for as long as Sam had been alive. He was rough around the edges, and yet, when it came to selflessness, he had always put the Waters family first.

Buckie was not just a cook, and certainly not just an employee. He was a friend.

No, a member of the family.

*Like an annoying uncle.*

Still, annoying or not, Buckie was coming from a place of having a genuine sense of being the family guardian. And unlike Sam, he was seeing clearly—very clearly—that there was something going on between Shelby and Sam.

It was time to find out.

What was between them.

It was time to find out if it was a one night thing, or if it was going somewhere.

Feeling like a warrior getting ready to stride into battle, Sam took a deep breath. He stepped out onto the dance floor. He pushed his way through a crush of people until, finally, he came to her.

He didn't have to say a word. His body language said it all. The men who had been clustered around her all night melted away.

Shelby looked at him as if she had been waiting, maybe her whole life, for this exact moment in time.

And he felt as if he had been, too. Nothing had ever felt quite so right as looking down at her flushed face and saying, "Could I have this dance?"

The music changed, just like that.

As if the whole universe had been waiting. For this. For this man and this woman to come together in this way.

It was a slow song, a love song. The mood in the room changed. The lights dimmed.

And when Shelby slid into his arms, and pressed against the length of him, it was as if she had been born to fit against him.

His hand found the small of her back. She tilted her head up to look at him. Her eyes were luminous.

"You're not my nanny, anymore," he said, his lips nearly on her ear.

"I told you from the start, I was never a nanny," she said, her voice husky.

But now it was official.

Just as he had thought, what was left of his barriers collapsed. He and Shelby stopped moving, leaning into each other, breathing hard. They stared at each other.

"I need some air," she said, her voice hoarse.

"Me, too."

# CHAPTER FIFTEEN

SAM'S HAND ON the small of Shelby's back, he guided her through the crowd, avoiding that meeting of people's eyes that would lead to the stop, the inevitable conversation. He'd lost her once tonight that way, he didn't intend to do it again.

And then they were outside. He felt like they popped out, like a cork freed of a wine bottle. They were free of the noise and the crowd. They didn't pause in Reykjavík. In fact, in just a few steps they were swallowed by the cool, dark crispness of a star-filled night. Just yards away from that sea of noise and light and movement, they floated free.

It was incredibly hot for this time of year. He could feel a crackle in the air—a coming thunderstorm—that mirrored what was going on between him and Shelby.

And with the same suddenness that storm would start with, there was no preamble. She kissed him full on the lips, bracketed his face with her hands, took his mouth as if she was ravenous, her tongue exploring the curve of his lips, and the edge of his teeth, plundering the hollow.

"I thought you needed air," he muttered into the corner of her lips. He was shocked he was able to speak.

"I do," she said, her voice a husky caress that made his blood catch fire, "I'm dying. I need mouth-to-mouth."

"Who am I to turn my back on a dying woman?"

Her hands snaked under his shirt, leaving a trail of excruciating heat in the wake of her exploration. Her right leg slid up the side of his own. She pressed hard against him, so hard he could feel her pulse in her femoral artery.

"Come on," he growled in her ear, "we've got to get out of here."

He took her hand again and led her to the pathway behind the barn that snaked down into the ravine.

The woods were so thick the moonlight could not penetrate them. But he knew every inch of this trail. He did not need light to guide him.

Soon, the activity and noise of the grad celebration were completely gone. She kicked off her shoes and carried them in her hand, her bare feet padding quietly along the worn trail through the trees.

It reminded him of the first time he saw her, coming toward him, her shoes in her hand. He felt he had known, even then, it was leading to this.

He led her to a clearing, and finally they were free of the thick canopy of trees and had moonlight again. At this place, his boyhood favorite, the creek babbled happily into a pool. A large, flat rock overhung the pool.

When he laid her down on it, the rock was still warm from the heat of the day. There was an urgency about her, as if she could feel the coming storm, but he made them both slow it down.

He undressed her with reverence, the moon revealing her body to him, painting each perfect curve in silver and light.

They were caught in an enchantment, in a spell of meant-to-be.

Because there was no shyness in either of them.

But instead, a deep sense of recognition. Of moving toward what was always destined to be, something born of the same ancient rhythms and cycles that made rain and wind, dirt that grew things, and sun that warmed the earth so that they could grow after an endless winter.

They were in the grip of something, both of them, that could not be denied by something so puny as a man's strength or a woman's desire for a promise.

There was no yesterday. It—and its history, its memories, its lessons—had been completely obliterated by the sweet savagery of complete sensation.

As thunder growled in the distance, they explored, tasted, worshipped each other, explored some more. There was no place that was forbidden, there were no taboos.

Finally, they joined. They became the stars and the moon, the earth and the creek, the untamed storm approaching. Every barrier between them and the world dissolved as they moved in unison with the forces that had created it all.

When they were done, the tenderness he felt for her was overwhelming.

"It's not going anywhere," she told him, whispering the words against his neck as if they were a promise.

He was a man who had had his belief in forever shattered, and she was a woman who had never believed in it in the first place.

Could there be a more perfect match than that?

There were no more words between them, as if the place they had gone to was too immense for such a small thing as words to penetrate it, too sacred to try and capture its essence.

They slid into the pool, their skin so heated that the icy mountain runoff felt refreshing, as if it had been put there for the sole purpose of preventing an inferno, of cooling them off just enough to start all over again at the beginning.

The storm broke all around them just as they had finished making love for the second time. Shelby took in Sam, the beautiful cut of his muscles, the perfection of his skin. He was illuminated by the lightning flashes, before being plunged back into darkness.

The rawness of the storm was a perfect reflection of what had just transpired between them.

It was so *real,* so elemental, no frills or gadgets or flowers. No first-time awkwardness or discomfort.

Coming from a place of deep connection to all things, just like the storm.

The rain came, and Sam tugged her to his feet. Laughing, showering her with kisses, he somehow managed to get her back into the dress. He pulled on his now-soaked shirt, and she had to help him with the jeans which, wet, were sticking and gripping.

He took her hand, and with the rain sluicing down around them, the lightning splitting the sky, and the thunder rolling ominously, he led her along a path that followed the creek.

She was still barefoot—she had no idea what had become of her shoes—and the mud oozing up between her toes felt exquisite, her entire body so open to sensation, every cell celebrating it.

She realized they had skirted the barn completely and they came out of the woods behind the house. Despite the exertion of navigating a path turned to grease by rain, she was shaking uncontrollably.

They ran, hand in hand across the lawn, and up the front stairs.

"I can't get mud of Alvin's floors."

They both chuckled that such a rational thought was even possible. Without hesitation, Sam swept her into his arms, nudged the door open with his foot, kicked off his own boots without setting her down, and then carried her across the threshold and up the stairs.

It was so dark, but lightning flashes, illuminated the bedroom he had brought them to. It was beautiful, masculine, in muted grays with an impressive, solid four-poster bed dominating the space. But he went by the bed and into the en suite bathroom.

He flipped on the lights with his elbow and, peripherally, she noted the spa-like beauty of the bathroom: white towels, marble surfaces, a huge tub, a separate shower with multiple heads.

Sam set her down.

"Mud," she started to say, but he placed a single finger over her lips, regarding her with wonder, as if he had been deaf and returned to hearing to find himself in the midst of a symphony.

With simple masculine mastery, he stripped the sodden dress from her.

"Obviously ruined," he said with a touch of regret.

*Worth it*, she thought.

Sam reached around her and turned on the shower. Water poured like the rain outside from a showerhead in the ceiling, pulsed from a mounted wand, spouted out of wall jets. And then he stepped out of his own clothes, and they were in the shower, the hot water pounding them. He knelt at her feet, lifted them one at a time, directed the wand until the mud sluiced off them.

And then he rose, and as the water cascaded around them, he captured her lips once again, and they tasted each other, explored, and then tasted some more.

They stepped out of the shower and toweled each other dry. Then, Sam lifted Shelby again, carried her to his bed, set her down to pull back the covers. She slipped into the pure decadence of Egyptian cotton sheets and a down comforter.

He came in beside her. "What kind of man makes love to a woman for the first time on a rock?" he whispered against her. "I think I better make up for that."

And he did.

Shelby woke in the morning with a feeling like she had never had in her entire life. Entirely relaxed. Satiated.

*Happy.*

The storm of last night had passed, and sunshine danced in the large paned window of his bedroom. She turned to look at Sam, appreciating how the strong morning light spilled across the perfect male contours of his body.

He was laying on his belly, his broad back bare, the comforter riding the line of two strong dimples right above the beautiful curve of his behind. One strong, tanned arm was splayed across her midriff, the other fell off the edge of the bed.

Sam's face, whisker-shadowed, was pressed into the pillow, and Shelby unabashedly, hungrily, studied the rumple of his hair. It was curling rebelliously at the tips even though it had been cut short. She took in the sweep of his lashes, the cut of his cheekbones and chin, the gorgeous curve of his lips.

As if he sensed he was being watched, he opened one eye, and then the other. He smiled at her with such tender and sleepy welcome she felt as if her bones were melting.

He put his hand on the back of her neck, pulled her into him, kissed her good morning. The kiss deepened.

"What about Buckie?" she whispered. "What's he going to say?"

"He has his own quarters, down by the bunkhouse. He has the day off today. It's Sunday. But it's not as if we're teenagers coming out of the hayloft all flushed with guilt and excitement."

"Well, maybe the excitement part."

"He wouldn't disapprove," Sam said, tracing the line of her cheek and her lips with a gentle finger. "In fact, he'll probably post banns at the church."

This was said casually, as if that would be quite all right with Sam.

For a flash, that familiar terror tried to rise. *Banns at the church?*

That sounded like a commitment. Is that where Sam thought this was going? She wondered what the future held, but then she decided there would be lots of time for thinking later. She had to go home today. She would think then.

Later, they were in his kitchen. She was wearing one of his button-up shirts. It had the subtle scent of laundry soap and him. It stopped just above her thigh, and it made her feel sexy and as if she was his. He was wearing the crazy boxer shorts that Hannah had lent her that first day in the sprinkler. It made him look sexy, and feel as if he was hers.

They made toast and smeared it with jam and fed it to each other.

"Don't go," Sam said, flicking a crumb off her lip with his finger. "Don't go today."

*Don't go. What she feared and longed for.*

"So tempting," she said, trying for a light tone. "If ever anyone was going to convince me to just throw the last two years of working and building a business to the wind, it would be you, but I can't. And I'm going to have to leave soon, within an hour or two. I've got to drive to Calgary and my flight goes to New York at three. And then I have to go to Mississippi for most of next week."

"Stay, just for today."

*Just for today.* Couldn't a person live their whole life like that?

"I'll get someone to take the car back," he promised. "I'll get the company jet to take you to New York tonight. You can sleep all the way."

He had stolen them a few more hours, and she was grateful for that. How easy it had been to forget, in the primal things that had happened between them, that he was *also* this. That he had companies and jets and a fortune at his command.

"That sounds wonderful," she said.

Several hours later, they took the helicopter and picked up

Hannah. When they got back Sam saddled horses and Shelby took the opportunity to remind Hannah she was leaving.

"Don't go," Hannah cried, an exact replica of her father's words.

"I have to," Shelby said. "Remember I told you about the party I'm planning for that young woman in Mississippi?"

"I remember," Hannah said sullenly.

"I have to go do that. But I'll be coming back here, because we're going to have my dad's birthday party at the barn in September."

It occurred to her last night had felt as if she didn't need to think about the future, but because of her dad's party, their lives would be intertwined for a while longer.

They couldn't be lovers! What would it do to Hannah?

"Do you know Sandra?" Shelby asked Hannah, avoiding even looking at Sam, sure Hannah would read some change and some truth into the way she looked at Sam.

"'Course. She's so pretty. I thought her dress was the prettiest last night."

"So did I!" Shelby said.

"Jimmy's her boyfriend," Hannah announced.

"He is?" Sam said, his brow furrowed.

"Everybody knows that. She's a really good horseback rider, too. Daddy, remember when she won the barrel racing at the high school rodeo?"

"I do. Would you be okay with Sandra coming to spend time with you when Shelby goes?"

The word *nanny* was carefully avoided.

"Oh!" Hannah said. "Do you think she would teach me how to barrel race?"

And that was how easily Hannah moved on.

"Let's go for a picnic," Sam suggested.

Shelby knew she should say no. But she was not that

strong. She would take these moments, even if they felt as if she was stealing them.

They took a simple sandwich lunch to the waterfall. The grass was still wet from the storm last night, and they spread a thick blanket over it.

While Hannah ran delirious circles chasing butterflies, they lay side by side, watching lazy clouds drift across the sky.

Hannah appeared and looked down at them.

"Are you going to be boyfriend and girlfriend now?" she asked solemnly.

Shelby shot him a look. He gazed back at her, and the understanding passed between them. This was their complication. It wasn't just about them.

Protecting Hannah had to be the priority.

"Grown-ups can be friends without being a boyfriend and a girlfriend," Shelby said carefully.

"How do you know about girlfriends and boyfriends?" Sam asked, not answering the question.

"I'm going to have a boyfriend, too."

"Really?" Sam said. He turned his head to Shelby and mouthed, *Over my dead body.*

"Shane Hardy," Hannah announced.

"He's twelve, for god's sake," Sam sputtered.

"I'll grow up a little bit, first."

"Would you?"

"He doesn't know yet." She cocked her head at her father. "When should I tell him?"

"When you're thirty."

"Oh. Really *old.*"

"Thanks," Sam said dryly.

And then a butterfly caught Hannah's attention and she was off, forgetting she had even asked that question.

# CHAPTER SIXTEEN

"WHEN AM I going to see you again?" Sam asked, an hour later, as they stood at the airstrip.

"I don't know."

Shelby felt as if she didn't know anything. She needed time away from him. She couldn't think straight around him.

What was unfolding between them was terrifying.

Even now, her eyes kept drifting to his lips, and wanting him made her feel as if her restraint from throwing herself at him was an elastic band, stretching tighter and tighter, getting ready to snap.

She glanced at Hannah and felt her resolve firm.

She took a deep breath. "We can't," she whispered.

He looked at her steadily. "I know," he said.

"Don't call," she told him.

"I won't," he said.

His agreement felt as if it tore her in two. She got on the plane to Calgary. She did not look back.

An hour later, she was on the jet to New York, in a supremely comfortable bed, thinking how unexpectedly she had arrived back at the life she'd been born to.

Only with such exquisite differences.

Sam was different from the kind of people she had grown up around. He was sophisticated, and yet that sophistication was layered with an authenticity, an awareness of his own power that money and station in life had not given him.

And she realized, gratefully, that she had that now, too. Since Eventually, she had come into herself in the most unexpected and lovely ways.

And all of it—the unexpected twists and turns of her life—felt as if it had conspired to bring her to this moment.

Where she was equal to a man like that, completely worthy of his love.

*Worthy of love,* a little voice taunted her. *Worthy of love.* It reminded her that Sam had not mentioned the word *love*.

And for some reason, she hoped he wouldn't, as if that could spoil everything.

Exactly one week from the day that she had become Sam's lover, Shelby was in the mansion in Mississippi putting together the final details for the debutante ball.

The house was beyond expectation. It had a ballroom, for heaven's sake, the wall-to-wall French doors thrown open to the evening breeze, letting in the scents of magnolia and honeysuckle and the sounds of crickets and cicadas, whip-poor-wills and nighthawks.

Everything was as perfect as she and Marcus and her crew had been able to make it, though at the last minute, she found out they were down two servers who had called in sick.

Still, every event had those kinds of glitches. She rarely felt this kind of tension over them.

Then Marcus said, "Ooh, la la, who is that?"

She turned and looked.

It couldn't be. But it was. Her world went from gray to color again.

"That's Sam," she told Marcus, trying desperately to keep her tone neutral.

"*That's* Sam Waters? No wonder you abandoned me for some ranch when we had all *this* to get done."

"I'm sorry. You have done an incredible job."

"Actually," Marcus said, suddenly serious, "I was only teasing. I've wanted, for a long time, to show you what I can do."

She made a note of that to herself: *let go of control.*

In the context of Sam's surprise arrival, she was not sure now was the time to contemplate letting go of control. Unfortunately, as she thought it, her eyes fastened on Sam, moving toward her, and she had a rather heated memory of letting go of control completely.

He was neither the cowboy nor the businessman tonight, dressed in slacks, a polo shirt and loafers.

"Sam," she said. "What are you doing here?"

She ordered herself to stop being pleased that he had remembered what the event was, that he had gone to the trouble of tracking it down.

"Anything you tell me to do," he said simply, his eyes drinking her in as if she was a long cool drink of water and he was a man dying of thirst.

"The man with a private jet waiting will do whatever needs doing?" she asked, trying to hide her pleasure at seeing him behind a skeptical note.

He nodded earnestly. "You need dishes washed? I'm your man. One of the debutantes drinks too much punch, and throws up? I'll clean it."

For heaven's sake. That was almost better than a declaration of love.

*Love.*

She could not let that word enter her mind. She couldn't. That word was a temptation, a witch holding out a poisoned apple.

It promised one thing and delivered another.

"What if the girls want a male dancer?" she challenged him.

"At a debutante ball?" he choked.

Sam was blushing. She wanted to make him blush. Lots.

"How's Hannah?" she asked, even though she had Face-

Timed her favorite little girl twice this week. She needed the barrier of his child between them. It was dangerous that Hannah wasn't here.

"She's great. I'll have to think of a great gift to bring her since I've abandoned her for the weekend. Though I'm not sure if she'll even notice I'm gone. Sandra couldn't be more perfect. Poor Rascal doesn't know what hit him. He's running the barrels half a dozen times a day. His tongue's hanging out so far, I had to warn Hannah not to let him step on it. They had plans to take in a local rodeo together this weekend."

"You can bring her back a Mississippi mud pie." She knew it would be a hit with Hannah.

"Don't get me thinking about mud," he warned her in a low voice.

She thought of him washing the mud from her feet a week ago.

"I promised to help," he said. "What can I do?"

"Well, um, I still have flowers in the sink…"

"Flowers?" Marcus huffed. "We're down servers."

"Or course he's not going to be a server," Shelby snapped. Marcus was taking this being in charge thing a little too far.

But Sam lifted a broad shoulder amicably. "Happy to do it. I think it sounds kind of fun, actually."

And just like that Marcus was hustling him off to get changed into one of the tuxedos they had rented for all the waitstaff.

The evening was absolutely glorious. Was it because she kept catching glimpses of Sam that it felt as if it might have been one of her best events ever? He slipped into the role as if he'd been doing it his whole life, and she loved it that these young women had no idea their "server" was a billionaire who had arrived in a private jet.

It made her feel as if she knew a secret.

In fact, she couldn't look at him nearly as often as she

wanted, because it made her remember all their secrets, and that made it very difficult to concentrate on work.

Finally, well past midnight, the last of the limos had pulled out ferrying the last of the debutantes and their guests.

Marcus handed her a box with leftover Mississippi mud pie from the evening snack and shooed her out, insisting he had it, winking toward Sam, and mouthing something extremely inappropriate.

She was going to insist on staying, but then she remembered the part about giving up control, and graciously accepted Marcus's offer to look after the wrap-up.

Sam had rented a four-wheel drive, and they rode with the top down through the muggy Southern heat. They came to a sleepy little town, the nearest one to the venue, where she had rented a hotel room.

It was not the kind of hotel room either of them was used to. When she opened the door the bed seemed like the only piece of furniture, beckoning them.

She tried for small talk.

"I can't believe how you handled being a server," she said. "I can't thank you enough."

"I'm exhausted," he said, giving her a mischievous grin that did not look exhausted at all.

"Oh, I think being waitstaff is way harder than people give it credit for."

"That part was a cinch. It was fending off Marcus and all those women that was the hard part. Hannah better not act like that when she's that age."

"Act like what?"

He emptied his pockets and dollar bills and little slips of paper fluttered out. She picked one up and looked at it.

It had the name Linda on it. The *I* was dotted with a heart. There was a phone number. She picked up another one. Different name. Bolder message.

"Good grief," she said, looking at the crumpled dollar bills scattered around him with the phone numbers. "They were tipping you? We have a strict no tip policy!"

"You forgot to tell me. I'm not sure I could have stopped them." He fished several dollars out from under his waistband, and then reached into the back of his shorts.

He was right. She could not have stopped these wealthy young women from letting them know they saw him, and wanted what they saw.

Everybody in the world saw that thing he had. That masculine potency, the pure confidence and power he carried himself with. He had it whether he was riding a horse, waiting tables or running a billion-dollar company.

And tonight, it belonged to her.

"Hey," he said, loosening the tie, "come here."

He pulled her into her arms and kissed her thoroughly.

"I have been wanting to do that all night," he growled.

"Me, too," she admitted.

"Ma'am," he breathed into her ear, in a slow, sensuous, bone-melting drawl, "what's your pleasure?"

He didn't wait for her to answer.

He decided *his* pleasure was eating Mississippi mud pie. Off of her body.

"You know what would make this perfect?" he asked her huskily.

It could be more perfect?

"A spray can of whipping cream."

After that, Sam and Shelby spoke often, both on the phone and video chat. They texted each other several times a day, little notes and jokes, the language of lovers.

Shelby realized Sam made her feel cherished, while not making her feel trapped or committed.

"I'd love you to experience the Calgary Stampede with

Hannah and I," Sam said one night. "Will you come for a few days?"

Shelby drew in a deep breath. "What will we tell Hannah?"

"I've booked us a suite. Separate rooms. The Stampede experience will definitely be G-rated."

She was ashamed to admit, even to herself, she didn't know how she was going to keep her hands off of him. At the same time, she loved it that he was protecting his daughter, who had already lost way too much, from potential hurt.

At some level, Shelby thought, he *knew*. It was fun. It was beautiful. But he knew that it couldn't last. Shelby was not the right woman for him. Or for anyone, if her past history was any indication.

He had suffered as much loss as his daughter. He wasn't leaving himself open to more.

They were having a fling, pure and simple. They would not complicate things with promises they did not intend to keep.

Shelby should have been glad that they were so much on the same page. But, somehow, glad was not how she felt.

Instead, she felt as if she was facing a hard truth.

She was not worthy of a man like Sam. She could not replace the perfect wife he had already had, the perfect mother Hannah had already had.

"So," she told herself, breezily, "the pressure is off. Just have fun."

But she was not so sure she had ever felt less like having fun in her entire life. Maybe it would be best if they called it off now.

And yet, she could not resist seeing him again. And Hannah. Why not indulge in the summer of love? Why not take every moment of happiness that was offered to her? A natural splitting point would be after her father's birthday party. Why cheat herself of moments with Sam before she had to?

The trick would be not to let Hannah see what was going

on between them, to make sure the child was not in any way affected by the final goodbye.

When she arrived at the Calgary International Airport, thoughts of goodbye fled her like late snow melting into nothingness on a sidewalk.

Sam greeted her with that oh-so-familiar grin, a lovely platonic kiss on the cheek, and by putting a beautiful white cowboy hat on her head.

"This is the Calgary version of a lei," he explained.

Of all the things she had experienced in life, it seemed to Shelby nothing had ever been sweeter than Hannah's excited greeting. When she swung the little girl up into her arms, Hannah showed none of her father's restraint. Shelby was covered in kisses.

Even though saying goodbye to Sam was inevitable, did she ever have to say goodbye to Hannah? They could always write, and call. As long as the little girl wanted to.

She decided not to think about it anymore. She surrendered to the simple bliss of being with them.

Hannah and Sam were already Stampede-ready in plaid shirts, jeans, cowboy hats and boots. They fit right in with nearly every other person in the airport, though they were probably the only authentic ranchers in the crowd. Shelby felt slightly out of place in the slacks and top she had chosen to be subtly sexy.

Sam had booked a large three-bedroom suite for them in a downtown Calgary hotel. As they drove there, Hannah chattered away about Sandra and Rascal, Buckie and Jimmy, new calves and the possibility of a bigger horse for her barrel racing career.

The hotel was super posh, and the suite was over-the-top, even for Shelby who had grown up in surroundings like this. Sam showed her through to the master suite.

"You take this one. I'll take the smaller room beside Hannah's."

"Thank you." When he closed the door to give her time to freshen up, she saw he had laid out a Western outfit for her. Just as that day they had shopped for dresses, he had guessed her size exactly.

She put on the jeans and plaid shirt, the new boots and the hat, then modeled the ensemble for her approving audience of two.

If she had thought she might feel foolish in her new "duds," as Hannah called them, she was dead wrong.

She would have been terribly out of place without them. The whole city had gone cowboy chic.

The hotel was at the very center of everything. Shelby quickly saw that Calgary, always vibrant, upped its ante for this ten-day Western extravaganza that always began the first Friday of July. It was called The Greatest Outdoor Show on Earth, and Shelby thought that might be an understatement.

She and Sam and Hannah gave themselves over to a whole city that was in party mode. They partook in street corner pancake breakfast served from chuck wagons, and danced on closed off streets. Shelby watched, open-mouthed, as Indigenous peoples in full regalia rode docile American paint horses through the middle of downtown.

By afternoon they had made their way to Stampede Park, where there were rodeo events, multiple concerts, and a midway full of rides, carnival food and attractions. Hannah rode on Sam's shoulders as they made their way through the throngs of people, trying rides and carnival foods that competed with each other to be the most bizarre. This year there were nearly sixty weird and wonderful offerings.

Sam, wisely, made Hannah stick to a traditional corn dog and some mini donuts. But at Shelby's challenge he gamely tried the ketchup and mustard ice cream, which they all took a lick of, and then they shared Shelby's spicy pickle lemonade.

As they laughed over the ice cream, Shelby saw people sending indulgent looks their way. They looked, she thought, like a family. She wasn't going to let the fact it wasn't true—and would never be true—spoil her experience. It was such an incredible day.

Sam had tickets for the chuck wagon races and evening show, but Hannah was worn out. In all that commotion, she fell asleep on her daddy's shoulder and so Sam and Shelby decided to return to their hotel. As they were exiting Stampede Park, he went over to a young couple, with a little boy, waiting in line to buy tickets. He gave them his.

It was such a nice thing to do. Shelby saw in that young couple's faces as they stared down at what were likely very expensive tickets and then looked back at him, the looks on their faces confirming what she already knew.

He was a good man, thoughtful and generous, in a world that needed so much more of both.

Back in their suite, Sam put Hannah in bed, came out and shut the door of her bedroom.

And then he took Shelby in his arms and kissed her until she was breathless.

"That couldn't have worked out any better," he said, not the least concerned about not using those tickets.

"I thought we weren't—"

"I thought we weren't, too, but Shelby, I'm just not that strong."

But he proved to her—twice—exactly how strong he was.

Later, they ordered food from another of Sam's favorite Calgary restaurants.

They made slow sweet love, again, behind the locked door of the master suite, in unison with the fireworks that ended each day of the Stampede.

# CHAPTER SEVENTEEN

THE NEXT DAY, they took in a few morning activates geared to children, but opted to take the afternoon off so that Hannah wouldn't be too tired for the evening show.

They played a board game in the hotel room.

After the sixth round, Sam said to Shelby, "I'm so sorry I packed this. The little fiend is torturing us."

"I'm not a fiend!" Hannah said. "And I win again."

Shelby did not think it was torture at all. She loved the lazy feeling of whiling away a hot afternoon in the air-conditioned room with two people she had come to adore.

What was she going to do when they were no longer part of her life? She warned herself, again, about spoiling what she had in the moment by worrying about the future.

They made their way back to Stampede Park in late afternoon. It was the last night of the chuck wagon races for the Cowboys Rangeland Derby. Sam had been invited by one of his neighbors, who owned and drove one of the chuck wagon outfits. This time they didn't need tickets. They wore passes on lanyards.

The barbecues and tables were set up just outside the stable area, right beside the track and underneath a grandstand reserved for families, friends, special guests and VIPs.

It was soon evident Sam fell into several of those categories, but probably mostly the friend one. He knew many of these people, and Shelby could see their respect for him and his for them.

The pre-race dinner reminded Shelby of the grad celebration that had been held in the Mountain Waters Ranch barn. Generations of families were hanging out here. Children, whom Hannah knew, and soon joined, were running in and out of the gathering of people.

The only difference was that in this barn, they were sharing it with actual horses. Shelby was taken under the wing of the chuck wagon driver's wife, who gave her an exclusive tour of the stall area. The horses were so friendly and gentle, putting their heads over the stall doors looking for a pat. Shelby was impressed with the extreme love and care lavished on the horse athletes that participated in this sport. It was evident the horses were considered members of these chuck wagon families.

After dinner, they took their place on the grandstand seats. The majority of the audience was sitting across the infield from them, in a covered grandstand that Sam told her was probably sold out for this final chuck wagon race of the Stampede, and that it could hold north of twenty-five thousand people.

"Have you been to a chuck wagon race before?" Sam asked her.

"I've never even heard of a chuck wagon race before."

"They're the best," Hannah said, with a contented sigh, leaving her seat and taking up on her daddy's lap instead. "If I don't become a barrel racer, I might be an outrider instead."

As the first heat of four wagons came out into the infield, Sam explained what was going on to Shelby. As well as competing for substantial prize money, the colorful canvases stretched over the ribs of each of the chuck wagons had been auctioned off to sponsor companies in exchange for advertising. The highest-winning bid this year had been for close to two hundred thousand dollars.

The first chuck wagon races had been held at the Stampede over a hundred years ago, and they were still a tribute to the tough, courageous kind of men and women who had tamed the West.

"The Rangeland Derby is the World Series of chuck wagon races."

Sam was so patient, intent on having her understand this sport that he had grown up with and that was part of his culture.

He was a good teacher. He told her each team consisted of a four-horse chuck wagon, a driver and four outriders.

"That means, in a few minutes, they'll be thirty-two horses running that track. At the starting horn, one outrider has to hold the lead horse steady, while the others throw on a barrel, a tent fly and posts in the back of the wagon. Then they'll all catapult onto their own horses and follow the wagon as he circles the barrels, and comes out on the track. The outriders are not allowed to cross the finish line before the wagon."

"I can't believe those are the same horses I was just petting!" she said.

The horses were practically breathing fire, fighting against the traces, prancing, lunging, wanting to go.

The teams were announced. The drivers seemed to all have cowboy names like Chance and Cody and Lane and Dallas.

And then the horn blew. Shelby could barely keep track, so much was going on. But by the end of the race she was up and cheering them on with twenty-five thousand other people, even though her heart was in her throat as the thirty-two horses thundered past the finish line. The wagons had come perilously close together. The outriders had been absolutely hell-bent.

She leaned into Sam's shoulder. It felt so easy to do that.

So right. She relished the evening light, the dust rising from the arena, the touch of his shoulder, Hannah on his lap.

It felt like a perfect moment, and she felt as if she loved life with an intensity made so much more exquisite by the feeling of belonging she felt with Sam and Hannah, and by the fact she knew she could not have it forever.

"You have to promise me, you will never, ever allow Hannah to be an outrider," Shelby whispered to Sam after the third heat of the evening. "I've never seen such daredevils in my whole life."

He laughed. "Funny. I find that less dangerous than those girls gone wild at the debutante ball."

Sam, Shelby and Hannah had now established a routine for watching the races. For each heat, they would all pick their own wagon to cheer for. Shelby picked hers by the names on the canvases, Hannah by how pretty the horses were, and Sam through knowledge—usually quite extensive—of the outfit.

He won most often, but that didn't prevent Shelby and Hannah from screaming themselves hoarse, cheering on their chosen wagons for each heat. When Sam's friend came out for his heat, they all chose him. They cheered and jumped up and down and pounded each other's backs with excitement. Sam's friend came dead last, and it didn't alter their excitement one little bit.

When the chucks were over, as day turned to night, the huge stadium lights came on and grandstand show began. The opening number could have put any of the best shows in Las Vegas to shame. But Hannah was worn-out from all the excitement. There was a brief period of crabbiness before she fell asleep on Sam. They, once again, walked back to their hotel with Sam carrying the sleeping child in his arms.

Shelby was not sure there was a sight in the world more lovely than that.

"Those people are death-defying," Shelby said, handing

him a cold beer when he came out from tucking the sleeping child in her bed. "That may have been the most exciting thing I've ever experienced."

He set his beer down without even taking a sip.

He picked her up as easily as he had picked up Hannah and carried her to the master suite. He shut the door with his foot, set her on the bed.

"I'm going to take that as a challenge," he growled.

"You won that challenge pretty handily," Shelby told him later. They were wrapped up in the thick, white housecoats provided by the hotel, sitting on their balcony. Sam was finally getting around to that beer she had opened for him earlier.

As they watched, the final fireworks of the Calgary Stampede lit up the city sky in a spectacular fashion.

"You were pretty good yourself," he said, wagging his eyebrows at her and then turning his attention to watch a huge rocket whistle upward, upward, upward. And then it exploded, and the sparks of color cascaded down. And then each of the sparks of color exploded and more fiery color dotted the sky.

She gasped with delight, delight that was deepened when his hand found hers.

"At least that good," he said, and then softly, "but I want more."

"You're insatiable," she said, deliberately misunderstanding him.

"I didn't mean more of that. I meant more of us."

"Didn't we talk about this?" she said, trying for lightness. "The song of youth? More, more, more."

The thing was, she didn't want more.

She wanted everything to stay exactly the way it was, right this minute.

"I think we need to talk about the future," Sam said softly.

"Please, not yet," she whispered. In her experience nothing could spoil a relationship more quickly than that particular discussion.

It occurred to her she was usually the one who spoiled it, too. Why? She had never been in a relationship like this one.

Why did it feel as if she was quite capable of sabotaging her own happiness?

Sam could not believe how quickly the summer was going by. He hadn't been sure how to follow up that amazing weekend at the Calgary Stampede, but then he'd been called to Switzerland for a business trip. Shelby had been able to join him in Bern.

He'd liked the three of them spending time together, but he liked this way, way better. He needed to protect his daughter as he and Shelby got to know each other more deeply.

As lovers.

As partners and equals.

And as friends. He hoped the discussion Shelby didn't want to have would finally happen.

This was new in his experience. Usually it was the woman who was pushing for a commitment. But Sam realized it was him who could not picture a future without her in it. He did not even want to try. And he knew it was time to do the honorable thing.

She had to feel the same way as he did.

Love.

He was not sure when that had entered the equation, only that he felt it truly and deeply. He was confident she did, too, though she had not said the words. Still, it was in the way she looked at him, and the way she touched him, and the way she expressed tenderness to him.

Neither of them had ever been to Bern before and the

beautiful European city was about as opposite to Calgary as you could get.

Being with Shelby made him feel so awake to the world. Open to new experiences, willing to celebrate the incredible differences that existed on the same globe. Everything felt brand-new to him.

This time, they spent grown-up time enjoying the gorgeous views of the Aare River, strolling hand in hand on the covered walkways, and availing themselves to the many charms of the Old City.

And then, once, when he found himself alone, he wandered into a jewellery store, and he saw it immediately.

The ring he wanted her to have.

That night in their room overlooking the river, the lights of the city reflecting in its inky darkness, he whispered the words to her for the first time.

Or tried to.

"I lo—"

Her finger had touched his lips, stopping him from finishing. Instead, she had finished it. They said actions spoke louder than words, and yet somehow the fact she had not let him say those words kept the ring in his pocket, waiting for the perfect moment.

But somehow, the moment never presented itself.

And then the next time they met, Hannah joined them again, this time in Shelby's territory, New York City. It was truly wonderful to explore that city that he was pretty familiar with through the eyes of his child.

"When I grow up, I'm going to work in this toy shop," Hannah announced, hugging her new teddy bear.

"I thought you were going to be an outrider," Shelby reminded her.

Hannah looked momentarily deflated.

"So much to do, so little time," Sam teased her.

But then his daughter brightened. "Outriding—or maybe barrel racing—is only in the summer. I'll work here the rest of the time."

"Hard no to my daughter working in New York City," Sam said to Shelby in an undertone.

"I turned out okay."

He smiled at that. "So you did," he said and felt a familiar bolt of heat race through him. He had that ring in his pocket, but he realized he didn't want to ask her to marry him with Hannah there.

Once they were a family, there would be plenty of time for the three of them. But for this—for his proposal—it needed to be just him and her.

They juggled schedules and locations all summer, meeting as often as they could, and still the perfect time never presented itself, though every encounter just cemented his certainty that Shelby was the right one.

The perfect partner for him.

The perfect mother for Hannah.

Even when they couldn't meet, he loved the sound of her voice on the phone, loved the texts she sent, sometimes funny, sometimes serious, sometimes so naughty they made him blush.

Still, though she was generous with the love hearts in her texts, Shelby had not said she loved him.

And yet everything said she did.

He was so glad when she came back to the ranch as summer dwindled to start getting ready for her father's birthday party. It occurred to him that this is what he'd been waiting for.

The perfect opportunity.

For him to propose.

He'd had enough of acting like guilty teenagers, he'd had enough of pretending to Hannah nothing was going on. He'd had enough of protecting his daughter and himself from the potential of hurt. Is that how he wanted Hannah to live? Afraid of all the things that could possibly go wrong?

It was starting to feel as if he was having an illicit affair, and lying about it. Lying to his kid! It was not like the Santa Claus lie, either.

It was lying about love between a man and a woman. He did not want his daughter to ever feel love was something to be hidden.

And it was time to lead by example.

# CHAPTER EIGHTEEN

SAM IMAGINED IT ALL. He would propose. Shelby would squeal her yes and declare, finally, her love for him.

He needed to play by all the rules. He needed to go by the book. As a father himself, he had to make it right. As old-fashioned as it was, Sam needed to ask Boswell Kane for the hand of his daughter.

Knowing that was the missing piece to his proposal, he was able to just relax and watch how seamlessly his and Shelby's worlds combined. He got to see all the behind-the-scenes work that went into an event, and how good she was at it.

The barn had undergone a cute transformation for the grad, but what Shelby did for her father's birthday elevated it to new heights.

She had briefly considered a Western theme for the party, but she had decided it could too easily become hokey. Instead, she had opted for a formal black-tie affair, and he watched as she transformed the barn to fit that vision.

As the day drew closer, Sam was aware of feeling increasingly nervous. He rarely got nervous.

But when he finally met Boswell Kane, he knew exactly why he was nervous.

This was the father of the woman he was sleeping with.

Shelby had, in such a short time, brought the light to a dark world.

Not just his world, but Hannah's.

He was startled to find the presence of her father made him a little ashamed that he had not done the right thing before now. For the longest time, he had allowed himself to believe that what was happening between him and Shelby was okay. Better than okay.

He had lost faith in forever. She had been the perfect woman because she didn't want it at all.

But it had all started to feel terribly off. Not right. As if he was not being true to himself by not offering his protection, his commitment, his life, to the woman he had come to love.

He avoided Shelby all night because he was sure if Boswell saw them together, he would see, very clearly, what was going on between them.

Finally, the opportunity he had been waiting for presented itself. Boswell slipped outside and Sam followed him.

It was a gorgeous night. Chillier than the grad night, fall already in the mountain air. The pool on the creek would be a good place to propose, even if there would be no swimming in the creek tonight.

He was glad it was dark. He was blushing thinking about it.

"Sam," Boswell greeted him.

"Sir," Sam replied.

"No, no, Boswell, please."

*Not until after he'd asked his question.*

"Unbelievable place you have here," Boswell said. "Like nothing I have ever experienced before."

"I'm glad you're enjoying it."

Boswell wanted to talk about business! He wasn't familiar with tech things and he probed Sam's expertise.

It occurred to Sam that he had done such a good job of avoiding Shelby tonight that her father had no idea what was going on between them.

"Uh, sir, I need to talk to you about something."

Boswell looked at him shrewdly. What was he expecting? A business proposal?

"Um, you might not be aware that Shelby and I are, um, dating. Seeing each other."

Boswell tilted his head, squinting at Sam. "My, my," he said, "are you the reason my daughter is blooming like an autumn rose?"

"Um, well, I certainly hope so, sir. I wanted to ask you…"

He suddenly wished he had thought about this more. Maybe looked up how you asked a father for his daughter's hand in marriage. Beth's dad had died when she was young. Of a cancer very similar to hers.

*Genetic*, the doctors had said.

And still Sam had not absolved himself. What could he have done differently? Was he really going to do this again?

*Yes, he really was.*

Sam had made million-dollar deals. He ran one of the biggest ranches in Alberta. He liked to think he *handled* whatever challenges were thrown at him.

But now he felt like a gauche boy.

"Yes?" Boswell asked, puzzled.

"I wanted to ask you if you'd be okay with me asking Shelby to be my wife."

Boswell ducked his head and didn't say anything for so long that Sam was afraid the answer was no.

He hadn't considered that possibility. At all. What would he do if Boswell said no?

But when Boswell lifted his head, Sam saw the reason that he had ducked it in the first place.

His eyes shone with tears.

"You could not give me a better birthday gift than this," he said softly. "Thank you for my daughter's happiness. I cannot wait to get to know you better, as my son."

It was 3:00 a.m. Shelby felt exhausted as the last of the limos had pulled out, the Mercedes-Benz bus was gone and only one jet remained on the tarmac.

Her father's.

Lydia came and took both Shelby's hands in her own.

"I cannot thank you enough. This has been one of the most memorable evenings of my life. I mean that, Shelby." She cast Boswell a look.

Shelby could not miss the pure love in that look. "I'll wait at the plane for you, Bosley."

Somehow Shelby actually *liked* the endearment now. She was glad he had Lydia. Love did that, she supposed, softened all the edges.

And yet she felt a little troubled by her love of Sam tonight. He had seemed off, preoccupied.

As if he was avoiding her.

Maybe he had read something into her inability to say the words *I love you*. She felt if she said those words, the enchantment would be broken, like the clock striking midnight at Cinderella's ball.

It was silly. It was superstitious. And yet she clung to that superstition as if it was a talisman protecting them all—her and Sam and Hannah—from a darkness that waited. To destroy all happiness.

She shivered. Where was this coming from? Except for Sam ignoring her, the evening could not have been more perfect.

That was a pretty big *except*.

*I wonder if it's over*, she thought, and a terror that she had mostly managed to tame over the summer roared back to life.

*Good things did not last*.

She had always thought the end of summer—this event—would be a natural concluding point for her and Sam.

But now that it was actually here, she did not feel ready.

Her father took Shelby's elbow. "Let's sit outside for a minute."

They walked to a bench that had been set up to overlook the ravine.

"I've been to so many parties in my life, I've lost count, Shelby. But what you just did tonight? It transcended. What an extraordinary gift to give a father. Not just the party, but an opportunity to see who his child has become. Seeing you in your element, I am just bursting with pride."

"Thanks, Dad. It was my privilege to do it for you. I have to confess something. I overheard you and Lydia at Christmas two years ago. Plotting to cut me off."

He chuckled. "And you beat us to the punch. That's my girl."

She was twenty-eight years old, and she was his girl. She still loved his approval. It occurred to her she would always be his girl. There was something extraordinarily comforting in that. She laid her head on his shoulder, and he put his arm around her.

"I had already started my company when I overheard the two of you talking. But up until that point it had been kind of a cute little distraction. Hearing you and Lydia gave me the impetus to take it to the next level. It started as *I'll show you* and it became *I showed myself.* Who I could be. What I could do.

"I have to confess, this party started kind of the same way. I wanted you to be proud of me. I wanted you to see me at my best. It felt like a lot of pressure to succeed."

"You achieved all those things, in spades."

"But something else became much more important to me. I started to look at it differently. I still wanted to show you, but I wanted to show you something else. It became not all about me, but about you.

"How much I appreciated you," she said softly, "I wanted to thank you for being a single dad, and doing your best all the time."

She realized her acute appreciation of single dads had a great deal to do with Sam.

"I spoiled you," Boswell said.

"I know. But it wasn't spoiling, like *oh, I'll throw some money at her and get rid of her,* it was spoiling like *I love her so much, and I just want to make her happy.*"

"Thank you for seeing that. It means the world to me."

"We don't say that much, do we, Dad? I love you?"

He shivered. "I'm sorry. I have an aversion to it."

Ahh, the things families passed on.

Silence sat between them for a few minutes.

"Your man is a fine man, Shelby."

"Oh," she stammered, "I don't know about *my* man." Especially since he'd been avoiding her tonight.

"Well, you better figure it out, because he had *the* talk with me tonight."

"I hope not," she said, trying for lightness. Where was this sense of dread coming from? From Sam ignoring her, certainly, but it had deepened since Boswell said he had an aversion to saying I love you. "*The* talk is what you had with me when I was eleven."

"He's an honorable man," Boswell said, pleased.

She knew, with sudden clarity, what *the* talk was. Of course Sam would be bound by tradition. He had done the old-fashioned thing. He had asked her father for her hand.

Where was the excitement? Why didn't it chase away the dread she had been feeling since she noticed Sam avoiding her tonight?

"Dad," she said, and her voice sounded as if it was coming from far away, "why can't I remember Mom?"

Boswell shot Shelby an uncomfortable look. "It's been such a nice night," he said, uneasily. "I don't want to—"

"Tell me," she said. "Please."

His discomfort, his uneasiness was already telling her something. That feeling of dread, intensified, shivering up and down her spine.

Her father sighed, took his hand off her shoulder, and knit his hands in front of him between his knees, and studied them.

"She just wasn't there, Shelby. Maybe that's why you can't remember her."

"What do you mean, she wasn't there?" Shelby asked. She could hear a funny squeak in her voice.

"There was something wrong with her," Boswell said, his voice faraway, remembering. "I didn't realize it until it was too late."

"What do you mean there was something wrong with her?"

"Even before you, Shelby, there was something in her. Restless and wild. It wasn't your fault."

*Her fault?*

"That she wasn't like other new moms. She never wanted to hold you, she didn't want to spend time with you. At first, I thought it was depression. That depression women get—"

"Postpartum," Shelby said, woodenly.

"Except it never went away. And you were like a little puppy, so anxious for her affection and approval, going to her for it again and again, only to be swatted away.

"She didn't act as if she was married and had a baby. She went out all the time, she partied hard. I suspect there were other men. That's all she wanted. The rush, the attention, the altered state of mind."

Shelby felt as if the cold started at her feet and moved slowly up, freezing her one cell at a time.

Her mother had not loved her.

Had not seen any value in her.

She had not been worthy.

Hadn't she always known that? Isn't that why she had chosen to have shallow relationships, easily left behind, before they discovered the truth?

She was not worthy. Even her own mother had seen it.

"The night she died, we had a terrible row about it," Boswell said, his voice low and tortured. "I always wondered if you had heard it. I'm ashamed to say, I don't know how you couldn't have heard. I practically lifted the roof I was yelling so loud."

And suddenly, she did remember.

She was a little girl, sitting on the stairs, her face pressed through the rails, her dolly clutched to her.

"It was the Beachwood Canyon house," she said, recalling the ornate wrought iron of the handrail.

Her father shot her a surprised look. "Yes, it was."

She remembered his voice, the rage in it. *Why can't you just say it? Is it so hard? I love you? All she wants is a little bit of your time. All she wants is those words. I think she'd be happy with a pat on the head every now and then when you walked by.*

And isn't that exactly what Shelby had accepted in every relationship? Pats on the head, crumbs of affection, believing, somehow, that's all she deserved.

But now, she had broken all the rules that that little girl had made that night sitting on the stairs, that terrible night that her mother had died.

She had run down the stairs. *Mommy, I love you.*

The look on her mother's face. Pity. Disdain, maybe.

No, horror.

*You're suffocating me,* she screamed. Her mother had slammed out of the house, angry. Shelby remembered screaming after her, as if it would solve everything, as if it wasn't suffocating her at all:

*I love you.*

*I love you.*

*I love you.*

Until her father had told her, sternly, sensing hysteria, to stop it. And then, not fifteen minutes later, they had heard sirens and seen flames.

# CHAPTER NINETEEN

AND SHELBY HAD KNOWN, to the core of her being, that her mother was gone.

She was *responsible* for the fact her mother and father had fought that night. It was her fault her mother had stormed out of the house, gotten in that car, taken one of the canyon twists way too fast, and sailed off the earth.

Those words *I love you* had chased her from the house and straight into the arms of doom.

"I don't know," Boswell said, softly, "if she'd been drinking that night, or if that's what she wanted all along. With the drugs and the parties and the men, and finally that. Just to escape."

A child's hungry love not enough to hold her, just one more bond she wanted to be free of.

"I'm sorry, sweetie. I should not have told you. It's not a good note to end such a spectacular night on."

Always he had done what he thought was right, protected her from the pain of the truth.

"It's okay," she said. "Really."

And it was, because every single cell of her, and particularly the ones around her heart were frozen solid.

"Are you going to New York tonight?" she asked. She felt as if she was floating above them, looking down. She could hardly believe that cool, composed voice was her own.

"Yes, a red-eye, for sure."

As if he was sitting in the economy seats, not able to sleep, and not stretched out in a white leather recliner that went all the way back, with a steward gently covering him with a blanket.

"I think I'll come with you," she said.

"What? Just leave?" Boswell cast a look at the mess left in the barn.

"Marcus is here. And…" She couldn't say his name. It might thaw the ice block around her heart. "The bunkhouse was offered for him and the staff. They'll look after it. They know what to do."

"B-b-but why? Is it because of what I just said?"

"No, of course not." She suddenly remembered what her mother sounded like, and it was exactly like that. That insincere falsetto, that high inflection as if something really exciting was about to happen.

*That did not involve a needy child clinging to her, screaming at her desperately.*

*I love you.*

"Don't you need to let Sam know?"

She took out her phone and wagged it at her father. "That's what we have these for. I was leaving tomorrow, anyway. It will be way more convenient to take the jet with you. I'll just go grab my bag and talk to Marcus for a minute."

Her father looked at her face and it seemed as if he wanted to say something else. But he didn't. He looked back at his hands.

She got up briskly and moved away.

She suddenly remembered that about her mother, too.

Always brisk. Always in a hurry. To get away.

That was part of Shelby. Half of her, actually. You couldn't deny it just because you didn't like it.

How could she do that to Hannah and Sam? It was only a matter of time until her defects became apparent, until she cracked.

Better, so much better, to leave now.

Thank goodness she had gotten wind of the proposal before it happened. How awful that would have been.

How nearly impossible it would have been to do the right thing.

To say no.

It was a near miss, really, for poor Sam and Hannah. He'd been about to pop the question! To the most unsuitable person in the whole world.

She felt a momentary stab of anger at Sam. Why hadn't he just left well enough alone? Why hadn't he just let them keep going the way they had been?

Why did everything have to change?

Sam woke up in the morning and reached for Shelby. Despite trying to keep things from Hannah, he had thought she would sneak into his room when she wrapped up at the barn.

*Sneak.*

He was so glad, that as of today, that part would be over. There would be no more sneaking.

Love needed to be celebrated. Announced. Not hidden away.

He was surprised to find the bed empty. She'd still been at the function when he'd left at one in the morning. He looked at her pillow, at her side of the bed. He realized she hadn't slept there at all.

For a moment he felt pure panic.

No, wait, breathe. It hadn't been a party in New York City where there might be a nefarious person waiting, watching for her to have a vulnerable moment.

And she had not been drinking at all. It was her father's party, but she had juggled expertly between being a family member and the complete professional that she was. While she'd socialized—she'd known most of her father's friends and associates since she was a child—she's also been making sure everything was perfect, doing all the hard work in the background that made the magic unfold with seeming effortlessness.

He was pretty sure she hadn't even noticed that he'd been avoiding her.

Sam picked up his phone from the bedside table and frowned. It was just after five in the morning. Had she curled up out there somewhere, exhausted? She wouldn't have gone down to the creek by herself, would she?

She was getting to know her way around the ranch, but it could still be a dangerous place, perched on the edge of the wilderness the way it was.

But then he saw he had a message and that it was from Shelby. His relief was instantaneous, until he tapped the text icon.

And then he didn't feel relieved at all.

Sorry. Something's come up. Had to leave unexpectedly. Caught a ride with Dad. Talk soon.

Strange. No *babe* or other term of endearment. No little red hearts. No smoochie emoji.

It was five in the morning. He couldn't call her. On the other hand, she was heading to New York. It was eight there.

He tapped her contact, listened to the phone ring and ring and ring. And then he listened to her voice mail.

He'd always liked hearing her voice on voice mail when he'd called her in the past. But he didn't feel that way right now.

He'd had a big plan for today. Her father had given him his blessing. He had the ring. He'd had it for way too long. He'd been thinking of things to say for way too long. He *needed* to give it to her. He *needed* to ask her the question.

Questions, really.

*Will you marry me?*
*Will you spend the rest of your life with me?*
*Will you be a mother to Hannah?*
*Will you have my children?*
It wasn't happening.
Not today.
He scraped a hand though his hair and headed for the shower. He hoped the hot water would dissolve the feeling in the pit of his stomach.
Of what?
He'd felt this way only once before in his entire life. Sitting in that doctor's office with Beth.
*Impending doom.*
Shelby's idea of *talk soon* was to ignore his calls for three days, and then to finally phone, something weirdly breathless in her voice, as if she was hurrying to catch a train or something.
"Sam," she said, "I'm so sorry I haven't returned your calls. Emergency at work."
What kind of emergency did planning parties leave you open to? He managed, barely, not to say that.
He respected what she did. He respected how she did it. But an emergency so compelling she couldn't answer her phone for three days? He was skeptical.
"Look," she said, "I have to tell you something."
What was with her voice? It made him want to ask, *Who are you and what have you done with Shelby?*
"It's been a fantastic summer, really it has. But my work is suffering. It's all pretty intense."
"Intense?" he said, stunned.
"It's suffocating me."
"What the—" He said a word that men say on a ranch a lot. Buckie's word for the letter *F.* He had never said it to a woman before.

"Of course, I'll call Hannah. If it's okay with you."

For a minute she almost sounded like herself.

"I'll just kind of wean her off of me. I don't want to hurt her. I'd rather die than hurt her."

She didn't sound like a woman who was suffocating. She sounded like a woman who was suffering.

"We need to talk," he said, trying to be reasonable.

"I can't. I mean to Hannah. But—"

"But not to me," he said tersely.

"That's correct."

Like a schoolteacher telling him he'd gotten two plus two right.

Shelby Kane had just told him he was suffocating her, and he was practically begging her to talk about it?

No.

He would not beg her to love him back. He would not. But if he stayed on the phone, he might. So he didn't say one more word. He disconnected.

Buckie waited two weeks before he addressed it.

"What is wrong with you?" He managed to get his word for the letter *F* in that short sentence three times.

"Wrong with me? Nothing."

"Don't give me that." He put his word for the letter *S* at the end of the sentence. "You're acting like a bear with a sore bottom. You got three hands and a cook fixin' to quit if you keep it up."

He didn't say anything.

"What happened between you and Shelby?" Buckie asked.

"I don't know, okay?"

He said that with quite a bit more heat than he expected.

"Did you have a fight?"

"No! She just left, the night of her dad's party. She left and she didn't say goodbye and then she called a few days later and said it was all too intense." He might as well say all of it. "She said I was suffocating her."

"You're dumb as a stick," Buckie said, all sympathy of course.

"Well, maybe that factored into it."

"She's lying to you."

"Maybe she lied to me before and this is the truth."

"Dumb as a stick," Buckie said, with a sad shake of his head. "It wasn't too intense, and she's not suffocating."

"How do you know?"

"You know, I might look as dumb as you're acting, but I ain't. I know human nature, and I know who that girl is."

"Yeah," he said sarcastically. "I remember. You saw it in her eyes."

"I know you been hurt, Sam. I know you suffered more loss in a short period than a lot of men get in their lifetimes. But you can't let it control you. You go talk to her."

"I'm so angry I wouldn't know what to say."

"Say that," Buckie said. "Say what's real. In your heart. If she still won't have you after you've had your say, at least you know you gave it everything. You didn't just quit. We don't abide a quitter around here."

Sam glared at Buckie.

"I'm willing to bet dollars to donuts that girl is hurting something fierce. If you love her, as much as I think you do, you'll go find out what's hurting her so bad, and you'll bring her back from it.

"That's what love does. It risks it all. It puts the other person first. It can hurt like hell. But it's still the only thing that can save us."

Sam said nothing.

"I need your word."

"You're asking me to be like a white knight, riding to the rescue of a maiden in distress."

"I am asking you that."

And suddenly, Sam was looking at things differently. He'd been so consumed by his pain and his anger that he had not thought about her feelings.

Was Shelby in distress?

Of course she was!

There was no way what had transpired between them over the last few months was not the truest thing that had ever happened to both of them.

Buckie was right.

Sam was just plain dumb. The truth had been right in front of him all along. Somehow knowing it didn't make him any less angry with her.

# CHAPTER TWENTY

SHELBY HEARD SOMEONE pounding on her apartment door. It matched the pounding in her head. She felt exactly as if she had a hangover, but she did not.

Unless emotion caused hangovers.

And then she deserved a doozy. After not remembering her mother for eighteen years, now it felt as if a dam had burst, and the memories would not stop coming, water pushing its way through every weak spot, rushing out.

Plus, she had just hung up from Hannah. She had done as she promised Sam she would. She had called every day for the first week. And then she'd eased off just a little bit. And now, three weeks after her father's birthday party, she was calling every third or fourth day. Usually she did a video call, but today she was pretty sure Hannah would have picked up on how hideous she looked.

So, she'd done a regular call. She'd sung *Old MacDonald*, she'd put extra enthusiasm into the oinking.

And she had hung up the phone and done what she did every single time she hung up the phone.

Cried.

She missed them so much. Hannah. Alvin. Rascal. She missed it all so much. Mouse pancakes and sprinklers and storybooks and games. She missed cows lowing in the distance, elk on the lawn in the morning, the cool, pure breezes coming from the mountains.

Sam.

Especially Sam.

She missed the look in his eyes, and his smile, his hair growing back in curly. She missed his hands: those beautiful, competent, strong hands that could fly a helicopter or throw a calf, and yet be so tender when holding her hand, or so on fire as they brailled her body.

She missed sharing worlds and jokes and ice-cream cones.

Shelby had not known until now that you could physically ache for a person, that you could want them so badly your teeth hurt, that you could feel a dark hole of emptiness inside of you that felt as if it could swallow you.

The pounding at the door came again.

It was unusual to get someone at her apartment door unannounced. Visitors to the building had to get by a doorman and a concierge.

She decided to ignore it, but it came again, insistent.

Maybe the building was on fire and they were ordering evacuation. Or a pervert had slipped in and he was going to tell her he needed to come into her apartment for some manufactured emergency.

She got up off the couch, padded to the door and threw it open, and didn't bother with the peephole. She thought, *Let fate take me.*

Shelby was stunned at where fate intended to take her. Sam stood there.

*Sam.* The relief she felt was intense, even as she tried to school herself not to show it. She was *saving* him. And Hannah. She could not throw herself against him, and wrap her arms around him, as if he was a knight who had arrived on his steed to save her.

Besides, nothing in his face invited that.

He looked furious.

Gloriously handsome, but furious.

Except for the night she had told him she was not really a nanny, she did not think she had seen Sam angry.

And this did not compare to that. It would be like comparing a campfire to a volcano.

He was a volcano, right now, on the edge of eruption.

There was something about a man who was furious, and doing his best to contain it, that was oddly enticing. Like that thunderstorm the night they had first made love.

She could not think of that right now.

"What the hell are you doing?" he bit out, his gaze raking her.

She realized she must look beyond horrible. Her hair tangled, her eyes puffy from crying, her uniform of sweatpants and an old T-shirt unchanged for days.

"What the hell are you doing?" she shot back.

He glared at her and pushed by her into her apartment. He stood there, looking around grimly. She saw it through his eyes. The curtains were closed. There were two empty ice-cream containers on the coffee table, and one half-eaten microwaved lasagna on a television tray.

He swung around and looked at her. "You tell me what's going on. Right now."

Sam was not making a request. He was giving an order.

Shelby closed the door, leaned against it, folded her arms over her chest.

"I told you what's going on," she said. "We had a great time. Loved every moment. But it was interfering with my career."

He cast another look around the apartment. "I can clearly see your career is a priority."

*Don't break*, she ordered herself, but she was breaking. It was as if she was full of cracks and his arrival was putting pressure on them, and they were opening. If she didn't get things under control, he was going to see how broken she was.

But, wait. That's what he needed to see. That she was way too damaged for him to want, for him to invite into his life, and the life of his daughter.

"The night of my dad's birthday party—"

"The night you left," he snapped.

"I asked him about my mom. I asked him why I couldn't remember her."

His whole expression changed. "What did he say?"

"You know why I didn't remember her, Sam? Because she didn't love me. She hated me. She hated every single thing about me. She hated being a mom."

For a moment, he stood there, absolutely frozen. And then in one long stride, he came to her, and his arms folded around her.

It felt as if she had been adrift on a raft in the middle of the ocean, hopeless, and the rescue craft had appeared.

It felt as if she had wandered, dying of thirst in the desert, and found an oasis.

It felt as if she had been lost in the deepest, darkest forest, and finally saw the light.

Of home.

That's what she felt as his arms closed around her. A sensation of being home.

If she would have had the strength she would have pulled away. But she had no strength left. She could not fight the relief of this: someone coming after her. She leaned into what he offered, and she wept. She had thought she had no tears left, but it turned out she did.

He lifted her easily into his chest, carried her to her sofa, sat down with her on his lap, stroking her hair, saying soothing things.

"Tell me," he said, and though his tone was more gentle than it had been before, it was still an order that brooked no argument.

"I can't stop remembering things. About my mom."

"Tell me."

She had not said a word about these memories to a single soul. It felt as if they were corrosive, eating away at her.

"I remember clinging to her leg as she was trying to get out the door to go to a party, and her prying my fingers from her slacks."

His complete attention was her antidote to the poison she had swallowed. She could feel the toxin within her dilute.

"I remember begging for a story and being laughed at. *Me? Do I look like I read stories? For god's sake, the next thing you'll want is a mommy who makes cookies.*

"I remember wearing my prettiest dress, wanting just to be noticed, just to be approved of, and her not even looking at me.

"I remember drawing pictures, signed with love hearts, that were glanced at, then tossed away with no comment.

"I remember her promising to be there for things like the Christmas play, my kindergarten graduation and never showing up.

"I remember her telling me if I stopped *pestering* her, she'd take me shopping, or out for iced hot chocolate, or to the park. But she never did.

"I've waited and waited for you to disappoint me. I was nearly delirious with joy each time you kept a promise. But the trepidation would start to build for the next time."

One by one, Shelby told Sam every single thing she remembered. She thought she would feel deeply ashamed, weak for sharing these memories with him. But instead, as she spoke the dam emptied, as if all the dirty, debris-filled water had to be cleared away.

Until she came to the last one.

"I remember screaming I loved her at her as she headed out the door. I think I have believed, my whole life, even though I didn't remember saying those words, that saying them had the power to kill."

"The exact opposite," he said firmly. "Do you hear me?"

"Yes."

"Good."

But still, she did not say them. "So," she finally said. "You can see why I had to go."

"I don't, really. I don't get it."

"Oh, Sam, she's half of me. Those parts of her are in me. My own mother didn't love me. Who could love me?"

"I could," he said, softly, and with such conviction. "I think you're looking at it all wrong, Shelby."

"In what way?"

"You are part of her. But you're the best part. You're her good thing, her one beautiful, good thing that she gave to the world. I don't know if there's a heaven, but I bet if there is, the best part of your mom, the undamaged part, her soul, is looking down, saying *See? I made it. The best part of me survived. I go on, in my daughter, in that beautiful, strong, resilient woman who took everything I gave her, who took all that coal I heaped on her, and mined it for diamonds.*"

She could feel his words seeping into her, like warmed wine, thawing all the places she had turned to ice.

"What if you're wrong?" she whispered.

"I'm not wrong. I remember what Buckie told me the first day you were there."

"What did he tell you?"

"He said, anybody who can't tell who that girl is from lookin' in her eyes is just plain dumb."

"Buckie said that about me?"

"Day one."

"You do a pretty good Buckie impression."

"I know. Don't tell him."

A small bubble of laughter escaped her. Five minutes ago,

she had thought she was facing a life without one more moment of laughter in it.

This had been the miracle of Sam from the very beginning: life having a different plan for her than she had for herself.

Thank goodness.

"I miss him. And I miss Hannah." She took a deep breath. "And you, Sam. I miss you so much. It feels as if my world has gone from full color to black and gray."

"I'm going to suggest something to you," he said quietly. "I'm going to suggest that what made you run away from us was not just remembering your mom.

"It was more than that. It's terror that love will let you down. That it will hurt you more than you can bear. That it will give something to you that you feel you can't live without and then it will snatch it away."

"That's you, isn't it? With Beth?"

He nodded. "It is. I'm terrified of this thing called love. But you know, when I was growing up, the cowboys taught me something. They taught me it's not courage if you're not afraid in the first place.

"Life, Shelby, is asking you and I to step up to the plate. To be courageous in the face of our terror. To say to that little girl we're going to raise together—with our actions as much as our words—that love is worth it.

"That love is everything."

"Love is everything," she whispered.

He slipped out from under her and got down on one knee before her.

It was a surreal moment. Her billionaire cowboy kneeling on a stained pizza napkin in front of her.

Sam slipped a ring box from his pocket and opened it.

There was not much light in her apartment, but what there was was captured deep in the facets of that ring and shone back out at her.

She could hear his voice saying, *Who took all that coal I heaped on her, and mined it for diamonds.*

Shelby was pretty sure she would hear his words, and the pure love in them every single time she wore this ring.

She stared at the sparkling diamond, and then at the sparkle that meant more to her than diamonds. The deep sparkle in his eyes.

Of strength. Honesty. Trust.

Love.

"I want you to marry me, Shelby Kane. I love you."

This then was life, too. He was right. Everything you cared about could be snatched away in a breath.

Wasn't that a reminder to make each breath count?

And as much as life could take things away unexpectedly, it also brought things unexpectedly. Her day had started with despondency and darkness.

And now she was here.

In bliss, in the Light.

She had to dig deep for the words. But when she found them, it was as if they had been waiting for her, a treasure chest buried deep, deep within her.

People said when you find yourself in a hole to quit digging.

But what if you quit before you found this? The treasure chest?

She reached tentatively for the chest. The lock on it opened beneath her fingers. The lid was heavy, and the hinges were rusted.

It took all her strength to do what she needed to do.

She opened the lid of the treasure chest within her. She was afraid, after all this time, it might be full of snakes, or monsters, or rot, or dust.

Instead, Shelby was almost blinded by the brilliance of what waited for her.

She said the words.

"I love you."

And her world did not fall apart. Just as Sam had predicted, the exact opposite happened. She could feel her whole world—and her bruised heart—sparkling like jewels, lit from within.

"Yes," she whispered to Sam, but also to the whole Universe, "yes."

# EPILOGUE

THE OLD BARN was filled to absolute capacity, the front and back doors thrown wide to let in the spring breeze. The early afternoon light drenched the space.

It was a year to the day that Sam had first seen Shelby, coming toward him, her heel digging deep into the dirt, his daughter shooting her with her Bobby-doll.

Sam stood at the front, on the raised dais that had been built for this moment, thinking, *This is what miracles look like.* He felt a shiver of pure wonder move up his spine.

Alvin stood beside him as his best man, and he glanced at him. Alvin looked surprisingly civilized in a black tuxedo, crisp white shirt, a neat bow tie, a clean new cowboy hat, boots that shone until they sparkled.

If Sam had been hoping for a shared glance that said Alvin, too, was feeling the utter enchantment of this moment, he was disappointed.

Without any change in the expression worthy of such a solemn occasion, Alvin winked at someone. Sam followed his gaze. The Duchess—or Countess—of Chanterbury was blushing under her extravagant hat. She and Alvin had met at Boswell's birthday party.

Sam's gaze moved from her and swept the crowd. The barn had never hosted such a diverse gathering.

Every race was represented. Shelby's assistant, Marcus, was there with his partner, sitting shoulder to shoulder with

Sam's ranch hand, Jimmy, and his soon-to-be wife, Sandra. They were all laughing about something.

There were celebrities, and some of the world's wealthiest people. There were his longtime business associates and friends from his university days.

The ranch community was out in full force. Ranchers and cowboys, their families, and the people who supported them, store owners and beef processors.

It was a meeting of worlds that should never have worked, and yet it *was* working. Looking out at that gathering, Sam felt as if he was having a little glimpse of heaven.

Joy hummed in the air.

This was the universal truth: everyone wanted love. The richest, the poorest, the most elevated, the humblest.

Whatever barriers usually stood between them were erased. This was the meeting place where everyone seemed to recognize each other at the deepest level.

Love.

The music began. A single violin played *Canon* by Pachelbel. The music soared, and as if on cue, two bluebirds, a bright male and his quieter companion, flew in the open front doors, over the assembled, and out the back ones.

Then Hannah appeared. She was wearing a pale blue dress made of lace and chiffon. Her hair had a band of wildflowers around it, but was loose and curled wildly around her flushed face. She was practically dancing down the aisle in her pink cowboy boots, scattering the wildflower petals that she and Shelby had gathered the day before.

Other violins joined the solo, and here *she* came through those open doors.

Shelby. The woman who had given him back his heart by taking it. Completely.

Her father was escorting her, and she was absolutely radiant. Her white dress was simplicity personified, like something a goddess would wear: a fitted lace bodice, with a deep V-neckline, tight at her tiny waist and then the long silk skirt flaring out, flowing behind her.

Every now and then, Sam would catch a glimpse of her pink cowboy boots, purchased specifically to match Hannah's.

Shelby's hair, like Hannah's, was loose, a band of braided wildflowers encircling her brow. The wildflowers matched her bouquet.

Her shining eyes saw only him. She arrived at him just as the music stopped, and they faced each other. He met her gaze, and everything else faded.

The barn. The light. The people. Alvin. Even his daughter.

In the clearness of Shelby's eyes, Sam saw the future. It was breathtaking. He saw babies and community, he saw Christmas trees and socks on the mantel. He saw a life that blended adventure and discovery with a place of safety and sanctuary.

When he looked in her eyes, he knew they had found the place the whole world longed for.

The place that love led one man and one woman, who had found each other against impossible odds, unerringly toward.

Home.

They had found home.

\* \* \* \* \*

# COMING SOON!

We really hope you enjoyed reading this book.
If you're looking for more romance
be sure to head to the shops when
new books are available on

## Thursday 14th March

MILLS & BOON

# MILLS & BOON®

## Coming next month

### IT STARTED WITH A PROPOSAL
Susan Meier

'So, where's the bride?'

He frowned. 'Bride?'

'Sorry. Where's your fiancée?'

He continued to look at her as if he didn't understand.

'The woman you're going to ask to marry you.'

His mouth fell open a little bit. 'I thought you were bringing her.'

'I don't even know who she is.'

'That's the point. There is no one. So just like the flowers and the mandolin players I thought you'd provide someone to fake propose to.'

This time her mouth fell open. 'I assumed you'd bring the woman from the restaurant.'

He squeezed his eyes shut. 'No.'

'Okay,' she said, thinking on her feet. There were three cute young women arranging the flowers, but they were dressed in dark trousers and golf shirts with a florist logo on the breast pocket.

'I…' She looked around.

He tapped her shoulder to bring her attention back to him. 'You're here.' He looked down at her dress. 'And you're dressed for it.'

Damned if she wasn't.

Antonio's voice brought her back to reality. 'Please. We've gone to all this trouble already.'

She took a breath. 'You're right. It's no big deal and technically I am dressed for it.'

'And you look beautiful.'

Her heart fluttered before she could remind herself that he'd only told her that because he wanted a favour.

She forced a smile, then turned to Jake, the videographer. 'I'm going to be playing the part of the fiancée,' she said, holding her smile in place as if it was completely normal that she was standing in for the role. Because it wasn't. This was a job. Period. Nothing more.

'Once I get to the centre of the gazebo, you start filming.' She faced the mandolin players. 'Same instruction to you.'

The three guys nodded. Jake scrambled to get into position for the best angle for the simple video.

Riley took a long breath and put her forced smile on her face again. She walked to the centre and turned.

Jake said, 'Action.'

The mandolins sent romantic music wafting through the gazebo.

Antonio started up the steps. He walked to her, got down on one knee and took her hand.

When his warm fingers wrapped around hers, she had to work to stop her heart from pounding. The man was simply too darned good looking and sexy.

'I love you, Riley Morgan. Will you marry me?'

*Continue reading*
**IT STARTED WITH A PROPOSAL**
Susan Meier

*Available next month*
millsandboon.co.uk

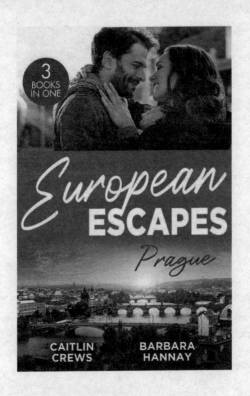

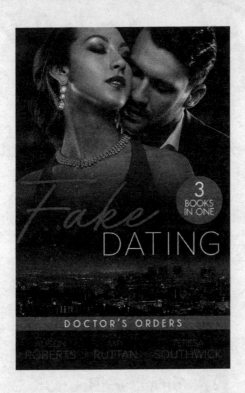

## LET'S TALK
# Romance

For exclusive extracts, competitions and special offers, find us online:

**f** MillsandBoon

**X** @MillsandBoon

**◉** @MillsandBoonUK

**♪** @MillsandBoonUK

Get in touch on 01413 063 232